NEVER TOO
OLD TO CRY

To Rod Seiler H.'S. 3-1
I salute you.
D. R. McWilliams
6-11-95

NEVER TOO OLD TO CRY

D. G. McWilliams

Northwest Publishing, Inc.
Salt Lake City, Utah

Never Too Old To Cry

This is a work of fiction.
Historical characters and events have been used to add verisimilitude.
All other characters and events portrayed in this book are fictional,
and any resemblance to real people or incidents is purely coincidental.

For information address: Northwest Publishing, Inc.
6906 South 300 West, Salt Lake City, Utah 84047
J. B. 12-14-94
Edited by: G. E. Bloomsburg

PRINTING HISTORY
First Printing 1995

ISBN: 1-56901-586-4

NPI books are published by Northwest Publishing, Incorporated,
6906 South 300 West, Salt Lake City, Utah 84047.
The name "NPI" and the "NPI" logo are trademarks belonging to
Northwest Publishing, Incorporated.

PRINTED IN THE UNITED STATES OF AMERICA.
10 9 8 7 6 5 4 3 2 1

Introduction

The novel you are about to read is fiction. It is a story about the lives of six young men and their friends who served together in the First Marine Division during World War II. It is a story about young men who grew to manhood in a short period of time, about fear and courage, sadness and laughter, and about their gallant and courageous struggle on the Pacific islands in the march toward Japan. It is a story of their early lives before they entered the Marines, how they met, how they fought, how they loved, and how they died.

It is a story about a Japanese family and how their lives entwine with the lives of the six Marines and their friends.

Three of the young men were seventeen years old when they enlisted in the Marines, another was eighteen, and the other two were nineteen. The young men were from different backgrounds, but they became friends in their early training, and their friendship helped them through the invasions of Cape Gloucester, Talasea, Peleliu, and Okinawa. When the war ended, the men were sent with units of the First Marine Division to China to disarm the Japanese troops that had occupied mainland China during World War II, and in early 1946, four of the young men in the story returned to the United States.

The novel is based on the experiences of Marines who fought with the First Marine Division. Many years have passed since my Marine buddies and I first met in 1943, but their memories of times, places, people, and things became a part of this book. I am grateful and appreciative of their help.

I also wish to express my appreciation to my friend John Gardemal of Dragonfly Art at St. Martinville, Louisiana for his superb drawing used for the cover.

I give a special thanks to my wife, Maggie, who gave me the support and encouragement to write this novel.

Finally, I wish to express my most sincere respect for all the men and women of the Army, Navy, Marines, and Air Force who united under a single cause during one of the most historically significant times of our nation.

Those who returned, as well as their relatives and friends, will recall with pride their own experiences. The sacrifices made by some are known only to themselves.

To all of them I say, "Thanks."
Semper Fi.

D. G. McWilliams

The author in China, 1945

PART I

1

Mack Williams, the next to the youngest of five brothers and five sisters, lived with his mother and father and a younger brother in a large rustic house on a sheep ranch. The ranch was more than thirty miles south of Crockett, Texas, a small ranching town, proud of its fame, the friendliest and richest little town in the state. Each year when the children attended school during the fall and spring months, the family moved back into town and lived in one of the most beautiful and spacious mansions along "Silk Stocking Row."

Mack's curly auburn hair complimented his ruddy complexion, freckled face, and pug nose. He was muscular, with wide shoulders and strong arms, five feet ten inches tall, and weighed one hundred fifty-five pounds. He had a reputation of stretching the truth, as he said, "to make a good story better," but his sense of humor and likable personality allowed him to make friends easily.

On a Saturday morning in February 1943, Mack finished writing a note to his roommate in the Texas Tech football rooming house. "I've got a ride home this weekend, and I'll be back Sunday night. My best friend is leaving for the Army, and I want to tell him good-bye."

He placed the note on the desk, remembered to gather up his dirty laundry, and stuffed it into his suitcase.

He walked to the front of the rooming house and crawled into the back seat of the waiting 1940 Chevrolet sedan. He should be home with his family in Crockett by late afternoon, and he looked forward to the supper meal his mother would have waiting for him. She always cooked his favorite foods when he returned home, and the supper table would resemble a banquet feast.

The Chevy cruised down Highway 87, and Mack pointed to the rows of plowed fields waiting to be planted in cotton. "All of this land used to be pasture. At one time prairie grass was knee-high, and the cattle drives passed somewhere along this highway. Irrigation wells have changed it all. It's better land than where we ranch in West Texas, but this year we've had good rains. The sheep and goats on our place have good grass, and our ranch looks the best it's looked since the depression. Back in 1929 my family almost lost everything: the land, sheep, barns, everything. You couldn't *give* some of the stuff away. Wool prices fell to nothing and the drought ruined the lands for years."

"How did your family keep the ranch?" asked his back seat companion.

"Well, no one could make any money by staying on the ranch," Mack said. "It was a dust bowl. Dad sold off most of the stock for whatever he could get, got barely enough to pay the taxes. He kept borrowing money, and the bankers couldn't afford to foreclose on his loans. He owed more than the ranch was worth at that time. Dad ran for sheriff, got elected, and the county said we had to live in the jail. We lived in the jail for six years. With ten kids, eight of them living at home, and a German shepherd dog, there wasn't much money left, but we saved and paid taxes on the ranch. Some of the ranch wasn't worth much for grazing, but we kept it all. The worst land is where most of the oil wells are now."

The driver of the Chevrolet laughed. "With that many kids, where'd you sleep, with the prisoners?"

"Not quite," Mack laughed. "The cells for the prisoners were on the second and third floor, and we lived on the bottom floor. We slept in three rooms, and Dad used to say he almost screwed himself out of a place to sleep."

The driver of the Chevrolet sedan said, "Some people have never known how it feels to be poor. Thank God none of us has to live like that anymore."

Mack nodded his head. "We don't, but there's still some that do. We've been lucky. We've come a long way since those days."

On the Williams Ranch, the adobe hut with its thick mud walls was cool, not yet heated by the sun that baked the tin roof each day.

No breeze stirred the cloth that hung by the door, and Felipe Ramirez raised up on one elbow and looked through the uncovered window. He could see the first faint glow of the morning, and he could see the silhouette of the ranch house on the hill.

It was quiet, except for the distant sound of a coyote lifting his head in one last mournful howl to the departing moon. Felipe lay back on the thinly padded mattress and closed his eyes.

Across the room, Carlos Ramirez rose slowly from his mattress. He stood for a moment, yawned, and reached down to rub his aching knees. He grimaced from the pain in his hands and fingers and took a deep breath before standing as erect as his bent body would allow. He put his legs through his worn and patched Levi's and tugged his boots onto his feet. He buckled his belt as he shuffled his way to the opposite side of the room where his son lay.

"Felipe." Carlos gently touched his son's shoulder.

"I'm awake, Papa." Felipe did not tell his father he had been awake for the past several hours. In some ways, he had looked forward to this day, the day he would leave home, perhaps for good. Yet he dreaded leaving his father.

As the last few years had passed, he had watched his father attempt to do the work of a much younger man, watched as he fought to stand on spindly legs, bowlegged from too many years of riding horseback on the ranch were he had lived and worked. He had watched the old man's crippled hands try to hold the rope on a bucking, kicking horse, watched his father's face, dried and sunburned from the wind, become more wrinkled, while his eyes lost the shine and sparkle of an earlier time.

Felipe looked around him as he dressed. He had saved his best pair of Levi's for this day. There wasn't much he could do about his boots, he thought. They were worn across the toe, but he had cleaned them as best as he could. He pulled on his denim shirt and started to put on his belt. There was a new buckle on the belt, a massive silver buckle. He looked at it carefully and saw his initials carved in the polished metal. He glanced up to see his father watching him.

"Papa, this is beautiful. How did you get such a wonderful thing? I can't believe it!" Felipe exclaimed.

"Do you like it?" Carlos asked. "I made it from the silver panel from my old saddle. Took some pounding though. Do you like it?" he asked again.

"Papa, you know I do. From your saddle? But you shouldn't have taken it from your saddle. You won that in Mexico City at the rodeo years and years ago. I remember when you told me about it. It was your greatest treasure."

"I wanted you to have it," Carlos said to his son. "I don't

know if the Army will let you wear it just now when you first go in, but perhaps there will be a time when you can. It will bring you good luck, as it did for me. Take it," he added, and turned away.

"Papa, I thank you, and I will find a way to wear it." He started to touch his father on the shoulder, to show in some way his appreciation, but his father, a sensitive, proud Mexican in his early sixties, backed away.

Felipe finished dressing and stepped to the door. He pulled back the cloth that hung by the opening and looked out. "It will be a fine day," he said.

Carlos asked, "Do you want me to saddle a horse? I do not believe Mr. Williams will mind. You can leave the horse at the feed store. I will come into town later to get him, perhaps tomorrow, when I go to the mission."

"No, Papa, it is a beautiful morning. I will walk. You would have no way to pick up the horse. If I start soon, I will be in town before the sun sets. The bus doesn't leave till late. I will have plenty time."

"I'm sorry I can't go with you," Carlos said. "I must repair the windmill today. And I saw that the fence by the barn is sagging. I must fix that also."

"I know, Papa. That's all right. I understand."

"Felipe, while you are away, you will remember to say your prayers?"

"Yes, Papa, and I will ask the Virgin Mary to ask God to keep you well while I am gone."

Carlos nodded his head. "And I will pray that you will stay well and that you will be a good soldier."

Felipe wrapped a tortilla in a brown paper bag and stuffed it in his pocket. He looked around him. Not much to say goodbye to here, he thought. But it was all he had ever known. Ever since his mother died when they still lived in Mexico, there had been just he and his father. He was very young when his father waded the Rio Grande River and carried him across the border into Texas.

Carlos started to work on the Williamses' ranch as a horse wrangler. He was given enough food for him and his young son, a place to stay, and ten dollars a month. Carlos knew in those hard years, just before and during the Great Depression, any kind of wages would have been satisfactory and preferable to the difficult life that awaited him and his son if they were ever forced to return to Mexico.

Felipe looked through the window opening at the seemingly unfriendly range he had known for most of his life. He had learned long ago to admire the mesquite and cactus-covered hostile land, forgiving only to those who came to know and respect it. He had grown to be a young man of eighteen, traveled every path, looked at every rock, and studied every animal that shared the barren lands with the people who dared to live in this particular part of Texas.

Felipe's eyes roamed across the room he had shared with his father, allowing his gaze to stop momentarily at the wooden table, the blackened wood stove, and the two beds. His eyes drank in the beauty of the Mexican woman whose framed picture hung beside the wooden cross.

He turned to his father. "It is time to go. Good-bye, Papa. I will write to you. Mrs. Williams will read the letter to you."

"Good-bye, my son. God be with you."

Felipe held out his hand, and Carlos extended his own. They stood for a moment looking into each other's eyes, then Felipe turned and walked from the adobe hut.

Mack pushed back from the massive oak dining table, still covered with food, some of it untouched. "Mom, that was the best meal I've eaten since I was here at Christmas." He patted his stomach. "I'd gain fifty pounds if I ate like that for very long. That was some feast. Your roast and gravy are the best this side of the Rio Grande."

Mack's mother smiled. "It makes me feel good to see you eat like that. I miss fixing your favorite foods. Do you want another piece of lemon pie?" She reached for a knife and pulled the pie toward her. "Here, let me cut you another piece."

"Oh, gosh no, Mom. If I ate another piece of pie, or anything else for that matter, I know I'd pop. I'm not even sure I can get out of the chair."

"Well, I'll just save it for you to eat for breakfast in the morning. Would you like biscuits and eggs or hot cakes and sausage? I can fix both if you want them. It'd be no trouble. I'll just do that," she said as she began clearing away the dishes. "I'll have Maria wash and iron your clothes tonight. We can spend the day together, talking about your school or whatever you want to talk about."

"I'm sorry, Mom, but I'll be leaving pretty early in the morning. It's a long trip back to Lubbock, and I've got some studying to do before Monday classes."

"I wish you didn't have to leave so early."

"Mom, there is something I want to talk with you about before I go back. You know I want to join the Marines, and I need your permission."

"You're determined to join the Marines, aren't you? Isn't it enough to have three of your brothers and a sister in the service already?"

"Mom, that doesn't have anything to do with me joining the Marines. What they did can't be a reason for me to stay out of the service. Besides, when I join, you'll have one of your children in every branch of the service, including the WACs. Think of all the fun we'll have when the war is over and we all start talking about which was the best: the Army, Navy, Air Force, the WACs, or the Marines. Of course, you and I know which is best already, don't we, Mom?" Mack smiled as he put his arms around his mother. "Tell me you love me best, Mom, come on, admit it. I won't tell the others."

"You know I'm not going to say that. I love you all the same. And quit trying to make me say that."

"Aw Mom, you won't say it but you know you do. Come on, just whisper it to me. I won't tell." Mack lifted his mother in his arms.

"Mack Williams, you put me down, and you better go to the bus station. You didn't come all this way to miss telling Felipe good-bye. The bus doesn't spend much time at the station, and you don't want to cause Felipe to miss the bus."

"Yeah, I know. Felipe had already left the ranch when I drove out to find him this afternoon. Carlos said he had left early this morning. I looked for him but never saw him. I'll wait for him at the cafe at the bus station. I may want to eat another piece of pie or something."

"Go on, get out of here," she smiled and pushed him toward the door, "and tell Felipe I send my love. Tell him to take care of himself, too, and if Carlos needs to write a letter, I'll help him."

Mack sat in the station cafe and sipped his cup of coffee. He glanced at the clock on the wall and knew the bus for El Paso should be arriving. Felipe should have already been there, he thought.

He walked to the pinball machine, started to play it, then instead walked to the nickelodeon. He scanned the list of records, chose "Green Eyes," and inserted a nickel. He watched the record fall from the rack and the needle arm bob up and down when the record turned and the music started.

"Mack," a voice behind him said. "I thought that was you when I walked inside. It's good to see you. Are you waiting for the bus too?"

Mack turned. "Felipe! I was watching for you. I didn't see you come in. Naw, I'm not waiting for the bus, I'm here to see you. You're late."

"How did you know I was leaving?"

"Mom called me. She talked to your father. He told her you were leaving tonight. There was no way I could get in touch with you out at the ranch, and I didn't want you to leave without me telling you good-bye. I drove out to see you this afternoon, but you'd already left."

"I'm glad you came."

"How are you?" Mack asked. "You're looking good.

Maybe a little thinner than the last time. Much thinner than I am, but you work harder than I do." He patted his stomach. "Mom added a pound or two tonight."

Felipe said, "You look good. College must be agreeing with you. Do you still like it?"

"Yeah, it's all right, but it'd be better if we didn't have classes," Mack laughed.

"I see your mother and father when they come to the ranch. I hope they are doing well. How are your brothers and sister in the service?"

"They're all fine. Roland is in North Africa with the 142nd Infantry. Mom said tell you hello, and she also said she'd help Carlos write you if he wanted her to. She sends her love. She'd be mad if I forgot to tell you that."

"She is a kind woman. Tell her that I said good-bye. And I would appreciate it very much if she would help my father. He wouldn't want me to say it, but he's looking older each day. I can see it in his eyes," Felipe said. "I hated to leave him."

"Why did you join the Army?"

Felipe looked at the floor. "I was drafted the day I became eighteen. Most of my friends have already left for the Army."

"I guess it's everybody's war. The sooner we get it over with, the sooner we can all come back to our own way of life," Mack said.

Felipe's fingers traced the initials on his silver buckle. "Yes, we can all come back to our own way of life. I am sure that is the way it will be."

"I'm joining the Marines when I get my mother's consent," Mack said.

"I didn't know. Will you enlist soon, before you finish your first year in college?"

"Well, I'm thinking now that I will," Mack answered. "Come on, I'll buy you a cup of coffee. I've already got one over at the table by the window."

Felipe looked toward the man behind the counter, then turned to Mack. "He…he won't serve me in here."

Mack walked to the counter. "Give me another cup of coffee."

The waiter looked toward Felipe. "You already have a cup, and I'm not serving any wetback in here."

Mack leaned over the counter, his face only inches from the waiter's face. "I drink a lot of coffee. Let me have another cup, and I like water, so give me two glasses of water."

The waiter hesitated, then shrugged. "Just so long as you drink them yourself. You owe me another nickel."

Mack carried the cup of coffee and the two glasses of water to the table where Felipe waited.

"He's a prick," Mack said, and pushed the cup of coffee toward Felipe. "I'm sorry."

Felipe said, "It doesn't matter, but thanks for what you did."

"Aw, forget it," Mack said.

"When you join the Marines, where will you go?"

"If I can get into the Marines," Mack said, "I'll go to the West Coast, no doubt to San Diego, but I'll go wherever they send me."

The lights of the bus pulling into the terminal flashed across the window where Felipe and Mack sat. Mack looked at his watch. "The bus is early. The driver must be trying to make up time."

Felipe pushed away from the table. "It's just as well. I guess we will say good-bye now. I hope all goes well with you. If you join the Marines, I hope you go through the war safely. Good-bye, my friend. It was good of you to come see me before I left."

"Felipe, you and I have been friends for a long time. We played cowboys and Indians when we were young. I went on my first deer hunt with you, remember? In fact, you taught me how to hunt and how to track. My first deer was that big ten-pointer! Remember? And I taught you how to swim in the water tank. That had to be the coldest water in the world. Our bare butts were covered with goose bumps."

"Yes, I remember, and you scared me when you made me believe a fish was going to nibble my worm." Felipe laughed with Mack as they started toward the door.

"We have done many things together," Felipe said. "You are my friend. You always took up for me, even fought for me when someone called me 'spic.' Someday perhaps I can show you and your family my gratitude. Well, I must go. I hope you stay well, and I pray you come back home."

"I hope we both do," Mack replied.

"*Vaya con Dios*," Felipe said, and walked toward the waiting bus.

Mack watched the bus leave the depot, then walked back to the table where he and Felipe had sat. He picked up the still full cup of coffee and turned it upside down. The coffee poured over the table and dripped on the chairs, then he walked toward the counter and looked at the waiter.

"I'm all thumbs. I spilled my coffee," he said, and left the cafe.

2

"Manny, help your little sister get in the wagon," Mr. King commanded. "We best be getting on to Benson Cove. The older kids already left with the belongings in the other wagon. Tell your ma as soon as I tie the chicken coop on the tailgate, we can leave out."

Manny, the seventh of twelve children in the King family, with four sisters and seven brothers, was ten years old.

"Pa, does our new farm have good land? Better'n this?"

"I'm told it's the best in North Carolina, fertile sandy loam, grows prime tobacco. Good rains most of the time. They say by the Fourth of July the cotton crop will be tall enough to hide a rabbit. We'll have plenty of land for winter wheat, too."

During the next eight years, Manny worked from before sunup till after dark six days a week in the tobacco and cotton fields, and his strong arms and shoulders showed the result of years of hard manual labor. He could cut down a tree with an ax as fast as any man his age in the valley.

His dark brown hair usually needed cutting, and when he laughed his lips pulled tight across his teeth. He was normally a quiet man, tenacious and determined.

The paint on the rough boards of the King farmhouse had long since peeled away, and like other farms nearby, the unpainted barns and outhouse were weatherworn and in need of repair.

In the early forties, parts of the United States had begun to recover from the Great Depression, but for the dirt farmers in rural North Carolina life was not easy. The sharecroppers felt the pains of poverty in their never ending effort to eke out a meager existence.

Electricity had not yet come to the King farm, and sometimes when the day's work was done, Manny sat on the front porch and read books by the light of a lantern.

The King family raised their own vegetables and had chickens to eat and enough eggs to sell those they could not use. The milk cow was getting to be more dependent on them than they were on her, giving less milk and smaller calves. She was getting too old to keep any longer, but the cow had been in the family so long she had become a revered member. Mr. King dreaded the day when he would either sell or butcher her; he knew none of the family could swallow the meat.

Mr. King, forty-nine years old, showed the strain of poor times and hard work. He raised some of the best tobacco and cotton in the valley but worked part-time as a carpenter when, as his neighbors said, he was not at home in bed with his wife. The other farmers would say that if Mr. King could raise cotton and tobacco as often as his wife bore children he could get three crops a year.

Manny's mother, a large woman, was almost as strong as

her husband and, with the help of her daughters, cared for the vegetable garden and did the cooking, cleaning and laundry.

She was a gentle woman, never complaining; even when angry, she kept her emotions from showing. Her low voice had a strong Southern flavor, and like her son Manny, she was stingy with conversation.

She raised twelve children, never asking for help from her husband. It seemed to her neighbors that she was always either pregnant or giving birth, and when the other women who lived in the valley came to help at the birth of her first babies, they discovered there was little they could do for her that she couldn't do for herself.

Until the beginning of World War II, all twelve of the King children worked on the farm, and then, one by one, the boys left home. Four of the boys joined the Navy and two other boys left to work in the shipyards in Newport News, Virginia.

"Manny," Mrs. King said on a Sunday morning, "go make sure your brother and sisters are ready for church. Your Pa has gone to hitch Josie to the wagon. Tell Karen and Sara to bring the babies."

Manny walked to the farmhouse and opened the door to the room where his sisters slept. "Ma said to hurry, and she said to bring the babies. Pa's hitching Josie to the wagon. He'll be mad if we're late."

When Manny returned, Mr. King was already sitting in the wagon seat. "Where's your ma and the girls? We're going to be late if we don't hurry."

"She was out here a little while ago. The girls are about ready. They're coming."

"Well, go find her, and tell her we best be starting for church. Besides, it's too hot to sit out here for long," Mr. King complained.

"I'll go look in the back. We'll come just as soon as I find her."

Manny walked behind the farmhouse, but stopped when he saw his mother standing at the corner of the smokehouse, looking out across the fields at the horizon, beyond the crest of the wooded hills behind their farm.

Manny watched his mother, not daring to make a sound or to break the silence that held her captive. He saw the trace of beauty still in her face, resembling only slightly the picture that hung on the bedroom wall. The years had taken away some of the beauty of the woman in the picture worn on her wedding day, but the same proud look was still in her eyes.

She looked at her rough, chapped hands and lifted the material of her faded, patched dress and looked at it as though she was seeing it for the first time.

Manny felt guilty standing there and quietly turned away and walked back to the wagon. "She'll be along in a minute, Pa."

Manny helped his younger brother and sisters get in the back of the wagon, and when Mrs. King returned to the wagon, she climbed into the seat beside her husband.

Mr. King looked at his wife, and when she nodded her head, he said, "Giddy up, Josie," and the black mule strained forward to pull the wagon the four miles down the winding dirt road to the church.

The dark gray dirt of the road lifted slowly, and the hot July winds pushed the dirt higher into the air, and the heat pressed their clothes to their sweating bodies.

Manny watched his mother sitting so erect and straight in the wagon seat. He looked at his little sisters and realized their dresses, like his mother's, were all made from feed sacks.

"Someday, I'm going to get her some pretty store-bought material," Manny vowed, "and it's going to have flowers and pretty buttons."

Frankie Rogers lived on a farm a mile from the King place, and on school days, Manny and Frankie had walked together and he had carried her books and a jar of buttermilk she took for her lunch. She's the prettiest girl in the valley, Manny thought.

He hadn't spoken for her yet, but Manny already had his eye on a piece of land at the far end of the valley. He knew the day was not far away when he would talk to Mr. Rogers about marrying his daughter.

Manny looked forward to Sundays and going to the Spring Mountain Baptist Church. Frankie would be there and they would sit together during the sermon. Manny wanted to go to church for another reason, and that was to hear Preacher Roe give what his father called the "hellfire and damnation" sermon. He had heard it so many times he could give it himself.

Preacher Roe's eyes searched the congregation, "his sinners," as he referred to them in his sermon, to see how many were still asleep. The tempo in his voice gradually increased, and Manny braced himself for the part of the sermon he liked best. When Preacher Roe slammed his Bible down on the top of the pulpit and shouted, "Praise the Lord," Manny laughed as some of the men who had dozed through the sermon fell from their seats. The sudden noise of the Bible hitting the pulpit made the sleeping babies cry, adding their wailing noise to the bedlam.

When the sermon ended, the congregation sang "Upon This Rock I Will Build My Church." Sister Roe was the only woman in church who could sing the high notes, and her voice pierced the air in a final screech. While they sang, their voices joined with the wails of the crying children, and pennies rattled in the tin collection plate as it passed down the rows.

On a Wednesday morning in August 1942, Mrs. King said to her oldest daughter, "Karen, go gather the wood for the fire. Be sure you don't get snake bit around the wood pile. You and Sarah carry enough water to fill the kettle, and then start a good fire."

The girls filled the large bucket with water, the pump squeaking with each stroke. They put a broom stick through the wire handle, and together they carried the pail of water to the fire. The large iron kettle, blackened through decades of being heated by wood fires, was propped up on three large stones, also scorched and black. A well-worn path extended from the well to the black kettle and then to the clothes-line which always needed tightening.

Mrs. King walked to the house to gather the dirty laundry, stopped on the back steps, shaded her eyes, and searched the cotton patch for a glimpse of Manny and the mule.

"Karen, when you get done with the fire wood, carry a jar of water out to Manny. Be sure you get it right out of the well just before you start out to the field. He should be about to the end of the patch of cotton by the Aker's place. And don't take all day. Sarah, you mind the babies until Karen gets back, then we got some canning to do."

It was a hot day, the thermometer nailed to the side of the barn registered ninety-two degrees, but the ninety percent humidity made it seem even hotter. Mule and man walked through the cotton field, the blades of the weed harrow cutting just below the ground level; weeds tumbled. Nothing better than the smell of freshly plowed land, Manny thought. He walked behind the mule, the dirt breaking around their feet as they plodded through the cotton field.

Sweat dripped from his body; his overalls were a little shorter than they should have been. His old straw hat, which could have been a reject from the garden scarecrow, was pulled low over his eyes to shield the hot sun's rays.

Manny saw the Mason jar of cold water his sister left for him at the turning row. "Whoa, Josie," Manny commanded, and took a soiled rag from the back pocket of his overalls and wiped the sweat from his eyes. He swallowed large gulps of water and then screwed the lid back on the jar. He walked behind the plow and popped the reins. "Giddy up Josie, we got lots of ground to cover before we head for the barn."

The mule seemed to understand, as she picked up her feet and moved at a faster pace.

Morning turned to afternoon, and Manny realized he had almost finished plowing the field. He would finish before the sun went down, and it would be too late to start in the tobacco field, but time enough for him to go to the Rogers farm to see his girl.

Manny trudged along behind the mule and tried to decide what he should do about entering the military. The young men of the valley were expected to be farmers, just like their fathers, and their fathers before them. Some had been given a dependency deferment, but most had been drafted into the Army, leaving their farms for the first time in their lives.

If I marry Frankie, he thought, I probably could get a deferment, especially if she got pregnant right away. If I don't get married and wait to be drafted, the war might be over before I have the chance to learn something besides farming. If I don't go into the service at all, I'll always be a farmer, that's for sure, he told himself.

The books he read had pushed open the door to a world that lived only in his imagination. He had read that some men who joined the military were given the opportunity to get an education; a man could learn how to become a radio operator, or maybe a clerk, or perhaps even an engineer.

If I enlist, he thought, only my younger brother and four sisters will be left to do the planting and the harvesting of the crops. I don't want to leave Pa to do the farming by himself, but I could send my pay home, and the money would be enough to hire some help.

"One thing I know," he said. "I don't want to spend the rest of my life behind a mule's ass."

Manny had the reins hung over his shoulder, one hand holding the leather strap and the handle of the plow while the other hand gripped the other handle, worn smooth through years of hard use. He stumbled, and the plow lurched and swayed as he struggled to keep the blades from cutting the young cotton.

He was lost in thought until he stepped in a pile of mule shit.

"You damn, stupid lop-eared son of a bitch," Manny muttered between clenched teeth. The mule responded by farting once more to show her disgust at hearing such vulgar language.

"Josie, you don't know it, but you just helped me make up my mind."

Manny unbuckled the plow and patted the mule's rump. He rubbed the animal's ears and head with the rag from his back pocket and said, "Let's go home, Josie, we've done enough for one day."

The mule was most anxious to head for the barn, knowing that her workday was over. As Manny and the mule began to trudge toward the barn, Josie hurried her walk to a trot, and the reins were suddenly jerked from his hands.

Manny started to run to catch the reins, but he was too tired to run. What the hell, he figured, she knows where she's going, and I know where I'm going, too.

3

Donald Woodson slowly got out of bed, pulled on his overalls, and felt around the floor for his shoes and socks. He heard a rooster crow and instinctively looked at his watch. "Five-forty, time to be at the barn," he said to himself. There was much to do that morning before he would catch the school bus to the Mineola High School.

He finished dressing in the half-light, walked as quietly as he could across the wooden floor of his room, and stepped out into the cool air.

The weathered, unpainted barn, like the four-room farm house, was in a state of neglect, and the door to the feed barn squeaked on rusty hinges as Donald opened it just wide enough to enter. He was strong for his age, eighteen now, and he lifted a bulky bale of hay and carried it toward the cow pen.

He walked through the black gumbo soil, typical of bottom land farms in East Texas. His shoes gathered more weight with each step. He unlatched the gate to the cow pen, broke apart the bale of hay, and scattered the feed for the waiting cow and calf.

He knew he should be alone, but to make sure, he looked carefully around the barnyard. Confident there was no one to see him, he stood at military attention, pulled back his shoulders, and expanded his chest to its fullest.

Donald Woodson became oblivious to everything around him. He was in his make-believe world where fantasies fashioned thoughts into reality.

He envisioned himself standing before a sea of human faces, all turned toward him, waiting for him to speak, and in his mind's eye, he saw the American flags that stood on either side of the seats in the row of honor immediately before him.

He looked into the imagined faces of friends, the military and government leaders of his country, and most proudly, into his mother's eyes. In so many ways, he thought, he would impress all those within range of his voice, and he secretly gloated over the thought that his words, fashioned into a speech he had rehearsed many times, would make some jealous of his success. Donald knew the person who would be the most jealous would be his stepfather, and that pleased Donald above all else.

Donald looked at his make-believe audience, feeling an attentive hush created by the importance of the occasion. In a voice just loud enough to be heard, he began.

"Mr. President, Commandant of the Marines, fellow Marines, friends, and loved ones. It's not often a man can speak to such an important group of people, and I'm proud that today I can do that. I see my high school friends and my teachers and my mother, all of you who've really helped me all of my life, and I thank you for believing in me."

Donald's eyes searched the empty expanse before him.

"When you're in war, like now, some people become heroes. Sometimes, you just have one chance in your whole life to do something really brave. And when that time comes, and you don't do it, then you might not ever have another chance to do something that good again."

He hesitated only a moment, straightened his shoulders, and continued, "My mother taught me to be brave and to help others. When I got to be a Marine, they learned me all over again. When I grabbed up that machine gun, and I picked up my buddy, and I carried him on my shoulders, and I saved his life, I wasn't afraid. When you do something like that, you're not supposed to expect a reward, you just do it because it's good and it's the right thing to do. A Marine has to be a man who people can depend on, and he's going to be there when he needs to be. Everybody has got to know that sometimes. People will learn to trust him."

Donald looked at his imaginary audience and waited for any applause that might be given.

"So, I thank you for giving me this award, the Congressional Medal of Honor."

Donald took two steps forward, saluted, and then turned to accept his imaginary award.

The chickens, if they heard the speech at all, showed no sign of understanding. The cow and calf swished flies with their tails and grazed on the hay Donald had earlier given to them.

The fantasy world ended abruptly when Donald's stepfather walked toward him with a bucket of feed for the chickens that had been, only moments before, part of Donald's audience.

Donald grabbed his hoe and hurried toward the garden he had been told to weed. He hoped his stepfather had neither heard nor seen him.

Tabor emptied the last bit of coffee from the tin can he carried, and stuffed chewing tobacco into his sagging mouth. "Hey boy," Tabor shouted, "ain't you done what I told you to do yet? I told you to finish the garden a long time ago. Hell, I know better'n to ask you to do somethin' that takes any brains.

You ain't done nothin' right in so long I don't know when. I can't depend on you to do nothin' right."

Tabor sneered, "You're dumb, boy, plain dumb. You hear me, boy? Dumb!" He spelled the word, "D-U-M," and squirted tobacco juice in the direction of Donald's feet.

"Now git out to the garden, and don't let me see no weeds left," he shouted, louder and louder with every word.

"Fuck you," Donald said under his breath. He viciously swung the hoe at the weeds, cursing his stepfather as he walked along the garden rows.

Ralph Tabor weighed over two hundred pounds and was five feet six inches tall. His clothes were too tight for his large stomach and even larger rear end. His black hair was usually uncombed, and when he walked his eyes darted from side to side. Donald thought he looked like a toad searching for flies to further fill his fat belly.

When Alice Woodson's husband left her, Tabor saw the opportunity to get free land and free screwing. Although Alice Woodson was not legally divorced, Tabor persuaded her to marry him and moved from his shanty on the edge of town into the farmhouse with Alice Woodson and her five-year-old son.

After the marriage, Tabor was cruel to Donald, beating him for the most insignificant reasons. He was jealous of Donald's right, as an heir, to part of the farm, and relished every opportunity to tell Donald how stupid he was and to humiliate him in front of others.

"Undependable bum," Tabor would yell. Alice Woodson never had the courage to defend her son and, to escape her husband's wrath, joined him in making sarcastic remarks about her son.

Ralph Tabor refused to legally adopt Donald and constantly reminded his wife that Donald's faults were of her own making. "His stupidity ain't from me. He was born dumb and he ain't improved none since."

Donald had few friends in high school. He had never dared to participate in sports and seldom attended any social or academic function, and if he did, he was ignored by his classmates.

He had failed the sixth grade but would graduate in May of 1943 if his teachers, who understood Donald's scholastic limitations, gave him passing grades.

When Donald's teachers gave him his midsemester report card, he crammed it inside the pocket of his jeans and walked home instead of riding the school bus as he usually did. He entered the house through the back door, changed into his work clothes, and went to the barn.

Tabor watched Donald walk to the barn, waited until the boy was out of sight, then slipped into his room. He looked again to make sure Donald was still at the barn and rummaged through Donald's jeans. "Ought to be some spare change in one of his pockets. He don't need money for smokes like I do," he grinned.

That night at the supper table, Tabor pushed the report card toward Donald.

Tabor scowled. "Didn't think I'd find out, did you? Ain't no never mind, schooling ain't that important to someone like you."

Donald glanced toward his mother, who only sighed and looked down at her plate. Tabor sneered, "You ain't got the brains of a jackass anyhow. I told you already you're dumb."

Donald clenched his teeth. God, how I hate him, he thought, and he pushed his chair away from the table and left the room.

Stephen Emmerson sat at his desk in room 107 at Mineola High School. He had just finished grading the last of his students' six weeks' algebra exams.

He looked at the pupils seated before him, and when his eyes fixed on Donald Woodson, he studied him intently.

Donald's large muscular frame more than filled the seat, and the too-small clothes he wore showed a lack of care. Neither his shirt nor his overalls had recently been ironed. His tanned face was framed by the dark brown hair growing long on his neck, almost hiding the collar of his shirt.

Emmerson looked again at Woodson's paper and shook his head in concerned exasperation. He walked to Donald's desk. "I need to talk to you. Come into my office after school. There is something we need to discuss."

"But Mr. Emmerson," Donald said, "I've got to catch the school bus. It won't wait for me."

Emmerson started walking from the classroom. "The bus won't leave for another ten minutes. I won't take long. Come to my room."

Donald reluctantly followed behind his teacher then stopped in the hallway just outside the door, partially blocking the hurried exit of the last students scurrying from the school.

"Get out of my way, Donald," one of the girls from his class muttered as she elbowed past him. He grabbed at one of his books, and a bundle of papers fell from his arms. He looked at the girl, but said nothing.

Emmerson waited. "Come on, Donald."

The boy looked down the hall toward the front door of the school and the waiting bus then looked back at Mr. Emmerson. I don't want to talk to him, Donald thought, he'll just give me a bad time about my grades.

"I'm sorry, Mr. Emmerson, but my bus will be leaving and I can't afford to be late getting home to do my chores. If I miss the bus, I don't have another way to get home and my stepfather will be mad."

"Then will you come back into the classroom for just a minute? It's very important that I speak with you, Donald. In private."

The room was now empty except for the two of them.

"Donald, of all my algebra students, your grades concern me the most. I've just finished grading the exam papers. I'm sorry, but you didn't do well, not well at all."

Donald looked at the floor. He was anxious for the conversation to end, and he wanted to leave as quickly as he could. "I'm sorry, Mr. Emmerson, I have to go." He moved toward the door.

"Don't you understand? If your grades don't improve, Donald, and if you don't get your assignments in, I just can't give you a passing grade. I'm very concerned you won't graduate with your class. You'll have to repeat your senior year if you don't pass. Do you hear what I'm telling you?"

"Yes, sir."

"I just can't give you a passing grade!"

"I try, Mr. Emmerson. I do, I promise."

"But that's what I mean," Emmerson replied. "I know you try, and I know you're much more intelligent than your grades suggest, but you need my help. On the test I just graded, you only got three of the fifteen problems correct. Donald, listen to me. I want to help you, but I can't if you don't let me. If you could stay after school, even one day a week, we can try to get you caught up. Would it help if I talked with your stepfather to see if you can stay some afternoons?"

Donald's eyes were wide. "No, don't do that, Mr. Emmerson," he groaned. "Please don't do that." He backed further away, and the chair slid behind him, making a sound like chalk on a blackboard. He stumbled, his loose-leaf notebook fell, the clasp opened, and the pages scattered.

"Please don't talk to my stepfather."

"Donald, wait," Emmerson pleaded, as the boy ran from the room.

Emmerson walked back into the room, wearily sat down, and pitched his pencil to his desk. He took off his glasses and rubbed his graying temples with his fingers. "Damn, damn, damn! He just won't let me help him. He's not dumb, maybe he just doesn't care," he sighed.

Donald stepped into the school bus, and walked to the back. He sat down in the empty seat by the window. His face was flushed, and he brushed a tear from his eye with the back of his hand. He knew that he would not graduate, and he felt nauseated. He swallowed and held his hand over his mouth to keep from throwing up.

The bus picked up speed, and Donald hummed softly. He

looked out the window and saw the large familiar recruiting poster of a Marine in dress blues. Another poster had been added of Uncle Sam pointing his finger directly at him, saying, "I WANT YOU!"

Each day as Donald rode past the recruiting signs, he had imagined himself as a Marine. On that particular day, he read again the words in large letters: I WANT YOU!

That night in March 1943, Donald packed a small suitcase and quietly slipped into the kitchen. He found an apple and a piece of bread and turned to leave.

The faint glow of the moon shined through the kitchen window, and Donald saw the tin cup his stepfather used to drink his coffee. He saw the coffee pot on the stove that Ralph Tabor fixed each night for his morning coffee. He smiled as he gently lifted the lid to the coffee pot and pissed into the water.

4

Billy Harris was a senior in high school in 1943 at Pampa, Texas. He was taller than most boys in his class, standing just at six feet. He weighed only one hundred forty pounds, too light to play football, but he played on the varsity basketball team.

His black hair was a stark contrast to his usually sun-burned, freckled face, and when he smiled his wide grin dominated his facial features. He was not handsome, but his friendly attitude made him a well-liked person. He was admired by his teachers and had been selected as "Class Favorite."

He wore a size eleven shoe, prompting more than one person to call him "Feets." He was neat and conservative in choosing his school clothes, and his favorite attire was a white shirt, black trousers and shoes, and a white scarf his mother had given him for Christmas the year before.

He had read every book that he could find about the military. He knew all the famous American generals and significant battles of the American Revolution, the Civil War, and World War I. He followed closely the beginning of World War II and read with special interest about the Marines at Guadalcanal.

On March 10, 1943, Billy would be seventeen, old enough to join the Marines.

The evening was cool, and the supper dishes were done. Billy and his mother sat on the front porch and watched the stars. They savored the stillness of the quiet moments they shared, contented with the peaceful feeling of a small rural town.

Wanda's favorite place was the porch swing, with the wooden slats and arms of the swing worn smooth from many years of use. Each time she pushed her foot against the wooden floor for momentum, the dull monotonous creak created a contrast to the melodious and almost rhythmic call of the tree locusts.

Mrs. Harris was not surprised when Billy broke the silence one evening and said, "Mom, I've been wanting to talk to you about something."

"About Laura?" she asked.

"How did you know that?"

"I've been expecting you to tell me about her. I knew that when you were ready, you would talk to me."

"Well," Billy said, "I guess you could tell I think about her, but she hardly knows I exist. She's in some of my classes, but she won't even look at me half the time. I used to talk to her, but this year she's changed. She looks different, she dresses different, and she even smells different. I'm going to talk to her, and if she doesn't say anything, I'm going to keep right on talking, no matter what she does."

"You do that. If you're friendly to her, I'm sure she'll talk to you. She won't bite you," she laughed.

"I know Laura's parents," she continued. "Mrs. Bently buys clothes from the dress shop, although I don't think I've waited on her in some time. Laura came in herself not too long ago, bought a little cotton dress, solid blue with a white collar."

"Mom, you've never talked much about Dad. You have only one picture of him that I know of. Do you remember what he was like, what he looked like?"

Wanda was not expecting such a change in their conversation. She stopped swinging, and the locusts, sensing the stillness, stopped their song, and the night was quiet.

Her voice was soft. "Yes. I remember your father. I remember what he looked like. His face is as clear to me now as it was before he died. I think about him, though not as much as I once did."

She began swinging again, and the locusts started their rhythmic chorus. "At first, after he died, it was hard to talk about him to anyone. You were only three years old when he died, and in those days, there was no one to talk to."

"Why did you ask about your father, Billy?" she asked, stopping the swinging motion once again.

"Oh, I don't know. Guess I just wondered." He hesitated. "You loved him very much?" Billy asked, then said, "Aw, I know you did. Did you know you loved him at first? Did he love you when you started loving him?"

"Yes, I knew from the very first. I'm not too sure he loved me then, but he did later."

"What did you do to make him start loving you?"

"Nothing that I remember," Wanda said. "I just started noticing little things he did and said, sometimes just a smile, a little gesture."

"Mom, how do you know, I mean really know, when you're in love?"

The swing moved slowly back and forth. "You know it when you think your entire life was meant to be for one purpose, to be together, to share, to know life would be so lonely, so wasted if you didn't share it with that special someone."

The night became quiet again except for the creak of the porch swing and the call of the locusts.

Billy Harris first met Laura Bently when she moved to Pampa and was assigned the desk next to his in the second grade classroom.

Until his senior year, he had never realized how pretty she had become. He looked at her when he didn't think she would see him, and during lunch at the school cafeteria, he sat as close to her as he dared. He watched the way she brushed her hair, and for some unknown reason, she always seemed to put on more perfume when he was near her. He mentally divided her in half, and for the moment, he decided he liked the top part best.

It was only a matter of time, he knew, before she saw him looking at her, and he had no idea what he would say. He thought, I'll just say, "Why, hello, Laura, how are you?" Maybe I'll just say, "Laura," and nod my head. That sounds adequate. No sense in letting her know I've been noticing her, he thought. It'll be a simple "Laura," nothing too forward and kinda like "Well, what more do you expect?"

He stood before the mirror in his room and practiced saying Laura in a deep voice, nodding his head in a nonchalant way. He used different voice inflections, then chose the deepest he could handle without choking. He smiled to himself when he felt he could do it with just the right touch. He decided he would speak to her the next afternoon, when they were in fifth period, the last class of the day.

The next morning Billy took an unusually long time getting dressed. He looked at his face in the mirror, opened his mouth to check his teeth, and wondered why his ears had suddenly become so large.

He turned his face so the light shined just right to see if there could possibly be a whisker on his chin. He took off his shirt, lathered his face, and searched for the razor he remembered was somewhere under the sink. He found it, still in the Christmas wrapping paper from last year.

He shaved half of his face before he noticed there was no blade in the razor. By the time the blades were located in the medicine cabinet, the inch thick lather had dried, so he washed his face and lathered it once more.

He couldn't remember on which side of his chin he had seen the whisker, but after he finished shaving and washed his face, he was satisfied he couldn't find the whisker again.

He put on his shirt again, then noticed his hair was sticking up in the back. He put so much oil on his hair it dripped on his collar, and he changed his shirt once more.

"Billy, it's getting late. Aren't you coming down for breakfast? I've got to be leaving for work in a few minutes, and if you want to have breakfast with me you'd better come on. Are you all right?"

"Everything is fine, Mom, I'll be down in a minute."

Billy polished his shoes and then decided his shirt didn't match his trousers and changed once more.

"Well, you look nice this morning," Wanda Harris said when Billy walked into the kitchen. She smiled. "Did you shave, is that what was taking you so long this morning? Do I smell after-shave lotion?"

"Yeah, looks like I'll have to start shaving every morning. The whiskers on my face are getting pretty tough."

"Well, I can't wait. I'm almost late for work. Kiss me good-bye," she said, leaning her face toward Billy's. "Mmm, you do smell good. Bye, love you. See you this afternoon, maybe late though. The Millers are having a party and they want their house extra clean."

She waved from the front door. "Bye again."

The morning classes were extremely boring to Billy, and he constantly checked his watch to see why time was moving so slowly. He did not dare look at Laura all morning.

Billy was unaware his name was being called until his chair was nudged by the student behind him. He looked up, startled to see his teacher standing by his desk.

"Billy, are you all right?" she asked. "You keep jerking your head, and I've called your name without your answering."

"I've just got a sore neck, guess I hurt it in basketball," he stammered, his face turning red.

Billy glanced at Laura, and he was sure she was smiling at him.

He was grateful for the sound of the bell and gathered his books to leave the class. Laura pushed past him. "Billy," she said, and nonchalantly nodded her head.

The following Saturday morning, Billy walked to work. He saw Laura and a girlfriend coming toward him.

Laura smiled and said, "Hi, Billy."

He wanted to say something, anything, but he was too embarrassed to speak. They met, and when they passed, Billy looked over his shoulder at the prettiest girl he had ever seen.

He stumbled over the curb, and Laura ran to help him. She held out her hand, and they both laughed at his clumsiness, and it was the most wonderful day in Billy's life.

Each day became a beautiful day to Billy. He looked forward each morning to meeting Laura at the doorway of the school, and they walked to class together. He sat beside her in the cafeteria, and during class he looked at her so often he felt sure he would make low grades if he didn't start paying more attention to what the teacher was saying. He worked up the courage to wink at her and then felt the blood rushing to his face when she winked back.

Laura Bently had become the most important person in his life.

The evening of his seventeenth birthday, Billy asked Laura to come to his house for ice cream and chocolate cake. The homemade ice cream and cake were placed on the card table in the backyard, and Wanda Harris spread an old quilt on the grass near the large pecan tree. The breeze that occasionally cooled the evening was a welcome relief from the unseasonable heat.

After the cake and ice cream, they sat on the soft quilt, cushioned by the thick grass. What was left of the ice cream had been packed in ice and salt and carried into the house. The conversation and laughter of a moment before seemed to slow in synchrony with the increasing darkness, and fireflies twinkled and flitted in a zigzag pattern around them.

Billy glanced at Laura and then at his mother. "Mom, you know I've wanted to enlist in the Marines but couldn't until I turned seventeen, and then only with your permission. We've talked about it. Now that I'm old enough, will you sign the papers? You promised you'd let me. It has to be in writing before they'll let me take the physical."

"When did you plan to join? Surely you want to finish your senior year in high school. You don't mean you want to enlist now, do you?"

"Yes," Billy replied. "I do."

Wanda Harris sat very still. She looked at Billy then looked away. She had hoped this day would not come so soon.

"Billy, if you want to go into the Marines, I won't stop you, and I'll give my consent as I promised, but I wish you would wait a while longer. Wait until the summer, at least till then. You are so young, and you don't have to go just now. You could wait until later. Let them call you and then enlist. You haven't finished high school; you only have a few more weeks."

"Mom, I don't want to wait. If they draft me, I'll have to go into the Army, and I want to be a Marine. The school has already said anyone can get a diploma who goes into the service with no more than six weeks left in their senior year and with grades of A's and B's. The principal told me if I go now, I'll get my diploma. I'll be fine, you know that, and I'll write, every day if I can, and I'll write you too, Laura, just as often as I can."

Billy's mother rose from the quilt. "If that's what you want, Billy. I think I'll go in now. Good night, Laura, I'm glad you could come. Good night, Billy." She leaned over for him to kiss her. "You kids don't stay out too late," she said and walked slowly into the house.

Laura looked at Billy in the darkness. She rose and reached for his hand. "Do you have to enlist? You've told me you wanted to, but I thought you might change your mind. We've had fun these past few months, now that we've gotten to know each other, kinda like we're going steady. Won't you wait?"

"Laura, as long as I can remember, I've wanted to go into the military, to make it a career. It's all I've ever wanted. I don't know what else there is for me to do. I want to do something more with my life than work here in a grocery store. I want to be somebody, go places, see things I've dreamed about. We don't have enough money for me to go to college. Oh sure, I've saved some money, and Mom would work harder and do without if I told her I wanted to go, but I can't ask her for help. I'm not sure I could earn a scholarship. I could work during school to pay for part of my expenses—I'm not afraid of work—but what I want is to be a Marine. I've thought about us, and I've thought about not joining, but when I do, I know I'm losing something I've wanted all my life."

"What about me, Billy? What about what I want? You've changed my life too, and if you leave now, I'll feel like I'm losing something I've wanted all my life."

"Laura, I've got to go. I'm leaving next week."

"Billy, I love you," Laura whispered. "If you go, I'll miss you, and I promise to write you every day, and I'll answer every letter you write to me."

Never before had she felt so helpless. She had never known such a feeling of despair. Tears formed in her eyes, but she made no attempt to hide them.

"I've never known what it's like to be in love, Billy, and I'm scared. Please don't go. I may never see you again, and I'd just die if anything bad happened to you, I know I would."

"Laura, don't cry, please don't cry."

Billy stood close to Laura, and she raised his hands to her moist cheeks and kissed the palms of his hands. Billy put his arms around Laura and held her close, then lifted the tip of his scarf and tenderly wiped away the tears that filled her eyes. He smelled the sweetness of her perfume and felt the softness of her hair against his face.

"Laura," he whispered. He sat down on the quilt and, still holding Laura's hands, gently pulled her down beside him. He kissed her cheek and tasted the bittersweet of her tears. He pushed her gently back until their bodies were together. He kissed her lips, softly at first, and then harder with each kiss. He felt her returning his kisses with the same intensity as his own. She held his head in her hands, her lips pressed against his, their faces moving from side to side as their passions grew.

"Oh my gosh," Billy whispered. He breathed harder and pulled her ever closer to feel her breasts against his body.

Laura felt his hand as he tried to unbutton her blouse. "I can't get it unbuttoned, you've got to help me," Billy pleaded, and Laura reached to help him. His hand found her brassiere. He began to pant. "Does this thing have a button too? How the heck do you get it off? Does it go over your head?"

"It fastens in the back," Laura said, and turned more on her side. "Use both hands. It's like two hooks."

"Laura, please, I can't get it apart. For gosh sakes, help me." Billy felt the sweat on his face.

Laura reached behind her back and, in one quick motion, unfastened her brassiere. "Do you have a…you know…one of those things?" she asked.

"I have one, but the darn thing is taped to the bottom of my dresser drawer in my bedroom."

She felt his hand on her breast. The pounding in her heart made her dizzy, and she kissed Billy with a force that pressed her lips against his teeth. Now her breath came in short gasps, and she kissed him again and again. "Billy, Billy," she moaned. Her face moved beside his, her lips kissed his ear, and she said over and over, "I love you, I love you, I love you."

Billy whispered, "Laura, I love you so much."

She felt his hand as he pulled her dress further up her thighs, and she kissed him again and again with burning desire. She breathed heavily as she felt him on her. Together they tasted the sweet moment of first love.

The following week, Billy bought his ticket for the early morning bus to Lubbock, Texas. He stood on the sidewalk, looked at the town not yet awake, and his hand felt the softness of the scarf he wore around his neck. He thought of his mother and Laura. The night before he had told each of them good-bye and asked them not to come to the bus terminal when he left the next morning.

In the dim morning light, he couldn't see the lone figure standing in the shadows on the next block.

The driver of the bus climbed into his seat, and nodded. "Let's go, son."

Billy picked up his small leather bag that belonged to his father. He took a seat by the window, tightened the scarf around his neck, and looked out at a still, quiet morning.

5

Gilbert Everson was six feet tall and. when fully dressed, weighed one hundred forty pounds. His blue eyes and blond hair were inherited from his great-grandparents, who had migrated to the United States from Sweden in the early 1880s and settled in the eastern part of the United States.

His lanky build and quick reflexes made him a star on the varsity basketball squad, and in his senior year he was chosen as first team center on the All-District squad. After he graduated from high school, he worked in a small store for forty cents an hour, stocking shelves, and carrying out groceries for the customers. Later he quit his job to work on a construction crew to build the Pyote Air Base for the new B-29 bombers.

The West Texas oil town of Pyote, with summer temperatures in the hundreds, with the sand and blowing dusty winds, always smelled of burning sour gas. Gil knew that when he was old enough to leave he would do so, and on December 5, l942, his seventeenth birthday, Gilbert Everson filled out the necessary papers to enlist in the military service.

In March 1943 he was told to report to the Marine Recruiting Office in Lubbock, Texas, for his physical and induction into the Marines.

Gil's aunt watched him pack his bag. "I patched your blue jeans if you want to wear them," she said. "They're getting too short, like the rest of your clothes, but they're clean. Your socks are rolled, and don't forget to put in an extra pair of undergarments. I don't know if they put soap in hotel rooms or not, so you pack a bar of hand soap."

Gil buckled the strap on the worn suitcase, and his hands rubbed the scared leather.

"Aunt Ida, I remember when Dad called us together to tell us we were coming here to live with you. That's the last time any of us ever saw or heard from him."

"Gil," his aunt said, "you were three years old when your mother died. It wasn't easy for your father to care for all of you. Jobs were hard to find in those days. He did what he thought best."

Gil closed his eyes, and his mind returned to a time of his life he had almost forgotten.

"Kids," his father said, "I want you to know I've tried my best since your mother died to keep the family together, to take care of you as she would have wanted. God knows I've tried, but I just can't do it any more. I can't make the money we need to live on, and it's not fair for me to move you from town to town. Some of you younger ones could continue to do it for a while longer, but you older ones need a place where you can stop and learn how it is to live in one town for a while, to make friends. I've failed you, I've failed myself, I've failed your mother. I didn't want it to be this way. As bad as I hate it, the time has come for us to make different plans."

Gilbert remembered his father walking from one end of the room to the other, all the time rubbing his hands together as though he was rinsing them under water.

"Your Aunt Ida has agreed for you kids to live with her. It's the only place in God's green world I know to keep you together until I can save enough money for you to come back and live with me. Sis, you'll need to help with the cleaning and do some of the cooking. You older kids can work to help pay for your keep."

The children sat without moving. Gil was frightened at the thought of leaving his father. One by one, each of the children moved to their father's side. Robert, the brother just older than Gilbert, wrapped his arms around his father's waist. "I don't want to live with Aunt Ida. I want to stay with you."

"Dad, we can make it, I know we can," Charles, eleven and the oldest of the boys, protested. "We can manage. We don't need anything we don't got already or nothing we can't afford. I'm almost old enough to work full-time on a drilling rig myself, see, I'm getting strong." He stuck out his chest.

"Kids, listen to me," Gilbert's father said. "It's not what I want, but it's what we have to do. You can't continue to move from town to town. You'll like living with your aunt, and you'll fit in just fine with your cousins. Gil, one of Aunt Ida's boys is just your same age, and Robert, you'll be about the same age as her other boy. Now, I've already got the bus tickets. Get your things together tonight so tomorrow you can leave. Sis, will you see to it everyone is ready when the bus leaves at ten o'clock in the morning? We'll have to walk. The rear tire on the Chevrolet is flat, and I haven't had time to patch the inner tube."

Gilbert's father knelt down to look directly into Gilbert's face. "I'll keep in touch and send money for your upkeep. I'll save some, too, so we can all get back together. It won't be long at all before we can be a family again." He wondered if his children knew what he said was untrue.

The next morning the children packed their clothes. Gilbert and Robert shared the same tattered, worn, and scratched leather suitcase, showing the effects of move after move.

Gilbert's sister had been very quiet all morning. She fixed their breakfast, a slice of toast and jam and one slice of bacon for each of them. Only once had she looked into her father's eyes, and when she did, he knew she understood this was good-bye forever. He patted her shoulder, put his arms around her, and squeezed her close to his chest. He looked into her eyes for only a second, turned away, and walked to the back door. The screen door was pulled and latched, and a large fly buzzed against the screen, trying to make an entrance into the kitchen, where it smelled the scent of the bacon and toast. Gilbert's father unlatched the screen, and the fly made a happy flight toward the breakfast table.

The backyard of the small rented house was cluttered with sticker burrs, and the rusting remains of a Model T Ford were partially buried in a pile of sand blown in from several wind storms. A half-filled trash can, leaning with the wind, was perched on the sand pile as though playing King of the Mountain. A large jackrabbit loped across the barren land and stopped at the edge of the tall weeds just beyond the yard.

Gilbert's father looked toward the railroad tracks that marked the edge of the backyard. He walked slowly toward the tracks, thinking of the many hours he had spent working as a railroad man. Even now, he missed the sounds of clanking wheels, the triumphant sound of a train whistle, the heat and smell of the engines, and from his younger years, the shoveling of coal into the fire bin. Those days were gone; only memories remained.

He bent over, touched his hand to the track and smiled when he felt the almost imperceptible vibration, telling him somewhere a distant train rumbled across the West Texas prairie.

He cocked his head, listened for the sound of a faint whistle, then turned and walked back to the house where his kids had finished packing their meager belongings and were waiting for him to return.

It was only a half-mile walk to the depot, and there was plenty of time before the bus left, but there was little reason to delay what had to be done.

"Well, Sis, guess if y'all are packed we better start leaving," he said. He opened the screen door, not noticing the large fly regain his freedom.

The children picked up the suitcases. Gilbert chose to carry the small box of sandwiches his sister packed for the trip.

Gil put his arms around his aunt's neck. "Aunt Ida, it seems like these last ten years went too fast. I'm sure going to miss you. You've been like a mother to all of us, caring for us when we were sick, holding us when we were hurt, loving us every day of our lives. How can I say how lucky I am to have lived here with you?"

"You've said it every day, Gil, by doing the little things that help make us a family. I couldn't love you more if you were my own. I'm expecting a letter from you, just as soon as you can write, and if you don't, I'll paddle your britches when you come home from the war. You will come home, I know that."

"I'll come home. I promise."

Aunt Ida drove the black Ford to the cafe where Gil would catch the bus. The wind was blowing, the dust swirling, and a large tumbleweed blew across the highway.

"I remember the day you and the others came to Pyote. I remember how dusty it was, how scared you were. You were only seven years old when you came to live with me. Do you remember that day?"

"Yes. I can still remember how lonely and scared I was when the oil field bus slowed and then stopped right here at the bus station. I remember the driver pushed open the door and said, 'This here's Pyote, kids, where you get off. I'll help you with your bags, then I got to get moving, bucking that head wind slowed me down. I don't envy you. This place has about as much life as a bent nail.'"

Aunt Ida laughed. "He was about right on that. It hasn't changed much since then, has it?"

Ten years before, when the bus had stopped, Gilbert looked at his sister. "Do we got to get off here? I don't see nothing 'cept tumble weeds. Is this where Aunt Ida lives?"

"Come on, let's get off. It will be all right," she answered. "Robert, Charles, come on." She held Gilbert's hand and stepped from the bus. She shielded her eyes from the blowing dust and grabbed her hat to keep it from blowing away.

The four children stood on the hot pavement as the driver unloaded their baggage. He pulled the last suitcase from the bus, "Is someone gonna meet you kids?"

Gilbert looked up at his sister, "Aunt Ida's gonna meet us, isn't she?"

"Yes, we'll be fine," she told the driver.

"Wait inside that cafe, if you want to," he said.

The driver crawled into his seat, turned to wave at the kids, and the bus moved away from the curb. The children picked up their suitcases and walked toward the cafe. When they reached the door, Gilbert's sister said, "Wait out here. I'll see if Aunt Ida is here yet."

"I gotta go pee," Gilbert whispered.

"Come on with me," she said. She looked at her other brothers. "Do you need to go too?" she asked. They shook their heads, and Gilbert and his sister entered the cafe. The walls were dirty; here and there the blue paint had peeled, showing dark green beneath.

Gilbert held his crotch. "I gotta go pee," he wailed.

"In there, the door on the left," she said, pointing toward a door. "The one that's marked Braves, and don't sit on the toilet seat without wiping it if you have to do number two." Gil ran across the dusty floor, still holding his crotch. She looked around the empty room and walked toward the door marked Squaws.

She waited for Gil to return, then held his hand, and they walked outside. She motioned for Robert and Charles to get up from the bench where they had been sitting and come to her. "Better go use the toilet, the door that says Braves," she said.

Robert shook his head. "I don't need to."

"Go use the toilet, both of you," their sister insisted, and the boys walked inside the cafe.

The wind was stronger, and the dust swirled and stung their faces. Gil spat and rubbed his eyes, "I don't like this place, do we have to stay? Where's Aunt Ida? When's she gonna be here?"

A black Ford turned the corner and stopped at the curb. A woman stepped from the car. "Kids! Over here!" she shouted. "Over here!" She ran to where the children stood.

She grabbed Gil and hugged him. "I'll bet you're Gilbert. You look just like your daddy, and you must be Robert, and that means you must be Charles." She looked at her niece. "No denying who you are, being the only girl in the group," she laughed.

"I'm sorry I wasn't here when the bus came. I couldn't get here any sooner, I intended to, but couldn't get away from the post office till my relief came. Get your bags, and we'll go home." She took the bag from Gil and put it in the car. "Are you hungry?"

Gil nodded his head. "Are you our Aunt Ida?"

The woman knelt before Gil. "I'm your Aunt Ida, and welcome to Pyote, Texas."

Gil smiled at his aunt. "It was a long time ago, wasn't it? Well, the bus is here. I'll tell you good-bye now, Aunt Ida. Thanks for all you gave me these past ten years."

"Gil, the world isn't always a pretty place, but we can make it better than it was when we found it. You can always make it a little better if you try to leave more than you take. My prayers will be with you."

Gil stepped from the car and placed his bag on the ground. He stepped back from his aunt's car and waved to her. When the car pulled away from the curb, he stood in the blowing dust and wondered if he was taking more with him than he had left behind.

6

George counted out the dollars, placing each bill on top of the last. "Twenty-one, twenty-two, twenty-three, twenty-four dollars and seventy-seven cents," George said proudly.

"Seventy-six cents," George's father corrected.

Mrs. Pappas smiled and reached across the edge of the kitchen table and kissed her son on the cheek. "That's good, George, you're a good boy."

"How much have I saved now, Dad?" George asked. "There should be quite a few dollars. I've saved all of my pay checks since I started at the plant."

Mr. Pappas folded the dollars George had handed him, put the money in a brown envelope, locked it in a small metal box, and placed it in the cabinet above the dishes. "Now, George, it's all here, along with the money your brother has added. It's best we don't count it too often, just need to save what we can so your younger brother can go to college when he finishes high school. Your brother doesn't have a steady job like you, but he manages to pick up some money from selling papers and odd jobs. It all adds up. We'll count it together at the end of the month, like always."

Mr. Pappas counted the seventy-six cents in change and handed it to George. "You can keep this. It'll add up pretty fast if you put it away, but you do as you please. Spend it if you want to."

George was the oldest of two boys and two girls in the Pappas family. His father owned a small butcher shop, and even in hard times, the Pappas family lived a comfortable life and always had meat on the table.

In the late 1930s, the steel mill on the outskirts of the small industrial town of Huxford, Ohio operated at half capacity, but with the beginning of World War II, a constant flow of red molten metal and heated cinders spewed from the furnaces, and tall smoke stacks belched dirty, black smoke, making one house indistinguishable from another. Dirty soot fell on the once green grass, and the yards became filthy, lifeless playgrounds.

George, older by two years than his friend Ed Blake, graduated from high school in 1941 and started to work at the plant as a manual laborer for the going rate of eighty cents an hour. He was promoted to crane operator, moving the pipe from the incoming freight cars to the flat-bed carriers which transported the pipe into the plant.

By the winter of 1942 most of the town's young men had gone into the service. George and Ed, friends from early childhood, often met in the evenings at the city park and talked about the war.

"I'm quitting school to join the Navy," Ed said. "I think I'd like being on a big ship. You going into the Army or Navy?"

"I'm thinking about the Marines, that's where the fighting

is," George replied. "I went to the picture show last Saturday and they showed movies about the Marines on Guadalcanal. I wish I could've been there."

In January of 1943 Ed quit high school and enlisted in the Navy. When the picture of Ed wearing his Navy uniform appeared in the *Huxford Daily Tribune*, George wanted even more to enlist. He knew if he waited he would be drafted into the Army and would lose his chance to become a Marine. He tried to talk with his parents about enlisting, but his father refused to discuss the topic, insisting he continue working at the plant.

George was determined he would wait no longer and, one night when the family finished eating supper, said, "Dad, I'd like to talk with you and Mom. It's important."

Mr. Pappas, seated in the brown leather chair in the living room, scanned the headlines, looked over his glasses, and asked, "What did you say, George?"

"I said I want to talk with you and Mom. Mom said she'd come in when she finishes in the kitchen."

"Umm," his father grunted and looked again at the paper.

George's mother walked into the living room, wiped her hands on her apron, and straightened a lace cover on the small coffee table in front of the couch. She smiled to herself at the delicate handwork, remembering the hours it had taken her to crochet the intricate pattern. She heaved a satisfied sigh as she sat in the chair nearest her husband.

George cleared his throat. "Mom, Dad, I want to talk with you about something…"

"You're not in any kind of trouble, are you, George?" Mrs. Pappas interrupted.

"No, Mom, I'm not in any kind of trouble. I just want to talk with you tonight, please?"

Mr. Pappas lowered his head, glanced over his glasses at George, and turned to the next page of his paper. "Seems like all a person can read about anymore is the war. Every day, it's the same thing. I have to look on page four if I want to find out anything about the local news. Meat prices are getting out of sight. This war, I don't like it. We never should have been in it and wouldn't be if the Japanese hadn't started it all. It's not going to be over any time soon, I'll tell you for sure, and there'll be more killing on all sides before it's over."

George stood in the doorway for a moment, then stepped closer to where his parents were seated. "Dad, Mom, it's the war I want to talk about and…"

George's mother nodded her head in agreement with her husband. "And I know so many fine young boys will never come back home. I saw Ed Blake's mother this afternoon, and she said Ed was sent to some Navy base and expects to be put on a boat and didn't know where he'd go after that. My lord, I feel so sorry for her. She told me Ed's father was almost beside himself over Ed leaving."

Mr. Pappas responded, "I know, I know. I don't blame him for being upset. The boy never should have quit school. His folks needed him to work and bring in money to pay the bills. The boy was selfish in leaving when he did. Looks to me like he could have stayed to help his family."

George sighed, "Dad, Mom, I'm wondering if…if…"

Mr. Pappas got up from his chair. "I think I'm ready for bed. I didn't sleep much last night. Damn dogs kept barking all night long."

George pleaded, "Dad…"

"I heard those dogs myself," George's mother said. "There should be a law about dogs barking at night." She frowned and looked back at her son. "What were you saying, George? Something about the war?"

"No, Mom," George sighed. "We'll talk later."

George left the room, hating himself for not insisting they talk with him about what was uppermost on his mind. He walked out on the porch and looked down the street. Lights began to brighten the darkened houses, and he walked down the path, kicking a pebble. "Everyone tells me not to enlist, but no one will listen to what I want to say or do."

He walked to the gate in front of Fay Moore's house, and just as he turned away to leave, Fay came out the front door. She was small with dark brown hair and walked so gracefully she appeared to glide.

When she saw George, she smiled, then looked away, embarrassed. She was fond of George, but not in love with him, she told herself. She had gone with him to the school picnic, and the memory of George trying to kiss her made her face flush. She had refused to kiss him of course, but later wondered if it was the reason he had not called.

"Hello, Fay. I thought I'd see if you'd like to take a walk, or maybe stop at the drug store for a soda."

"Hello, George," Fay replied. "I'm going into town, if you'd like to walk with me."

"Sure. I'd like that," George said, and pushed open the gate. "Have you heard from Ed lately? I talked with his folks the other day. They said Ed will be going to sea in a couple of weeks. Maybe you already know, since he writes you every day."

George pulled his shoulders back and consciously made his thirty-four-inch chest as large as possible. "I'm thinking about joining the Marines. They're the toughest. That's why I want to be a Marine."

"I didn't know you wanted to enlist," Fay replied.

"Fay, when I join, I'd like to write to you, like you're my girl. Of course, I know you write to Ed, since you're his girl."

"No, no, I'm not Ed's girl. I do like him, of course, but only as a friend. He's written me, not every day as you said, and I've answered his letters. The picture in the paper of him in his uniform made him look so handsome, didn't you think?"

George felt uncomfortable with his chest expanded so large and gradually let it return to its normal size, hoping Fay didn't notice.

"Well, I'm not saying you're my girl 'cause Ed and I are friends, but I'd like to write to you, and I'd like to get letters from someone besides Mom and Dad, especially if I get into combat and maybe even get shot or something. While I'm in the hospital, I'll write to you if you'd like. Of course, I might get wounded so bad I can't write, maybe hurt real bad."

"Oh George, don't go talking that way. I don't want to hear you talk about getting shot. It's bad enough to talk about the war at all."

George pictured a beautiful nurse wiping his brow, reading to him, holding his hand, telling him how brave he was. She would probably fall in love with him, he thought, and he would have to tell her he had a girlfriend back in the States. He could almost feel his biceps bulge with strength and power.

"If you want to write to me, I'll write to you, and I'm not Ed's girl, either. I'm nobody's girl, just yet anyway."

George reached for Fay's hand, and she started to pull it away, but then walked along the path with her hand in George's.

He expanded his chest once again and sucked in his stomach, and his trousers almost fell.

"Ed wrote that when he completed boot camp, he'd be assigned to a destroyer in the Pacific," Fay said.

The morning was cool and crisp, with still a hint of winter, and George had promised Fay he would walk with her to church. He knocked on the door, and when Fay opened it, she stood staring at him, her eyes red from crying.

"Fay, what's the matter? What's wrong?"

"Ed has been killed. His ship was hit by a torpedo from a Japanese submarine. I'm so sorry," she sobbed. "Ed's parents got the telegram just a while ago, and Mrs. Blake called. I'm going over to their house. Will you go with me?"

George stood stiffly, his hands clinched. "Oh my god." He swallowed, fighting to keep from crying. "He was my best friend, my buddy, your friend too. I can't believe he's been killed. He only left the States a couple of weeks ago."

George held Fay close. "Oh god, his ship must have been hit on the way over. Fay, I've got to enlist—tomorrow. I'm nineteen years old. I don't care what my parents think or what anyone says. Working in a steel mill isn't the same as fighting the Japs. I feel as though I'm letting others do the fighting in this war and I'm not doing my part."

The next day, George took his preliminary physical for enlistment in the Marine Corps and was told to report to the Marine Recruiting Office in Raleigh, North Carolina for his final examination and induction into the U. S. Marine Corps.

As he waited outside the Raleigh recruiting office, George studied the way the Marine in the enlistment poster was holding his bolt action .30-caliber rifle. He moved closer to the poster and looked at the medals, ribbons, and the battle stars on the tunic of the Marine. George straightened his shoulders and pretended he was holding a rifle at "present arms."

"Looks pretty tough, don't he?" a voice behind him said. "Don't look much over our age either. I'll bet he was a farmer before he went into the Marines. Look at those muscles, you can see them through his uniform. My name is Manny King, and I'm from Benson Cove. You going to enlist?"

"Yeah, I'm George Pappas, from Huxford, Ohio. Where's Benson Cove?"

"North Carolina, not too far from here," Manny replied.

"I took my first physical back home in Ohio," George said. "I came in with some other guys last night. We were told to report here for another physical."

"I got orders to report here, too," Manny said. "We were told that if they don't find anything wrong with us we'll be sworn in and head out. I don't want the war to end before I get a crack at whipping the Japs."

"I wanted to enlist earlier but never got around to it," George said. "I had a friend who joined the Navy, killed on his way overseas, probably a Jap sub hit them. I don't think he ever saw any action."

"Is that why you're joining the Marines?" Manny asked.

"No, but when my friend got killed, I decided to join.

Besides, the draft board would put me in the Army if I didn't enlist, and I wanted to be a Marine. What about you?"

"I stepped in a pile of mule shit," Manny answered.

Pappas frowned. "Oh. Well, that sounds like as good a reason as I can think of."

"Down our way most folks don't think the war will last too long," Manny added. "Don't see how it can, with Japan being such a little island and America being so big. I don't see why we couldn't just circle their island with our ships and keep them bottled up till they surrendered."

When George and Manny entered the recruiting office, they handed their papers to the recruiting sergeant and followed him into a large room.

When the examination was finished, Manny asked, "Was your first physical like that?"

"It wasn't as complete. I'm glad I put on clean shorts this morning. I'm not sure what they were doing with all that feeling around, but I think I lost my virginity," he laughed.

"I wonder what they're looking for when they look up your butt?" Manny said. "I don't have anything I hide there."

Manny and George were immediately inducted into the U.S. Marine Corps. A quarantine had momentarily been placed on Camp Lejeune, and all new enlistees were ordered to report to the Marine Recruiting Depot, San Diego, California.

7

The four young men who stood outside the Marine Recruiting Office in the early morning of March 15, 1943 shivered as the cold wind and rain whipped the awning over the front of the Sears and Roebuck store.

Mack Williams pulled his leather football jacket tighter around his neck and nodded his head at the boy wearing a pink satin basketball jacket with the words Pyote Braves sewed across the back.

"Hi, my name is Mack Williams. What's yours?"

"Gilbert Everson. My friends call me Gil."

They both waved at the tall, freckle-faced kid with big feet behind them.

Billy Harris smiled broadly at Gil. "I'm Billy Harris, from

Pampa, Texas. I see you played basketball. I did too, when I could keep my feet from getting in the way," he laughed.

Mack looked toward the man standing near the door of the building. "Who's your friend?"

"I haven't met him," Billy replied. "I just got here."

"My name is Donald Woodson, from Mineola. I'm here to join the Marines."

"Yeah," Billy added. "We all are. I want to get into the infantry, that's where I'd rather be, but it'll be my luck to end up as a cook. I've never shot a gun in my life, never even held a gun, but I hope it won't matter. I can't cook either, so maybe it won't make any difference what I don't know. I'll be starting from the bottom no matter where they put me." He pulled his sweater around his chest. "Boy, this rain is cold."

Gil tried to look startled. "Is that what this is? I'm from West Texas, and I was ten years old before I saw my first rain. It was the last time too. I fainted, and they had to throw sand in my face to bring me around."

"You never saw rain until you were ten, and that was the last time? You must be kidding," Donald said.

The rain fell heavier, and the boys moved further beneath the awning. "Look at the girl in the store window," Mack said, pointing to the store next to the recruiting office. All four boys watched her pull a pair of sheer panties on the long slim legs of a mannequin.

Mack stepped closer to the glass. "How much do those cost?" he asked. "If they don't cost too much, I might buy you a pair, providing you model them for me."

"She probably can't hear you through the glass," Gil said.

She looks familiar, Mack thought, but I can't place her. In a louder voice, Mack repeated what he had said.

The girl in the store window stared at Mack, then a broad smile crossed her face. "Mack? Mack Williams? Stay right there. I'll come outside."

She ran from the store. "You don't recognize me, do you?"

"Anna Robbins! Sure I remember you now. I knew you looked familiar. I can't believe it. My gosh, how many years has it been?"

"Four years—since we moved from Crockett. I wondered if I'd ever see you again."

"You've changed so much since I saw you that I didn't recognize you at first," Mack exclaimed. "What happened to the braces on your teeth? You've let your hair grow long, and you're…you're more beautiful than I thought you'd be."

"Is that a compliment?" Anna said, casting her eyes about in a provocative manner.

"I didn't mean it the way it sounded. I just meant that you're even more beautiful than I could have imagined. What I meant is…," he stammered.

Anna tilted her head back and laughed, her long black hair swinging over her shoulders. "Oh, I know what you meant. I was just teasing."

Mack looked down at her neckline and then, embarrassed, quickly looked back into her eyes. "You have filled out in all the right places."

Anna's eyes sparkled when she laughed. "Girls do that, you know. You still look pretty much the same. You've grown taller, but I recognized your curly auburn hair."

"You heard me through the glass, didn't you?" Mack laughed. "Why didn't you say something when I spoke to you a minute ago?"

"I was too surprised. I didn't expect to see you."

"I've thought about you so many times since you moved away," Mack said. "It's good to see you again. It's been a long time."

"Yes. It seems a lifetime. Oh, it's so wonderful to see you."

They stood looking at each other, both feeling the magic of the moment.

Anna was the first to speak. "Still live in Crockett?"

"Yeah, my folks do. I'm a freshman at Tech."

Anna looked at the Marine recruiting office. "Are you joining the Marines?"

"If I pass the physical. Look, I need to go inside. I don't know how long I'll be there, but when I'm through, I've got to see you again."

"I'd like that. I'll be here," Anna said.

"Your boyfriend wouldn't mind?"

She smiled. "I don't have a boyfriend." When she walked toward the store, she turned and blew him a kiss. Mack pretended to catch it.

"I'll keep that until I see you again. So long, Anna."

Inside the recruiting office, a staff sergeant in dress blues was seated behind a desk. Two rows of battle ribbons with battle stars and an expert rifleman's medal were pinned to his chest.

"We want to join the Marines," Billy said.

The sergeant rose from his chair. "Good. Come in, you've picked the best."

Donald was standing as straight as he could, arms to his side. He saluted the staff sergeant. "Aye aye, sir."

"You've had military experience?" the sergeant asked.

"No, sir, not yet."

The sergeant's eyes moved from Donald's head to his toes. "You don't need to salute an enlisted man."

The sergeant handed them papers from his desk. "Fill these out, then return them to me. If you have any questions, let me know."

When Mack handed the form to the staff sergeant, the sergeant frowned. "You're only seventeen and you spent six years in jail? When was that? For what reason?"

Mack laughed. "My father was sheriff, and we lived in the jail for six years."

"You don't understand," the sergeant growled. "We're not playing games." He ripped the paper into tiny pieces. "Fill out another one and bring it back."

The sergeant studied the recruits. "Three seventeens and one eighteen. OK, come on, let's see if you can pass your physicals."

He motioned for them to follow him into another room. A corpsman nodded. "Morning, Sergeant. New blood?"

"Start these men on their physicals. Captain Frazer has some papers to sign, and then he'll be in."

The corpsman told the recruits, "I'll take your blood pressure, temperature, and give you an eye exam, and then I'll take a sample of blood for our lab work. Captain Frazer will give you a chest x-ray, short arm inspection, and a rear-ender. Any questions?"

When Captain Frazer entered the room, he spoke to the corpsman. "Morning Charley. How you doing? Finished with the prelim?"

"Morning Captain. Yes, sir. Everything looks all right to this point."

The captain faced the boys. "So you want to be Marines? You look like you're in good health, and I hope all of you pass. The Marines can use young men like you."

The doctor motioned to Billy. "What's your name, son?"

"Billy Harris, sir."

Frazer looked at Billy's feet, "I'm not too sure we have shoes your size, but if you can find shoes in civilian life, we can in the military. Maybe you'll be lucky and get assigned a desk job. I don't think the infantry will take you with feet that big."

Billy said, "Captain, I'm not joining the Marines to sit behind a desk. I want to get into the infantry."

"Well, then, I hope you get in the infantry," he replied.

When the physical exams were completed, the staff sergeant stood before the recruits. "You're free to leave. If you passed, you'll be notified when and where to report for induction."

Donald stepped closer to the sergeant, "Sir, I mean, Sergeant, when can I find out? I'd like to get into the Marines as soon as possible." In a lowered voice, he said, "To be honest, I've just got to have passed. I can't go back home. My stepfather wouldn't let me. I have no place to go."

"I'll have the results for all of you by 0900 tomorrow." When they left the recruiting office, Mack said, "Well, I don't think any of us have to worry about not passing the physical, and we could all be on our way tomorrow."

He looked toward the store window where he had first seen Anna. "I don't know what the rest of y'all are going to do, but I know what I'm going to do."

"Can you tell me where I can find Anna Robbins?" Mack asked a clerk at the front of the store.

"Anna works in the women's department, down this aisle and to your left."

When Mack saw Anna, he stopped. Her long black hair fell in soft waves about her face, and the silk blouse she wore was pulled tight across her breasts.

"Hello, Anna," Mack said.

"Mack, I'm glad you came," Anna exclaimed. "I was about to think you weren't coming. I have to leave early today, and I was afraid I'd miss you."

"The physicals took longer than I thought. I came as soon as I could. I'm glad I got here before you left."

"I've been thinking about you ever since I saw you this morning," Anna said.

"And I've thought about you too," Mack admitted. "I never realized until I saw you this morning, how glad I am to find you again. I couldn't leave without talking with you." Mack reached across for Anna's hands. "Anna, there's a lot I'd like to say to you. Can you go out with me tonight?"

"Mack, I wish I could, I really do, but I can't, not tonight. Mom has asked me to do something for her that I can't put off. I'm truly sorry." She hesitated. "Maybe tomorrow? Will you come by the store tomorrow?"

"There might not be another tomorrow for you and me, Anna. I may be leaving right away. Are you sure you can't change your plans for tonight? I'd really like to see you. It's been too many years since you moved away, and there's not enough time left to say all the things I'd like to say. Can't you go tonight? Please?"

"Mack, I've thought about you all day. I'm glad I've seen you again, but if you're going into the Marines, as you must be, then you and I don't need a one-night stand. You'll be gone and I'll be left with nothing but a few more memories. I don't want just memories. You might come back, then again, you might not, and for the rest of my life, I'd think of dreams that might have been. No, you go fight your war. Come back if you can, and then I'll have that date with you. I told you good-bye this morning. It's harder to tell you good-bye now. I don't want it to be any harder, and it would be if I went out with you tonight, even if I could. The next time I see you, I want to tell you hello, rather than good-bye. Can you understand?" Anna slowly pulled her hand away. "I'm sorry, I really am. Will I see you tomorrow?"

"I'll be back at nine in the morning to find out if I passed my physical. I'll come as soon as I know."

It was a beautiful night, the rain had ceased, and Donald and Billy walked down the wet sidewalks, looking into store windows.

"I think I'm going to the motel," Billy said. "Where are you staying tonight?"

"I hadn't planned on spending the night here," Donald replied. "I haven't had time to find a place yet."

"You can stay with me," Billy offered. "It's not fancy, but the room is clean, and there are two beds. You're welcome to share my room."

"You're sure you don't mind? I'll pay my part," Donald replied. "I've got two dollars, if that's enough for my share."

"I guess you've wanted to join the Marines a long time, just as I have," Billy said. "I've planned on this moment almost since my father died. He died when I was young, and I don't remember him much. Are your folks still living?"

Donald could not say the things he wanted to say. No one had ever talked to him about their own personal feelings as

Billy was doing, and he had never dared to share his own feelings with anyone.

"No, I don't have any parents."

They walked in silence, then Billy continued, "Mom didn't want me to join the Marines, but she signed the papers so I could. I have a girlfriend, and she didn't want me to leave either, but after Pearl Harbor, I knew I'd join the Marines when I turned seventeen."

They were in front of the motel, and Billy stopped. "Donald, have you thought how it will be when we go overseas and get into combat? I have, and I wonder if I'll be brave or not. Do you ever think like that?"

Donald wanted to tell Billy about his fears of how he would act under fire, how he had nightmares of getting wounded, maybe killed. He wanted to tell the truth, but if he did, he wondered, would Billy be like the others, telling him how unreliable he was and how he would fail in all the things he attempted to do?

"Combat won't be too rough for me, and I'll be as brave as anyone, maybe a lot braver than most. I can handle it," Donald answered.

"You're going to make a good Marine, Donald. I hope we can stay together," Billy said.

Donald looked away. He didn't want Billy to see his face and know that he was lying.

8

Mack kicked the covers off his feet, sat up in bed, and looked at the twin bed across the room. He could see only the top of Gil Everson's head, a bit of blond hair sticking out from beneath the covers. "Rise and shine, the recruiting sergeant told us to be at the office at nine o'clock. If we pass our physicals, we might be on our way to San Diego before the day is over."

Gil yawned and pushed the covers back. "I hope so."

"You hungry for bacon and eggs with some hot biscuits, butter, and homemade jam?"

Gil had two dollars in his pocket. That was all he had brought with him, leaving the rest of his wages with his Aunt Ida when he left home the day before.

"I don't eat much in the mornings," Gil lied. "I'm not hungry. I'll skip breakfast."

"Suit yourself. I have a meal ticket, and I can't get my money back if I don't use it up. You're welcome to join me."

"To tell the truth, Mack, I'm so hungry I could eat the south end of a northbound polecat, but I just have a couple dollars, and I've got to make it last."

"Gil, if I've got something and we can share it, we will. From now on, we need to be honest with each other. If we both get in the Marines and end up in the same outfit, we'll need to depend on each other, so let's get something to eat."

Gil extended his hand. "Mack, I hope we do end up in the same outfit. I think we'll do pretty well together. I don't think either of us need to worry about flunking the physical, but you never can tell. My best friend came to Lubbock to join the Marines and couldn't pass his physical. He thought he was healthy, but the doctor found out he had a bad heart. You got anything wrong with you?"

"Only thing wrong with me is I got one nut that hangs down low."

"As long as it's not your pecker that hangs down to your knees you'll probably be all right," laughed Gil.

The boarding house was a large frame house with wooden floors and high ceilings, and inside, the smell of bacon cooking and the aroma of coffee invited everyone to a table covered with dishes of scrambled eggs, buttered toast, and jelly.

Gil sniffed. "Do I smell Irish stew? Ahh...I love Irish stew. My aunt could cook it better than anyone. Maybe I can get the cook to let me sample it."

The cook gave Gil an extra large bowl and served him four eggs and stacked bacon on his plate.

"Gil, I know you're not a big eater," Mack said, "but if you're sure you don't want anything more, we better get to the recruiting office, it's almost nine o'clock."

"Well, I could eat another bowl of stew, but if you're in a

hurry, I guess I'm through. You sure you don't want to get there early so you can see Anna?"

Mack smiled. "I intend to talk to her before I leave."

Mack and Gil walked to the recruiting office and saw Donald Woodson sitting on the curb.

"How long you been here, Donald?" Gil asked.

"Awhile, maybe an hour. I came down early so I'd be here when they open." He looked at his watch. "We still have a few more minutes to wait."

"Are you nervous about passing the physical? You look healthy to me," Gil said.

"Yeah, I guess I am, but if I didn't pass, I can't go back home, and I don't have any other place I can go," Donald said.

"Quit worrying, now you're making me nervous," Mack said. "The doctor probably didn't see anything when he looked up your butt, and he might not have seen anything except space when he looked in your ears."

Donald frowned. "I'm serious, Mack. I don't know what will happen if I didn't pass the physical. Well, hell, it's nine o'clock, and here comes Billy. Let's go in and get it over with."

The Marine sergeant was sitting at his desk when the four boys entered the recruiting office. "Men," he said, "your travel orders have been cut. Departure time will be at 1300 hours from the Lubbock Greyhound bus station. Don't miss it. Woodson, you're in charge of the travel party. Here are the papers, meal chits, and a voucher for your hotel room tonight in El Paso. Report to the Marine recruiting office in El Paso at the office location shown on your travel orders and be sworn into the United States Marine Corp. That's all. You're dismissed."

"Does that mean we passed the physical?" asked Donald.

The sergeant scowled. "I said you were dismissed. It also means to get the hell out of here."

"Come on, Donald," Billy said, pushing Donald through the door and out into the street, "You passed your physical. Let's go, and since you're our leader, all you need to worry about now is getting us to El Paso. Any orders, sir?" he joked.

Gil and Mack snapped to attention and saluted.

Donald said, "Yeah, as a matter of fact there is. All of you be at the bus station at twelve o'clock. That'll give us one hour before the bus leaves. The bus won't wait if we're late. You heard the sergeant say so."

Billy grinned at Donald. "Hey, don't take this leader stuff too seriously. We haven't been sworn into the Marines yet."

"Well, you heard the sergeant, and it says right here on our travel orders that I'm in charge."

Mack looked at Gil, then at Billy. "I'll be on the bus when it leaves, but don't expect me to be there an hour early. I've got something special to do. See you guys at the bus station."

"Hey, wait up, Mack," Gil called as he followed Mack to the front door of the Sears department store. Mack slowed down until Gil was beside him. "Can you beat that crap Donald was trying to pull?" Mack asked. "Who the hell does he think he is, the Marine commandant?"

"Aw, he didn't mean anything," Gil replied. "He's just relieved to have passed his physical and now he's trying to collect his cool."

"Well if he thinks he can pull that crap with me, he's crazy. Look Gil, I've got to be by myself to tell Anna good-bye. I want to talk with her, alone, OK?"

"Sure, go ahead. I'll see you at the bus station if not before. Don't be AWOL or Donald will report you!"

"I'll be there, but if I'm not, send me a postcard from Japan," Mack laughed.

There was a chill in the air, and fluffy snow flakes fell. The ever present West Texas winds made the morning air seem even colder, and the sky darkened as the sun hid behind the white clouds. Mack turned up the collar of his football jacket, stuffed his hands in his pockets, and walked toward the department store where Anna worked.

He entered the store, and when he saw Anna, she seemed even more beautiful than before.

He walked close enough to hear Anna talking to a gray-haired woman. "Here's your package, all wrapped with pretty paper. Your husband is very fortunate to have such a beautiful wife. He'll be thrilled when he sees you in that sexy nightgown."

"I wish he'd get more than just thrilled," she said and smiled sweetly. "But I'm afraid he's lost the sparkle in his Roman candle. Still, it might just do the trick. Last month I laced his buttermilk with gin, but he fell asleep taking off his pants," she giggled.

Anna leaned close and whispered, "Let me know if it works." She laughed.

Anna smiled and waved when she saw Mack walking toward her.

"Anna, I passed the physical," Mack said. "I'm leaving on the bus this afternoon at one o'clock."

Anna looked at her watch. "That's only a few hours from now."

"Can you get off?" Mack asked. "I have to talk with you, and this is no place to say what I want to say."

Anna spoke to the clerk in the next aisle. "I'm taking off. I'll be back when I can."

"You'll need a coat. It's getting colder outside and it's beginning to snow," Mack said.

Anna grabbed her coat from the rack and pulled it over her shoulders. "Where do you want to go? There's a park just down the block."

"Anna," Mack said, "I'm leaving this afternoon, so this could be the last time I'll ever see you. I may never come back from the war, and even if I do, you may not be here. Can't we go some place where the pigeons won't crap on my head while I'm kissing you?"

"Do you want me to get my umbrella?" Anna laughed and reached for Mack's hand. "Come on, there aren't many pigeons, and if we have to, we can sit under General Sherman's horse."

Mack thought, the first time a pigeon craps on my head, we're leaving, and I'll be damned if I'll spend my last hour under the belly of Sherman's horse. I'll just bet he's a low-hung stud, and wouldn't that be a romantic setting, making love, and all the time looking up at a pair of balls?

Anna led the way to a park bench beneath the branches of a giant pecan tree. "The snow isn't falling too hard, we can sit here."

"Do you come here often?"

"Yes. I like to come here in the winter when the weather is cold and there's no one else around. In the spring when the trees are full of leaves and birds are singing, it's nice too. It's one of my favorite places. It's pretty here, isn't it?" Anna asked.

"Yes," Mack answered. "I'm glad we came."

"When we moved away, I wrote to you. Do you remember? I've thought about you many times since then."

"Yeah, I remember you writing. I answered your letter, and the letter came back, saying you had moved. I didn't know where to send it on to you, and I lost track of where you were."

"So that's why I never got a letter from you? I wrote you another letter, but I never mailed it," Anna said.

"If I write to you when I leave, will you answer my letters?" Mack asked.

"Yes, I'll write to you. I'd like to know how you are too, and if you can, let me know where you are."

"Anna, there's so much to talk about and not enough time to say all I'd like to say."

A gust of wind swirled around them, and Anna brushed the hair from her face. "I want to say things too, Mack. When I saw you yesterday, a special forgotten feeling came over me. It was like it was when we were freshmen in high school."

"Anna, I wish we could have met again before now."

"But we didn't, and we can't worry about that now," Anna said softly.

Mack stood and pulled Anna beside him. "When we were freshmen in high school, there was a girl I thought was the prettiest thing I had ever seen. I didn't think she knew I existed. I sent her unsigned notes, and once, on her birthday, I left a box of chocolate covered cherries on her desk. Do you remember getting it?"

"That was from you?" Anna asked. "Of course I remember, but I didn't know who had sent it. I wish I had known."

"I loved you very much then, as I do now. You were my first love. Some people call it puppy love, but to me it was as real as any love can be. Of course I wasn't the only boy that thought you were cute. Every boy in the class had a secret crush on you," Mack said.

"You used to blush every time I looked at you. You were shy then. I don't believe you are now," Anna laughed. "You've changed in other ways, too, I believe, these past four years.

"This is a corny thing to say, but I'm going to say it anyway. I don't know how long it takes to fall in love. I think I've loved you all these years. I'm not asking you to wait for me to come back from the war, and maybe you wouldn't want to. I'm not sure I could ask you to, but I will write to you, and who knows, maybe when I do get back…"

Anna stood on her tiptoes and put her arms around his neck. She looked in his eyes for a long moment. Her cheek touched his face, and she held him close to her. She knew this was a special, wonderful moment in her life she could never live again, and the thought made her want to stay in his arms.

She slowly pulled her arms from around his shoulders and backed away, holding his hands in her hands until they were at arm's length.

"Mack," Anna said softly. "When my family moved from Crockett, I thought I'd just die. I thought about you every day for a long, long time. I've dated many boys since then, but I never felt about them as I did about you. It was as though you were the only boy in my life. You've made me feel different than any boy I've ever known. These last two days have meant so much to me. When you come back from the war, I'll be here."

"Don't promise something you don't mean, Anna," Mack said.

"I mean it," she whispered. "When you go through the war, I hope you'll think of me. I know I'll think of you. When you read my letters, try to pretend we're together and I'll do the same when I read your letters. Perhaps we can feel each other's presence, and we can pretend we're holding hands just as we're doing now. I'll say a prayer for you to come back—to come back to me."

"Just promise you won't come here with anyone else while I'm gone. If you do come here with some other boy, I hope the pigeons crap all over both of you."

Anna started to laugh and then kissed him. In a low voice, she whispered, "Let's not say good-bye. I don't know how to say good-bye to someone I may never see again. I don't know what I'm supposed to say. I don't know what to feel. You came back into my life so quickly, and now you're leaving the same way. I didn't want it to be this way. I almost wish you had never come back into my life because this may be all it will ever be, and yet, without you, my life would never have had this moment I know I'll never forget."

The tears formed in her eyes, and she brushed them away as they started to roll down her cheeks. She tried to laugh. "Why am I crying? This isn't like me to do that."

Anna held Mack close and murmured softly, "Why did you have to wait so long to come back into my life?"

"Anna," Mack said, "I plan on coming back. Every man plans on it. I hope I can. I hope you're here when I do."

He looked at his watch. "I have to go now."

"When you leave, will you just walk away? I don't want to see you leave. Will you kiss me good-bye? I'll close my eyes so you are the last thing I see until you're gone."

Mack held her in his arms, and she closed her eyes. She felt his lips on her mouth, tenderly at first, then his lips pressed harder. Her hands, soft and cold, touched his face, and he kissed her again and again. The tears, escaping from her tightly closed eyes, rolled down her face.

Finally, she no longer felt his lips against hers and, for a brief moment, felt his fingers wipe away the tears she no longer tried to hide.

She heard his footsteps as he walked away, and when she

opened her eyes, there was no one in sight. She wanted to run after him, to hold him in her arms once more, to tell him how much she loved him. For a long moment, she stood looking in the direction he had gone, and a feeling of loneliness filled her heart. The March wind seemed very cold, and she tightened her coat around her neck. She sat on the bench and watched the snow cover the world around her.

9

Mack picked up the small bag he had packed with a change of clothes and his toilet articles. He took one more look around the room in the football dormitory where he had lived these past several months and walked to the bus station.

"Where is Gil?" Mack asked Billy.

"Inside. He's got a bad case of the runs. He thinks it must be the Irish stew he ate for breakfast. You ate breakfast with him, didn't you? Did you eat the stew too?" Billy asked.

"Nope, I didn't have any, but he had at least two helpings. How bad is it?"

"He's gone to the toilet at least four times in the past hour."

"He better get over it before he gets on the bus," Mack replied. "I don't think the driver will stop along the road, and it's a long way between towns from here to El Paso."

Gil came out of the terminal and gradually eased himself down on the wooden bench by Mack and Billy.

"I don't feel so good," Gil groaned and wiped the sweat from his forehead. "I'm not sure I can even get on the bus. I feel like I'm going to throw up again. It's hell to be running off at both ends at the same time. My butt is so sore it'd hurt to touch it with a powder puff. I may try to catch a later bus to El Paso."

"There isn't another bus to El Paso until tomorrow," Mack said. "Maybe the driver will let you sit by the door so you can be the first to get off the bus when he stops."

"I assure you I'll be the first off the bus," Gil sighed.

"Maybe you could get a couple of paper bags and sit at the back of the bus," Mack suggested. "One to throw up in and the other to crap in."

"This isn't a time to joke. I'm really sick. Oh hell, I better go to the toilet again before the bus starts loading."

The driver finished checking the boarding passes and moved behind the steering wheel. Gil leaned over and whispered to the driver, "I've got the runs, and if I say I've got to go, you'd better stop the bus unless you want me to shit all over the seat. I mean it, too."

The driver looked at Gil with a frown on his face. "Son, I stop for railroad crossings and bus terminals. If you mess up my bus, you'll clean it up, and I mean that too."

When the bus pulled into the terminal in El Paso, Billy was the only passenger awake. He had been unable to stretch his long legs or find a comfortable spot to place his feet and had only dozed. Mostly he sat thinking about his mother and Laura, wondering what they might be doing at this time of night.

Billy touched the scarf that hung around his neck. He liked the cool feel of the cloth on his skin, and the scarf, his good luck charm, brought back memories of his first date with Laura and of other good times when he had been wearing it. He closed his eyes and pictured her as she was when he told her good-bye the night before he left to join the Marines. He could still see her face, could almost feel her body close to his as he held her in his arms.

He remembered when they talked of his leaving. She had cried and he had wiped away a tear with the tip of his scarf. Now he found the end of his scarf and lifted it to his nose, and a trace of perfume was still there. He knew sooner or later the smell of her perfume would fade from his scarf, but it would never fade from his memory.

The bus slowed, made a wide swing into the driveway of the bus terminal, then stopped. The four young men pulled their baggage from the overhead rack and stepped off the bus into the hot Texas border town of El Paso.

The next morning, Donald was the first to enter the Marine recruiting office where other young men in their early twenties were already waiting. The other fellows showed up soon.

Boog Marshall was a big man, by far the largest in the room, and to Mack, he looked like the pictures of Charles Atlas, the body builder. His size discouraged anyone from being too inquisitive about his dress, his hair, or for that matter, anything else.

His sport coat reached almost to his knees, and his long blond hair was combed back so it reached well beyond his collar. A long key chain with gold beads hung beneath his coat. He tossed a coin in the air with his right hand, caught it, then tossed it again. Every now and then he would blow a bubble with his chewing gum.

Mack nodded as their eyes met, and he extended his hand. "Hi. My name is Mack Williams."

There was a long pause before the big man stopped tossing the coin and held out his hand. "Name's Boog Marshall, from Houston. Where you from?"

He flipped the coin again and blew a bubble inches from Mack's face.

"Crockett, a little town in west Texas. Mostly sheep country."

"Ever cuddle a sheep?" Boog grinned.

"Hell, Boog," Mack laughed, "the town isn't that little, we got women as well as sheep."

Boog frowned. "You ain't laughing at me, are you?"

Mack's smile faded as their eyes held. "No," Mack said slowly. "I'm not laughing at you, and the answer to your question is no, I haven't cuddled a sheep as you call it. I shear sheep, and I eat them, but that's all."

Boog shrugged his shoulders, and a smile appeared on his face. "Seems like it wouldn't be too bad, huh?"

They both started laughing, and Boog began to toss the coin in the air again and again.

The Marine recruiting sergeant looked as though he enjoyed eating nails. His eyes moved from one new recruit to the next, deliberately pausing when he saw Gil's pink and black basketball jacket, Mack's Levi's trousers and boots, Billy's white scarf, and Donald's faded shirt.

When he saw Boog flip his coin in the air, he walked from behind his desk and stood with his face an inch from Boog's nose. His eyes looked down at Boog's feet, then very slowly inched upward, stopping at the long hair brushed back to the top of his collar. Boog swallowed hard, more like a gulp, and his eyes glazed over as the wad of gum almost choked him as it slid down his throat.

There wasn't a sound in the room, not even breathing. The sergeant's eyes were penetrating. Not a word was spoken, but the message of disapproval was there.

The sergeant turned away and walked back to his desk, and the recruits started breathing again.

The sergeant picked up a list of names from his desk. "Sound off loud and clear when I call your name."

Just as he finished calling the names from the list, a young Marine lieutenant walked briskly into the room. The sergeant snapped to attention. "Ten-hut!"

The group of men, yet unfamiliar with military protocol, made an attempt to come to the rigid attention displayed by the sergeant.

"At ease. You men are about to be given your final physical examination. Since you passed the preliminary physical at your local recruiting station, it is unlikely that you will not pass the physical here. If you pass, you will be inducted into the United States Marine Corps. All of you in this group have volunteered to enlist for the duration of the war and six months thereafter."

The morning was spent bending over, saying "ah" and coughing, as some doctor studied their most intimate parts.

Billy's feet got the usual stare, but no comments were made. Donald no longer doubted that he would pass, believing that if anything had been wrong, the doctors in Lubbock would have found it. Gil, no longer concerned about being too small, only dreaded the rear end examination.

As the men stood naked, everyone took the opportunity to size up his fellow recruits. Mack noticed that although Boog was powerfully built, he would have a difficult time "cuddling" a sheep, as he had phrased it. Mack decided to keep his thoughts to himself.

After the recruits were dressed, the Marine lieutenant who had spoken to them earlier entered the room. "Ten-hut!" The sergeant snapped to attention, and this time the recruits did a more professional job of following the same rigid example set by the sergeant.

The lieutenant walked to the center of the room and surveyed the men in front of him. "At ease," he said, and the men relaxed. "I have the results of the physical examination, and all of you are physically fit to be Marines. After you take the oath this morning, you will be given your travel papers to proceed to the Marine Recruiting Depot in San Diego, California, where you will take your boot training and be assigned for further duty."

The lieutenant studied the men for a moment. "You don't look like Marines now, but you will. Your drill instructors in boot camp will either make you or break you. They will be the ones who decide if and when you can be called a Marine. I will read the oath to you, and you will repeat it after me, saying your own name at the proper place in the oath. Raise your right hand."

Gil smiled as he saw one young boy first raise his left hand and then quickly lower it and raise his right hand.

The men repeated the oath and gave their last name, first name, and middle initial as instructed. They had become the property of the United States Marine Corps.

10

The train carrying George Pappas and Manny King sped across the southern route from the east to the west coast on its way to San Diego, California, with almost one third of the entire trip traveling through the widest part of Texas.

George sat by the window, watching the barren West Texas miles pass beneath the clanking, monotonous beat of the wheels.

"Jesus Christ, we've been in Texas for the last three days. This train is either too slow or Texas is too big. I've never seen so much of nothing. Why would people live down here? I haven't seen a single factory like we got back home. Hell, I haven't seen a town in two days. I wonder what's the name of this place we're coming to?"

"The sign back there said El Paso," Manny answered. "Maybe we'll pick up more recruits."

The train slowed, and great puffs of steam belched from the engine when it stopped. More military recruits boarded the cars. Manny nodded to the tall blond boy wearing a satin jacket with Pyote Braves emblazoned on the back.

George nudged Manny and pointed to the young man wearing boots, Levi's, and a western hat. "They wear funny-looking clothes in Texas, don't they?"

After Mack and Gil boarded the train, they pushed their way through the recruits standing in the aisles. Some were laughing and talking about their hometown or girlfriend, but some men gazed out the windows of the train with faraway looks in their eyes, already missing someone they might never see again.

George Pappas sat by the window and watched the brown grass and spindly, twisted mesquites of Texas change to the darker brown stretches of flat New Mexico wastelands. He gazed at the sand and rock and saw swirls of dust skip between yucca plants that resembled silent sentinels guarding the lonely cactus and clumps of prickly pear. The flatlands gradually surrendered to the jutting buttes of Arizona, where parched and barren stretches of multicolored desert sands waited for rain that seldom fell.

He shook his head in disbelief. "I wonder what possible use this land could be to anyone."

"Maybe the Indians could live in this desert," Manny agreed, "but no one else could."

The panorama beyond the windows of endless terrain seemed to stretch the horizon, and Mack and Gil, tired of watching the empty wasteland, wandered up and down the aisles of the cars.

When they reached the end of the train, the last car was empty except for one man sitting alone on the last row of seats. They turned, ready to make the trip back to their car, when Gil said, "Hey, isn't that Donald Woodson? I haven't seen him since we boarded the train in El Paso. Let's go speak to him."

Donald, his eyes closed, half-asleep, rocked in his seat in rhythm with the train's movement.

Gil and Mack walked toward him, when suddenly the train swayed violently as though it were leaving the tracks. Gil grabbed for the back of the seat, missed, and fell into Donald's lap.

Startled, Donald jumped up from his seat, glaring, and swung his arms in a sudden motion that knocked Gil to the floor of the train.

Mack grabbed Donald's arms. "Hey, knock it off. Gil didn't mean to fall on you, take it easy."

Donald unclenched his fists and relaxed his tensed muscles. "I'm...sorry, Gil," Donald stammered and helped Gil to his feet. "You surprised me. I think I was asleep. I didn't know what was happening."

"It was my fault. I lost my balance when the train swayed," Gil replied. "I'm sorry."

Donald looked embarrassed. "I hope I didn't hurt you."

"We wondered where you were," Gil said. "There's some empty seats where we are. Do you want to come join us?"

"No, I'd rather stay back here. I can see where we've been when I look out the back. I like it when it isn't too noisy."

"Suit yourself," Mack said, starting toward the front of the train.

Gil turned to follow Mack. "If you change your mind, come on up."

When they had returned to their car, Gil said, "Donald is a strange guy, isn't he? He seems lonely, but he won't let anyone get near him. He'll have a tough time if he doesn't make friends with someone. I hope he finds a friend when he gets in boot camp."

"Screw him," Mack muttered. "I don't know what's on his mind, but sure as hell he isn't friendly."

For the next day and night and on into the late afternoon of the following day, the view from the windows changed

from the rock and sand of the Southwest into rolling hills
covered with grass, and the window panes were no longer hot
to the touch. Towns and, eventually, the buildings of San
Diego replaced the yucca plants of the desert, and the young
men crowded the seats by the windows.

The evening shadows stretched to their farthest reach of
the day as the train slowed to a crawl. The wheels came to a
stop, and the train seemed to sigh as steam escaped from
beneath the great engine.

When the men stepped from the train, they were greeted
with shouts of "You'll be sorr-eeee." The enlistees waved and
smiled, unaware of a stocky Marine corporal briskly walking
toward them, swinging a swagger stick, his shoes so polished
the rays of the setting sun seemed to reflect like diamonds. On
his chest were two rows of battle ribbons, with two Bronze
Stars centered in the Pacific theater ribbon, an expert rifleman's
medal, and the shoulder patch of the First Marine Division.

They were still smiling as Corporal C.C. Allen came to a
halt and, in a loud and authoritative voice, shouted, "Over
here, lads, step lively, line up in rows of three."

There was mass confusion as the men lined up in four
rows: some in pairs, some slouched, some looked at the girls
passing by, and some made no effort to move at all.

The corporal's chin rested on his green tunic, his eyes
flashed, and he said through clenched teeth, "Over here, lads,
over here, rows of three."

Some of the recruits tried to get into what they thought was
a military formation, but a few were still talking and made no
effort to do as they were ordered.

In a voice slightly louder than a whisper, the corporal said,
"I'll bet, by God, you feather merchants better listen up." It
was the first time any of them had ever been called a feather
merchant. They didn't know what a feather merchant was, but
the way the corporal said it, it must not be good.

The men assigned to his platoon would soon realize that in
the next eight weeks it would be the kindest thing they would

be called. Those near enough to hear his hushed command grasped the sternness of his voice and stood at their best imitation of attention. The men still standing in groups noticed the sudden change of those around them. Smiles faded, shoulders straightened, and three rows quickly formed.

Allen surveyed the menagerie of men before him. He muttered to himself, "Some of these shit birds just got off a watermelon truck and couldn't pour piss out of a boot, and some will be assigned to my platoon! This has to be the ugliest, most stupid gathering of human flesh in one small group I've ever seen."

To the men, he announced, "My name is Corporal C.C. Allen. I'm a drill instructor, a DI, at the recruit depot. If any of you shit birds are fortunate enough to be in my platoon, I'll make Marines out of you." His voice was soft, but the recruits clearly understood his words.

Gil leaned toward Mack and whispered, "I wonder what's the difference between being a shit bird and a feather merchant. Is that a promotion or demotion?"

"The first row of men will board the first bus, the second row will board the second bus, and the third row will board the third bus. Column left, harrrch!" Allen commanded.

Some of the recruits turned right, others left, some changed from left to right, and others remained where they were, too confused with all the turning to know what to do. "One, hup drree four, drree four ya left, one hup drree four, drree four ya left," the corporal shouted, and stepped smartly toward the row of waiting busses.

Billy started walking in the direction Corporal Allen marched toward the buses. Donald started in the opposite direction and bumped into Mack, and Gil tripped and fell to the ground. Boog Marshall didn't move, then ran to catch the rest of the platoon.

Gil and Mack sat in the first empty seats of the first bus. "I wonder if we're all going to the same place," Gil said. "Did you see which bus Billy and Donald got on?"

"They might have decided to get back on the train. I'm not too sure that wouldn't be the smart thing to do," Mack said. "Corporal Allen looks tough. Maybe it's not too late to crawl out the window and make a run for it."

11

The buses weaved their way through the streets of San Diego, and the recruits, who only a short while ago had been laughing and waving to the girls at the train station, suddenly turned quiet.

The buses stopped at the gates of the Marine Recruit Depot. Marine guards on each side of the gate saluted, and allowed the buses to enter the base.

The buses stopped in front of the camouflaged green and brown barracks, and when the buses opened their doors, Allen shouted, "Off the buses, line up in rows of three. Step lively."

Gil stepped from the bus, and his foot slipped off the bottom step. He stumbled and fell into the DI's arms, and both men fell to the hard pavement.

Allen scowled. "You fucking boot, get in rank."

Gil ran to the back of the platoon, as far away from the DI as he could get. Mack's shoulders shook with laughter, and Gil muttered, "I'll kick your butt if you don't quit laughing."

Allen's chin was held tight to his chest, giving the impression no sound could be emitted, but there was no mistaking the gravel voice.

"Line 'em up, lads, line 'em up. Form columns of three."

When the columns formed, the DI ordered, "Column right, harch! One, hop, dree, four, dree, four ya left, one, hop, dree, four, dree, four ya left!"

Somehow, Billy thought, this must be some type of code for marching. He couldn't understand the words, but there was no misunderstanding their meaning. Billy stepped with his right foot first, and Allen shouted, "Your other left, shit bird! Your other left!"

Billy did a double shuffle to change feet, and Donald, not sure who was and who wasn't a shit bird, was still trying to get in step as they entered the barracks.

A large room was filled with double bunk beds, one stacked on top of another. A folded mattress, two sheets, and a green wool blanket with USMC stenciled in black letters was on each bunk. "Find a bunk and stow your gear," the corporal ordered.

Mack pitched his bag on the top bunk. "Let's try out the showers, Gil. I'm ready to get some sleep. There's no telling when we have to get up in the morning."

When Gil returned to the bunk after his shower, he spread his sheets and blanket and crawled into his bunk.

"Man, this feels great," Gil admitted. "I'll be asleep in five minutes."

Corporal Allen walked into the room, and his eyes squinted into narrow slits.

"I never gave the order for you to hit the sack," he shouted. "Get your asses out of those sacks and stand by your bunk until you're told otherwise. I'll teach you feather merchants the Marine Corps way to make up a sack."

Billy was out of his bunk before Allen finished giving the order.

"What's your name and where the fuck did you come from?" Allen snarled at a man wearing blue pajamas.

"Stokes, Wilber, from Pine Point Arkansas."

"Your last name Stokes or Wilber?" Allen sneered.

"Stokes is my last name, sir."

"Stokes, do you know how to make up a sack, the Marine Corps way?"

"Why, ah suppose ah can put a sheet and a blanket on a bed, maybe not the Marine Corps way, 'cause ah don't know as ah ever knew there was a special way," Stokes replied. "Back home, my mamma just spreads a sheet on the mattress, tucks in the sides so's they don't flap too much, then throws the blanket on the bed so's the sheets don't get too dirty as to when you sit on it."

Corporal Allen licked his lips. "When I ask you a question, shit bird, I don't want a stupid, smartass answer, and I'd better hear 'sir' when you're talking to me. Do you think you can understand that much so far?"

The smile on Stokes's face faded. "Yes sir, ah think ah got that pretty straight."

The DI jerked the sheets and blanket from Stokes's bunk. In quick fashion, he spread the lower sheet on the mattress, neatly cornered the ends, tucked in the sides, and quickly did the same for the top sheet. He pulled the blanket tight, took a coin from his pocket, tossed it onto the bunk, and the coin bounced in the air. "Now then, Stokes, do you think you can do that?"

"Yes sir, ah reckon ah can do that, sir," he said. He picked up the coin and tossed it on the bunk as Corporal Allen had done. "Like that, sir?" he asked.

Allen's face was flushed. He jerked the blanket and sheets from the bunk bed and glared at Stokes.

"You fucking shit bird. Make it up the Marine Corps way."

Stokes folded the corners of the sheets and spread the blanket. He saw the blanket was not pulled tight enough to make a coin bounce. He pulled the sides tighter, but when he pulled one part of the blanket, another part became slack.

He tried again and pulled the blanket on one side then the other with the same result as before.

"Ah guess you going to have to show me one more time, sir, how you got that blanket to be so darn tight, sir."

"No, I'm not going to show you one more time, Stokes. You'll make and tear down that bunk twenty times, and by then you better get it right."

"I want each of you other feather merchants to make up and tear down your bunk ten times, and I might remind you when you hear taps, it means lights out. Is that understood?"

Corporal Allen walked briskly from the room, confident he had accomplished his objective of making the recruits aware that he was the owner of their very souls and that military life was nothing like they had ever dreamed.

When the order sounded for lights out, Donald was still making up and tearing down his bunk. It was long after many of them had finally gone to sleep before Stokes crawled into his bunk, not bothering to pull the blanket back to get in between the sheets.

All too soon for the sleeping men, the blaring sound of a bugle sounded reveille, and Gil jumped straight up in bed and rammed his head on the springs of the bunk above him. "What the hell is going on?" Gil rubbed the top of his head. "It's not even daylight. Don't tell me it's already time to get up."

The lights came on and Allen walked into the room. "Hit the deck. Turn loose your cocks and grab your socks. Fall in for muster, outside, on the double! Move!!"

A mass of humanity hurried to find clothes casually thrown off the night before. Shoe laces tangled at first touch and socks disappeared in the darkness.

Mack jumped from the top bunk to the floor and landed on top of Gil. He reached for a pair of trousers, and Gil grabbed them out of Mack's hand. "What are you doing? These are my pants. Find your own."

Mack found his trousers and pulled his boots over his bare feet. He stuffed his shirt into his trousers and ran from the room.

Corporal Allen yelled, "Form three columns, move it! When you hear your name called, sound off so I can hear you."

When roll call was completed, the raw recruits marched to a large mess hall, and Allen ordered the men to sit at a row of tables. Mess hall recruits from earlier arrivals placed large containers of scrambled eggs, bacon, butter, jams, and pitchers of cold milk on each table.

Billy piled the food on his tray and drank two glasses of milk before he started eating. Milk pitchers on the tables were filled again and again.

"Do you think we'll get this kind of food all the time?" Billy asked Gil from across the table. "If we do, I'll stay in the Marines the rest of my life." He put another helping of eggs on his tray, then put down his fork.

"Gil, I'm ready to get back to the barracks," Billy said. "Let's get out of here. I can't swallow another bite."

Gil and Billy moved toward the door, food trays in their hands. When Gil started to walk out of the mess hall, the corporal who stood by the door stopped him.

"Boot, at this base you leave no food on your tray. You eat what's there before you leave the mess hall."

Gil stepped to one side, and without saying a word, pushed the food into his mouth.

Billy stuffed eggs into his mouth and gagged when he tried to swallow. He took another bite of bacon, gagged, swallowed again, and crammed the last bite of food into his mouth. Billy's cheeks were bulging when he showed the corporal his empty tray and then staggered through the door and spit the food from his mouth.

Gil held his hand over his mouth to keep from throwing up. "That's the last time I'll ever take that much on my tray. Thank God it wasn't Irish stew."

As soon as the recruits returned to their barracks, Allen marched them in platoon formation to the supply depot for issue of standard military clothing and equipment.

The shoe size was a mix between a guess and a glimpse, and men who had worn tennis shoes, boots, or loafers to the induction center were unaccustomed to the heavy "boondockers" they pulled on their feet for the first time.

Each man was issued two sets of dungarees, pith helmet, socks, skivvies, first aid kit, mess gear, and toilet articles.

"This is my first razor," Gill admitted.

"Not me," Billy said. "I had to start shaving a long time ago."

When they marched to the base barbershop, other boots who marched by with their heads shaved shouted, "You'll be sorr—eeee," and the new recruits understood why.

Mack walked behind Boog Marshall when they entered the barbershop. "I hear you can throw your pith helmet in the air and have your head shaved before it comes down," Mack whispered.

As Boog moved down the line toward the waiting barbers, he put his hand on top of his head and covered the long blond hair that fell below the collar of his dungaree jacket. "They'll have to whip me before they shave my head."

Mack watched the barber shear Boog's head. In just three swipes, Boog's head was shaved, and Boog gathered up part of his hair from the floor when he got out of the barber's chair. "Hey Boog, you going to paste it back on?" Mack laughed.

When the recruits left the barbershop, Gil looked at Billy's head and started laughing.

"If you think I look funny, you should see yourself. You look like a peeled onion," Billy said.

Gil continued to laugh. "You'll look all right, if you don't take off your cap for a month or two."

"Yeah, and you'd better not go near a pool hall. Your head looks like a cue ball. If someone yells 'rack 'em up,' you'd better run," Billy answered.

"That barber that shaved Boog's head was really fast," Mack said. "After the war, I might give him a job out on the ranch. If he can shear sheep as fast as he cuts hair, there might be a better profit in the wool market."

Sixty-four recruits were assigned to each platoon, and sixteen men were assigned to one of four huts reserved for each particular platoon.

Privates Williams, Everson, Woodson, Harris, and Marshall were assigned to Platoon 224, and to the same wooden, single-story hut. Their DIs, Pfc. W. W. Mills, Cpl. C. C. Allen, and Sgt. L. A. Jefferson, were quartered in an adjacent hut. For the next eight weeks of boot camp, the DIs would possess the men—body and soul.

The following morning, Platoon 224 gathered outside their barracks. The three DIs stood before the recruits to observe their newly inherited platoon members.

Sergeant Jefferson's face was expressionless, but a close look into his squinted eyes revealed a man of stern discipline. His mouth was as much of a slit on his face as were his eyes. His nose was long and thin, his face scarred and pockmarked from some childhood disease. He was no more than five feet nine inches tall, but his small waist made his shoulders seem large. The medals pinned on his starched uniform were impressive, and his polished shoes glistened in the early morning dawn. He looked every bit the part of the Marine in the posters on the walls of the recruiting stations.

Mack knew it would not be wise to disobey or question the authority of Sergeant Jefferson, the senior noncom in the trio of DIs who stood before them.

Corporal Allen, second in command, demanded the same respect the recruits held for Sergeant Jefferson. He was tough, sarcastic, and displayed two rows of combat ribbons on his huge chest. His tailored uniform was contoured to fit every muscle of his body. His face was almost round, his pug nose flattened against his face, and his chin rested on his chest, even when he was not at rigid attention.

His gravel voice was loud and clear when he wanted it to be, and when he wanted the recruits to pay particularly close attention, he lowered his voice to a whisper so they strained to hear every word. When he marched beside the platoon, he walked with a swagger, slightly rocking his shoulders from side to side.

Pfc. W.W. Mills was older than the other two drill instructors. He was large in build but not especially muscular. His voice lacked the ring of authority that was apparent in the other two DIs. His uniform was not as starched, and his shoes were less polished. His "father image," not surprisingly, commanded less respect. The recruits, even from the beginning, would not fear this man as they did the others.

Of the three DIs, Mack knew if ever he had a choice to be in combat with any of them, he would choose Jefferson. His intelligence could mean the difference between life or death for those serving with him. In hand-to-hand combat, however, Allen's brawn could prove to be a better choice than Jefferson's brain.

"Ten-hut!" Sergeant Jefferson's eyes traveled from one recruit to the next before he ordered, "At ease."

"Those of you who with any college education, take one step forward," he ordered.

Well how about that, Mack thought, my semester of college has already given me an advantage over these other recruits. He and five other recruits stepped forward.

"Fall out and follow Corporal Allen," ordered the sergeant.

Corporal Allen said, "You men will follow me to the base officers' quarters. Left face. One hup dree four, dree four ya left."

Mack gave Gil a faint smile as he marched behind Corporal Allen to what he thought would be an easy office assignment.

Allen led the college-trained recruits to a supply tent and told them to pick up a bucket and a broom. "You shit birds have just volunteered to police the area around the officers' quarters. When I return, I'll inspect the area, and if it's not clean, I'll personally pound sand up your ass."

After Allen left, one of the other recruits looked at Mack. "How could the fact that we've been in college have anything to do with picking up butts?"

"The DIs want us to understand that it's not what we learned before we enlisted," Mack said, "but how much and how fast we learn as a Marine. I've learned I won't volunteer for anything again."

On the evening of the sixth day of boot camp, darkening clouds formed on the horizon and the skies were heavy with threats of rain. The humidity in the air increased as the evening hours surrendered to dusk, and the first spring rain fell softly on the Marine base.

Jason Balleau was from San Angelo, Texas. His face was brown, and thick eyebrows shadowed his dark eyes. He took a chain from around his neck and rubbed the smooth sides of a coin between his fingers. He let the coin swing, and as it twirled, the Mexican peso reflected the overhead light. Jason smiled to himself as he watched Billy stare at the coin. When Jason grabbed the coin and held it in the palm of his hand, Billy grinned. "That's some coin you got there. What is it, a good luck charm?"

"It's a charm my grandmother gave me a long time ago. I keep it for good luck. I wear it like you wear that white scarf. Where'd you get it? Does it bring you good luck?"

"I guess it does," Billy said. "My mother gave it to me. A lot of good things have happened since I started wearing it."

"Like what?"

"Well, there is this girl I had known for a long time, and then one day I realized how pretty she was. I was wearing my scarf the day I asked her for a date." Billy smiled. "There are other good things that have happened, but I guess since I wear it all the time, everything that happens can't be because of the scarf. I like to wear it anyway, good luck charm or not."

"I have a girlfriend back in Texas, and she's as hot as a jalapeño pepper. She looks great in a sweater, you know what I mean?" Jason laughed. "Say, Billy, I need somebody to help me try something, something that'll make the other guys laugh."

"What do you want me to do? I'm not good at making people laugh. When I try, they laugh at me instead of with me."

"All you have to do is watch the coin, and I'll tell you what to do next. That's all there is to it."

"That's all, nothing more?" Billy asked.

"Oh, I may tell you to do something funny."

"Like what?"

"I don't know yet, but I promise I won't hurt you or anyone else. Now watch my coin as it swings from the chain."

Billy had already started looking at the coin. "Don't look away until I tell you," Jason said in a soft voice. "And after that you'll hear only my voice, no one else's. When I snap my fingers twice, you'll wake up. Let's see if you can do it. I've tried it on some and they can't concentrate long enough. I'll bet you can."

Without waiting for a response, Jason started swinging the peso back and fourth, and light reflected from the twirling coin as though it were a blinking light.

Billy's eyes stared without blinking, and Jason touched Billy's hand. "The room is very warm. You are so hot you want to take off your trousers."

Billy loosened his belt and unbuttoned his trousers, and they dropped to the floor. Donald saw Billy's trousers fall. "Hey what's going on, Billy?"

Billy stood motionless and showed no evidence of hearing Donald's voice.

"You are an ironing board. You can't bend your body," Jason said softly. He walked behind Billy, and put his hands on Billy's shoulders, and then leaned him backwards until his rigid body was almost level with the floor.

Other recruits now gathered around Billy and Jason. "Pick up his feet, Gil, and let's raise him up," Jason said.

Gil hesitated, and someone said, "Go on, Gil. Let's see if this is for real."

Gil lifted Billy's feet and Jason lifted his head. Billy's body was stiff. There was no bending at the knees or waist. He was completely rigid. Donald laughed when Jason told Billy he was a duck and for him to waddle and peck corn off the floor.

"Quack," Jason said, "and flap your wings."

Billy quacked and flapped his arms, pecking at the imaginary corn on the floor.

Donald said, "Aw, he's just acting. He's just pretending to be hypnotized. What else can you make him do, Jason? Make him do something that we know he wouldn't do if he wasn't hypnotized."

"Billy," Jason said softly, "go out the door, out into the rain, and walk over to the DIs hut. Open their door, don't knock or ask for permission to enter, just walk into the hut, untie Corporal Allen's shoes, and throw them out the front door into the mud. Is that clear?"

Billy started walking toward the door.

"Don't do that, Billy," Mack said. "Corporal Allen will be so mad he'll put you in the brig. Billy, don't do it."

Billy didn't appear to hear Mack's voice or feel him touch his arm.

"Jason, if Billy gets in trouble, I'll make sure you'll never want to hypnotize anyone again," Mack promised.

"Come on, Mack," Donald said, "let's have some fun. Billy and Jason probably have this all planned anyway. He's not hypnotized. Billy won't go into the DIs' hut."

Jason and Mack stood looking at each other for a moment, and then Jason remarked, "He's not going to get hurt."

"Just remember what I said," Mack replied.

All of the recruits followed Billy out into the rain. They knew if this was just an act, Billy wouldn't dare open the door of the DIs hut without knocking. Every recruit looked on their DIs as second only to God, and there were a few who placed them first.

Billy walked through the door, and out into the rain to the DIs' hut. He opened the door without knocking and, with mud clinging to his size eleven boondockers, walked into the room where several DIs from other platoons had gathered.

When Sergeant Jefferson saw a half-naked boot enter the hut, his mouth fell open. Corporal Allen, lying on his bunk with his feet hanging just off the edge of the blanket, stared at Billy in disbelief. His feet dropped to the floor, and he tried to say something.

Billy walked to Allen's cot, untied his shoelaces and, before Allen had a chance to stop him, threw the corporal's shoes out the door and into the mud.

A DI from another platoon realized that the recruit was not from his own platoon and began laughing. Jefferson's face turned red from anger. His eye's squinted and his jaw muscles tightened.

Mills saw the recruits standing outside the hut in the mud and rain and was the first to understand what was happening. "I'll be damned, he's hypnotized. He doesn't know what the hell he's doing. Look at him."

"By God, you're right. That's it, he's hypnotized," Jefferson exclaimed.

Allen walked in his stocking feet to the door and looked out at the recruits standing in the rain. "OK, the fun is over. The shit bird responsible for hypnotizing this man will find my shoes, and when reveille sounds in the morning, they better be clean and polished. I better not see any evidence they've ever been even remotely near water or mud. This will be the last time something like this will ever happen."

He slammed the door shut, and the wet recruits ran back to their hut, none doubting that Jason had hypnotized Billy.

Billy stood in the rain, and Jason touched his shoulder. "Billy, go back to your hut and put on your trousers. When I snap my fingers twice, you'll wake up."

After Billy put on his trousers, Jason snapped his fingers twice, and Billy opened his eyes wide and rubbed the water from his head.

"How come I'm all wet?"

"You don't remember anything you just did?" Donald asked.

"The last thing I remember I was talking to Jason and looking at his coin. What'd I do? Jason, you promised you wouldn't get me in trouble."

"We just had some fun with Corporal Allen. You didn't get into trouble, but I've got some shoes to clean and polish before reveille."

The rain continued all during the night, and the sound of rain on the roof of the hut was accompanied by the sound of a shoe brush, moving back and forth across a pair of shoes that glistened like never before.

By morning, the slow rain had become a driving torrent. Sergeant Jefferson finished morning chow and looked at the plate and utensils in front of him as though inspecting a recruit's rifle. He wiped a glob of butter from his knife onto another piece of bread and swirled the bread in the remaining syrup on his plate.

He wiped his mouth with the back of his hand. "Corporal Allen, this is an excellent day to see how much stamina our recruits have. It will be a fine day for a long march, I'd say about twenty miles, don't you agree?"

Allen glanced at Mills, knowing they would be the ones to take the platoon on the march in the rain; therefore, he did not share Jefferson's enthusiasm.

"Well, it will be a chance to check them out, that's for sure. They're shaping up, particularly the younger ones, and the Indians in the platoon are in super condition. Chief Wings of Birds is about as tough as any recruit I've ever seen. I doubt if he'd ever get tired during a march, and I know for sure he'd never show or admit it if he did. Hell, he grew up and lived his entire life on a reservation in Arizona, so he thinks boot camp is a pretty easy life. Some of the older ones will find it tough, but they know they'd better get in shape for combat training. They'll damn sure be surprised to go on a twenty-mile march in this miserable weather. They'll be mad as hell."

Jefferson smiled as he drained the last swallow of coffee from his cup. "That's part of the benefits of being a DI."

Allen pushed away from the mess table. "Well, let's get them moving."

The sound of Allen's voice, as piercing as the bugle call for reveille, ripped into the thoughts of those who dared hope the rain would postpone their physical exercises.

"Platoon, fall in! On the double!" Allen shouted. The rain was now falling heavier than it had been, but the recruits hurried to take their customary positions in the platoon ranks.

Streams of water rolled off the corporal's pith helmet. "Platoon 224 will fall out at 0730 with full packs for a forced march," he growled. "And I'd better not find any shit bird not properly dressed or equipped. Platoon, fall out."

The recruits were falling out, falling in, and falling over each other as they scrambled to put on their equipment and gear.

Donald muttered under his breath, "Allen ordered this march. It was his idea, and it's all because of what happened last night."

Jason Balleau kept his head down when the platoon began to march in the pouring rain. He could feel other recruits staring at the back of his head. Maybe I can hypnotize Corporal Allen and make him think he's a monkey and have him scratch fleas off his balls, he thought.

The mud caked on the soles of the recruits' boondockers, and each step became more difficult than the one before. Water dripped from their helmets and ran down their necks, and their packs slid farther down their backs.

Chief Wings of Birds, at the first of the long line of recruits, walked with a smooth steady gait, almost a glide. A faint smile softened the normally stern look on his face as he remembered those years on the reservation in the hot Arizona stretches of barren rock and spindly cactus. The reservation was the only life he had ever known, and, when the war was over, he knew he would return to his homeland. He knew of no other place to go.

Chief Wings continued through the day with the same smooth gait he had taken when the march began. Corporal Allen, in superb condition, matched his own stride to that of the Indian.

The older men breathed harder, and the distance between them lengthened. "Close it up, close it up," Mills shouted. The ranks tightened, and those toward the rear of the single file broke into double time to fill the gaps.

Robert Munday was from Kansas and, at thirty-four, was the oldest boot in Platoon 224. He was overweight, and although he had lost several pounds, there was still more fat than muscle, and he couldn't keep up with the rest of the platoon.

Pfc. Mills walked beside Munday and, when the space widened, prodded him to walk faster, and the recruits behind him had to walk faster to catch up with the one ahead.

"Munday, fall out," Mills ordered. "The rest of you close ranks."

Munday stopped and breathed hard, shoulders bent slightly forward, his chest heaving each time he took a long breath.

"Munday, fall in at the end of the platoon," Mills directed as he and the other men moved on.

The rain gradually slackened and changed to a drizzle, and when the order was given to take a break, the recruits gladly did so. Mack searched the long file of men behind him for Billy and Gil. He waved at them and saw the white scarf around Billy's neck. Mud or no mud, Billy wouldn't leave that scarf behind, he thought.

Mack could see that they were no worse off than he was himself. Their youth and excellent physical shape paid dividends.

Behind the platoon, Robert Munday moved in a slow walk. He was almost to the last man in the single file of recruits when Allen gave the order to move on, and the men gradually moved out ahead of him. He never slowed his walk as he trudged behind.

The rains finally ended, the sun came out, and the humidity became oppressive. The platoon was soaking wet, and steam rose from their wet dungarees and backpacks. The slick ground made walking more difficult, and the men drank more and more water from their canteens.

Mack took a swallow from his canteen and realized it was empty. They had not stopped for water since the platoon left the base early in the morning, and Mack was certain the other men had emptied their canteens. Mack was sure Allen and Mills had also drained their canteens, and the platoon would soon stop for water.

An hour passed, and Mack found it difficult to swallow. What he and the rest of the recruits didn't know was the DIs still had plenty of water in their canteens, and they had no intention of stopping for water until the platoon returned to camp.

By late afternoon, the recruits were exhausted. They were thirsty, their feet were tired, and their backs ached from the weight of their packs. Only the Indians kept pace with Corporal Allen.

Allen ordered a rest break, and Billy took advantage of the extra time to pull off his heavy boondockers and rub his aching feet.

Munday reached the last of the line sprawled along the road and continued walking until he reached Mills, who was near the middle of the long file of men.

Munday stopped, took a long breath, and kept moving his feet. "Sir, if we're to continue marching, just tell me which way to go, and I'll get out ahead of the platoon. If we're going back to camp, I'd like your permission to start back now."

Mills frowned. "We're returning to camp, but you look like you need to rest. Take off your pack and rest until we start back."

"Sir, if I sat down, I wouldn't be able to get back up. I'll make it if you'll let me start back now."

Mills saw the look of determination on Munday's face. "Permission granted. A relief truck will come along to pick up those who can't make it back to camp. When it comes by, get on it."

"Thank you, sir," Munday said, and started back down the narrow trail that led to camp.

When the relief truck pulled alongside Munday, the driver stuck his head out the window. "Hey, boot, hop on, and I'll give you a lift back to camp."

"How many you picked up so far?"

"You're the first. Get in."

Munday shifted his pack on his shoulders. "No thanks. I'll keep walking."

"Suit yourself. It's a long way back."

Two hours after Platoon 224 returned to camp, Munday staggered into his barracks. The pack slipped from his shoulders and he fell on his bunk.

When the last man returned from the march, Jefferson asked Mills, "How many rode back in the relief truck?"

"No one got in the truck," Mills replied.

Jefferson looked at Mills and Allen. "Either these recruits are in better shape than I thought they were, or they weren't very tired when they returned," Jefferson said.

Mills took off his muddy clothes and sat on his bunk. "They were tired all right, but scuttlebutt says that after they returned, two of them got into a fistfight."

"Who was it?" Jefferson asked.

"Williams and Balleau."

"Balleau is bigger than Williams. Who won the fight?" What were they fighting about?"

"I didn't hear what it was about. Scuttlebutt is they fought until neither of them could get up. I'd call that a draw," Mills replied.

The sergeant smiled. "Platoon 224 might be a pretty good bunch of recruits after all."

12

During the eight weeks of boot camp, the drill instructors—masters of all training tactics—cursed, taunted, belittled, humiliated, frightened, and drained all self-respect from the men. They were unrelenting and pushed or pulled the recruits through the most difficult physical training of their lives. Fat was replaced with muscle. They took the men on long gut-wrenching marches through the hot summer days of 1943 and made them believe that if they emptied their canteens of water, more was available, only to tell them later there was no more.

The boots were fed the best food some of them had ever eaten, but at other times, served tasteless rations. Navy beans were served every Wednesday for breakfast, and horse meat,

Spam, and corned beef hash—better known as "shit on a shingle"—were consistent menu items.

They spent long hours on the rifle range, snapping in on dummy rounds, learning to hold their breath and squeeze the trigger so that later, when live ammunition was fired, the rifle did not jerk. The DIs demanded that every member of the platoon score either as a marksman, sharpshooter, or expert rifleman before boot training was completed and taught them that learning to shoot a rifle could be the difference between life or death in combat. The men dreaded the humiliation of scoring a "Maggie's Drawers," a total miss, but were proud when the bull's-eye signal was waved from the rifle pit.

For many, the rifle range was their first exposure to the cracking sound of rifle fire, the shattering sound of a bullet, and the destruction it could bring.

Boot camp was more difficult for some than it was for others, but to quit was never an option. Pride of accomplishment pushed the endurance of many beyond expectations. In just eight short weeks, the recruits had become Marines, confident they were unequaled as fighting men. With bravery, stamina, spirit, and determination, any goal could be reached and every obstacle could be mastered. They were taught to believe there was no parallel for winning and no excuse for losing.

There had been times when the boots feared, hated, admired, and respected the NCOs who dictated their every move, but on the final day of boot camp, the men of Platoon 224 knew they were no longer boots. They were Marines.

A full dress parade would officially end boot camp for all the platoons completing their basic training. This would be the moment when the DIs marched beside the men they had trained, men they had cursed, men they had shamed for a task not properly completed. It was the day when every platoon competed for the distinction of being the best.

Mack sat on the side of his bunk and polished his shoes for the final parade of platoons.

"After the parade this afternoon," Mack said to Billy and Gil, "Platoon 224 will scatter, but I hope we stay together. I'm glad boot camp is over, but these past eight weeks haven't been too bad."

"There were times when I didn't know if I could do what the DIs told us to do," Gil admitted. "I learned one thing: if one of the DIs told us to do something, we at least tried. When Allen made me jump from the high platform into the water, he didn't believe me when I told him I couldn't swim."

"Yeah, but you did after that," Billy laughed.

"We didn't waste water in West Texas by swimming in it," Gil continued. "I can laugh about it now, but at the time, it wasn't funny. I almost drowned. At least I remembered to loosen the chin strap on my helmet before I jumped. Donald forgot, and when he hit the water, his head was almost jerked off his body."

"I learned one thing," Boog added. "The DI could call me a shit bird, feather merchant, or a top-ranked fuck-up, and he got no argument from me."

"I never could figure out which of the three I wanted to be," Mack laughed. "Boog, remember when the recruiting sergeant in El Paso scared you so bad you swallowed your gum?"

Boog grinned. "He did scare me, that's for sure. I almost choked, and ever since, I've been afraid to chew gum."

"The DIs were tough, but they taught us how to fight," Gil said.

"And how to stay alive," Mack added.

"I hated it when I had to stick a bayonet into a dummy dressed in a Japanese uniform. I hope I never have to do that," Billy grimaced.

"You still want to be a career Marine?" Gil asked.

Billy looked at the white scarf around his neck, lifted it to his face, then tucked it inside his dungaree jacket. "Yeah, I do, but someday, when the war is over, I want to go back home."

The parade was about to begin, and Platoon 224 stood at parade rest. Sergeant Jefferson stood before his platoon. "This will be the last time I will be talking to you as recruits. When the parade is over, boot camp will officially end. You'll be Marines and, when you're dismissed, report to base headquarters for further orders."

Jefferson looked at the three rows of men, remembering the way these same men had looked only a few weeks before. "For the past eight weeks, we've done our best to train you to be good Marines. Some of you may think we've been unfair or too tough on you. It was our duty to prepare you for when you get in combat, and when you do, you'll be the judge as to how successful we were. Your life may depend on what and how much you've learned."

Jefferson stepped back and Mills stepped forward.

"At ease. When we started out eight weeks ago," Mills began, "you didn't show us much, but Platoon 224 turned out to be a pretty good group. I'm proud of you, and you should be proud of yourselves. Good luck."

Corporal Allen strutted to the front of the platoon. "Platoon, ten-hut!" he ordered. His eyes moved from one boot to the next. His face was as stern as it had ever been. He walked slowly down the ranks. "You've finished basic training, and we've toughened up your bodies, and I hope we've prepared your minds for what lies ahead."

Every man strained to hear his words. "Some of you will begin special training in the fine art of how to kill a man, and some of you will be trained in some service group, but you're all Marines. You are in a war you didn't start, a fight that at least some of you didn't ask to be in, but you're here, and you have a job to do. I expect nothing less than the best from each of you.

"It will be a long time before some of you get back to your homes. Some of you will never get back, and those of you who do will find the world you left behind is not the same as it was. You may not think so now, but I don't believe you'll want it to be the same. Before you get back, your girlfriend will probably marry a 4-F or some dogface stationed in a camp where she lives.

"Until this goddamn war is over, you'll go through things you never wanted to, see things you don't want to see, do things you hate to do, and for some, there will be memories for the rest of your life of things you wished you could forget."

Corporal Allen walked back to the front of the platoon. "This afternoon, after our final dress parade, you will be allowed to go on liberty for the first time since you arrived at the base. I have an idea what most of you have in mind, so I'll just warn you not to be too stupid about it.

"At some time, when you walk down the streets or when you're in a bar, we may meet again. If any of you think I was too tough on you and feel like you want to try to whip my ass, I'll always be ready. I hope that, instead, you'll be ready to shake my hand as one Marine to another. Platoon, DIS-MISSED!"

When the U.S. Marine Corps Band began playing, the platoons on the parade field were called to attention. Platoon 224 stood ready to outshine all the other platoons. It was a very solemn moment.

"Platoon, ten-hut." Sergeant Jefferson's voice was loud and clear. "Platoon, forward march," and Sergeant Jefferson led Platoon 224 for the last time. Every platoon on the parade field stepped forward in one inspiring step, each determined to be the best.

Sergeant Jefferson, Corporal Allen, and Pfc. Mills strutted before the platoon. The DIs had all been in combat in the Pacific before they were assigned the duties of being a drill instructor. Their chests were covered with battle ribbons and battle stars earned while at Guadalcanal and other faraway places. Allen's chest stuck out, his chin rested on his shirt collar.

When the parade was over, Platoon 224 had been judged as one of the best on the parade field. Basic training was over, and the next phase in becoming a Marine, special training, would begin.

"I've been assigned to the infantry," Billy beamed when the duty roster was posted.

"Yeah, looks like we're all assigned to the infantry," Gil said.

"Not Chief Wings of Birds," Mack replied. "He's assigned to communications, all four of the Navajos in our platoon were. The Navajo language is unwritten, and the Japs never have been able to decipher it."

"Billy, how does Donald feel about being in the infantry training?" Gil asked.

"He didn't say. I think it's what he wanted, but I'm not sure. I know I am. I was afraid I'd be sent to cooking school."

"Your chances of coming back alive would have been better as a cook," Gil said.

"Maybe so, but I joined the Marines to fight a war, not to peel potatoes."

13

The first day after assignment to infantry training, Platoon 224 prepared to go on their first liberty.

Gil, Billy, and Mack, still just seventeen, knew they would not be allowed to enter a bar for a drink, but alcohol was not their first priority. After eight weeks with only the sight of men, they were anticipating a night in San Diego to rejoin the human race.

Boog asked, "Where's everybody going on liberty?"

Mack winked at Billy. "We're going to the Hollywood Theater. Come along if you'd like. Gil's never seen a burlesque show with naked women, and I'll have to explain everything to him."

"I'd be surprised if you've ever seen anything naked except a goat," Gil responded.

"Donald, do you want to go with us?" Billy asked.

"No, I've got other plans," Donald replied. "I'm thinking about seeing a friend from my hometown."

"I feel sorry for Donald," Billy said later. "I think he's lonely."

"He doesn't want to make friends, not with any of us, anyway," Mack said. "I tried to be friends with him when we joined the Marines, but he made it pretty clear he didn't want to be sociable."

"He doesn't need to be sociable," Billy said defensively. "He needs someone to be his friend, someone to talk with."

"If he doesn't want to go with us to the Hollywood Theater, that's his problem," Mack said.

"Well, I've got plans for our next liberty that don't include going to the Hollywood Theater," Billy said. "And the plans include both of you. How would y'all like to go over to L.A. on our next liberty? We could go to Hollywood, maybe see some of the movie stars."

"Hey, that's not a bad idea," Mack said enthusiastically. "I'd like that. We could go to the Hollywood Canteen, maybe dance with Ginger Rogers. I could show her the Texas two-step, maybe the cotton-eyed Joe. How about it Gil?"

"Heck yeah, count me in. How do we get there? By bus?" Gil asked.

"Bus, I guess," Billy answered.

"Wait a minute," Mack said. "I've got an idea. If we put on our dress blues, we can hitch a ride, maybe get a ride with a good-looking gal. We can save our bus money to spend once we get there. I used to hitch rides all the time going from college back home. Hitching a ride is easy, believe me."

Billy looked at Gil. "What do you think?"

Gil shrugged his shoulders. "It might be all right, but the bus will be the safest and surest way to get there. Let's take the bus."

"Nah, trust me, we can hitch a ride and save our money," Mack promised. "Saturday morning we can catch the military bus from the base to the place closest to the highway, and be in L.A. in a couple of hours. So, it's settled, we hitchhike to Hollywood."

The following Saturday morning, Gil, Billy, and Mack waited for the bus at the base entrance. Mack brushed a speck of lint from the sleeve of his uniform and looked at Gil. "You look pretty sharp," Mack said. "You look good in dress blues. You too, Billy."

"You look pretty good yourself, Mack. Your uniform really looks sharp. I can tell you worked on your shoes. I've got to admit you may be right, Mack, about being able to hitch a ride. We look sharp. What do we do if some good-looking girl comes along and wants to pick up just one of us?" asked Gil.

"I think we should all stay together," Billy said. "If we don't, we'll get separated. There'll be a lot of servicemen and women at the Canteen. We'd never find each other. You agree we stay together, Mack?"

Mack thought for a minute, trying to picture the instance where he would turn down a ride with a good-looking girl. "Let's make that decision if and when we have to. No sense getting too far with our plans until we need to."

They rode the military bus to within a few blocks of the L.A. highway, waited until the bus moved far enough away so the dust wouldn't get on their uniforms, then walked confidently the three blocks to the highway. They stood on the side of the road.

"Mack," Billy said, "you show us how."

"It's better if just one of us stands here. I've always been real good at catching rides. As sharp as we look, we won't have any trouble, I promise." Mack stepped closer to the pavement and held up his thumb. The first car passed him by, as did the second. The soldier in the third car held up one finger when he went by, and Mack gestured with his fist. After the fourth car passed, Mack looked back at his friends. "It takes just the right person to come along. When you hitchhike, you gotta be careful who you ride with." As the Greyhound bus headed for L.A. sped by, Mack looked out the corner of his eye to see if Gil or Billy had noticed.

Mack held up his thumb when the next car approached. The car had dented fenders, one hub cap was missing, and the paint needed a good wax job. The car slowed and the driver rolled down his window. "Where you boys going?" he asked.

Billy and Gil walked toward Mack.

"Going to L.A.," Mack shouted.

"I'll take you there, but I got some boxes in the back seat. One of you will have to sit on a lap, but I guess you could trade off."

Mack shouted, "No thanks, we'll wait for another ride." Gil and Billy watched the car move down the road.

"What'd you tell him that for? We could have all gotten in his car, it'd be better than standing out here in all this dust," Gil said.

"His car was too dirty, and besides, we got to wait for the right car, one with good-looking chicks in it," Mack replied.

Two hours later, Mack walked back to where Billy and Gil sat on a fence post. "Why don't one of you try for a while. My thumb's getting tired. Go try it, Gil. I need to sit down. I don't want to be too tired to dance when we get to the Hollywood Canteen."

One hour later, Gil walked back to the fence post where Billy and Mack sat. "Billy, you try it for a while. I'm getting hot standing out there. This darn uniform is tight around the collar." He looked at the dirt covering his shoes, then stared at Mack.

"Sometimes it takes longer," Mack muttered.

"Yeah, we been out here over three hours already. I'm getting hungry," Gil said.

Billy stood, brushed his uniform as best he could, and started walking to the side of the highway. Mack looked at the seat of Billy's trousers, and shook his head. Black tar had stuck to the blue material. Gil had seen it too and was frowning when he looked at Mack. Mack shrugged his shoulders and said nothing.

"I figure three hundred and forty cars have come by, and not one has stopped," Gil said.

"One car had women," Mack said defensively.

"With four sailors in the back seat," added Gil. "If we don't get a ride soon we might as well go back to the base. We can't get to L.A. in time to do anything. Great idea you had, Mack."

"It's my turn. I'll try again. Maybe out here in California they use something besides the thumb," Mack said.

"Don't try what you're thinking, Mack. Some of these people out here won't take kindly to that sort of thing. I'm too little to fight and too tired to run. Stick with the thumb," Gil said.

A pickup slowed and pulled off the road. Gil and Billy ran toward Mack. "Don't turn it down if he offers us a ride. We'll take anything."

A man wearing a baseball cap stuck his head out the window. "Hi boys, need a lift?" His grin showed several teeth missing. Billy and Gil ran toward the truck. "We need a ride to L.A., so if you're going that way we'd appreciate you letting us get in," Billy said.

"Front seat's full, you'll have to get in the back, but you're welcome to that."

Gil and Billy crawled in the back, and Mack held out his hand for them to pull him up. "Whew, I wonder what he's been hauling?" Billy asked.

Mack looked at the back of the pickup, sniffed, and looked at Gil and Billy.

"Pig farmer," he said.

When the truck pulled up to the first stoplight in L.A., Mack suggested, "Y'all think we should get off and try to find out where we are? Every time we slow down, the flies get pretty thick. I wonder if they've followed us all the way from San Diego, or maybe they're new ones each time. Sure have the same look, don't they?"

A red convertible pulled up beside them. Three blondes were in the front seat, and they smiled at the Marines. The blonde sitting behind the steering wheel sniffed the air, frowned, held her nose, and the car sped away. "See, that's the ride we should have had," Mack said. "I'll bet they just drove in from San Diego. If we'd waited a little longer, they would have given us a ride."

The farmer stuck his head out the window, "I turn up here at the next light. You'll have to get off unless you're going on with me. Main part of town is on down the road."

The three Marines were trying to decide what to do when they saw a city bus coming toward them. "Hey, look what's coming. We can ride the bus into town," Gil exclaimed.

"We could save our money if we…," Mack said, then saw the expression on Billy's face. "Yeah, let's get on the bus."

When Gil dropped change into the coin box, he asked the driver, "Will this bus take us near any hotels?"

The driver nodded. "I go near three or four hotels on up the way."

"Can you let us know where to get off? We need to find a room."

Several minutes later, the driver looked over his shoulder. "At the next corner, two blocks east. There's the Star Hotel, and across the street is the Randolph. There's a couple more, but I don't remember the names."

Gil returned to his seat. "Let's get off up here and find the hotel. We need to get cleaned up before we go to the Hollywood Canteen—if it's still open by the time we get there. It's too late to do any sight-seeing." Billy nodded, and when the bus stopped, the three Marines stepped to the street.

The first three hotels were full, and the fourth hotel had only the bridal suite available. The clerk at the fifth hotel told them he could put each of them on a cot in the hallway. "How much?" Mack asked.

Before he had a chance to reply, Billy said, "We'll take it. Where can we take a shower and use the toilet?"

"You'll have to use the toilet in the gym. Paper's not always there. You can use a shower on the second floor."

"And what floor will our cots be on?" Mack asked.

"Sixth," the clerk said. "You'll have to pay in advance. Rooms are generally twenty dollars, but I'll let you sleep in the hallway for twelve. I'll get your cots up soon as you pay."

"That's for all three of us?" Mack asked.

"Twelve dollars apiece."

An hour later, after they had showered and cleaned their uniforms as well as they could, Billy said, "We haven't eaten anything all day, and I'm hungry. Maybe the clerk knows of a good place we can eat."

"There's a hash house down the street," the hotel clerk told them. "They make good Irish stew."

"Where's another place? Irish stew is out," Gil interrupted.

"We can eat at the Hollywood Canteen, and dance, too," Mack suggested. "How do we get to the Canteen from here?" he asked.

"The Canteen's all the way on the other side of town. A bus will take you there, but it'll take you awhile. Easier if you take a cab, that's the best way."

Gil looked at Mack. "No, don't even suggest what you're thinking. We'll ride the bus."

Billy said, "When we get to the Canteen, we all need to save enough money so we can get back to the base."

"Maybe we can hitchhike," Mack said, and the three Marines started laughing.

"I'm not riding in the back of another pig truck, even if I have to walk," Billy said.

An hour after they entered the Canteen, Mack found Gil and Billy. "Talk about luck! I was talking to a Marine supply sergeant who's stationed at the Base. I told him about all the trouble we've had and how we were short on money. He has a car and said we could ride with him tomorrow morning when he goes back to San Diego. He'll take us back to our hotel tonight."

Gil asked, "What's it going to cost us?"

Billy watched Mack's face, then said, "What did you promise him in return for the ride back to the base?"

Mack laughed, "Now wait a minute, do you think…"

"What and how much did you offer him, Mack?" Billy asked again.

"The sergeant needs two men to help him load some boxes in a warehouse tomorrow, so I told him you two could help him. That's all, and just think, Billy, you don't have to ride back on a pig truck after all."

A week later, when the first rays of sunlight were just beginning to shine across the sky, Mack shook the bunk bed where Gil was sleeping. "Get your butt up, Gil. The Marine Corps doesn't put up with a lazy ass. Rise and shine. I don't want to miss chow call. The scuttlebutt is we're having mountain oysters and Irish stew. I know how much you like both. Come on, get up."

"I don't feel good. I'm sick. I think I have a fever. I feel like I got the flu. I'm not kidding, Mack, I'm feeling terrible. I'm going to sick bay."

Mack helped Gil sit up. "You do look pale. Your skin feels hot. You really are sick."

"I can put on my clothes, but you'll have to help me get to sick bay," Gil confessed.

When they walked into the sick bay, Mack motioned to a corpsman to help him. "I've got a sick buddy. He's got a fever and stomach cramps."

"If you got cramps, it's not the clap. What's your problem?" he asked.

"You're supposed to tell me," Gil replied.

"I'm just learning. All I know how to do is give out quinine and I'm pretty good at giving shots of penicillin to guys coming back from liberty," the corpsman admitted.

"Yeah, well don't give me one in the left nut with a square needle."

That evening when Mack and Billy visited Gil in the infirmary, the corpsman said, "Your buddy has cat fever, and he'll be in the infirmary for several days, maybe a couple of weeks. He's not going anywhere for a while."

"What the hell is cat fever?" Mack asked.

"Asiatic flu," the corpsman replied.

"Mack," Billy said, "if Gil is in the hospital for a couple of weeks, they may put him in another group when he gets out."

The corpsman shrugged his shoulders. "He'll be here for that long, and you're probably right about him not staying in your group. Cat fever is tough."

"Are you sure it isn't pig fever?" Mack asked.

PART II

14

Vice Admiral Naha Koturu sat behind his large wooden desk at the naval headquarters in Tokyo. Papers and reports covered the top, leaving little room for him to write the letter he had started the previous day to his youngest son, Lieutenant Commander Nakoka Koturu. He started to seal the envelope, then removed the letter and wrote, "I pray that our ancestors and the Merciful Buddha will protect you."

A picture of his three sons was almost hidden by the files marked TOP CONFIDENTIAL, and the admiral pushed the stack of folders to the side so that he could get a better view of the three men dressed in their military uniforms.

The admiral would never admit to anyone that Nakoka was really his favorite, and he never showed partiality, although Nakoka's brothers, Kono and his older brother Kushi Tameichi knew it was true. The admiral recognized in Nakoka's reckless nature and arrogance the same traits he had possessed as a young man when entering the naval academy prior to World War I. "Perhaps that is why I favor Nakoka with such joy," the admiral admitted to himself.

Kono, his second son, always careful and pragmatic, exhibited the same air of confidence in the photograph that he did in real life. Kushi Tameichi, the eldest son, was the top student in every school he ever attended, and graduated with the highest honors from the Japanese Army Military Institute in Tokyo. The admiral's wife believed that he was the most dependable and caring of her three sons, and it was he that she always mentioned first in her prayers to Buddha.

The old officer gently touched the picture with his thumb, wiping away a small speck of dust from the glass. It had been taken two years earlier, just after his eldest son had been promoted to major and was home on leave from his Army post in Burma. Nakoka, dressed in his white Navy uniform, was slightly smaller than Kono. The admiral smiled and nodded his head in obvious pride. Other than his emperor, his three sons were the most important people in his life.

He looked across the room at the framed kakemono his eldest son had made for him. It was a handsome scroll, with exquisite fine lettering on the softest silk cloth, much like the fine lettering of the many scrolls that his own father had taught him to make. No father could be more rewarded, he thought, and he thanked the gods every day of his life for such blessings.

A small, spectacled naval officer knocked on the admiral's door. "Admiral Koturu, you requested that I advise you of the meeting with the commander in chief."

"Yes, thank you, I will go now," the admiral said. He rummaged through his desk drawer, and found the report marked Target A. He quickly found another file marked I and R.O. class submarines among the stack of papers on his desk and stuffed them into his briefcase, straightened his coat, and left the room.

The officers were seated at the ornate teakwood table in the war room. Maps lay sprawled over the polished surface. The commander in chief of the Japanese combined fleet rose slowly from his chair. He turned to those on either side of him, first to the left, then to the right, bringing them in like peasants in a commune. He walked toward the map of the Pacific Ocean hanging from the lighted wall. Small flags pinned to it showed the location of strategic islands and bases.

"When the Pacific war started," he began, "the American submarines were inferior to our own, and their warships, including their cruisers, destroyers, and even their battleships and carriers were, for a while, ineffective in combat with our own vessels."

He pointed to the Solomon Islands. "The balance of power has shifted." He touched his finger to the map, pointing at New Guinea. "Here, and here, and here, the American forces have established footholds that are a threat to our success in winning the Pacific war." He jabbed his finger to the location of the Bismarck Sea. "Here and at Midway," he shouted, pounding the map with his fist, "our Imperial Navy has suffered losses of our ships that cannot be replaced."

He paced in front of the teak wood table, staring at each of the officers. "This council's responsibility is to develop a strategy to assure that Japan will regain superiority over the Allied forces. I will study plans you present and listen to your comments."

Admiral Koturu nodded to the commander in chief, rose, and walked to the map on the wall.

The admiral was a strikingly impressive officer, almost of mandatory retirement age. His thick white hair was disheveled, and his white eyebrows covered the top of his thick glasses. His body, thinner now than before, was nevertheless as straight as ever, and his voice still commanded the authority of an old and tested warrior.

Koturu knew all too well the fragility of power in the Japanese military. Officers of high rank, including the all-powerful chief of staff for the Army and Navy, were not immune to danger from the younger officers with fanatical political beliefs.

History had recorded that a prime minister had been killed because he did not share the same ardent philosophies of the rebellious, impatient military antagonists, and as recently as 1936, the vice-president of the privy council had been shot because younger subordinate officers considered him a bad influence on the emperor.

Koturu knew he must be cautious in what he was about to say. If the young officers took direct political action with their guns and swords, he would be helpless.

He began, "It is true that Japan has suffered losses, but we have not abandoned our immediate objectives of capturing Australia and the Hawaiian Islands. We have not lost the war, but we have already lost many opportunities to defeat the enemy."

Koturu paced the floor in deep thought. "It is wise to remember the past," he said, "if we are to plan for the future. Many years ago, in 1921, when the Americans and British forced Japan to sign the disarmament treaty, we, as a nation, were subjected to humiliating terms. Some of you will remember that no Japanese ship could exceed 10,000 tons, and I cried when we were ordered to sink those warships that exceeded the maximum size the Americans and British would allow."

Koturu's voice grew stronger with emotion. "They even restricted Japan's access to the raw materials, oil, and rubber of the Dutch East Indies, Sumatra, and Burma. Without those materials, we could not insure the life of our nation. That is why our war lords have engaged our nation in this struggle for survival with the American and British forces.

"I need not remind you of the industrial might of the United States and their unlimited supply of the materials needed to fight this war. Materials, unfortunately, that Japan does not have."

Admiral Koturu faced the commander of naval operations. "The length of Allied supply lines in the Pacific and the

infinite expanse of the ocean is of great advantage to the
Japanese Imperial Navy. The first priority of our submarine
fleet should be to attack the Allied troop and merchant ships,
for without men and supplies, the Americans cannot fight."

The officers sat motionless. Koturu continued, "We have
awakened a sleeping giant, and if we are to win this conflict,
we must do so before the Americans concentrate all their
power into a single path of determination. We should never
underestimate the power of the American fighting forces."

Koturu took a long breath, "I propose that we unite our
military forces under one central command. There is no single
control. Our Navy and our Army do not join together to fight
the common enemy; they fight their own war, and in doing so,
we lose men, ideas, equipment, and valuable time, precious
irredeemable time."

He paused and then added softly, "And with each day that
passes, we move toward the end that only Buddha can know.
If we continue to hold our main fleet of warships in home
waters, we sign a death warrant for the soldiers on our island
outposts.

"I am proposing that henceforward, all our cruisers, destroyers, carriers, and battleships, certainly our submarines
move out of home waters and engage the enemy wherever we
find him."

A junior officer in the Imperial Navy, stunned to hear
Koturu's proposal, started to rise from his chair, but Koturu
motioned for him to sit down.

"In the beginning," Koturu said, "when the Pacific war
started, Japan had more carriers and cruisers than the Americans, and our naval personnel were better trained. Their
submarine fleet outnumbered ours almost two to one, yet they
were not efficient or effective in protecting their ships when
crossing the Pacific. We had the initiative, but at Guadalcanal
our Army lost valuable territory, and at the Battle of Midway
our Navy lost the supremacy of the seas.

"The momentum has shifted in favor of the enemy, and to

regain what we have lost, we must engage the enemy with all our might in every advance they make. We must show more than token resistance to the ever advancing assault forces of the American military."

The commander, visibly irritated at Koturu's comments, interrupted, "Admiral, we fought gallantly in the Solomons and at Midway. How can you suggest we made only token resistance?"

"There is an old Chinese proverb that says a lion uses all its might in attacking a rabbit. At Guadalcanal," Koturu replied, "the Army waited too long to commit enough soldiers and the Navy waited too long to commit enough ships to win the battle.

"When the enemy attempts to land Marines on New Britain, or on Bougainville, or any strategic island, and they most certainly will, we should immediately defend them with all our resources and all our might. It is on these island outposts that we must defend our nation. If we lose there, we lose here as well. It is sad that while our military forces fight on these far-away places, we keep our main fleet anchored in home waters."

It had been the commander's decision to hold the mighty First Fleet in the Sea of Japan, and this assault on his integrity and the implied lack of leadership was tantamount to loss of face.

The commander's voice shook with emotion. "We are all responsible for the future and glory of winning this war, and if we do not succeed, we are all accountable. We are equally responsible for the actions we take to achieve success."

Admiral Koturu had given much thought to the position he was taking, and he had carefully weighed the consequences of his words. It was too late for him to become timid.

He swung around to face the commander. "We lost the opportunity of establishing naval superiority over the Americans when the war started and we were not able to destroy either their carriers or their submarine fleet at Pearl Harbor. It is a loss for which we now must pay the price."

The atmosphere in the room was tense. The other officers

sat stiffly in their chairs, unwilling to accept what some of them also secretly believed.

"We are faced with a problem like the two sharp sides of a Samurai sword," the admiral continued. "One is the ever advancing American ground forces, and the other is the increasing loss of our merchant ships. One side is as dangerous as the other."

"And," an officer interrupted vehemently, "which side do we defend against?"

Admiral Koturu responded, "It is possible, for now, to defend both. Since Japan depends entirely on imported oil, further loss of our supply vessels will be devastating.

"We are losing ships we cannot replace, and we can never afford the loss of trained and experienced men to guide them. We must not lose our island outposts, for if we do, we will lose supremacy of the seas, and then we will lose supremacy of the skies. We must not allow that to happen.

"The outcome of this war depends on the balance of our combined air and sea power rather than on manpower alone. When we engaged the enemy at Pearl Harbor, we knew that Japan's Imperial Navy could fight strongly for two, possibly no more than three years. If we continue on the course we are now taking, our country will fall."

The officers were stunned. "Admiral Koturu," one young officer demanded, "do you propose we leave the shores of our homeland unprotected while we send our greatest defense, our main naval forces, to engage the enemy in any island outpost? We cannot leave our shores unprotected. Never!"

The highest ranking officers vehemently disagreed to the plan that would leave the shores of Japan unprotected and shouted their disdain for Koturu's proposal. Only one other officer supported Koturu.

Admiral Koturu studied the officers sitting at the great teakwood table. Some had not been in combat, and their only contribution to the war effort had been voicing approval of the commander's words.

Three of the officers had been no closer to the fighting than the map on the wall. He did not doubt their courage, but he questioned their reasoning. The admiral ran his hand through his hair and stared at the floor, determined he must convince the council of his plan.

"The priority of securing the natural resources necessary for the continuation of the war is greater now than it has ever been," Koturu argued. "The growing air supremacy of the enemy and their use of radar are taking a heavy toll on our merchant ships. The enemy's industrial superiority increases every day, and if we are to win this war, we must do so before it is too late."

"So...the enemy's air supremacy is growing. Just how do you propose we solve the problem? How do we balance our air and sea power to win the war?" the commander of naval forces demanded angrily.

Admiral Koturu replied, "We must build carriers, not battleships. Our Zero fighter is superior to anything the Americans have. If we put better pilots in these planes, we can destroy more of their planes than they can destroy ours. The training of our pilots must be accelerated, and while we still have the facilities and materials, our factories must produce more planes and more carriers."

Koturu could not stop his words from flowing. He must express his thoughts even if it meant removal from the council, or possibly his death by a fanatical subordinate.

"We must act at once to destroy as many of the American ships as we can or it will be too late. We must keep secret the location and movements of our carriers. We must strengthen our initial air assaults.

"The American ships have been equipped with radar since the beginning of the Pacific war, and that single factor has rewarded them with victorious sea battles that should have belonged to Japan, but now, we also have the knowledge to install radar in our ships.

"Our greatest advantage is our top secret oxygen-fueled

torpedoes that run without leaving a trace on the water. This knowledge must never be shared with the Americans."

"And what else must we do?" sneered another officer.

Koturu replied defensively, "Establish a 'ring of fire,' with our submarines as the first line of defense, traveling in packs, like the Germans do in the Atlantic." He stepped to the map on the wall and with a finger traced an arc across the Pacific Ocean.

"The construction of more I-class and R.O. submarines should be a top priority. With a cruising range of over 12,000 miles, they can travel as far as the shores of California and then back to their base in Rabaul. We can control beneath the seas, and then we control the seas themselves. When our submarines destroy the Allied ships, the American ground forces cannot fight."

The admiral paced the floor, deep in thought, confident he was correct, persuasive in his argument. His fingers sifted through his gray hair. He stopped and faced the council. His clenched fist pounded the air, emphasizing his words. "Our second line of defense will be our carriers and cruisers, protected by at least half of our destroyer fleet. Our carriers will engage the enemy when they attempt to establish a foothold on the strategic islands in the southwest Pacific. Our destroyers must probe for the merchant ships that pass through our submarine net and protect our carriers and cruisers."

The officers waited. The admiral finally said, "Behind the circle of cruisers, our battleships will be our final line of defense."

"And what happens if these rings of defense are broken?" asked the commander. "Have you forgotten the battle of the Bismarck Sea?"

"Our Navy captains were less brilliant than they should have been. We do not need to repeat mistakes of that magnitude," Admiral Koturu answered. Almost in a whisper, he added, "And if our ring of defense is broken, then our soldiers must be prepared to die on the beaches of our homeland."

The room was quiet. The commander in chief rose from the table and walked to face Vice Admiral Koturu. "Admiral, you know General Tojo will not approve what you have proposed."

"No," Koturu said, his voice more quiet than before. "General Tojo won't approve the plan unless you support it."

The commander said, "Part of what you propose, I will recommend to the war ministry and to the Joint Chiefs, but I will not allow our main fleet to leave the shores of Japan, nor will I support putting all our military forces under one central command. If the American forces are successful in reaching our home waters, our fleet will repulse them. We will fight them on the beaches, if need be, and our Glorious emperor will someday dictate the settlement of this struggle to the American people. No, I will never agree to our main fleet leaving our homeland unprotected. That is final."

Admiral Koturu bowed to the commander and returned to his chair.

15

On the afternoon of October 23, 1943, the Twenty-seventh Replacement Battalion was ordered to stand by, and all leaves were canceled. Those Marines who had recently completed special training following boot camp were transported to the San Diego harbor, and boarded the USS *Rochambeau*, a "Liberty" troop transport converted from a cargo ship to carry men and their combat equipment to the Pacific.

The Marines carried heavy sea bags on their shoulders to their assigned compartments belowdecks where long rows of canvas-bottomed bunks, stacked one on top of the other, filled the cargo quarters. The top bunks were only inches below the maze of pipes that crisscrossed the ceiling of the compartment. The Marines sweated as they stood in line in the crowded passageway, waiting until those in front moved to their assigned quarters.

A compartment loudspeaker blasted the ears of the already frustrated Marines. "Now hear this! Now hear this! All Marines move to your assigned compartment! Keep the passageways open! On the double!"

"How in hell can we keep the passageways open when we can't even move? I'll bet it's 110 degrees in this damn cargo hold. I'm about to pass out," Mack said angrily. "Come on, move up there!"

"Blow it out your ass, we're moving as fast as we can," a voice ahead of Mack yelled back.

When they reached their compartment, Mack wrestled his gear to one of the top bunks. He removed his cartridge belt and strapped it around a large steam pipe immediately above his bunk. The canteen attached to his cartridge belt hung almost to his face.

Billy crawled into the bunk below Mack, his dungarees soaking wet. The confining space between his face and the sagging canvas bunk above him almost restricted him from turning over. "It's so hot in here I'm about to throw up. I gotta get some fresh air, I'm going up on deck."

Mack leaned over the side of his bunk. "Let's go," and he was already on his way down when Billy slipped from his bunk. They crowded by other Marines still stowing their gear and headed for the upper deck. "Oh man, this fresh air feels good," Billy said. The sweat began to evaporate when the wind blew, cooling his face.

Mack took several deep breaths, and moved to the railing. "I may sleep topside on this trip." He grabbed the rail. "Do you feel that, the ship is moving! We're already underway."

Further out to sea, the sleek, gray destroyer USS *Topeka* waited with other ships to form the convoy that would take so many young Marines to the Pacific war. Others who had come topside joined Billy and Mack on the deck of the USS *Rochambeau*.

"Guess this is so long to the good ol' United States for a while," Billy said. "I wish Gil was here too. We could have all stayed together if he hadn't gotten sick."

"Yeah, I wish he was with us too."

The two friends watched the disappearing California coast. "The coast line is getting smaller. I wonder how long it will be before we see it again?" Billy asked.

"Those are questions none of us can answer. At first, in boot camp, I just thought about the training and didn't really think about the day we would board ship. The war seems much closer now, doesn't it?"

Billy looked down at the blue water. "Some of us won't come back."

"I've got a feeling I won't come back," Mack said. "Do you ever have that feeling?"

"I haven't thought about it, and I don't want to think about it now," Billy replied. "We joined the Marines to fight the Japs. I don't think I'd want it any other way. I just hope I won't ever be a coward. That would be worse than dying. I could never live with myself if I turned coward when I got into combat."

"Billy, that's the stupidest thing I've ever heard you say. You'd be the last person to ever be a coward."

"Mack, if I don't make it back, will you write Mother and tell her I wasn't a coward and I wasn't afraid? Don't write Laura. I wouldn't want her to find out from a letter. Mother could tell her."

"All right, if you'll make the same promise to me."

The loudspeaker over the ship's intercom blasted the evening air. "Now hear this! Now hear this! All Marines report to your compartment."

Billy tightened the scarf around his neck and Mack took a final look at the shoreline, now only a faint blur above the blue Pacific water.

"Well, so much for the fresh air. Now it's back to that damn, hot cargo hold, smelling each other's farts and BO. I dread to think what it will smell like when people start throwing up. And now that I think of it, and I wish I hadn't, I'm feeling the ship's movement just a little bit."

When Billy and Mack returned to their compartment, the corporal in charge of their section was calling roll. "When I call your name, sound off loud and clear."

Billy and Mack were assigned to a cleanup detail to keep the topside decks swept. Donald was assigned to the mess hall.

"Sweepers, man your brooms!" came the order over the intercom. Billy said, "I guess we start our sea duty on the stupid end of a broom. The only good thing about being on a work detail is we get three meals a day."

George Pappas stood in front of the latrine. "Come on, just a few drops, anyway. Come on," he pleaded.

"Who you talking to?" asked a Marine standing next to him.

"I can't pee," Pappas moaned. "I need to go, but I can't, and I'm sick to my stomach. Jesus Christ, what a miserable feeling."

"You're not the only one that's seasick. Some usually feed the fishes the first day aboard ship," the Marine told Pappas. "It'll be a few days until most of the Marines get their sea legs, but some never will, and some end up in sick bay for the duration of the trip. You may be just lucky enough to be one of them. No shit details and better chow."

"You call being seasick lucky? Not being able to pee? Jesus Christ! What do you know about it anyway?" Pappas said.

"This is my second trip over. You need to get food in your belly," the Marine advised. "You better have food in you when the puking starts."

Evening chow was called over the loudspeakers, and those who could formed a long line that began on the upper deck and wound down to the galley below.

"I wonder if this line is ever going to move?" Billy asked.

"We're moving some, but I see two Marines up ahead

trying to cut in line. They can go to the end like we did," Mack said.

When one of the Marines stepped in front of Billy, Mack said, "Hey, Marine, you weren't in line. Move to the rear or squeeze in front of somebody else, but not in front of my friend." Mack placed his hand on the shoulders of one of the Marines and firmly pushed him to the side.

"The hell you say. It don't hurt you any for me to get in line here. There must be plenty of chow for everyone. You'll get served," the Marine replied, and stepped ahead of Mack.

Mack insisted, "I don't know what they're serving, and I may not like it when I get there, but you're not going to cut in the line ahead of me."

The two Marines were similar in build, although Mack was ten or fifteen pounds lighter. They stared at each other, trying to decide if it was worth fighting to see who would be first in line.

"Get out of the line," Mack repeated.

"Make me," the Marine challenged.

Mack swung his fist at the stranger's face. It landed with a thud, and the Marine swung from his waist with a right that caught Mack in the chest. He grabbed Mack in a bear hug and they rolled to the deck.

Mack pulled on top and swung again. Blood ran down his face. Mack swung again, but the Marine grabbed Mack's arm in midair, and they wrestled on the deck. His fist hit Mack again in the chest and another blow landed on his stomach. Mack doubled over with pain, the blow to his chest numbed his shoulders and the blow to his stomach made him nauseated.

From a half-crouch, Mack swung as hard as he could, his fists hitting the Marine in the face and neck. The fellow groaned and gasped for breath, his mouth open, trying to pull oxygen into his lungs. He fell and grabbed Mack's legs, pulling him down.

They wrestled on the deck, first one on top then the other, swinging their arms and fists as they rolled closer to the edge of the deck.

Billy yelled, "Help me pull them apart. They'll roll into the ocean if we don't stop them." He grabbed Mack's legs and pulled as hard as he could. George Pappas grabbed the Marine's legs and pulled in the opposite direction.

"All right, that's enough," Billy shouted. "Stop fighting, or you'll both end up in the ocean."

Mack got to his feet, breathing in short gasps, fists clinched, and spit blood from his mouth. The other man wiped his nose, blood streaming down his face, covering his dungarees. He held his mouth open, taking long breaths, and glared at this man he had just met.

Billy stood between the two men. "Come on, that's enough. Y'all quit fighting."

Both men straightened, their breathing slowed, and their muscles gradually relaxed.

"Whew, you're good with your fists, that was a tough fight. You ready to quit, or do you want to fight some more?" the Marine asked.

"I'm willing to stop if you are," Mack answered, feeling one of his front teeth. "Boy, you've got a punch like a mule." He rubbed his chest and extended his hand, "Don't squeeze it, my left hand feels like it's broken. My name is Mack Williams, hope that nose isn't broken."

"It's too sore to tell. You don't waste much time in a fight do you? Where you from?"

"Crockett, Texas. Where you from?"

"I'm Manny King, from Benson Cove, North Carolina. I think I've seen you somewhere before, but I don't remember where."

Mack winced as Manny grasped his sore knuckle. "Who's your friend?"

"I'm George Pappas, from Ohio."

"I'm Billy Harris, from Pampa, Texas, and y'all can get in line ahead of me."

Manny glanced at Mack. Mack shrugged. "If Billy says you can, that's all right with me. You can get in line just behind me."

Mack rubbed his sore chest and moved to close the gap that had opened in the chow line while he and Manny were fighting. "It'll be our luck for them to be serving shit on a shingle anyway."

When Mack could see the food being served on the trays, he turned to Manny. "Guess what we're having?"

"Shit on a shingle?"

"You guessed it," Mack said, and they both started laughing.

The sleeping compartments got hotter and more smelly, and the four friends met several times on the upper deck. Freshwater showers were allowed for a short time in the early mornings every other day, but were so crowded that most of the Marines could not use them. Saltwater showers left a sticky feeling, and many of the Marines preferred to skip bathing altogether. The smell in the compartments got worse each day.

Saltwater soap was issued, but it was impossible to make the soap lather, and the only way the men could clean their dungarees was to tie them on a long line and drop them overboard into the pounding sea. Billy discovered after the first washing that the one place not to drag his clothes in the water was immediately behind the release of the refuse from the heads.

Woodson was assigned KP duty when he came aboard ship, but since the ship's galley was one deck above where his bunk was located, he could go topside after his KP duty was completed. He knew what foods would be served and told Billy that turkey, dressing, and pumpkin pie with ice cream would be served on Thanksgiving.

The heat and stench in the hold of the USS *Rochambeau* made sleeping difficult. Mack Williams and George Pappas, clad only in their skivvies, lay sweating on the top bunks of adjacent rows.

The ship rolled from side to side, and the rise and fall of the bow became more pronounced. The waves grew larger, the wind more severe by the minute.

"This must be one heck of a storm we're getting into," Pappas groaned. "The ship is rolling so much it's getting harder to stay in the bunk. I'm getting sick."

"Yeah, I've heard that some of these Pacific storms get pretty rough. I'd go topside but they put a stop to that when more men were sleeping on the top deck than in the hold. You know of course our compartment is below the waterline. What scares me is that if we got hit by a torpedo, it'd hit us about where our bunk is. Boy, we wouldn't have a chance to get out, would we?"

"Jesus Christ, what the hell did you have to bring that up for? Isn't the storm enough to worry about without you talking about getting hit by a torpedo? It scares me just to think about that, so don't start talking about getting torpedoed, and lay off the crap about the storm. I had a buddy killed on his first trip to sea. That was one of the reasons I joined the Marines when I did." The ship rolled sharply. "Oh god," Pappas moaned. "My head hurts and I'm getting seasick sure as hell."

Mack looked at Pappas' face. "You're turning green. Try concentrating on something besides the storm, just don't think about getting seasick." Mack grinned. "And George, don't think about greasy food or puke. Get your mind off of throwing up and gagging."

George groaned louder and held his hands over his face. Mack saw George's cartridge belt and canteen that hung over the water pipe only inches above their faces.

"George," Mack said, "did you know the ship is rolling so much it makes your canteen swing back and forth?" He pushed the canteen, and the roll of the ship kept it swinging.

Pappas watched the swinging canteen, and Mack touched the canteen again, harder this time, and it swung with more momentum.

"Oooh, I think I'm going to throw up!" Pappas moaned.

"Watch out below," Mack yelled, but the warning was too late. Pappas managed to partially lean over the side of his bunk, and breakfast and the evening meal came up together, showering not only the bunks below but everyone unfortunate enough to be in the way.

"Ooh, my head, my stomach, my ass," Pappas groaned, and again he leaned over the side of his bunk and sprayed those below him.

"Goddamn it, you up there," someone in the lower bunk screamed. "Get off your damn bunk and get to the head. You just covered me with your puke. I'm...I'm...," he choked, as he too began to vomit.

"Whew, that stinks, Pappas, I think you threw up in your own bunk too." Mack felt himself getting dizzy and hot, but managed to get down from his bunk and race toward the head to splash water on his face. Pappas, slumped almost to his knees, hung over the latrine, the dry heaves wrenched his body as he tried again and again to throw up.

"Oooh," he moaned through gasps of breath, "I think I'm dying!"

Six thousand yards ahead of the convoy, Commander Ledley J. Oberson of the American destroyer escort USS *Topeka* noted the drop in barometric pressure and ordered his crew to make all necessary preparations for the approaching storm.

"We must be heading into a real live one," he said to his first mate. "We'll continue on course unless the storm gets so severe we're required to do otherwise. If there are any Jap subs around, they'll submerge. They won't like this storm any more than we will."

The *Rochambeau* rolled and plunged into the waves, and the Marines clung to the sides of their bunks, wondering if the ship would stay afloat. Seasick Marines filled the head and gagging men lined the latrine.

The night was pitch-black, and the thick low clouds touched the white fury of the sea as the troopship headed directly into one of the most severe storms many of the crewmen had ever experienced. The waves towered above the bridge, and great rolling mountains of water threatened to break the ship apart.

The ship climbed steeply as each wave crashed with more fury than the last, and each time her bow hung in the air before dropping into the next trough. With each lunge, the sea buried the hull and shock waves added to the vibrations of the propellers racing madly as they came out of the water.

All through the night, the storm intensified, and Donald Woodson grasped both sides of his bunk with an ever tightening grip. Perspiration formed on his face, his eyes stared at the canvas bunk only inches above his body, and with each roll and plunge of the troopship, his forehead tightened into a deeper frown, and each moment he became more frightened. His heart beat faster and he had difficulty swallowing. He tried to think of something, anything that would take his mind away from the fear that gripped him. He had felt fear before, but never in his life had he experienced such stress and anxiety.

He had feared his stepfather and the beatings his stepfather gave him, but they had not threatened his life as the storm did now. He listened to the moan and creak of the ship as it battled with the hurricane winds, and he wondered if the ship was built to withstand such a pounding, and if the ship broke apart, could he fight his way out of the hold to the upper deck where he would have a chance of survival.

He couldn't remember where the nearest lifeboat was located, and cursed himself for not knowing. He wondered if there were enough lifeboats, and if they had to abandon ship, would the crew members get into the boats before the Marines?

He did not know how far below the waterline his sleeping compartment was located, nor did he know how far the hull of the ship lay below his compartment. He cursed himself again for not thinking about those questions before the storm hit.

He could feel the pounding of the waves against the bow when it dipped ever lower into the hissing fury and knew the power of the storm had increased. He tried to get out of his bunk, but the motion of the ship and the almost instantaneous feeling of nausea forced him to grip the sides of his bunk.

He hated the tight and crowded compartment, and he dreaded the fury of the sea. He pulled his life jacket over his head and hummed softly.

All the next day and following night, the ship rolled and plunged, and the sound of the hurricane winds joined with the moan of men and metal in a frightening and anxious symphony.

On the day before Thanksgiving, the fury of the storm began to subside, but the ship still rolled and occasional gale force winds kept the Marines belowdecks. By now, the hold was so hot and smelly that those who had managed to stay well had to use maximum willpower to keep from getting seasick.

Many of the men lay in their bunks, not daring to get to their feet for fear they would get sick again, and only the more stalwart ventured topside for fresh air. Only those "salty" Marines with their sea legs went for morning chow.

By Thanksgiving morning, the frothy whitecapped waves lost most of their fury, and by midafternoon, the storm winds weakened, and the roll and plunge of the *Rochambeau* diminished. Those who could went topside.

It was still difficult to stand on the deck, and Mack grasped the railing. Billy and Manny stood nearby along the bulkhead behind Mack and looked out at the still churning sea, the whitecaps on the waves still three to four feet high.

"I've never seen anything like that storm, and I never want to see another," Manny said, as he held tight to the bulkhead. "I hope the other ships came through the storm. I'll bet even the destroyers had a tough time. I wonder what a submarine does in a storm like that?"

"How is Pappas doing, Manny?" asked Billy. "I've never seen anyone as sick as he was. Anybody that didn't get sick in that storm is a real sailor. I threw up once, but after I got back on my bunk and closed my eyes I felt better."

"Yeah, Pappas was sick all right. He must have eaten something that didn't agree with him. Maybe Irish stew," Mack said.

Manny tied the strap on his life jacket. "Pappas went to sick bay. He had the dry heaves. He kept vomiting, and I told him if he threw up something round and brown with hair on it he better stop 'cause that would be his asshole. He said he had already thrown it up."

"Has anybody seen Donald?" Billy asked. "I don't know where his bunk is, and I haven't seen him much. Maybe we should check on him."

"Who is Donald?" asked Manny.

"He joined with Billy and me and with a guy named Gil Everson," Mack answered. "Donald is a loner, a real oddball as far as I'm concerned. Gil was a nice guy. I really liked him. He got sick before we shipped out, and they put him in another replacement battalion. We were hoping we could all stay in the same outfit, and I'm sorry he got sick. He'll be a good Marine."

"Hey, look," Billy exclaimed. "Here comes Donald now. Hey, Donald, how are you? Where've you been hiding? We were just wondering how you made out in the storm. It was pretty rough, wasn't it? Were you scared?"

"Naw, I didn't get scared. The storm was rough for a while, but I didn't get seasick," Donald answered. "I'm a pretty good sailor."

"Well, all I can say is that I'm glad we made it through the storm. I don't know if we were even close to breaking up, but I don't want to get that close to ending up in the ocean on our way over," Mack said.

The same storm front that battered the American convoy spread across the Pacific in a curtain of wind and rain. The U.S. Naval weather advisories placed it in the major storm category, making it one of the most deadly of the season.

The storm that had already battered the convoy was yet to reach the Japanese I-class submarine that slowly cruised the Pacific waters in a northwesterly direction of the USS *Rochambeau*.

For three days, Lt. Commander Nakoka Koturu had

watched the falling barometer and darkening skies. The strengthening wind forewarned of a major storm, and the height of the waves had increased as the wind velocity grew stronger. A weather advisory from Kuru confirmed what Koturu already knew. "The waves are increasing," he said to his first mate. "The clouds suggest a significant storm will occur before we complete our search for enemy ships and return to Kuru."

Lt. Commander Koturu, the youngest son of Vice Admiral Koturu, was also the youngest officer in the Imperial Japanese Navy to have full command of one of the I-class submarines. He had graduated from the Imperial Naval Academy at Eta Jima, one of the most highly competitive institutions in Japan, and ranked fourth out of a class of 150 graduates.

He had studied at Staff College in Kuru, and his superior grades qualified him for the coveted assignment to a battleship, cruiser, or destroyer, but instead, Nakoka had requested submarine duty. If there were war between Japan and the American and British nations, he thought, I want to get into the fighting as soon as possible.

For the past two years, he had been assigned to one of the older R.O. class submarines and had been praised for outstanding performance as a junior officer. He recalled how proud his father had been when he received special recognition from the commander in chief of the Japanese combined fleet.

Koturu had been ordered to sail from the Naval base at Kuru and join with other recently commissioned submarines to form a defense line that stretched across the Pacific. It was the first combat opportunity for Koturu as chief officer of the recently commissioned submarine I-28. His specific orders were to "intercept and destroy" American merchant and troop convoys.

Near the end of 1943, the new radar system already common on most American ships had been placed on many of the Imperial Navy's battleships, but due to technical problems, some commanders reported their radar to be unreliable. Before the I-28 had sailed on its maiden voyage from Japan, radar had been installed, but already the radar equipment had malfunctioned. Koturu's crew, technically inexperienced with radar equipment, was unable to locate the problem.

Koturu banged his fist against the radar screen. "You must fix it," he commanded his chief technician. "We cannot achieve our mission unless you do so. The Allied ships have radar. Why can you not repair it?"

"I am sorry, Commander, the radar unit overheats and must cool before it functions properly. We do not have the necessary spare parts."

Koturu was extremely disappointed that on his first voyage as captain of the I-28 he had been unable to locate a single Allied ship, and he did not wish to return to the fleet home base without scoring a significant victory.

On the night before his submarine left Japan, he had promised his father, Vice Admiral Koturu, that he would sink many Allied ships. His father had answered, "A successful maiden voyage ensures that Buddha has bestowed his blessings, and he will grant special protection to the ship and crew members." Commander Koturu knew he could never face his father if his ship returned to Japan without a victory.

The young commander ordered the first mate to have the crew inspect the torpedoes and all firing mechanisms and to make preparations for the coming storm. He doubled the lookouts to search the darkening horizon and then joined his men in the conning tower.

The rolling motion of the narrow cigar-shaped submarine made the crew's routine chores more difficult in the cramped quarters. Reluctantly, he said, "There is nothing we can see. We will submerge and ride out the storm."

The I-28 pitched into the heavy Pacific swell, and then began its descent below the gathering tempest.

After the storm passed over the I-28, the submarine surfaced and renewed its search for enemy ships. The observer standing on the conning tower looked through his powerful binoculars, scanning the sea around him. Suddenly, he spotted the silhouette of ships in a convoy.

"Enemy convoy sighted on the horizon," he exclaimed. "Target bearing ten degrees to starboard, range approximately thirty-five kilometers."

The skipper hurried to the radar. He cursed. The radar equipment had overheated again, and the convoy was not visible on the screen. "All hands to battle stations. Reduce speed to eight knots, mark range of target at ten thousand meters," Koturu ordered, and set the submarine's course directly toward the convoy.

Koturu knew the low profile of his submarine would make visual detection difficult by the convoy. He would use his boat's low silhouette and fast surface speed to get closer to the target range of the convoy. He changed his mind. The prize was too great, he thought, to take any chance that his presence could be detected by the American radar, and he decided he could not stay on the surface. "Prepare to dive," he commanded.

The submarine quickly submerged, and Koturu swung the periscope toward the convoy. He was elated. "We have spotted an enemy convoy on my very first command. Surely Buddha is with me," he proudly said to his crew.

He whispered to himself, "How very proud my father will be of me now. Victory is mine, as I promised it would be. I'll be a hero! My children and their children will remember me in songs, and stories will be told about me for all ages! And most important, I'll have the admiration of the emperor!"

The sonar officer reported, "All sonar gear now functioning properly. Mark range at ten thousand meters, bearing dead ahead."

"Prepare torpedoes fore and aft for firing," the young officer ordered. Koturu reasoned that the troopship carried several thousand Marines bound for the Pacific islands. "If I can sink this one ship, then many of my countrymen will live to fight yet another day," he said with passion.

In his excitement at finding such a prize, the skipper of the I-28 made two critical decisions. He would move within the circle of protection established by the American destroyers before he fired his torpedoes, and second, he would not notify other Japanese submarines to join him in the attack on the American convoy. "I will share the glory of such a victory with no one. This prize is mine, and I will not share it. Buddha has answered my prayers and has chosen to bless me," Koturu murmured softly.

Most of the Marines aboard the troop transport were no longer violently seasick, and in spite of the constant rolling of the ship, some could think about food without turning green. The scuttlebutt was confirmed that turkey and all the trimmings would be served.

None of them was aware of the impending disaster that awaited them, or that a young Japanese submarine commander had chosen to stalk the troopship as his prime target. They did not know that he would wait for just the right moment to send his deadly torpedoes toward the troopship carrying the Twenty-seventh Replacement Battalion, and that the fate of thousands of Marines aboard the *Rochambeau* now rested in the hands of Lt. Commander Nakoka Koturu.

When chow call sounded, the troops from each compartment made their way through the corridors and formed in line. The chow line weaved along the deck and bulkheads toward the ship's galley below, and Mack, Billy, and Manny cautiously moved their feet on the slippery deck. Spirits were high, and the thought of eating turkey and dressing put most of the men in a happy mood.

"Mack, do you think we'll get to choose which part of the turkey we'll get?" Billy asked.

"If we do, I hope Donald isn't on the serving line. I know which part he'd put on my tray," Mack replied.

"I'm hungry enough I'd eat any part; I'd even settle for the wing." Manny said. "It won't be as good as my mamma makes, but I'll eat whatever I get. I remember the pumpkin and sweet potato pies she used to make, and she always cooked biscuits for supper. Pa used to put sorghum syrup on his plate before he put anything else, then he could make a biscuit disappear faster than anybody. My mamma was some good cook, that's for sure. Just thinking about all she used to cook is making me hungry."

"I'm from a big family, and the oldest kids ate first and the youngest got what was left," Mack said. "I was in college before I knew a chicken or turkey had anything except a neck, two wings, and a tail."

Mack, Manny, and Billy eagerly held out their trays for the mess men to load them with turkey and dressing, gravy and mashed potatoes. They braced their legs to keep from falling and balanced their bodies against the still-rolling ship. They found a table where they could stand, placed their trays on the mess tables, and began to eat.

Only a few feet from where they stood, a Marine who had ventured from his bunk for the first time in over a day swallowed a mouthful of dressing. He tried to take another bite and stared down at his tray. He looked at the pieces of turkey, gravy, and mashed potatoes and was reminded of what he had been throwing up for the past several hours.

The sick Marine vomited, filling his tray with what little food remained in his stomach. The ship took a dramatic roll, and the tray slid toward the end of the table and stopped before Mack and Manny. Mack stared at the tray, gagged, and then added to the filled tray in front of him. The three men stumbled topside and lost the rest of their Thanksgiving turkey.

On board the I-28, Lieutenant Commander Koturu decided he would take no chances for a miss and would close to within five thousand meters of his target before he fired his torpedoes. He knew that if he could direct his deadly explosives into the hull of the troop transport, thousands of unsuspecting Marines would be trapped below the waterline, and then soon afterwards, when the ship sank through the murky, churning waves, the sea would be littered with the bodies of young American boys.

Koturu was sure that in a time frame measured in minutes and seconds, his success could delay an American landing on a Japanese-held coral island and change the balance of power for his countrymen fighting in the steaming jungles of the South Pacific.

The Japanese torpedo crew looked questioningly at their commander. They knew that the range of their oxygen-fueled torpedoes was well over twenty-five thousand meters, and they could not understand why the order to fire had not been given.

Young Koturu calculated the time it would take for the torpedoes, traveling at a speed of forty knots, to hit the troopship. He wanted to get so close he could make a direct hit on the troopship. He would release torpedoes at two second intervals from the forward tubes in his first salvo, and he would still have time to direct his next charges at either the merchant ships or fire again at the troopship. There would be no time to reload his torpedo tubes before making his escape from the American destroyers circling the convoy.

On the port side of the convoy, the sonar operator aboard the destroyer USS *Topeka* said, "Commander, Commander, we got contact. It appears to be a single submarine."

Commander Oberson nodded his head. "Roger, acknowledged."

Oberson knew from previous experience he could rely on the experience of his sonar operator to distinguish between the different pitches caused by a submarine and those coming from shoals of fish, whales, or even different layers of water. He also knew that in rough water and at speeds above eight knots his skill in tracking the enemy submarine would be put to a severe test.

Oberson wasted no time in sounding general quarters. "All hands, man your battle stations! Increase speed to thirty knots. Alert convoy on bearing and range. Give me a confirmation as soon as you have it. There's not supposed to be one of our subs in these waters. Nothing else on the screen?"

Seconds passed, and the sonar operator reported, "Sound confirms single submarine, range closing to nine thousand yards."

"Stand by depth charges. Give range every ten seconds," Oberson said. "Hoist flags to let the convoy know of action being taken."

There was no mistake, the convoy was being stalked by an enemy submarine. But why at such close range? thought Commander Oberson. Oberson was puzzled. He had not expected to see a Japanese submarine so close to the convoy in this area of the Pacific. The convoy would not reach their destination of New Caledonia for several more days, and they were still in what were generally considered to be safe waters.

"Keep a sharp lookout for torpedo trails, not likely with their oxygen-fueled torpedoes, but you never know." Commander Oberson turned to his first mate. "No torpedoes sighted?" he asked.

"None, sir. The Jap skipper is either dumb, foolish, or careless to be this close without firing his fish," the first mate said.

"Maybe all three," Oberson answered.

"The son of a bitch must be nuts! He's gonna be a friggin' sitting duck. He must think we're all asleep not to be able to spot him. Doesn't he realize the range of our radar and sonar equipment?" the first mate added.

The sonar man aboard the *Topeka* spoke again, "Target closing within a thousand yards, bearing forty-five degrees starboard." He continued to report angles and distance as the *Topeka* closed on the Japanese submarine, "Range eight hundred yards, ten degrees to starboard."

Oberson said, "Set speed to twenty-one knots and bearing ten degrees starboard. Prepare to launch depth charges." A seaman stood by the rack of depth charges, ready to send the explosives into the white waves.

The troopship was now only five thousand meters from where the Japanese submarine waited, and Koturu knew the troopship would soon be within his chosen range. His torpedoes were aimed so there could be no chance to miss such a large target. Koturu looked through the periscope at the approaching convoy, his eyes and concentration riveted on the troop-laden *Rochambeau* moving toward him.

The convoy neared, and once again, in the excitement and anticipation of becoming a national hero, the commander lost his usual good judgment. Koturu took long, deep breaths. "Reduce speed to five knots. We'll let the convoy come to us. Steady, steady, just a little closer."

He was unaware the USS *Topeka* was only yards away.

"Just thirty seconds more," Koturu said, his voice scarcely above a whisper. Koturu's lips eagerly but silently formed the words to fire the first of his deadly torpedoes.

Oberson ordered the *Topeka* to change bearing, and the destroyer raced directly toward the Japanese submarine. The range between the Japanese submarine and the American destroyer closed quickly.

Too late, Commander Nakoka Koturu became aware that the American destroyer was almost upon him. "Dive! Dive!' he shouted, and the submarine shuddered as it attempted to obey the sudden thrust of engines. It's bow quickly tilted toward the bottom of the sea, fighting for the safety of the ocean depth.

Seconds later, Commander Oberson gave the order to fire six depth charges, set to explode at fifty feet. The canisters cascaded into the churning sea and sank below the white caps, then exploded with devastating rumbles.

The sonar man aboard the *Topeka* said, "Lost track of submarine," and the crew members applauded loudly. Then almost immediately, the sonar operator added, "Target re-sighted, moving at nine knots dead ahead."

The sweat formed in little beads across Koturu's brow. For the first time in his life, he felt fear. The first depth charges exploded so near they brought the reality of death to every man aboard the submarine. The captain listened in the deadly quiet for the grinding noise of propellers to tell him the American ship was approaching. He heard the rhythmic beat of the destroyer's engines getting louder as it came directly overhead.

The Japanese crew waited in absolute silence as the seconds passed. Then suddenly, the roar and crash of the depth charges exploded all around them. The ship shuddered from stem to stern, and the quiet inside the submarine was shattered by compartment doors banging and glass shattering.

The submarine began to sink rapidly. Koturu watched in horror as the needle of the depth indicator moved with frightening speed. "Full ahead, both motors. Hydroplanes hard up. All crew move aft," he shouted frantically. Every man not manning a critical position moved through the bulkheads to transfer the weight in an effort to lift the bow.

Commander Oberson gave the order to turn his ship 180 degrees and prepare depth charges for another assault with torpedoes set to explode at a greater depth. Oberson frowned; his first depth charges had missed. "Boost speed to twenty-three knots, prepare to fire four port depth charges," he ordered. He looked at the second hand on his watch. "Prepare to release charges."

The commander of the I-28 fought to steady his submarine and gain control of the plunging ship. When the submarine responded to the emergency actions, he ordered a damage assessment and cursed when the chief engineer reported a leak in the forward compartment. The shock of the charges had smashed all light fixtures and broken glass lay on the deck. The leak would mean precious reserves of air must be blown into the tanks to keep the boat in trim.

Koturu watched the gauges carefully. Sweat rolled down into his eyes, and he wiped them with the tips of his fingers. The salty tears burned his eyes, and he rubbed them again as he pondered his next move. He could order the submarine to lay dead in the ocean depth and pray that the American destroyer could not locate him, or he could order the release of more air and allow the submarine to sink to the bottom of the ocean. The depth gauges and the ever increasing flow of water into the forward compartment warned him that the steel plates could not stand further pressure from a greater depth.

The seconds ticked away, and the sound of the destroyer's engine became louder. The crew crouched where they waited, as though anticipating the explosion of more depth charges that could end their world. They held their breath as they heard the destroyer passing three hundred feet overhead, then they heard it continue beyond, and the sound diminished.

Koturu felt his heart pounding against his chest. Perhaps we can elude the American destroyer if we move as quietly as possible; if Buddha is merciful, he thought, we can still escape.

Oberson was not to be fooled. He ordered a turn and began another pass over the enemy. His sonar operator held contact as the Japanese submarine attempted to escape. The sonar operator gave Oberson the information he needed. "Target steady at three hundred feet."

"Set target depth three hundred feet," Oberson ordered. The crew prepared the charges. "Stand by to release four more charges, starboard side." Seconds passed. "Release charges," he said and then ordered full right rudder and speed reduced to fifteen knots.

Koturu heard the clank of a canister strike the hull of his submarine. His eyes closed and he shivered with fear as he waited. The thunder of the explosion was deafening. The sides of the submarine crumpled from the pressure, and the sea moved to claim the I-28. Koturu felt the water rushing over him. "Buddha, help me!" he screamed. Water filled his lungs; there was no air left when he tired to scream again.

Moments later, black oil rose to the surface. Oberson ordered the destroyer to put about and saw the surface of the water covered with thick diesel oil. Oberson felt sure the Japanese submarine had been sunk, but he knew sometimes submarines released diesel to try to induce pursuers to believe they had been sunk. He ordered the area searched again and surveillance continued by the sonar operator. The sonar operator hesitated only a second to announce, "No target in sight."

Debris floated to the surface, and large patches of bubbles released the foul smell of fuel oil. Bits of wood, cork, clothing, and rope ends, and bodies of Japanese sailors, drenched with fuel oil, floated to the surface and became part of the turbulent, restless waves. A Japanese seaman, coughing up sea water poisoned by the fuel oil that covered him, clung to a wooden panel and then sank below the surface.

Oberson gave a thumbs up signal to his executive officer and grinned as he turned to the sonar operator. "Not a bad way to end this Thanksgiving evening, wouldn't you say? Let's get back to the convoy."

16

In the summer and early fall of 1943, the First Marine Division moved from Australia to advanced staging areas at Oro and Milne Bay, New Guinea, and in November, unit commanders welcomed the replacements from the Twenty-seventh Battalion from Camp St. Lokukis, Nouméa, New Caledonia.

Pfc. Harris and Private Woodson were assigned to the Seventh Infantry Regiment, Company I, Third Battalion, and Williams, Pappas and King, to the Fifth Infantry Regiment, George Company, Second Battalion.

"Good-bye, Billy," Mack said. "I wish we could have stayed in the same regiment, but at least we're in the same division. Don't volunteer for any shit details."

Billy tucked his scarf inside his dungaree jacket and lifted his sea bag to his shoulder. "So long, Mack. You do the same. Don't forget your promise to write Mom if anything happens to me. If it does, don't write Laura, just ask Mom to tell her."

"Don't worry, Billy. We'll drink a beer together when we get back home, if they'll let us. We still may not be old enough to buy a drink," Mack laughed. "I'll be seeing you. Donald, take care of yourself. Good luck to you too."

Donald slung his rifle over his shoulder. "Be seeing you, Mack."

With the addition of the replacements from the Twenty-seventh, the First Marine Division made final preparations for the invasion of Cape Gloucester, a Japanese stronghold located in a hot, humid jungle on the western tip of New Britain. The assault troops made practice landings at Cape Sudest, and after days of maneuvers the men were anxious for the practice to end and the invasion to begin.

The invasion of Cape Gloucester, code named "Dexterity," was originally planned for November 15, 1943, but was postponed to November 20, and then to December 26.

On December 14, Lt. General Frederick D. Post, Marine commander of the southwest Pacific area, requested Brigadier General Wilford T. Adams, commanding officer of the First Marine Division, to bring his regimental commanders and meet with him for an urgent planning session. Intelligence groups from the Sixth Army were also invited to attend.

General Adams, Colonel Edward Taggart, Colonel Alfred Jacobs, Lt. Colonel Jack Jackson, and Lt. Colonel Robert R. Armstrong were escorted to General Post's briefing room.

Adams saluted. "Good morning, General Post. It's good to see you, sir." He saluted the Army officers and introduced himself and his commanders.

General Post wasted no time in preliminaries. He unrolled a map and placed it on the table in front of the officers. "General Adams, I understand that you have problems with the Sixth Army's plan for taking New Britain."

"Not so much a problem, General, just an alternate proposal. We agree the key to New Britain has to be Cape Gloucester. We agree on the objective; we just differ on how to do it."

One of the Army officers wearing captain's bars grimaced and pushed his chair from the table. "The Army's plan is the result of weeks of study, and I don't believe it should be questioned at this late date."

"Captain, my Marines will be the ones facing the Japs, unless of course you want to come along. I'm sure we could use your intelligence as a forward observer. I know the Army has given a lot of time to this plan, but any action we follow will be approved by me and my staff before we land at Cape Gloucester."

The captain swallowed, his face turning red. Colonel Jacobs concealed a smile.

"We do have new information that could cause us to make changes, even at this late date," Post admitted. "Army Intelligence has learned that the Japanese Supreme Commander, General Iwao Matsuda, has enlarged the troop strength in the vicinity of Cape Gloucester to over 10,800 troops, with another 85,000 troops available as reinforcements from various land sites."

Post leaned over the table across from Adams. "There's one more piece of information you should know, General. I just found out about it this morning. Army Intelligence has learned that the Japanese forces at Cape Gloucester will be under the command of a Colonel Torao Osaka. We don't know much about him, other than the fact that he was promoted as commanding officer of all troops in the southwest sector of New Britain. Matsuda would surely put his best officers in command."

"So does the Marine Corps," Adams said.

Post smiled and nodded. "Well, Matsuda knows we're coming, and I'm sure he's prepared to stop us."

The senior Army officer, Colonel F. J. August, spoke for

the first time. "The most important thing will be to secure control of the airfield on the western tip of the island. We believe the Japs intend to enlarge it into a strategic air base. Make no mistake about it, the enemy doesn't want to lose control of any part of New Britain. Right now, Rabaul is the main Navy control center for the entire southwest Pacific, and if we gain control of any part of New Britain, their base will be in jeopardy."

"Their forces will number over ten thousand," repeated Post. "How many more will depend on our success and how quickly we take our objectives."

Adams and his regimental commanders crowded around the table and studied the map of New Britain, a rugged volcanic island, roughly crescent-shaped, 370 miles long and forty to fifty miles wide. The general tugged at his lower lip and studied the targets and major terrain markers.

Adams pointed to the southwestern part of the island, and his finger tapped the map where the volcanic cones of Mt. Talawe and Mt. Tangi were located. "Well," he said, "these can give us problems. Talawe is over 6,600 feet, and Tangi is over 5,600 in elevation. We damn sure better get control of them as soon as we can."

The map showed that to the east, both mountains fell away toward the jungle valley of the Itni River, and the Government Trail, constructed by native labor under Australian supervision, was the main roadway.

Colonel Taggart pointed to the dense jungles and swamp forests along the coast. "These could give us a lot of trouble too. Some of the streams are unpredictable. They'll be difficult to cross with heavy equipment, especially after a hard rain."

Adams looked at General Post. "From what you tell us now about the greater size of the Japanese Army, I'm convinced some changes should be made from the Army's plan."

"You do realize the invasion of New Britain is imminent?" Post said. "We don't have much time to formulate new plans."

"Sir," Adams said, "we are not opposed to parts of the Army's plan, but you should listen to what we propose. We've given considerable thought to what we want to present to you."

Post frowned. "Let's hear it."

Adams nodded to Colonel Jacobs. "Go ahead, Colonel."

Jacobs began, "If there are as many Japanese troops as you say, we could get clobbered if we try to take this island by landing just one infantry regiment. We must plan for greater Japanese resistance, and we don't like the idea of landing artillery further westward to establish fire support. That may be one way of taking an island, but it's not the Marine way. We propose to have our infantry carve out a beachhead and then let the artillery come ashore. We don't believe a parachute regiment should be launched on the airdrome. If the Japs cut them off from the rest of the division, they'd be helpless to move and would be slaughtered by enemy mortar and artillery. They wouldn't have a chance."

Colonel Taggart stepped to the table and pointed to the map. "Yellow Beaches One and Two aren't very wide, and we could have severe casualties if we can't move inland in a hurry. From the minute our men get ashore, we'll be faced with the swamp, and then an almost impossible jungle. The swamps are obviously fed by streams after big rains, and we'll need more amphibious equipment than the plan calls for now. If we're stuck in the swamp, the Japs will have a field day, even after we establish a beachhead."

Lieutenant Colonel Jackson said, "Colonel Taggart is right. The swamp forests will be hard to get through, but what concerns me the most is how close the beachhead is to Mt. Talawe and Mt. Tangi. If the Japs aren't knocked from those high points, they can kill us with artillery and mortar shells. The Navy must blast those targets before we go in."

"Gentlemen," Colonel August said, "Army Intelligence reconnaissance patrols have thoroughly studied the best possible landing sites. Under cover of darkness, they have walked those same beaches where you will be landing your troops. We are all well aware of the landing obstacles you will face. Some, such as the proximity of the beachhead to the mountains, we can't do much about now, can we?"

"As I understand it, our purpose here today is to see how we can solve our problems, and that's what my men are trying to do," Adams said. "Given the information of the added strength of the Japanese forces, I think it wise that you hear more of our plan to achieve our objective."

Colonel Jacobs looked at General Post. "Go ahead."

"We've worked on this as an alternate landing strategy for some time. We know there are only fourteen more days before the scheduled invasion and time is running short, but if you and the Sixth Army approve, we're convinced we can make it work. Our plan will allow us to take our objective with a minimum of causalities."

"Give me details," Post interrupted.

"We'll utilize three combat teams. Combat Teams B and C will be the primary invasion forces, coming ashore here," he said, touching his forefinger to the landing sites of Yellow Beach one and two.

Adams interjected, "The Seventh, commanded by Colonel Jacobs, will spearhead the invasion with three battalions. Their objective will be to seize the beach on the eastern edge of the landing area.

"The First, commanded by Jackson, will drive westward down the coast with three battalions and will capture the airfield at Cape Gloucester.

"The Fifth, designated Combat Team A, commanded by Colonel Taggart, will be held in reserve until I direct them to land and consolidate an enclave sufficient in depth to defeat any Japanese counterattack. Two battalions can be brought up from Milne Bay to be used as quick reinforcement for operations on Cape Gloucester if and when reinforcements become necessary.

"Each infantry regiment will be supported by units from the Eleventh Artillery with its five battalions and the Seventeenth Engineering with three battalions, all under my central division command."

"Go on," General Post said.

"We need a heavy barrage against Mt. Talawe and Mt. Tangi from the Navy's big guns until we get a beachhead established," Colonel Jackson said. "We don't want the Japs pounding us with artillery and mortars when we come ashore. If the Japs come out of their caves after the Navy does their pre-landing shelling, our planes must keep that area busy until we get our men ashore."

General Post, only fourteen days before the scheduled invasion of Cape Gloucester, scrapped the original plan presented by the Sixth Army and agreed to the revised plan presented by Adams and his staff.

In late November 1943, Japanese intelligence concluded the American invasion of New Britain was imminent and strengthened their air power all along the Bismarck Archipelago.

When Admiral Page, U.S. Navy Supreme Commander, Pacific Operations, learned of the Japanese air defense plan, he refused to commit any vessel larger than landing ship tanks (LSTs) to the upcoming landing. Rear Admiral Lesley Higgins, fleet commander for the invasion force, requested and received permission from Admiral Page to add patrol torpedo (PT) boats from Task Force Seventy, four heavy cruisers, and two light cruisers to the invasion fleet. Higgins advised General Adams he would direct all naval operations from his flag ship, the USS *Covington.*

By December 20, most of the combat equipment at Milne Bay that would be used by the invasion forces had been loaded on the LSTs standing just at the water's edge, and bulldozers, trucks, jeeps, rations, ammunition, and various supplies crowded the decks, leaving just enough room for the troops with their personal gear to come aboard ship.

At Milne Bay, New Guinea, Pvt. Donald Woodson lay on his cot in the tent he shared with Billy Harris. "Billy," Donald said, "do you think the scuttlebutt about us going to New Britain is true?"

"Who knows? Someone said New Britain has jungles like here on New Guinea, so that's a good guess. Wherever it is, it's some place similar to this, that's for sure. They wouldn't have us training in these jungles just for the fun of it."

"I wouldn't bet on it," Donald muttered. "I know one thing, if we stay here much longer we're going to need some replacements. Some of the guys have malaria and the running shits. They sure as hell can't fight like that. Now I know how Gil must have felt when we were going to El Paso to enlist."

"Yeah, I know. Some of the guys throw away their Atabrine tablets. I can't stand the bitter taste, but I get them down. I haven't gotten sick yet."

"Hell, how can we get sick? We've taken shots for dengue fever, tetanus, typhoid and typhus, and that's just the shots I know about. They've given me a shot for everything that could affect my head, my stomach, or my asshole."

Donald got up from the cot and walked back and forth across the tent, then flopped down on his cot. "What a fucking way to spend a day," he said, and closed his eyes.

Billy watched Donald try to sleep. Since they had been assigned to the same company, Billy had managed to get Donald to talk a little more about his life back in Mineola, but recently, Donald had become more withdrawn. He would not mix with other men and would talk only if someone asked him a direct question.

Billy at times doubted the truthfulness of the things Donald had said about his life before becoming a Marine, but more than that, Billy felt Donald needed friendship and understanding more than anyone he had ever known. He had gained some degree of comradeship and trust with him, and in spite of his brusque and antagonistic ways, Billy wanted to like Donald. He knew Donald was a good rifleman, and during training maneuvers no one had tried any harder, but for some reason that Billy couldn't explain, Donald never allowed him to be a close friend.

"Donald, let's go down to the beach. I heard the Red Cross women are giving out lemonade. One of them is real pretty. Want to go down with me?"

"I don't think so. I've got something to do."

"Aw, come on. We don't have anything else to do. I've cleaned my rifle so many times I've almost worn it out. Come on."

Donald reluctantly stood and, without a word, walked with Billy toward the beach. When they neared the stand, Billy pointed to the two women dressed in their Red Cross uniforms. "See, I told you they had lemonade."

Billy took his first taste and wanted to spit it out. He made a face. "Gosh almighty, that stuff is sour." He stepped back from the stand and other Marines crowded forward. He knew they were there to look at the women more than to drink the synthetic lemonade, and after his first taste, he was willing to allow them to do both.

The younger of the women smiled at Donald. "You can have more. Do you like it?"

Donald returned her smile. "Oh, it's good, might need to be a little sweeter, but not too bad. I kinda like it this way," he lied, feeling his lips pucker.

Billy was surprised to see Donald drink a second cup, and even more surprised to hear him talk with the young nurse. The Red Cross nurse smiled at Donald. He's not bad-looking, she thought. There was something about him that really interested her. He seemed different from the others.

Donald said, "My name is Donald Woodson, from Texas."

"I can tell you're from the South and could have guessed you're from Texas. My name is Sarah Randolph. Bet you can't tell where I'm from."

Donald had no idea and said so.

"Iowa. A small town in the western part of the state," she volunteered. "You been in combat yet?"

"Not yet, but soon it looks like. I'm ready to go."

For the next hour, Donald and Sarah exchanged comments about various topics, and Donald was elated to find someone who seemed to enjoy talking with him. He drank several more cups of synthetic lemonade, and his mouth became so puckered, nearly every word started with a *p*. The urge to urinate got stronger, but he would not leave the stand.

Finally, his inflated bladder could take no more. "I better be going now." He awkwardly held out his hand. "I sure have enjoyed knowing you. Wish I could stay, but you're busy, and I got some things I need to do, so good luck. Maybe I can get back down here to see you again."

Sarah clasped his hand. "Thanks for stopping by, and thanks for the conversation. I'll have lemonade any time you come," she laughed. "And you don't have to drink it if you don't really like it."

Donald replied, "It's...well, it is pretty sour, isn't it?"

Sarah laughed. "It's the only thing we have, but yes, it is pretty sour."

Donald hesitated. "I know you're real busy most of the time, but could I come see you, ah, maybe visit you? I really enjoy talking with you."

Sarah replied, "You could come to the Red Cross quarters. Lots of Marines do, and sing and listen to some phonograph records we have. We have Bing Crosby singing 'White Christmas.' It's hard to believe Christmas is just days away, isn't it? We have a tent back up the beach. It's not difficult to find, just up the road leading down here, up about a mile." She pointed in the direction of her tent. "You're welcome to come tonight if you can. We even have more lemonade," she laughed.

"I'll be there," Donald replied, and hurried from the stand. As soon as he could, he ran behind a truck to relieve himself and then ran all the way back to his camp area.

When Donald entered the tent, Billy saw the smile on his face. "Well, I was wondering if you were coming back. I thought maybe you'd decided to take out squatters' rights at the stand."

"Guess where I'm going tonight?" Donald exclaimed. "Sarah invited me to come see her. She said they had good music to listen to and things like that. She said there'll be others, but I think she wants me to come tonight."

He rubbed his chin. "I better shave." He rubbed his fingers through his hair. "And I gotta do something about my hair. My hair always looks wild if I don't put something on it. Back home I always had to keep it oiled. I don't have a damn thing to put on it." He tried to part his hair. "I wonder what I could use?"

"Heck, Donald, it's not long enough to worry about. I remember when I was a little kid my mother would sometimes put a stray hair in place by using spit, and it stayed put."

Donald looked at Billy in disgust. "I know what will work. I'll use Skat. It's got a greasy feel."

"Skat? Mosquito repellent? You can't use that!" Billy exclaimed.

"Why not? We put it all over our face and hands, so it can't be harmful. We smell of it all the time anyway. I'll use Skat—that's what I'll use."

Donald used an entire bottle of mosquito repellent on his head. "I always say that if some is good, more is better." He rubbed the oily liquid on his hair and tried to comb it with his fingers. His hands were as greasy as his head, and he rubbed his hands on his face and arms. "How do I look?"

"It may work. One thing about it, you won't have to worry about a mosquito getting within a hundred yards of you tonight."

Donald made no effort to hide his eagerness for the late evening to arrive so he could see Sarah again and looked at his watch at least every fifteen minutes to make sure he would not be late.

When Donald located the Red Cross tent, he stood outside for several minutes. He could see lights inside the tent and hear music and singing and a woman's laughter. He started to leave, but the desire to see Sarah again made him walk back toward the tent. He stopped and tried to build up the courage to go inside.

"Hey, Marine," a woman's voice called. Donald saw Sarah standing in the doorway. She waved, and Donald walked toward her.

"Hi," she said. "I'm glad you came." She touched his arm. "Would you like to come in?"

"I'd rather just talk with you. I'm not much at singing."

"Fine. Let's talk then. Want to walk to the beach?" she asked.

"Aw, the beach is too crowded with the trucks and all that other stuff. I'd rather not go there."

"I know another place, come on," she said, and reached for his hand. "I know just the place."

They walked along the beach road until Sarah turned away from the shore toward a grove of coconut trees. They followed a narrow path that led to a clearing. "Some of the Marines come here during the day to play basketball or throw a football. There's some logs across the way where we can sit if you'd like."

"I don't really know how to talk to a girl," Donald stammered.

Sarah turned her head to look at Donald, "You didn't have any problem today down on the beach."

"That's not the same. There were other people around then. Why did you want to come here with me?"

"You said you wanted to talk. No, that's not the reason. I don't know why I came here with you. Maybe I find you different from the others," she replied.

"I've…I've been different from most everyone my entire life," Donald said.

Sarah studied his face in the half-light of the moon. "I didn't mean it that way. I meant you're different in a nice way."

Donald looked at Sarah. "I think you're the nicest girl I've ever met."

For a long time, they sat on the log, and Donald asked Sarah about her family and about her home.

"Your parents sound like good people," he said.

"And your parents?" Sarah asked. "What about them? I'm sure they're good people too."

Donald waited a long time to answer. "No, they're not. I never knew my father. I can't really say I've ever known my mother. I ran away from home to join the Marines, to get away from my family, to get away from anything and everything."

Sarah touched his hand, and he took her hand in his. "I'd rather talk about you than about me," he said, and Sarah found herself talking about when she was a child, about things she had almost forgotten, about things that seemed insignificant but wanted to share.

"I've really unloaded on you," she said finally, getting up from the log. "I don't know why I just kept talking. You should have stopped me," she laughed. "I think we'd better go back. They'll be sending out a search party if I don't get back pretty soon."

"Yeah, I wouldn't want them to do that," Donald said.

When they stood in front of the Red Cross tent, Donald felt embarrassed. "Sarah, could I come again, tomorrow night?"

Sarah moved closer to Donald. "I'd be darn mad if you didn't."

"I've never kissed a girl," Donald said.

"You're not just saying that, are you? You really mean it? You've never kissed a girl?"

Donald looked down. "I never knew a girl I wanted to kiss. There's never been a girl that would let me if I did."

Sarah put her arms around Donald's neck and kissed him. "Good night, Donald."

The next morning, the mosquito repellent had matted, and Donald poured water on his head, trying to wash the sticky substance out of his hair.

Billy came running into the tent. "We're moving out. Word just came. We're supposed to get our gear and be ready to board ship. The orders just came. Come on, let's get moving."

Donald looked at Billy in disbelief. "You're not serious. We've been waiting right here all this time, and you tell me we're shoving off now? I don't believe it."

"The heck I'm not serious. Sergeant Smith said to spread the word. You better believe me whether you want to or not."

Donald slammed his helmet to the deck. "I'll be go to hell. Just my fucking luck!" He strapped on his shoulder pack, picked up his M-1 rifle, and walked with Billy to join with the other Marines preparing to board the LSTs.

17

On Christmas Eve 1943, Combat Team C and accompanying units boarded ships and rendezvoused in Buna Harbor. At 0600 on D-1, Amphibious Task Force 76 began moving northward.

The weather was hot, and the heat was particularly intense belowdecks. Many of the Marines tried to sleep topside, and some decided to get a head start on using the new issue jungle hammocks by tying them from one piece of field equipment to another. The hammocks were comfortable, and the design of the hammock with a zippered mosquito net and waterproof rubberized cover had great promise of being better than sleeping on the wet ground in a poncho.

On December 25, 1943, Combat Team B completed loading and prepared to join the main convoy on its way from

Buna, and at 1600 hours, the Buna and Cape Cretin contingents joined and proceeded toward New Britain and their mutual destination, Cape Gloucester.

On board the USS *Covington*, Rear Admiral Higgins stood on the bridge, peering into the dark night. He had ordered his destroyers to form a protective ring about the main convoy and to be particularly alert for a possible submarine torpedo attack. No enemy activity had been reported. Satisfied the present operation was properly underway, he turned his thoughts momentarily to a more personal nature.

Higgins was deeply disappointed that he had not been promoted to Vice Admiral. The promotion was overdue, and Higgins could not understand the reason. It could not be a lack of trust, because Admiral Page had chosen him to lead the naval task forces in this invasion of Cape Gloucester, and Page was not one to risk failure due to an incapable leader. What must I do to get Admiral Page to approve my promotion? he thought. He had done all that had been asked of him in the Cape Gloucester planning. There always seemed to be an awkward tension between the two, Higgins thought. This perplexed and bothered him. If this operation goes smoothly and we are successful, surely I'll get the promotion, he assured himself.

"Admiral Higgins, sir," an ensign said, "General Adams aboard the USS *Martin* has sent this message for you."

Higgins smiled as he read the message, almost in the form of an order: "Get my Marine units safely ashore and I'll make Operation Dexterity the next island victory on our way to Tokyo. Signed, Brigadier General Wilford T. Adams, First Marine Division."

"No reply necessary," Higgins said to the waiting officer.

Admiral Higgins and General Adams had been friends since the early 1930s. They had met at the White House at some meeting with President Franklin D. Roosevelt. Higgins couldn't remember the reason for the meeting, but he recalled seeing for the first time the pug-nosed Marine captain with a flat bulldog face, round head, and an unusually fleshy mouth.

Adams must have been born with some skin left over and it ended up on his lip, Higgins remembered thinking.

The general's appearance had proven to be deceiving, and in later years, he earned a reputation that under the ugly exterior lay an intelligent, almost brilliant, military mind with unquestionable loyalty and compassion for his men. He was totally dedicated to his job as a Marine officer. The only resemblance his doglike face bore to the man's character, Higgins thought, was that of tenacity; he always held on until he wanted to turn loose, and that was only after he was sure the victory was his.

During the early hours of December 26, the main convoy turned to starboard from the Strait of Vitiaz, passed around Rooke and Sakar Islands, and set destination for the island of New Britain.

On board the first assault ship in the convoy, Donald Woodson again looked at his watch and turned restlessly in the canvas bunk. He stared at the stretch of canvas above him and thought of Sarah. Surely, he thought, she would know he had boarded ship on Christmas Eve and would understand that was why he could not return as he had promised. "I wanted to see you again, Sarah, I really did," he said in a low voice.

Donald traced the beauty of her face in his mind as he remembered the night with her on the beach. She had been the first, in fact, the only girl, he thought, to show him true friendship. She had mentioned that her family lived in Iowa, but he didn't know where. "Why didn't I get her address?" he cursed himself for not knowing where to write. "Aw, it doesn't matter," he muttered. "She wouldn't answer my letter even if I did write. But maybe someday, when this war is over, I'll look for her. Maybe I can find her again."

He closed his eyes, but he could not sleep with the fear of what could happen if the ship were hit by a torpedo. The stale air of so many men was oppressive to him, and he had difficulty breathing. He felt a choking sensation and began to cough and gasp for air.

"Aw hell, I can't sleep, no sense trying," he cursed, and slid from his bunk. He made his way through the narrow compartment corridor and climbed the steep passageway leading to the darkened upper deck. He walked to a deserted portion of the ship and looked into the empty darkness toward the bow, knowing it would be in that direction the approaching invasion would occur.

He leaned against the ship's railing and looked at the glistening sea. He hummed softly as he watched the phosphorescent waves leap to escape the ship's bow as it sliced through the dark blue water.

Donald heard other Marines talking in soft voices with their buddies. He heard someone laugh, and somewhere, far away it seemed, a Marine with a deep Southern drawl sang an old love song. Donald tried to remember the words; he had heard his mother sing the same song, but the voice was too far away for him to hear the words clearly. He hummed the tune as he listened to what now seemed to him the only voice in the night. "Mother, why couldn't you have loved me?" he whispered and brushed an unwanted tear from his cheek. He was ashamed and hoped no one saw. I'm too old to cry, he thought.

He saw the faint glow of morning and knew the invasion was only hours away. He gripped the railing tight with both hands. Sweat formed on his face as he thought about the impending day. He couldn't swallow, even in the fresh night air, and his heart raced when he thought of that moment when he would leave the ship and take his first steps under enemy fire. Some of the other Marines must feel the way I do about going into battle—they have to—he thought, but he knew his fear was like none he had experienced. He was glad the darkness of the night hid his face.

He reluctantly left the railing and returned to his quarters belowdecks. The yellowish glow from the bulkhead lights cast an eerie cover over the crowded compartment, and the only sounds were the squeaking of the canvas-bottomed bunks and the soft moans of men in restless sleep. He weaved his way through the aisles, crawled into his bunk, and waited for the night to end.

Billy lay awake in the early morning hours of D-day. He had watched Donald leave the compartment and started to go topside with him, but decided to stay in his bunk, and his mind wandered back to his home, to his mother and to Laura.

He wondered what they would be doing this morning, December 26 across the international date line, still Christmas day back in the States. He hoped they had received the small gifts he mailed to them from New Guinea. He had given a bar of candy to a native on New Guinea for a necklace carved from a Kunu tree for Laura and his last few American dollars to an Australian plantation owner for a silver cross for his mother.

He gently stroked the scarf around his neck, his good luck charm, and he thought of his first date with Laura and the night, still so vivid in his memory, when Laura had cried when he told her he was joining the Marines, and he would be leaving her. "Only for a while," he had said.

He wiped the tears from her cheek with the scarf, and the sweet smell of perfume became part of the tears that rolled down her face. "Please don't go," she begged. He could see her face so clearly, and when he held the scarf to his face and closed his eyes, the scent of perfume still lingered.

He held it to his lips and whispered softly, "I pray the Lord my soul to keep."

When the first distant glimmer of dawn paled the sky, the brooding, ominous bulk of Mt. Talawe loomed ahead through the disintegrating shadows.

Restless Marines stood by the railing near the bow and squinted in the direction toward the gray mass of land that would be New Britain.

Donald's fears leaped with the realization the landing would soon be under way. He tried to swallow, but his throat was dry. His hands felt clammy and almost slipped from the railing as the ship's bow dipped beneath the silent sea.

18

On the island of New Britain, the first rays of the rising sun were still hidden beyond the horizon. Japanese soldiers manning their posts along the coast could faintly see the small whitecaps riding the waves as they rolled up onto the sandy shore. The rhythmic sound had a soothing effect on the sentry manning Post 104, and the soldier yawned as he stood and stretched his arms above his shoulders. He shook his head in an effort to force his heavy eyelids open. His eyes searched the darkness, and satisfied there was nothing to see, he sat back on the wooden crate beside the shore gun he manned. His eyes gradually closed, and his head lowered until his chin rested on his chest. A faint smile twisted his lips as he thought of his homeland, and soon his thoughts turned into dreams.

Five hundred yards from the sleeping sentry, Colonel Torao Osaka, commanding officer of the Japanese forces, southwest sector of New Britain, finished buttoning his uniform. He had gotten up early on this morning of December 26, 1943 impatient for the day to begin. He had not slept well and, since he could not sleep, decided to go to the command room in the adjacent bunker and review the island's defenses.

Colonel Osaka was a graduate of the Imperial Army Military Training Academy at Tokyo, class of 1929. He had served in China, Sumatra, and later at Okinawa before he assumed command at New Britain. His strong and aggressive body matched his personality. His eyesight was corrected by glasses, the thick lenses magnifying his dark and narrow eyes.

Osaka gave a final tug to the bottom of his coat, straightened his shoulders and, as was his habit, stood at attention and faced in the direction of his homeland for a moment of prayer.

Osaka entered the command bunker, saluted the sentry, and saluted again the officer of the day, his second in command, Major Kono Koturu.

Koturu was the second son of Vice Admiral Naha Koturu. He was an experienced combat soldier and had fought in Burma with the famed Eighty-fourth Imperial Japanese Division before being assigned to the Pacific Command under Colonel Osaka. For many generations, the men of Major Koturu's family had been honored and revered military leaders. His grandfather, like his father, had held a very high command in the Imperial Navy, and his great-grandfather had been a general in the Imperial Army.

Koturu stood five feet nine inches tall, almost four inches above his commanding officer. When they stood together, Koturu purposely lowered his stature in a respectful submission to authority. Koturu's black hair, always neatly combed, grew low on his forehead, and the wire-rimmed glasses framed his dark, intelligent eyes. His nose divided his face not quite through the center.

"Good morning, Major. You slept well, I trust?" Osaka said.

"Good morning, sir. Yes, the night was calm, thank you, Colonel."

Osaka stepped toward the small wooden table at the far side of the room, sat down, unfolded the worn and tattered map of the island defenses, and looked intently at the familiar network of paths that linked one installation to the next.

Koturu walked to the table where Osaka was seated. He handed a report to Osaka. "Excuse me, Colonel, this report was received from Rabaul Headquarters."

The colonel read the report, folded it carefully, and placed it on the table. The news about Japanese military successes in mainland Asia pleased him, but it was Tokyo's custom to severely censor unfavorable reports of military losses, and there was some apprehension as to why there had been no mention of recent successes in the Solomon Islands or at New Guinea. He knew the Japanese armies had been in fierce combat with American Marines at Guadalcanal and, for the past several months, with the American Army at New Guinea, but no victory had been reported. He expected at least some minor defeats for the Japanese armies in the South Pacific, but the report did not state any had occurred.

Koturu watched Osaka. "Excuse me, Colonel, is the report from Imperial Command good news? I am sure our Imperial Armies are achieving many victories and our Navy is sinking many Allied ships. Would you not say the war is going well?"

Osaka continued to look at the map on the table and tried to direct his attention to the situation at his particular island of concern. He picked up the bulletin and read it again, more concerned about what the report didn't say than what it did say. Major Koturu watched the troubled expression on Osaka's face as he read the bulletin for the second time.

Osaka turned toward Koturu. "Major, here in the southwest Pacific, here on New Britain, is where the real battle, our war, is to be fought. Our Imperial Armies and Imperial Navy are invincible. I am confident of that."

Koturu hesitated, then said, "That is true, but there have

been many unexplained delays these past few weeks in getting supplies. Lately, our supply ships have not been coming through."

"Our supply of ammunition and food is adequate to withstand a long siege, if that becomes necessary," Osaka remarked.

"Yes, that is so," Koturu replied.

"The Americans will attempt a landing somewhere on this island of New Britain," Osaka added, staring at the map. "Our reconnaissance patrols have even found American ration cans, some with food still quite fresh. From a military viewpoint, it is certain they will attempt to take this island. Where the landing will be, however, is not certain."

Major Koturu removed his glasses and wiped them with a cloth. "The invasion could occur further up the coast, perhaps at Kokopo or even at Rabaul."

Osaka replied, "Yes. If the Americans land here, the jungle and swamps will slow the invasion. We have strengthened the defenses along the most logical landing sites, but if they come ashore, our brave soldiers will give us victory."

Major Koturu straightened his shoulders. "My father once told me, in order to win the war, we must defeat the Americans quickly. He said if the fighting lasts longer than two years, we cannot expect to win. We must avoid a major defeat here on New Britain."

Osaka interrupted, "That is why we must honorably defend this island." Colonel Osaka studied the floor, then reluctantly turned to face Koturu. Their eyes met, and Osaka confessed in a hushed voice, "No, Major, the war is not going as we had hoped." He paused for a long moment. "I am sure we have already lost a major battle in the Solomons. We must defeat the Americans here on this island. To lose will be the beginning of the end."

He stood silent for a moment. "Perhaps that ending has already begun." He abruptly moved away from the table and walked to the small slit in the side of the bunker where he could look out into the early dawn. His intelligent mind sensed things his eyes sometime failed to see. His eyes told him this day would be blessed by clear skies, but his mind warned him of approaching darkness.

The significance of Osaka's last words caused Koturu to remember something his father had once told him. Many years ago, when he first became a soldier, his father had stood before him and looked into his eyes. He had placed his leathered hand on his son's shoulder. "Kono, my son, when you face the enemy for the first time, you will fight for the glory of your emperor, not for yourself. The outcome is not as important as the way the battle is fought. If you live or die, that is not so important, for someday you will surely die. You must preserve your honor and that of your noble family. Your greatest danger will not be from the enemy, but from your own breast and the dreadful fear you might betray the faith that others have placed in you. You are part of a long and honorable legacy, my son, a part of the military history of your honorable country. Never has one of our family betrayed the trust and confidence of our glorious country. No son of mine will be the first to break that loyal trust."

Colonel Osaka paced the floor, impatient to receive the morning reports from the outposts along the coastline. He suddenly turned to Koturu. "The reports are late. They are not here. Why?"

Koturu quickly looked at his watch. "Colonel, it is not yet time. The reports are not yet due. All outposts are instructed to begin sending their reports at 0600."

The colonel walked to the table, picked up the tattered map of the island, and glanced at it. He threw it back on the table and resumed pacing the earthen floor of the bunker while he waited for the day to begin. Major Koturu was all too aware of Colonel Osaka's impatient nature, and he repeatedly looked at his watch, hoping the reports from the outposts would soon reach the command headquarters.

The convoy of ships sliced through the warm Pacific water

and held a steady course toward the island of New Britain. The Marines were now on full combat alert for the pending invasion.

Pfc. Billy Harris and Pvt. Donald Woodson stood in chow line with the other men from I Company, Seventh, and the darkness of the morning wrapped around them.

"I'm not hungry this morning," muttered Harris. "I don't know why I'm down here waiting in line."

"I don't think I can eat," replied Woodson. "I may be getting the bug or something. My stomach hurts."

Donald carried his food to a table. He looked at the spam and powdered eggs and pushed his tray away. "Stuff smells greasy. I'm going up on deck. Goddamn, you'd think the fucking Navy could have broken out some of their fresh eggs for us this morning. In a little while we're going ashore, and I'll bet they're going to eat fresh eggs and fresh meat. I wish some of these selfish Navy bastards had to go ashore with us."

"Aw, heck, Donald, you coulda joined the Navy if you'd wanted to. It isn't their fault, and don't forget those 'Navy bastards' as you called them will be taking you into shore."

"Well it isn't fair, goddamn it. The Marines always get the sharp end of the stick. I'd like to stick a sharp end right up that mess cook's ass. Hell, he only gave me one piece of spam."

"You didn't want to eat that, Donald. Quit your bitching. Let's go put on our gear, it's almost time to go."

Brigadier General Wilford Adams, and the Navy commander of the USS *Martin* watched the island of New Britain come closer. Adams was impatient to get his Marines ashore and tugged at his lower, fleshy lip as he watched the designated hour of 0600 approach.

"General," the commander said, "the weather forecast is for fair skies and mild winds. We should have a smooth landing. Perhaps the casualties will be light."

"Yes, I'm glad for my men the weather is right. We can use any help we can get. Some of these young Marines, as well as the Japanese soldiers on New Britain, are going into combat for the first time. I'm confident my men will fight with both courage and honor."

The general thought for a moment. "Every time I take men into combat, I know some will be wounded, others will die. I wish I could change that, but I can't. In a few hours, their fate will be in the hands of God, not mine."

"Sir, it's still Christmas day back home. Over here there is no holiday from war, is there?"

Adams shrugged his shoulders. "I guess one day is no different than another when it comes to dying."

The Japanese observer at Station 104, on the westernmost outpost of New Britain, wearily forced his eyes to open. The night was clear, and the sea appeared to be empty and serene. He stretched his arms and shoulders, then picked up his powerful binoculars and swept the horizon. It was still too dark to see beyond the shore.

The vast and endless sea stretched out before him, and through sleepy eyes, the sentry watched the dawn push the darkness from the sky. Distant ocean swells reflected the light from the moon, about to relinquish its domain to the rising sun.

He picked up the binoculars once more, but the only visible sight was a school of flying fish that leaped from the grasp of the blue water. He watched with interest as the fish leaped and gracefully sailed through the air, only to be beckoned by the gentle waves to return to the safety of the sea. It had been a long night.

With a start, the sentry spotted the dim silhouette of gray ships just above the distant horizon. In panic, he bent forward, refocused his binoculars, and then grabbed the radio transmitter. "Station 104 reporting! The enemy is here!" he shouted.

Major Koturu's body stiffened. He jumped to his feet and looked through the small ground level opening inside the command bunker. "I see nothing."

He grabbed the transmitter. "Station 104, this is Major Koturu. What do you see?"

"A large convoy of ships is on the horizon, Major. There

are hundreds of ships," the sentry screamed hysterically.

"Can you describe the type of ships?"

"There are many ships: cruisers, destroyers, and battle-ships! The sea is filled with ships!"

Colonel Osaka listened to the conversation between Major Koturu and the outpost. He cursed the sentry for not reporting earlier. "Major, check with Station 105 and ask them to confirm the size and types of ships!" Osaka ordered.

Osaka had been expecting an invasion force just as reported. New Britain was too close to the fighting in New Guinea and the Solomon Islands to expect otherwise, and when Station 105 confirmed the report that the Americans were approaching through Borgen Bay, Osaka knew the enemy would land at Cape Gloucester.

Osaka and Major Koturu studied the map. "It is a large convoy," the colonel said. "If the present course is maintained, they will come ashore here!" He pointed at a spot on the map. "At Cape Gloucester!" Then with a quick, clipped voice, he issued his first combat order for the defense of the island stronghold of New Britain.

"All units! Attention all units! This is Colonel Osaka speaking! An American convoy has been sighted approaching the northwest shores! All personnel! Man your battle stations! All personnel! Man your battle stations!"

Colonel Osaka wheeled around. "Major, I want all unit officers to come here at once! Send word to Captain Gasamata to alert all beach installations near Kokopo. If this is a ploy, the Americans could land somewhere on the northern beaches!"

On the bridge of the USS *Covington*, Rear Admiral Higgins was conscious of the noise his watch made as the second and minute hands moved to join the hour hand at 0600. He held his binoculars to his eyes and searched the waning darkness ahead of the bow. Tension mounted as anxious personnel manned their battle stations and waited for the order to commence firing on the island fortress. Higgins dared not show the nervous tension he too felt.

The convoy, under audio and visual blackout, moved steadily toward the landing site. Higgins knew he was responsible, as Commander of the Fleet, to use the full might of the Naval task force and destroy the Japanese shore guns so that the Marines could land on the beaches with minimum resistance. His hand shook as he held the transmitter to his mouth and gave the command to his cruisers and destroyers. "All units, this is Rear Admiral Higgins. Prepare to commence firing on my command!" His eyes focused on the sweeping hand on his watch as he counted off the seconds. "Six, five, four, three, two, one. Commence firing!" he said, and the battle was underway.

In the early dawn, six cruisers and fourteen destroyers opened fire with their big guns. A fuel supply dump near the end of the airstrip exploded in a great burst of fire, and the sky opened to the flames.

A formation of B-24 Liberator bombers flew overhead, opened their bellies, and dropped the first of many tons of explosives. Great masses of lush green jungle, rotted trees, and chunks of Mt. Talawe and Mt. Tangi lifted in the air, then fell again. B-25 medium bombers flew lower and dropped their payloads with precision accuracy. A-20 fighter planes, their .50-caliber guns chattering, strafed enemy positions along the landing sites.

Higgins listened to the distant thunder of the exploding shells from the cruisers, battleships, and destroyers and heard the bursting bombs, shaking and shattering the air in waves of concussion that reverberated across the Pacific. "My God, what a blasting the Japs are taking," he whispered.

The Japanese bunkers were heavily fortified, covered with several feet of dirt, logs, and sandbags. Colonel Osaka knew only a direct hit could destroy them, yet he instinctively ducked as the bombs exploded. A shell hit just outside his command bunker, sending a spray of rock and dirty sand through the small opening near the ground level. The desk shook as the ground above groaned from the devastating assault.

"The American forces will be coming ashore within the next few hours!" Osaka shouted to Major Koturu. "They must not take our land. They will pay dearly. We will not give an inch without taking a life in return."

"Yes! Yes!" Major Koturu exclaimed. "Our brave and honorable soldiers will not let the Americans come ashore."

Through the deafening roar of the exploding bombs and cannon shells pounding the sandy beaches and dense jungle, Koturu heard his father's voice: "Faith and honor for our family, and the glory of dying for our beloved Emperor Hirohito."

The landing was scheduled for 0745, H-hour, and one minute later, landing craft infantry, mounted with multiple rocket launchers and loaded with men and their weapons, moved through the wide opening in the barrier reef, and the landing at Cape Gloucester was underway. The assault personnel ships came next, and the leading waves transferred into landing craft that circled and formed into assault groups destined for the beaches ahead.

Billy Harris and Donald Woodson, with thirty other men of the Third Battalion, Seventh Division, hugged the sides of Landing Craft 176. Woodson kept his head down, afraid to face the next few moments. He held his hands over his ears to shut out the roar of shells exploding on the waiting beaches. His head hurt from the sounds of the landing craft's powerful engines, and he closed his eyes as tightly as he could. He made a feeble, unconscious effort to hum, but no sound escaped from his throat.

The sky was filled with planes camouflaged in shades of green, gray, and yellow that searched for their island targets. The attack group bombed and strafed Yellow Beaches One and Two for fifteen minutes, then one squadron came in low, making sure their payload of phosphorous bombs exploded on Target Hill.

Mt. Talawe and Mt. Tangi were pounded by the Navy's

big guns, and the white smoke from the bombardment shielded the first wave of Marines from the view of the Japanese defenders.

The assault troops surged through the churning water toward the beach. Donald huddled near the side of the craft, and as they neared the shore, the sounds on the island pounded in his ears. He was unaware that he had urinated and the crotch of his dungarees was wet. He tried to swallow, but there was no saliva in his mouth. He had no sense of feeling, only a fear of what the next few moments would bring. He repeated over and over to himself, his lips quivering, "Oh dear God, Oh dear God, Oh dear God." He became violently seasick.

The men and their equipment were covered with white foam and cold mist by the waves that splashed over the sides of the boat. Billy kept his head low, swaying in rhythm with the movement of the boat as it dipped and lifted for the next surge toward land.

Naval gunfire shifted inland and to the flanks of the approaching Marines. The fighter planes strafed the beaches just ahead of the first wave, and when the Marines were five hundred yards from shore, the squadron silenced their .50-caliber machine guns and banked their planes out to sea. Billy looked up from his crouched position and saw the attack squadrons dip their wings in one final salute to the Marines as they neared the shore.

LCN-176 headed for its assigned landing at Yellow Beach Two. The entire shore was engulfed with dense smoke, hiding the incoming waves of men from the eyes and fire of the Japanese defenders.

A Japanese mortar shell made a direct hit on one of the landing crafts. Its coxswain hung grotesquely over the controls; its cargo of men tangled in a mass of blood and pieces of flesh.

Waves pounded LCN-176, and the coxswain, blinded by the burning phosphorous smoke, rubbed his eyes and fought to steer his craft away from the lifeless boat beside him. The

176 spun and rolled, and Donald jumped to his feet and struggled to get to the side of the craft, his eyes searching for some way to escape this maddening world of fear.

He stumbled, and his M-1 rifle fell to the deck. He lunged over another Marine and reached for the side of the craft. He tried to climb over the side, but his feet slipped in the thick layer of puke from the huddled Marines. He struggled to pull himself up the side, but his hands slipped on the wet metal.

"Donald!" Billy screamed. "Get your head down! Donald! Don't! Wait, Donald!" With all the effort he could gather, Billy pulled Donald down beside him.

"Donald, what the hell are you trying to do?" he shouted as he held Donald's arms and looked into the face filled with terror.

A mortar shell exploded nearby, and when the boat tilted, Donald and Billy fell to the deck. Once again, the boat surged toward shore. Billy lay beside Donald and put his arms across his shoulder. He felt Donald's body shake and heard him sob.

LCN-176 was still four hundred yards from Yellow Beach Two, and the coxswain fought to turn his boat toward shore. The waves created by the other nearby craft collided with those of the sea, and confusion and panic gripped the coxswain, and he steered for the nearest shore.

As the landing craft crowded the shore, a mortar shell exploded just off the starboard side, sending a cascade of water over the crouched Marines. The firm beach should have been an ideal landing, but the frightened coxswain panicked and dropped the ramp. The leathernecks pushed forward, unaware they were still almost twenty yards from the beach. The coxswain rammed his gears into reverse and began to back away as the men stepped from the ramp into shoulder deep water. Some fell below the surface and struggled toward shore and for survival in the churning sea.

Billy gasped for air, and when he felt the shore beneath his feet, leaned forward to keep his pack from pulling him under again. The beach had a firm underfooting of black sand, almost entirely free of coral, and he fought to regain his balance.

The surging waves washed over his face. His heavy pack pulled him down again as he struggled to regain his footing in the waist-deep water. He was fearful he would lose his rifle in the sea and struggled to keep his weapon above his head.

He staggered ashore and blindly ran across the beach toward the mass of jungle that lay ahead. He lay panting, breathing heavily. He lifted his head and, with the back of his hand, wiped sand from his face and eyes.

Donald lay on his back near the edge of the water, his arms outstretched, his hands with open palms as though crucified. Donald slowly lifted his hands to his face and rubbed his forehead, then his hands fell back to his side. Somehow, someway, he thought, he had gotten ashore.

The shrapnel hit Sergeant Wally Smith, I company, in his left leg, and he fell at the water's edge. He crawled ashore and tried to get to his feet, but the sharp pain in his leg made him fall back. He tried to move his foot, and the pain intensified. The salty sea water burned the open wound, and he breathed hard for a moment.

He staggered to his feet. "First platoon, git off'n tha beach. Come on, let's go," Smith shouted, and hobbled as fast as he could on his wounded leg toward the cover of the jungle.

He grimaced in pain and then looked toward the sky, "God, ah'm shore as hell gonna need some hep ta whip these friggin' Japs. Don't think ah'm gonna need much, but ya never know."

Bullets thudded into the sand, and Smith fell behind a rotted tree trunk and looked at the blood on his dungarees. He reached for his K-bar knife and ripped his pants leg to look at the wound. "Don't look too bad," he said, then looked toward the sky. "Thank ya, God."

Before the Marines had boarded ship for the invasion of Cape Gloucester, the officers of the First Marine Division had briefed the NCOs on their objectives and responsibilities. In the hours since that final briefing, Sergeant Smith had studied the map of Yellow Beach Two where he and his platoon were to come ashore, and he knew every inch of the terrain. He remembered that Yellow Beach One was about five hundred yards long, bounded on the east by a thousand-yard stretch of rocky shoreline where jungle grew out over the water. Yellow Beach Two was approximately seven hundred yards long and terminated some twelve hundred yards west of the tip of Silimati Point.

Smith surveyed the beach as he opened his first aid pack and sprinkled sulfa drug on the bleeding wound, then wrapped a bandage around his leg. He studied the jungle and black sandy shore along the way. There was nothing that looked familiar, and Smith was certain that he and part of his platoon had been dumped ashore on Yellow Beach One instead of Yellow Beach Two.

"Dammit ta hell," he muttered. "Tha Navy was shore in uh hurry ta dump us an' git their li'l tails off'n the beach. He was so much in a hurry ta git his little ol' ass out ta safety that he done put us where we ain't supposed to be. Can't much blame tha li'l bastard, 'cause if'n ah was him, ah'd of most likely done tha same thing."

Smith saw that most of his platoon had made it, but some men were lying face down in the water that pushed them back and forth against the black sandy beach. He could count at least fourteen men, and he shook his head. "Pore fellers didn't know what hit 'em," he muttered, "but ah can't worry 'bout 'em now. Gotta worry about these here with me. Gotta find tha rest of muh company." He looked one last time at his men floating in the water. "Ah'm real sorry."

Further up the beach, Pfc. Wilber Stokes dragged two wounded Marines by the collar of their dungaree jackets into a bomb crater.

"Harris!" Smith shouted. "We got landed somewhere on Yeller One. We oughta be on Yeller Two. You git yore squad moving into cover of tha jungle and then work that-away t'ward Yeller Two." He pointed over his shoulder. "Ah'm gonna hep Stokes."

Smith knew the Japanese would concentrate their mortar and artillery fire on the shore. He also knew the wounded Marines needed his help, and they needed to move quickly to the protection of the dense jungle.

He looked again at the part of his platoon still stranded on the beach. "Pore bastards may stay right where they's at and git tha hell blow'd out of 'em if'n ah don't hep," he said under his breath. "Sometimes ah wonder if'n their folks done told 'em noth'n 'bout taking care of their little ol' butts."

He gently placed his foot on the sand and found that the pain was not as bad as it had been. He pushed harder, placing more weight on his leg. "Yep, ah reckon ah kin handle that," he decided.

The sergeant adjusted his pack and picked up his M-1 rifle. He almost fell as he put his weight on his injured leg, but regained his balance and limped toward the crater where his men were trapped. He looked back at Harris and said to himself, "Harris, ah shore as hell hope ya git yoreself and them other gyrenes into tha jungle where there's some cover."

A mortar shell exploded only a few yards away, and Smith ducked his head but kept running. "Seems like muh men must be scattered all up and down tha beach," he muttered.

The soft sand made running difficult, and he stumbled over a waterlogged tree that had washed ashore. He fell, then staggered to his feet. "If'n ah kin, ah aim ta git 'em go'n in tha right direction. Shore as hell don't want 'em charging tha ocean 'stead of tha jungle."

Smith weighed over two hundred pounds and, when he stood to his full height, was six feet four inches tall. Everything about him was big, even the *Semper Fi* tattoo on his left arm was big. His shoulders were several inches wider than his small waistline, and his muscular arms and strong thighs showed him to be a powerful man. He had played fullback at the University of Mississippi in 1938 and 1939, just before he quit college and joined the Marines.

He had blue eyes, and his thick red hair was almost always in a wild, uncombed mat that partially covered his freckled face.

His men liked him, and the morale in his platoon was exceptional. Smith had personally trained every man in I Company for this invasion, and he had trained them well. Every man under his leadership respected him and was proud to serve with him. He was friendly, as long as nobody mistook his friendliness to be a weakness of character. That didn't happen often, and never twice to the same person.

No one ever made fun of his southern drawl or the way he talked, not since the Yankee from New Jersey had laughed at him and woke up in sick bay with a broken jaw and a nose several inches wider than it had been. No one doubted his physical strength, and the more experienced officers valued his understanding of military tactics more than they trusted most of their younger officers. The officers of I Company never assigned unnecessary work details to Sergeant Smith's platoon.

A string of bullets from a Japanese machine gun kicked the sand behind him. He leaped into a bomb crater and winced as the pain shot up his wounded leg. He heard the whine of bullets splattering the beach and trees of the nearby jungle, and crouched low and waited for the burst of fire to stop. A mortar shell exploded behind him, and he cautiously peered over the crater where, only moments before, Harris and the rest of the Marines had been waiting.

The artillery shells from the Japanese defenders began to hit the black sandy beach with increasing accuracy. Smith knew he had to get his wounded men off the beach and into the limited safety of the jungle.

The sergeant crouched low, his dungarees wet from exertion and, using all his strength, lunged out of the crater and zigzagged across the remaining few yards toward his stranded men. Machine-gun fire flicked the sand around him, and he leaped feet first into the middle of the startled and frightened Marines. The pain of his injured leg cut through him as if he had stepped on broken glass. He groaned and grabbed his bandaged leg.

Smith panted to catch his breath. "Hey, y'all, tha rest of tha company is back down yonder, so why don't we git our little tails in tha cover of that jungle up tha way there so's we kin join 'em. It shore as hell will beat stayin' here in this sand pile." He brushed the sand from his face. "Stokes, ya hit anywhere?"

"I'm OK, Sarge, but shrapnel hit both of them in the legs. They can't run by themselves, and I can't carry both very fast, not at the same time anyway."

Smith frowned when he saw Private Balleau's left leg and foot covered with blood. Part of Private Jacoby's foot was missing, and he was bleeding from several places on his leg. "Is there any more gyrenes from first platoon on up tha beach?"

Balleau shook his head, "Don't think so, Sarge. We're the last of our platoon to come ashore here."

Smith breathed slower. "Aw'right, now in jist a minute we're gonna git up and run like holy hell right straight t'ward that bunch of trees, what's left of 'em anyway, and we're not gonna stop till we git inside that cover, and then we're gonna stay real low till we git tha next chance ta move back down tha beach ta join the rest of tha company. Anybody that stays here is gonna git tha hell blow'd out of 'em when tha friggin' Japs finish gittin' tha range on those mortars."

The two wounded Marines made an effort to get to their feet, but before they could do so, Smith held them back. "Jist lie still, don't make yore bleeding any worse than 'tis aw'ready. Y'all both gonna be aw'right jist as soon as we kin git uh corpsman. Yore not gonna be left here, that's for sure. Don't worry none about runnin' on them legs. Ah kin carry all three if'n ah need to. Stokes, ya big enough to carry one of 'em?"

"Yeah, Jacoby for sure. He don't weigh as much as Balleau. Hell, back home in Arkansas, we got hogs that weigh more'n Jacoby," Stokes grinned.

Sergeant Smith reached over and patted each wounded marine on the shoulder. "Then y'all take a deep breath 'cause when ah git up to run, ah'm carrying Balleau, this'n right here." He patted Balleau on his helmet. "And Stokes, ya kin carry Jacoby, and we're gonna run like hell. No sense giving the friggin' Japs an easy target ta hit. Git ready, 'cause ah'm 'bout ready ta git out of here."

"Ready when you are, Sarge."

"Aw'right, then, let's go." Smith picked up Balleau and gently put him on his shoulder. He felt the pain of his own wound tear at his side, and his leg almost buckled beneath him. He waited to move until he saw Stokes lift Jacoby to his shoulder. Together, they moved away from the sea that had almost claimed their lives and ran with their human cargo toward the cover of the jungle ahead.

Smith reached the edge of the beach and entered the thick jungle. He stopped and gently lowered the wounded Marine from his shoulder. He saw it would be impossible for them to make their way very far into the heavy foliage. "Only good thing 'bout this friggin' jungle is that if'n tha Japs can't see ya, they can't shoot ya. At least if'n they can't see ya and then kin still shoot ya, it'll be just plain dumb friggin' luck. Ah figure my luck in not gittin' shot is every bit as good as my luck in gittin' shot."

The second and third waves were coming ashore, some landing not too far from where Smith and Stokes knelt by the two wounded Marines. Smith watched them coming ashore. "At least, tha Navy is lettin' them walk ashore rather than makin' them swim like we did." He waved at a corpsman running to shore. "Corpsman! Corpsman! Over here!"

"Sure as hell ah'm glad ta see ya," Smith said as the corpsman reached them. "Ah got two of muh men that need some of yore help. Ah need ta git on up ta be with muh company, so if'n you kin fix them up and see ta it that they's taken off the beach, ah'll be much obliged."

The corpsman kneeled beside the two wounded Marines. "I'll do what I can, Sarge, and see that they get picked up on the first boat going back out to the hospital ship." He cut away the dirty, matted trousers from Jacoby's leg. Smith winced as he saw Jacoby's leg almost severed from his body, and part of his foot was missing. "Good God," he whispered under his breath, as the corpsman gave Jacoby a shot of morphine, wrapped a tourniquet around Jacoby's thigh, and covered the wounds with sulfa drugs. The corpsman gave Balleau a shot of morphine and removed Balleau's left shoe; part of his foot came off with the shoe. Balleau moaned as the corpsman wrapped his foot with bandages.

The corpsman looked at Smith's bloody dungarees. "Looks like you've been hit too, Sarge. Need any help?"

"Naw, ah'm aw'right," Smith replied. "Jist a scratch."

"Sarge, that wound needs a fresh bandage. I can evacuate you too, if you'll go."

"Naw, ah reckon ah'll stay. Jist do what ya kin so ah kin git going."

The corpsman sprinkled sulfa drug on Smith's wound and wrapped it with a bandage from his medical supplies.

"Don't wait too long before you let someone take a good look at that, Sarge. All this jungle shit can do a lot of damage. Infection can start in a hurry."

"Yeah, sure. Thanks Doc," Smith replied.

"Let's git going, Stokes. You and me gotta git back ta the rest of tha company." He straightened his pack and picked up his M-1 rifle. He saw that Jacoby was now unconscious, and he gently patted him on his shoulder.

"Sarge," Balleau said, "me and Harris went through boot camp together. Tell him I'm going home, back to San Angelo, Texas. Tell Harris I meant no harm. He'll understand what I mean."

"Yeah, ah'll tell 'em. Take care now, ya hear?"

"Sarge, Wilber," Private Balleau said softly, "I thank you both. Good luck."

Smith bent over to shake his hand. "Yeah, same ta you. Come on, Stokes, let's go find our platoon."

Stokes ran to catch Smith. He looked back over his shoulder. "See you back in the States," he yelled.

The Japanese defenders located further inland were still being pounded by shells from the big Navy guns. Mangled bodies of Japanese lay near the installations that had taken direct hits from the American Liberators, but the early bombardment had spared some of the bunkers near the shore, and Japanese soldiers began to crawl out of their caves.

A deadly symphony began. First, the staccato of American machine gun and rifle fire answered by the chatter of the Japanese machine guns. Next, the increasing crescendo of both Japanese and American mortars, and finally the explosive thump of the American artillery. In the background was the scream of the fighter planes that strafed the jungle where the Japanese defenders waited.

To those Marines still on the beach, the faraway drone of bombers made the battle seem remote until the sporadic whistle of a mortar shell passed overhead, followed by the shattering crash as the shell exploded.

When Billy Harris and Donald Woodson left the beach, they found the jungle ahead of them almost impassable. The hip-deep stagnant quagmire added to the difficulty and misery as they fought their way through the blackened swamp.

Heavy underbrush beneath the giant, towering trees competed for the skimpy sunlight. Billy was helpless to move through the thick kunai grass. He could hardly breathe in the foul stench of rotting trees. The savage vines, as thick as a man's arm, tangled with the undergrowth into a web of resistance that became a natural defense of the island.

Donald Woodson struggled to keep from falling, and sloshed through knee-deep stagnant water. A Marine just ahead of him crumpled and fell, and his anguished cry, muffled by the dense jungle, contrasted with the intermittent deep rumble of the heavy artillery. The battle sounds intensified as the leathernecks moved forward and gained a foothold on the shore of New Britain.

Harris pulled his machete from its webbed holder. He began to hack through the curtain of vines and underbrush as each step became more of an effort than the last. He saw

Donald trying to hack his way through a thick mat of under-brush, and he cut his way to where Donald stood. "Gosh almighty," Billy gasped. "I sure didn't expect the jungle to be like this, did you? We didn't do this in boot camp, that's for sure."

Donald took long breaths, his mouth open to help him pull air into his lungs. He shook his head. "This is the shits." He planted each foot deep in the muck before taking the next step. A sickening, indescribable odor from the decay of the vegetation bubbled to the surface when he pulled his foot up for another step.

Donald and Billy walked together, too exhausted to speak, and struggled through the water and mud. Billy fought to free himself from the tangled vines that held his legs.

Donald swung his machete at the mass of vines and pulled Billy by the hand until they both were free. Billy grinned. "Thanks, Donald. We'll make it yet. That looks like some kind of a clearing just ahead."

When they reached the clearing, Donald fell to the ground. Billy took off his shoulder pack and knelt on one knee, then slumped to the ground. Donald lay on his back. "I'm so tired I don't think I can ever get up. I'm beat." It was the first time Donald had rested since he left the beach. Billy took a long breath. "Me too. I hope I never see another jungle like that."

Smith and Stokes staggered into the clearing. Smith removed his helmet and ran his hand over his matted hair. "Stokes, we found 'em."

Both men dropped to their knees, and Smith, still gasping for breath, said, "Well, now that y'all have had plenty time ta rest, ah think we better git up and start movin'. Tha rest of tha company probably don't know where we're at, and we better git with 'em if'n we're gonna do what we're supposed ta. We're supposed ta be killing Japs, not cutting weeds."

Billy got to his feet and reached down to help Donald get up.

"Y'all git on your feet, let's git go'n. Come on men, let's git movin'," Smith ordered. "Come on, Woodson, off'n yore ass."

Sgt. Wally Smith listened to the groans of his men as they rose to their feet. He grinned. Ah'd be bitching too, if'n ah were them, he thought.

He helped one man get up. "Come on, up and at 'em. Let's go." He watched them struggle to their feet and pick up their gear. He grinned, thinking, they're real fighters.

The sergeant and his men moved forward around the giant trees, some over two hundred feet tall. One private tried to duck under a limb, and his shoulder pack caught the limb, and it broke and fell to the ground. Hordes of scorpions and termites crawled from the rotted wood and searched for a better place to hide.

One of the towering trees, battered from the naval bombardment, teetered on a rotten trunk, and crashed to the ground. Billy yelled, "Donald, watch out!" He grabbed Donald by the arm and pulled him away just as the tree crashed to the ground. The tree fell on another man, and Billy and Donald staggered through the brush and pulled him from beneath the tangled and decayed branches.

Billy and Donald stayed as close together as possible, "God, this stuff stinks," Billy said, his breath coming in short, wrenching gasps. "My gosh almighty, I've never smelled anything like this before."

Donald, too exhausted to talk, staggered forward. Mosquitoes swarmed over him, and he swatted at them as they stung him on his hands and face. He lost his footing and fell, his leg tangled in a submerged vine. He tried to get up, and as he did, he saw giant spiders that hung from webs stretched across the trees.

Donald screamed, "Oh shit! Oh goddamn! Look! They're all over the fucking place! Look at them!"

He swung his hands fiercely at the huge spiders that dangled in front of his face. "Get away from me!" he cried. His head reeled and his heart pounded as a snake, almost four feet long, slithered through the stagnant water around him. He almost fell again as he floundered in the muck that seemed to pull his boondockers from his feet. He stumbled again and fell, then struggled to regain his footing. He fell to his knees once more in the stinking sludge before he could stand. Mud dripped from his body, and fragments of vegetation clung to his face and arms.

He was no longer concerned about being hit by a Japanese sniper and moved forward in an effort to escape the nightmare of the jungle around him. Billy ran to him and helped him to his feet. "Donald, are you all right?"

"I'm just so tired." Donald sighed, removed his pack, and sat back down in the mud and jungle slime.

At 1600, on board the USS *Martin*, General Adams stood by the large oak table in the Command Quarters. The star on his clean starched uniform glistened in the bright lights. He had ordered Colonel Taggart, temporarily assigned as division coordinator, and the liaison officers from the First and Seventh to confer with him on the progress of the assault troops.

"OK, Taggart, what's the word from Colonel Jacobs?"

Taggart replied, "The landing on Yellow Two went very well. The beachhead is secured. Colonel Jacobs reported that the Japanese came out of some of their caves along the beaches, but our causalities were light. The first assault groups had some losses, but not as many as expected. Fox company got hit the worst. Two landing crafts took direct hits, and George company lost eleven men from that."

Taggart looked up to see Adams staring as though not listening. He saw General Adams brace himself against the table and slump to his chair. "Sir, are you all right?"

Adams rubbed his temples and winced at the sudden pain behind his eyes. "Go on, Taggart. What about the Japanese?"

"Well…" Taggart started to say then saw Adams push back from the table and turn away from his officers.

"Go on, dammit," Adams said.

Taggart looked at the other officers at the table. "The…the Jap machine gunners and riflemen retreated to the bunkers just up from the beaches."

"Go on."

"First Regiment reported some noncombat casualties—falling trees, and one man got chewed up by a goddamn crocodile. Beyond that, better than we had hoped. Nothing too serious at this point."

Adams had turned so that the officers could not see his face. The pain behind his eyes felt like a knife cutting through his brain. He squeezed his eyes shut and rubbed them with his fingers. He held his breath until the pain diminished. He tired to swallow, but his mouth was dry. He began to breath normally again and said, "What…were you saying, Colonel?"

Taggart started to get up from the table and walk toward the general, but as he did, Adams motioned for him to get back. "Get on with it, Taggart."

"Naval and air surveillance confirms that our preinvasion bombardment kept the Japanese in their caves and bunkers. Mt. Talawe and Tangi took a hell of a pounding, and we don't see any resistance coming from those two points. Some of the Seventh landed on the wrong beach, but all units have moved inland."

"What about First Battalion?"

"General," Colonel Taggart replied, "First Battalion was slowed more by the jungle than by the Japs, but they got through the swamp, and are already at our target for D plus two. They took Target Hill and Silimati Point. Depending on the amount of fight they get from the Japs, First Battalion will continue inland or hold and await further orders."

"Good, tell them to hold until we know about Third Battalion," Adams said. He looked at the executive officer from the Seventh Regiment. "What's the status there?"

"Sir, Third Battalion secured the right flank, and Second Battalion secured Yellow Two. They went through some of the worst part of the swamp, but they have a position they can hold."

Adams straightened in his chair, and looked at his officers. "Well, other than the fuck-up of landing some on the wrong beach, it sounds like the invasion of Cape Gloucester is better than we planned."

Adams pulled at his lip. "I'm moving my command ashore. I'll set up field command right here!" He poked his finger to a spot on the map. "Right here."

Colonel Taggart had learned long before that once General Adams made up his mind to do something, he did it regardless of the circumstances, but he felt it his duty to give his opinion.

"Sir, the operations are moving damn well. All units are moving inland. We're already at D plus two, even D plus three in one area, but Jacobs reports that his men are meeting sparse, but increasingly tougher opposition. The beachhead is established, but the Japs damn sure haven't been whipped. They probably have reserves hiding in the caves. We don't expect they'll move them out of the bunkers, but the bastards don't always do the logical thing. A strong counterattack could put our beachhead in jeopardy. We should wait until we secure the airfield before the command headquarters is moved ashore."

"Bullshit!" Adams said with agitation. "How the hell can I direct the campaign if I sit out here on this damn ship? I need to be where my troops are. Make the necessary arrangements to get me ashore."

From December through March, yearly monsoon rains always lashed New Britain, and General Adams ordered every unit to move inland as far as possible before that happened. The hot and humid climate was like nothing the Marines had ever encountered before. Even the veterans of Guadalcanal began to wilt under the oppressing conditions.

On December 28, a major storm battered the coast of New Britain, and torrential winds roared in from the Bismarck Sea. Thunder and lightning added to the misery of the troops. Camps were flooded, field equipment bogged down in the mud, and combat was more miserable than the men of the First Marine Division had ever imagined it could be. Rain fell continually, day after day. A solid wall of water fell as the

Marines lay in foxholes amid the tangled underbrush. Billy lay in the leach-infested water and tried to get his rifle to work properly.

The continuous rain slowed the forward movement of the assault troops. Only the amtracks could work through the swamp and jungle. With every drop of rain that fell, getting food and ammunition forward and bringing back the wounded became more difficult. Japanese snipers, armed with light Nambu machine guns, climbed tall trees and fired on their favorite targets—the Marines who struggled to bring supplies to the front lines. Casualties mounted, and the movement of supplies slowed to a crawl. Despite the increasingly stubborn Japanese resistance, the First and Third advanced further inland.

Colonel Osaka, concerned that his troops could not hold back the advancing tide of Marines, gathered his officers to discuss their defense strategy.

"Major Koturu, despite our brave effort, the Americans continue to move forward. We can no longer defend the shore. We must move our men to higher ground."

"Yes, Colonel," Koturu agreed. "They keep coming. More of the enemy come ashore each day."

Osaka looked at the map on the small table, then walked to the far end of the room. He stood looking down at the floor, then returned and studied the intricate connecting passageways of the many caves and bunkers where the Marines had come ashore.

Osaka looked at one of his officers. "Soon, our soldiers must defend their positions in the caves and bunkers. Some have no escape exit. Your men in these caves must kill as many of the enemy as they can before their bunker is destroyed. They must not leave their stations."

"They will not leave, Colonel. They will fight until the end," the officer replied.

Colonel Osaka said, "Many months ago, when our troops strengthened our defenses, we had to rely on the natural terrain. We knew that if the Americans came to our shores, their objective would be to capture the airfield, and it is there we must defend. If the Marines break through our shoreline defenses and move inland from the beach and swamps, they must follow certain routes to get to the airfield. Our defensive strategy now depends on which routes they use."

Osaka had assigned Major Koturu the responsibility of devising the island's fortifications, and a series of four bunkers had been constructed along the route I Company, Third Battalion, had now taken. Each bunker was armed with machine guns, nestled in a system of rifle trenches. Each bunker would lend support to the others, and a cross fire could inflict heavy causalities to the enemy making a frontal assault.

"Colonel Osaka," Major Koturu replied, "our soldiers are determined to defeat the enemy. They will defend their positions, until death, if need be."

Sgt. Smith led I Company through the thick underbrush. Suddenly, a burst of machine-gun fire cut through the branches and splattered against the rotten trees. Each time the men attempted to advance, the staccato sound of the hidden Nambu machine guns could be heard, followed by the muffled moan of a stricken Marine. Men fell to the ground, while others searched for cover from the chattering guns.

"Git down! Find cover!" Smith yelled. His eyes squinted against the semidarkness of the green foliage, trying to see a branch move or a waft of smoke from the enemy gun placement.

Woodson lay face down in the swamp, afraid to lift his head above the rotten jungle floor. He lay motionless, fearing any movement would draw the enemy fire toward him. "Oh please, God," he whispered.

Billy heard another burst and peered through the vines and tree limb. "Donald," he called softly. "Up ahead, I saw the flash from the Japanese machine gun." Donald slowly lifted his head. Billy pointed. "Behind those tree branches, about thirty yards." Donald lowered his head and lay as still as he could. Billy lifted his rifle and aimed at the spot where he had seen the burst of flames.

Twenty feet ahead, Sergeant Smith turned his head toward the Marine beside him. "Wings of Birds, git word ta tha lootenant that we need some bazookas and flamethrowers up here. We can't move up till we do. Tell him that, ya hear? Tell him we sure as hell need them quick."

Without a word, Wings of Birds slid along the ground until he came to a thick tree. He got to his feet, then disappeared in the shadows.

Billy crawled to where Smith lay. "Keep yore head down, Harris, ya don't want ta git it blow'd off. Where's Woodson?"

"Back about twenty yards, Sarge."

"Y'all keep down. Jist hold yore position, but watch for a banzai. No telling how many is up there."

"What are we going to do?"

"We're jist gonna wait till we git some hep, so stay put."

When Wings of Birds returned, men carrying bazookas were with him. Smith motioned for them to stop and crawled to them. "Good work, Wings," Smith said and then spoke to the two men with bazookas. "There's uh bunker jist ahead and uh Jap with a Nambu. Don't know if'n there's more than one. Ah think if'n yuh git up jist a li'l, yuh kin git aimed." He pointed to the place he had seen the fire from the gun.

The two men with bazookas worked their way so that they were directly in front of the opening of the bunker. The noise from the bazooka shells shattered the air, and then the jungle was quiet.

Marines with flamethrowers strapped to their backs cautiously crawled toward the hidden bunker. A tongue of fire scorched the air, and the Japanese screamed as the searing flames covered their bodies.

Woodson sniffed the air. "What the hell is that smell?

"I smell it, too," Billy said. "It's different from what we've smelled before. It's not just rotting trees. Maybe it's that stuff

they burn in the flamethrowers." Only later would they learn
it was the sweetish, roast-pork smell of burning flesh.

Sergeant Smith now knew the location of the other three
bunkers and directed his men to work their way around them
and drop hand grenades through the narrow openings. A few
Japanese soldiers attempted to crawl out as the grenades
exploded. One Japanese soldier climbed from a concealed
opening, his uniform hanging in shreds, his face and arms
badly burned, and aimed his rifle directly at Smith's back.

Billy brought his rifle to his shoulder and fired. The sound
made Smith duck his head, and then he saw the Japanese
soldier fall. Smith jerked around and saw Billy, his rifle still
pointing at the dead Japanese.

"Well, thank ya, Harris, that was quick shootin'. Ah owe ya
one. Guess ya learned somethin' 'bout shooting uh rifle after all."
He grinned. He looked up and said, "An thank ya too, God."

Smith ordered his men toward the second bunker, and
Billy threw a hand grenade into the opening. Two Japanese
men started to run from the covered shelter and were torched
by the flamethrowers. There were no prisoners taken. Sergeant
Smith signaled for his men to advance.

Billy and Donald walked around the blackened bunkers.
They saw the charred and smoking corpses, burned beyond
recognition. One of the Japanese was lying on his back, his
burned clothes hung in smoldering shreds from his body, his
arms lifted upward as though reaching to grasp an outstretched hand. A flame still burned on a piece of his trousers,
and Donald stepped on the flame with his foot, extinguishing
the blaze. Billy and Donald stared at the burnt, upright piece
of flesh that once had been the soldier's penis. Donald was
nauseated and gagged. He held his hand over his mouth to
keep from vomiting as he staggered past the smoking bunker.

Further to the west, George Company, Seventh, encountered deadly cross fire from another series of hidden bunkers.
Unaware that George Company could not advance, I Company moved further into the jungle, leaving a gap between the

two companies. Osaka was quick to see an opportunity and ordered his troops to fill the opening, breaching the American front line.

At 1800, December 28, Col. Alfred Jacobs, Seventh Regiment, sent a message to General Adams: "The front line has been breached. A counterattack is expected. Third Battalion has been ordered to fall back to the main beachhead. Reserves from the Fifth Regiment are urgently needed."

Adams conferred with his executive officers, then ordered Colonel Taggart to bring his troops ashore. Two platoons of medium tanks were added to the assault. He then ordered Colonel Jacobs to have I Company, Third Battalion, resume the thrust toward the airdrome.

Sergeant Smith removed his helmet and scratched his head. "Ah believe every tick on tha island has found uh home on muh head," he murmured. He studied his men. They were covered with mud from the swamp, and their clothes were wet from the torrential rains of the past two days. Some of his men had fungal infections, and some had dysentery. Two of his men, suffering from severe malaria, had been evacuated to the field hospital. He didn't feel too good himself, but was determined not to let his men know. The wound in his leg bothered him and would not heal.

There had been causalities from the Japanese mortars and machine guns. Four of his men had been killed by snipers hidden in the tall trees. His men had been on the lines for three nights and four days, and his platoon had lost thirty percent of its original strength. He knew he would lose more of his men when they returned to the front. They had not had a hot meal since they landed. He wondered how much more his men could take before they were relieved from the lines.

Smith hated to tell his men what he had been ordered to do. He muttered to himself, "Ah shore don't want ta have ta tell ya, but I got ta." He walked among his men. "Hey, y'all, we're goin' back up ta finish whuppin' the friggin' Japs. As soon as we git that done, we kin git us some dry clothes and hot food.

Right now, ah shore as hell would like that piece of fried Spam ah left on muh mess gear back 'board ship. Ah'll never fuss at uh mess cook again, so hep me! Y'all git your gear on, 'cause we're goin' to be movin' out. C'mon, Stokes, git off'n yore fanny. You too, Woodson, yore ass ain't married ta that stump yore sitting on. Let's git yore gear on, 'cause we're movin' up."

19

The LST carrying the Fifth Marines cut through the Pacific waters toward the shores of New Britain.

George Pappas sat on the blanket, his legs folded, and dealt the cards for another game of pinochle. "Jesus Christ, we've been aboard ship so long we should get paid for sea duty. Aren't we ever going to see any action? Cape Gloucester will be secured before they let us go ashore. Why did the Fifth have to be the reserve regiment?"

Manny picked up his cards. "Hell, George, for all we know the First and Seventh may still be on the beach. I'd rather be here than where they are. They haven't put us ashore for a reason, and I hope it's because they don't need us."

"Well, I hope we don't stay out here until the island is secured."

Mack looked at the cards he arranged in his hand. "Pappas, did you ever stop to think that reserves are called to the front only when the fighting gets tough? You're either dumb or braver than I thought you were, and I can't decide which it is. After you've been in combat, you can tell me why you were so frigging anxious to go ashore. Your blood runs red just like mine, and I'm not anxious to see that happen. The first thing we learned in boot camp was never volunteer for anything. You'll get into combat soon enough, and I'll bet when you do, you'll wish you were back out here."

"Didn't you join the Marines to get into combat, Mack?" Pappas asked defensively.

"I thought I did, but I'm not too sure about that now."

Pappas threw his cards down and got to his feet. "Bull, you want to get ashore just like I do."

"You want to go ashore just to get off the boat, because you get seasick just looking at water." Mack laughed and gathered the cards and put them in the box. "I'm ready to get off the ship, but I'm not all that anxious to get into combat."

General Post at Supreme Headquarters gave his approval to Adams's request for the Fifth Regiment to go ashore, and on the morning of December 29, during a relentless rain storm, the Fifth landed unopposed at Blue Beach.

Williams, Pappas, and King were in the second wave and after they cleared the beach area, entered the same muddy swamp and tangled jungle that had slowed the First and Seventh Regiments three days earlier.

Colonel Jacobs ordered his regiment to hold their positions until relieved by the Fifth, and F and G Companies, Second Battalion, Fifth Marines, started toward the airstrip.

Japanese soldiers, supported by antitank guns and 75 mm field pieces, waited in bunkers and rifle trenches on the far side of the airdrome. A Japanese officer watched the leathernecks approach and, when they stepped from the jungle cover, ordered his men to open fire. Bullets from their guns raked the jungle's edge by the airstrip, and their 75 mm shells pounded the runway.

Adams, anxious for his men to resume the offensive, ordered the Marine Eleventh Artillery Regiment to return fire with their 105 mm howitzers. Seconds later, a heavy barrage hit the fortified bunkers, and Colonel Taggart's infantry regiment stepped forward.

On the far side of the airstrip, amtracks from the regimental weapons company broke through the mortar barrage and wheeled onto the landing strip. Sherman tanks rumbled onto the coral-packed runways, and the clanking sound, muffled by mud sticking to the tracks, broadcast to the enemy that the Marine infantrymen were coming.

Pappas and King trotted beside one of the Sherman tanks, pushing as close to the side for protection as they could. A land mine exploded beneath the front track, and coral rock and shrapnel filled the air around them.

"Jesus Christ," Pappas said. "What do we do now?"

"We stay here until we have to move," King replied. "You and your gung ho crap about getting into combat!"

A few yards away, other tanks rolled across the airstrip. Sniper fire flicked the coral rock of the runway, and Platoon Sergeant Tucker dashed for cover. "Over here, over here," he shouted to the men behind the stalled tank, and Pappas and King ran toward the moving tank.

Artillery shells shrieked overhead, and the cracking sound of mortars added to the whine of tracer bullets. Williams hugged closer to the moving tank and winced at the continuous twang of bullets hitting the thick armor.

They were now almost across the airstrip. Sergeant Tucker yelled to his men, "Stay close to the tanks."

"Sarge doesn't need to tell me to stay close," Pappas panted. "If I was any closer I'd be under the tank."

Williams looked at Pappas. "You still rather be here than back on the LST?"

Osaka's men had scattered land mines along the runways, and when the tanks stopped for the mines to be cleared, Japanese mortar and light artillery shells rained on the airdrome area. The tanks and the men behind them inched forward, and when the day ended, F and G Companies had reached the far edge of the airdrome.

Colonel Osaka saw with mounting fear that his mortar and rifle fire were not enough to stop the enemy's infantry and tank troops, and in spite of all his defensive planning, his men could not repel the attack.

Osaka and Major Koturu stood together on the ridge beyond the airstrip. "Major, select two hundred of your men from the bunkers. Form them into a single line beyond the edge of the airstrip and, before first light, on my order, have them attack with all the strength they can bring forth from their bodies and all the fury and courage from their hearts."

"I will lead them myself," Koturu said.

"No. I need you with me. Tell your men what I have ordered them to do. They do not need you to lead them."

At sunrise, before the jungle steam lifted above the tangled muddy ground, Koturu's troops waited for the order to begin the banzai attack. When the order came, they ran across the battered airstrip, shouting, "Banzai! Banzai!"

The Marines, startled by such a suicidal mission, fired their weapons at point-blank range to stop the attack, but the fanatical Japanese overran the American lines.

Each man fought in hand-to-hand combat with his enemy. A Japanese soldier ran toward Manny, and when Manny tried to move to the side, his foot slipped and he fell to the ground. The Japanese aimed his bayonet at Manny's shoulder and was only two feet away when Pappas swung the butt of his rifle above his head and hit the soldier in the face. The soldier fell to the ground, his face covered with blood, his cheek bones crushed. Pappas turned just in time to see another enemy soldier coming from the other direction and swung his rifle again, breaking the soldier's neck. Manny scrambled to his feet and stood beside Pappas, and they fought side by side until the battle ended.

Major Koturu and Colonel Osaka listened to the shouts of

"Banzai," and as their men fell to the enemy fire and hand-to-hand combat, the sound of the battle became sporadic. Finally it ended. Koturu, with a sinking heart, knew the attack had failed.

"Farewell, my soldiers, your sacrifice has given you eternal life. I am sorry I could not have fought at your side," he murmured softly and turned away.

Captain Slator, G Company, walked among his men. He saw Pappas sitting on the ground and King beside him. "How'd it go over here? Either of you hurt?"

King shook his head. "Not that we can tell, Sarge. Have you seen Williams?"

"Yeah, over there." He pointed. "He's OK."

"We lost a lot of men, Sarge," Manny said.

"Yeah, casualties were pretty heavy. It could have been worse. As best I can tell, there's 150 to 200 Japs dead. Be on the lookout for another banzai."

"George, did you play baseball before you enlisted?"

"When I was a kid I did. I batted .300 on the high school team. Why?"

"The way you swung your rifle like a baseball bat, I thought you had. Did you know you can shoot bullets from the other end of that M-1?"

The next morning the Marines were ordered to extend their control of the area beyond the airdrome. The Shermans fired point-blank into the bunkers, and Slator's men started across the runway toward the battered control tower.

Some of Koturu's men, knowing they were predestined to die, left their caves and charged toward the approaching Marines. Slator's men caught them in a deadly cross fire. There were no survivors.

Lt. Col. Robert R. Armstrong's Eleventh Marine Artillery Regiment braced for another banzai attack. Armstrong ordered the resumption of the devastating 105 mm and 75 mm howitzer barrage.

Taggart sent the Third Battalion to the southeast side of the

airstrip to isolate the Japanese forces defending the airfield
from the other forces further inland.

The Japanese colonel was quick to see that his troops were
in great danger of being trapped. If Taggart's men were able
to encircle his men in the bunkers, there would be no chance
for their survival. Osaka dreaded what he had to do, but he
knew he had no choice but to sacrifice some of his men so that
the main body of men could escape.

He called Captain Takamatsu, one of his most devoted and
trusted officers, to his side. "Captain, we can no longer defend
the airfield, and the enemy is at this moment moving to isolate
and trap our soldiers. We must move our main forces to a more
defensible position before it is too late. This is what I propose.
You must take two companies of soldiers up there." He
pointed toward the caves and bunkers in the steep sides of a
narrow ridge-like barrier that rose 1500 yards above the
airfield. "You must hold the enemy long enough for our main
body of troops to move to safer terrain.

Captain Takamatsu bowed. "Yes, to keep our main forces
exposed here would not be wise."

"I must leave you there to fight the enemy. I will not be
able to help you. When you open fire, you will delay the enemy
and give our troops a chance to escape."

Takamatsu bowed his head. "I will do as you command,
Colonel Osaka. It is my prayer that we defeat the Americans,
but if that is not possible, my men and I will die with glory for
our emperor and for our beloved Japan."

Colonel Osaka watched Captain Takamatsu lead his bloody
and tattered troops up the slopes of the steep hill and into the caves
and bunkers. "I pray that Buddha is merciful," he whispered.

On the evening of December 30, General Post at Supreme
Headquarters received a dispatch: "On this New Year's Eve,
we have captured the airfield on Cape Gloucester. Happy New
Year, signed General Wilford T. Adams, Commanding General, First Marine Division."

Captain Takamatsu cursed as he watched the Marines

hoist the American flag over the severely damaged airfield. He crawled back inside his cave and waited for the beginning of the Marine assault and the inevitable end.

20

Once the airdrome was secured, the Japanese guns became strangely quiet. The American command suspected the main strength of Japanese forces had retreated to the rugged, more strategic, and defensible terrain further up the coast from the initial landing.

General Adams knew the Cape Gloucester campaign would not be successful until all Japanese resistance was found and eliminated, and he ordered the Fifth to search out and destroy the scattered pockets of fanatical Japanese soldiers that continued to harass the patrols. The Second and Third Battalions led the frontal assault through the dense swamps and streams, cut by trails too narrow for anything but foot passage.

The Fifth, joined by a detachment from weapons company, and First and Second Battalions, Seventh, advanced with only token resistance from the Japanese troops, and several strongholds were isolated and destroyed.

Before the Americans invaded Cape Gloucester, Colonel Osaka had ordered Major Koturu to locate and design a defensive strategy for all key military points. Koturu had recognized the military advantage in defending a winding, steep-sided ditch, filled mostly with shallow water, that cut its way north and south across the island. Koturu's men had taken full advantage of the natural terrain and ordered machine guns placed and sighted toward the most obvious crossings, using jungle vines, brush, and trees to hide them from view.

During the preinvasion bombardment from artillery and aircraft and from mortar shells in the landing assault, the Japanese machine guns along the banks of this putrid, dormant pond had been shielded by the thick forest cover. The bunkers were vulnerable only to a direct frontal assault by infantry and tanks.

G Company hacked its way through the jungle, and Mack Williams straightened his back and rubbed the back of his neck. His dungarees were soaked from perspiration, and his boondockers were covered with thick mud. "This frigging jungle never seems to end. Every time I cut a vine, another grows in its place." He looked behind him. "The damn jungle grows so fast I can't even tell where I've cut."

Manny King swung his machete at a thick clump of brush. "I wish I had some of this good dirt back home in North Carolina. We'd grow the biggest tobacco and the best cotton in the state. Right now I wouldn't mind being back home out in the fields with Josie."

"Is Josie your girl?" Mack asked.

"Josie's my mule."

The sudden crack of rifle and automatic fire startled the Marines, and they scrambled for cover.

"Where the hell are they?" Mack asked. "Son of a bitch, I didn't expect the Japs to be so close."

"I guess we've found what we've been looking for," Manny said.

Sergeant Tucker crawled on his stomach to where he could get a better view, then crawled back to where Captain Slator waited. Slator rubbed his face and brushed a wad of mud from his matted beard. "What's up there, Sergeant?"

Tucker knelt on one knee and scraped mud from his boondockers. "Best I can tell, the shots came from only one place, so it could be just one or two snipers, but it's hard to say. They must be on the other side of a ditch, maybe fifty yards from here, probably have some sort of bunker built in the bank of a ditch or stream bed. We crossed one about eighty yards back. It might be the same one crossing us again. It'd be a natural place to put a man with a machine gun."

"We've got to take them out, no matter how many there are," Slator replied. "Send a patrol and let's see if we can tell."

Three times the patrol attempted to cross, and each time, machine-gun fire raked the jungle and the men were forced to move back. Tucker crawled back to report to Slator.

"Captain, there's two, maybe three pockets of Japs on the other side of a deep ditch. We can't get across, and we'll lose too many men if we keep trying. The ditch is too deep and wide for us to get close enough to throw grenades. We're not going anywhere without tank support."

"Yeah, I'll get Taggart to send a Sherman. Have your men hold where they are."

Mack, Pappas, and Manny wearily sat on the rotting jungle floor. Mack pulled his legs up, folded his arms across his knees, and rested his head on his knees. Swarms of mosquitoes circled above their heads, and millions of the insects landed on their mud-caked dungarees. Mack slapped his hands and face then searched in his pack for the bottle of mosquito repellent. "I don't think this stuff does all that much good, but it's all we have." He rubbed the repellent on his face and hands then watched a mosquito land on the bottle cap. "Look at that," he muttered, slapping the cap with his hand. "You little bastard."

Pappas lay on his back, too weary to fight off the mosquitoes that covered his dungarees. "Who you calling a little bastard?" he murmured.

Mack slapped his hand again. "These damn mosquitoes."

"Fuck 'em," Pappas sighed.

Manny raised up on one elbow. "You two worry about the small things. Me? I worry about the big things, like will my girl be going to a party tonight at the County Square, or maybe going to a picture show and then to the drug store for a coke. I can't say as I'd like for her to be staying home, but I don't want her out on a date tonight either."

Pappas raised his head, squinted one eye at Manny, gave him a questioning look, and lay back down. "You better start worrying about those Japs up ahead and hope the tanks can locate the bunkers. They must have a network of caves that runs under this whole island."

"Yeah," Mack added. "I'll swear I heard a voice under the ground a minute ago."

Moments later, Pappas asked, "Mack, are you asleep, or just lying there with your eyes closed?"

"I'm not asleep. I'm too tired to sleep. Why?"

"I've been thinking, you know, thinking about home. I guess I never appreciated what home meant until now. I miss my family, but most of all, I miss being with Fay. I used to tell her how brave I was and what a good Marine I was going to be. I don't know if she believed me. I don't know if I believed it. My folks didn't want me to enlist. They wanted me to stay home and work in the mill. That all seems like it's another world now."

"It is another world," Manny said, "and this war will change us. It already has. I don't know if it will ever be the same again for any of us. It seems a long time ago when I told my folks good-bye. I don't mind saying I miss them, and I miss my girl too, no denying that. I even miss my mule."

"You miss your mule?" Mack laughed.

"Yeah, when I was working in the field, I used to talk to her. I'd tell her about things I'd never tell anyone else."

"You know what I'd be doing if I was back home?" Pappas asked. "I'd be out with Fay. We used to go to this little place downtown. Some people danced, but we didn't do much of that. Fay doesn't like to dance, but the music was soft, and we used to sit there for hours. I'd order us a drink—Fay liked cherry Cokes best—and we'd spend a lot of time just listening to the music. You got a girl back home too, don't you, Mack?"

"Yeah, I've got a girl. I'd like to be with her now. Someday, maybe I will be," Mack said softly.

"Yeah," Pappas said. "I wish I was back home, too. I hope I will be someday."

Manny said, "We all wish for something."

Sherman tanks, mounted with 75 mm cannons, lumbered through the thick underbrush and, when they sighted their cannon on the nests of machine guns, opened fire.

Tucker shouted, "Let's go, G Company. Up and at 'em."

"Guess the tanks did the job. We can cross the ditch now," Mack said, getting to his feet.

Manny helped Pappas get up. "Come on, get your butt up, we're moving out." The three buddies pushed through the tangled underbrush and stepped into the stagnant creek.

Halfway across the stream, a single Japanese soldier waited. His left leg and arm had been hit by shell fragments, and blood drenched his uniform. He knew he could not run from the advancing Marines, and he knew he would never surrender to them. He watched them get closer and reached for a hand grenade on his belt.

Pappas was the first to crawl out of the green water and step toward the concealed Japanese soldier. He was only two feet from the soldier when he saw the brush move and saw the grenade roll toward Manny.

"Manny!" he screamed. "Grenade!"

Manny, unable to see the grenade at his feet, fell to the ground and covered his head with his arms.

Pappas leaped toward the grenade, picked it up, and threw it back at the Japanese soldier in the underbrush, then fell across Manny and covered him with his body. The sound of the explosion shattered the air, and pieces of vines, brush, and flesh from the Japanese soldier covered Pappas and Manny.

Pappas took a deep breath. "Whew, that was close."

"Are you OK?" Manny asked.

"I'm too scared to feel," Pappas replied. "I think I am. We were low enough to the ground that the shrapnel flew over us."

Manny got to his feet and held out his hand to Pappas. "My aching ass, that son of a bitch would have killed us both if you hadn't seen that grenade."

The two Marines stood looking at each other a moment, then Manny said, "You saved my life, Pappas."

Pappas breathed hard. "Yeah, I guess I did." He grinned. "Save mine sometime."

21

On January 8, Colonel Osaka summoned Major Koturu to his command bunker. When Koturu entered the cave, Osaka stood waiting. "Major, when you and I talked the morning the Americans appeared on the horizon, I told you we must defend our land with honor and that if we lost the battle, it would mean the beginning of the end. The end, for you and me and for our soldiers, is now. There are too many Americans, and they fight with courage and more determination than I expected. Our troops have also fought with courage, and we have done the best that we could, but men can fight only so long, and soon the battle will end."

The major shook his head. "Perhaps the battle, but not the war. If we lose here, we will fight on the next island, and if we lose there, we will fight on the next. We may someday fight the Americans on the sacred beaches of Japan, but we will never allow the Americans to win. They will never take our land."

"Yes, we may someday fight the Americans on the shores of our beloved nation." He breathed deeply. "It is now time to divide our force. Tonight, I will take the largest number of men and defend the eastern ridges. You must take your men to defend Nigi Yama and the southern ridges. The enemy will be strong in their effort to defeat our troops, but we must defend our positions as long as we can.

"Major, you have served your country well. You have been a gallant officer. Your father and mother should be very proud."

Koturu's eyes were moist. "My father is a very wise man, and he taught me the wisdom of life. You, too, are very wise, and you have taught me the wisdom of war. You are a great leader. I am privileged to have served under your command."

Osaka straightened his shoulders, saluting his young friend and officer. "I pray Buddha will be kind to you."

General Adams pulled at his lower lip as he studied the captured document which revealed a large cache of Japanese weapons and ammunition at a place identified as Nigi Yama, somewhere on Nigiri Ridge.

He looked at the preinvasion maps. "Damned if I can find it marked on these maps. Get Division Intelligence to find the location of the ammunition depot. We have to know."

All during the night, Division Intelligence poured over the maps and studied the captured documents, and the following morning, Adams learned that Nigi Yama had been located. He ordered Colonel Taggart to send his Second Battalion, Fifth Marines to the front.

The Japanese Nambu guns, concealed among the roots of trees and heavy brush, were impossible to spot until bursts of fire betrayed their location. Each time the Marines moved forward through the tangled underbrush on the ever steepening incline, Japanese forces increased their resistance, and the Marines paid a costly price. The struggle to survive and the capture of the strategic ridge became as desperate for the Americans as it was for the Japanese.

Darkening shadows made the jungle more sinister, but the Marines managed to take a strategic position on the ridge. Time and time again, Koturu's men counterattacked, and each time they almost pushed the Marines off the hill, but the leathernecks fought desperately and held their position. By the end of the day, the battle-weary Marines had almost reached the limit of their physical endurance.

Just after midnight on January 10, Koturu went among his men. His soldiers had not eaten for two days, and they were weak from hunger and dehydrated from lack of drinking water. Their medical supplies were reduced to but a few remaining bandages, and their open wounds festered and bled in the scorching sun. Their dead could not be removed from where they had fallen two days before, and the rotting corpses filled the air with a foul odor that choked and gagged the Japanese as well as the Americans.

Koturu looked at his shattered left arm, hanging useless by his side. He lifted it with his right hand and looked at the bones, crushed from the bullet that had hit him the previous night. The dried blood was caked and matted with the remnants from the sleeves of his uniform.

He refused to use one of the last bandages for himself and used his teeth to hold one end of a strip of cloth tied above the elbow to keep the blood from draining from his body. With his right hand, he pulled the cloth as tight as he could. The pain made him weak, and he sat down on a rotted stump. He looked at his men and realized they could fight no longer. Most of his garrison had been killed, and those still alive had been wounded. The end was inevitable, but they had long ago decreed their souls to their emperor, and the glory of dying far outweighed the sacrifice to be made.

Koturu had two options, neither of which he wanted to take. He could ask his men to surrender and thereby save their lives, or he could ask them to make one last effort to drive the Americans from the hill. He knew to do so would mean all his men would die, for they would not quit fighting until every soldier was killed. His men, he knew, preferred to die rather than surrender.

He managed to stand and stood as straight as he could as he walked among his men for the last time. His men looked through bloodshot eyes at their leader when he spoke in a hoarse voice.

"Brave men, together, we have drunk bloody water on the battlefield, and your honor and your bravery have carried us through many conflicts. We have conquered pain and death. It is now time for us to make peace with our souls and give a final prayer for our beloved country and for the safety of our emperor."

He walked from one man to the next, and as he stood before each one, looked into his eyes and, with an unusual sign of respect for a Japanese officer to make toward his men, slightly bowed his head. The gesture of honor made each Japanese soldier bow his own head, and those who could rose to their feet. Each soldier knew what was being asked of him and was ready to make a supreme sacrifice, the final gift of life to his emperor.

Just before dawn, the Japanese made one last, desperate counterattack on the exhausted Marines. The fighting was fierce, and all along the ridge, men faced each other in one final battle. The war had narrowed to hand-to-hand combat between the Japanese soldier and the American Marine, each fighting for the right to live.

Captain Slator, George Company, inspired his men by his own courage and bravery. "Hang on, men. We've got to keep hanging on, this is their last attack. It's the last they can make! Hang on."

When the first rays of light broke across the tangled jungle at Nigi Yama, those Marines who were still able to stand stared through glassy eyes at the bodies of the Japanese soldiers. There was not a single Japanese survivor in this final bloody counterattack.

Williams knelt beside the Japanese major and looked down into the still face. The major's left arm was nothing but shreds of flesh, and his chest was riddled with bullet holes.

"Well, Major," Williams said in a hoarse voice, "it was either you or me, your men against ours. I'm glad I'm looking down on you instead of the other way around."

Williams staggered to his feet, and blood dripped from his face. His dungarees were splattered with the major's blood, and he fought to keep from fainting. He looked again at the still figure on the ground before him. "You gave us all the fight you could. It was almost enough."

When the area was secured, an elaborate network of caves containing weapons and ammunition was found. It had been a strategic observation point for the entire northwestern end of the island.

Colonel Taggart reported back to General Adams, "No wonder the Japs fought so hard to hold Nigi Yama. They used a trail as their main supply route that connected their headquarters and the principal bivouac areas with the Borgen Bay supply dumps and landing points. Without those supplies, the Japs couldn't fight a long war."

Brigadier General Adams relieved the Fifth Regiment from the front, and the haggard men, with muddy, unshaven faces and sunken eyes, trudged down the muddy slopes from Nigi Yama.

When they reached the now secured airfield, the most seriously wounded were evacuated to the hospital ship USS *Hope*. Those less seriously injured were treated at the field hospital and rejoined their units.

King, Pappas, and Williams stood in the chow line for their first hot food in almost two weeks, too tired to feel the rain or notice the water that dripped in constant streams from their camouflaged helmets and rolled down their ponchos.

The rumble of mortars and artillery in the distant hills, and the faint, quick staccato sound of a .30-caliber machine gun were too impersonal to matter. The only sound the exhausted men heard was the metallic clanking of mess gear against canteen cups and the sucking sound of their boondockers as each foot lifted from the thick jungle mud. The line moved in a slow step toward the mess tent, and after their mess gear was filled, Mack and Manny sat on a soggy tree trunk, and Pappas sat cross-legged on the wet ground. Cold rain mixed with the hot food, and Manny sighed, "I never liked shit on a shingle before, but this sure does taste good."

"I'd eat hot food now if it was a fried skunk," Mack chuckled. He punched Manny. "Look over there at Boog, he fell asleep with his mess gear in his lap."

Later, when the jungle hammocks were tied, the Marines crawled through the zippered openings and slept without fear for the first time since their initial landing.

The following morning, fresh troops from the Twenty-ninth Replacement Group came ashore. Their clothes were in stark contrast to those dirty, wet, torn, and bloody dungarees worn by the Marines who had landed, just two weeks earlier, on the beaches of Cape Gloucester.

Mack watched the approaching group of replacements and remembered the greeting when he first arrived at boot camp. He started to say, "You'll be sorr-eee," and then recognized a tall, blond, skinny Marine.

"Well, I'll be, it's Gil Everson!" Mack waved his hand and ran toward his friend from boot camp.

"Mack, is that you?" Gil shouted. "I never thought I'd see you again. This is really something! I can't believe it!" They grabbed each other in a bear hug.

"What outfit are you in?" Mack asked.

"George Company, Second Battalion. I was told to report to Sgt. Sammy Tucker."

"That's us!" Mack exclaimed. "This is George Company! I can't believe it." Mack laughed and slapped Gil on the shoulder, "Sergeant Tucker is a good NCO. He's smart, but tough. We're sure glad to see y'all coming in."

Gil looked at Mack's unshaven face, his auburn curly hair, matted and clinging around his neck, the dungarees caked with mud and grime. "Looks like you've been having it pretty rough. You doing OK?"

"I'm OK, but it's been pretty miserable in all this damn rain. I never knew it could rain so much and for so long. I'm thankful to be off the lines for a while."

"Many casualties?" Gil asked.

"Our battalion was hit pretty hard, but I don't know if you knew any of the ones who got hit. If anybody thought this was going to be an easy campaign, they didn't know the Japs very well."

"Are Billy and Donald here too?"

"Billy and Donald are in I Company, Seventh."

"Have you heard how they're doing?"

"No, but scuttlebutt is the Seventh lost the most men. The Seventh relieved us from the front yesterday, but I didn't see Billy or Donald."

"How about some of the other guys from our platoon in boot camp?" asked Gil.

"Munday and Boog are here. I don't know of any from our platoon that have been killed. Most of our old platoon ended up in the Seventh Regiment. You remember Jason Balleau, the one that hypnotized Billy when we were in boot camp?"

"Yeah, I remember. You had a fight with Balleau about that, too," Gil laughed.

"Yeah, I did. Well, he and Jacoby—you remember the little kid from the Bronx?—they were both hit pretty bad coming ashore in the first wave. Do you remember Wilber Stokes, the guy from Arkansas with the blue pajamas that Corporal Adams had making up then tearing down his bunk that first night at the recruit depot? Sergeant Tucker heard that Stokes is in for a Silver Star. But tell me how you've been. The last time I saw you, you were at sick bay, just before we shipped out. You were pretty sick—cat fever, or was it pig fever?" Mack laughed. "I sure hated to ship out without you. Can you believe we're together again? Come on over, I want you to meet some buddies."

"Pappas and Manny, this is Gil Everson, we joined the Marines together back in Texas, and we went through boot camp together. Gil, this is George Pappas, from Ohio, and Manny King, from North Carolina."

Manny held out his hand. "Name's Manson King. My friends call me Manny. Mack's talked about you before."

George Pappas shook Gil's hand. "Hi, Gil, you sound just like Mack. Youse guys from Texas all sound alike. How come nobody ever taught you to speak English?"

Gil laughed, "Nobody but a damn Yankee says 'youse guys.' Where'd you say you're from?"

"Ohio," Pappas said. "You coming into our outfit?"

"Yeah," replied Gil. "Mack says you got a good bunch of Marines."

"We got some good and then we got Texans," Pappas laughed. "The thing I want to know is, is there a Texan that ain't full of bullshit? And that reminds me, I want you to clear something up for me that Mack said. Tell me if it's true. I told Mack that when we rode the train from the East Coast to California, we went through West Texas, and I saw the damnedest-looking animal I'd ever seen—like a mixture between a kangaroo and a dog with long ears. Mack said it was a cross between a chicken and a rabbit, and…"

Gil said, "He told you right. We got a lot of 'em in Texas. What else did he tell you?"

"Well, that's not the question I was going to ask," Pappas replied. "He said you ship them up north and sell them for Texas Prairie Chicken, and the only good meat was on the legs 'cause their ears are too tough. He said the ranchers have a hard time growing them because they're so hard to catch. Is there any truth to any of that? I can't tell when he's bullshitting or when he's telling the truth, which he seldom does."

"Sure he's right. You've probably eaten them yourself many times," Gil laughed.

"Like hell I've eaten them," Pappas replied. "Youse Texans are all alike. If bullshit sold for a dollar a pound, you'd all be millionaires!"

22

General Adams ordered Colonel Alfred Jacobs's Third Battalion, Seventh, to make the final assault of the campaign, the taking of Hill 666.

Captain Britt, I Company, and his men found it especially difficult to advance across the terrain of deep gulches, fallen trees, jungle underbrush, and boulders strewn through parts of the hillside. Parts of the hill were so steep they had to sling their weapons and crawl up the slope on all fours. Torrential rains kept the surface so slick it was difficult to stand. It became impossible for the heavy artillery to make any forward progress in the muddy terrain.

Billy Harris, exhausted after hours of climbing, sat on the muddy ground. The rain came in torrents, and water rolled from his helmet and down his poncho. He removed his helmet to adjust the strap and turned his face to the sky. He used both hands to wash the mud from his face and then put his helmet back on. He sat for a minute more, then staggered to his feet and joined the others as they doggedly continued toward the crest of Hill 666.

Snipers hidden in the rugged terrain continued to harass them, and the physical exertion sapped their strength, but they pushed forward.

All during the day, 105 mm howitzer shells bombarded the entrenched Japanese, and mortars pounded the hillside. The defenders answered with their own mortars and sporadic rifle fire, and the sound of Nambu machine guns punctuated the soggy night. Casualties mounted, and, when the last rays of sunlight faded, the leathernecks were ordered to hold their positions.

At the base of Hill 666, Billy rested on his back in the shallow foxhole he had managed to dig, looking at the tattered trees and shattered jungle foliage around him. Three feet away, Donald Woodson lay face down on the ground. He felt the rain rolling down his back, but he was too tired to care. He turned over and closed his eyes but could not sleep. His weary eyes burned, and he tried to shield them from the constant drizzle that fell on his face, his body too wet to feel the muddy jungle floor beneath him. He struggled to stay awake for he dared not sleep. He sat up and crawled toward Billy's foxhole.

"Billy," Donald whispered. "Are you awake?"

"Yeah, I'm awake."

"Can I talk with you?"

"Sure, Donald." Billy raised up on his elbow to look at Donald. "What do you want to talk about?"

"I…I'm afraid of tomorrow." The rain and the dark night hid the terror on Donald's face.

"You're not the only one that's afraid, Donald. I think every man in the company is. I don't know what will happen tomorrow. I've prayed that we'll be all right."

"I don't know how to pray. I did once, when I was little, but I never got what I prayed for. Maybe I asked for things I wasn't supposed to have."

"The fighting on Cape Gloucester is almost over. The Japs can't hold out much longer. We've got to hold on too," Billy said.

"I...I...can't hold on much longer. All this rain, the jungle, the misery of it all."

"We've made it this far, Donald. We'll make it."

"Billy, I was scared when we landed on the beaches. I was afraid of getting killed. I still am."

"We're all afraid that could happen, but that doesn't mean it will."

"I just wanted to tell you that...that you've been a good friend. I wanted you to know that." He looked at his watch. "It's not too long till daylight. Tomorrow is almost here." Donald started to crawl away.

"Donald," Billy called, "don't worry about tomorrow. We'll make it."

The dark night gradually turned into a gray morning, and Billy lay there, thinking of Laura, wondering what she might be doing at this very moment. He squeezed water from the scarf around his neck and tucked it back inside his dungaree jacket.

Colonel Osaka commanded the Japanese defenders on the crest of Hill 666. He realized the desperate battle would be decided before the next night began. His ammunition was almost exhausted, and he knew his soldiers could not defend their position indefinitely against the unrelenting advance. When the shadows of the night began to fade into the early rays of morning, in one last calculated defensive maneuver, he ordered his men to increase the mortar and machine-gun fire against the Marines.

Fox Company was the hardest hit by the deadly fire from the concealed Japanese positions, and Colonel Jacobs ordered more heavy artillery from below into action. He then ordered I Company to move up to reinforce his besieged men.

Sergeant Smith's beard was as red as his hair, and it was difficult to tell where one ended and the other began. He scratched his face with his fingers and walked among his men. "Aw'right, let's git yore gear on. We got uh job ta do. Git up now, let's go fight some more Japs."

Billy started to get to his knees and looked at Donald, sitting a few yard away, with his legs crossed and his rifle resting across his knees. Water dripped from his helmet onto his slumped shoulders. His eyes were wide and unblinking, staring as though he could see into the jungle's depth. His pale, unshaven face was covered with grime and mud.

"Donald, are you all right?" Billy asked. Donald stared at Billy but made no reply. Billy got to his feet and stepped nearer to where Donald was sitting. He squatted down so that he was looking into his eyes. "You OK, Donald? Donald, you all right?" he asked again. "Come on, we gotta go back up front. Come on. Here, I'll help you," he said, and grasped Donald's arm to help him get to his feet.

Donald wearily rose to his knees, then slowly stood up. He licked his lips and tried to swallow. His lips mouthed the words, "I can't. I can't go back up."

Billy saw the fear in Donald's face as tears rolled from his eyes down through the mud that caked his face. Billy reached for Donald's hand and said gently, "You're doing great, Donald, let's go. I'll walk with you. I'm here if you need me."

Billy felt Donald shiver. and then he crumpled to the ground. Billy grabbed his arm and pulled his face out of the mud. Donald began to speak, almost in a whisper, and Billy moved his ear close to Donald's lips.

"What did you say?" he asked. Donald's words were barely audible, his teeth almost clenched: "Mr. President, Commandant of the Marines, fellow Marines, friends, and..." His words were slurred as he repeated them again, then mumbled them over and over.

As Sergeant Smith lifted his pack, he saw Billy reach for Donald's hand. He heard Donald's slurred voice as they sat huddled in the rain, and he slowly shook his head. He had seen the same faraway look in the eyes of other men. He pretended not to see the tears that rolled down Donald's face. He knew that now, for Donald, the war was over.

Billy looked in Donald's face, and he understood the hopelessness and grim despair unfolding before him. Billy put his arms around Donald, and together they cried as they sat in the mud and rain.

23

Colonel Osaka stood on the hillside and looked toward the shore where the Americans had landed. He called his officers together. "Our food and water are almost gone, and our men cannot fight much longer. Our ammunition supply is too low to defend our position much longer. Perhaps we cannot defeat our enemy, but we must fight one last battle."

When the Japanese opened fire, the Marines sighted their 60 mm mortars on the front line of Osaka's men and, with the longer range of 81mm mortars, dropped their shells on the far side of where his troops were concentrated. The Japanese were squeezed between two deadly barrages. As the lines of exploding death moved toward each other, Osaka's men were blanketed in a murderous cross fire, and the Marines fought their way toward the crest of Hill 666.

The last remaining stronghold was captured. The Cape Gloucester campaign, which seemed an eternity for the exhausted First Marine Division, had lasted only two weeks.

Osaka knew to fight any longer was futile, and the struggle was over. He ordered his men to abandon their positions and retreat down the steep and treacherous backside of the hill, determined to lead those he could into the dense and tangled jungle beyond.

He could see only the thick foliage of the jungle, but he knew the enemy was there. For over two weeks, his troops had fought in the most brutal terrain and in such deplorable weather that they were now exhausted. Only an estimated two thousand soldiers remained from his original garrison of twelve thousand men.

With the loss of Nigi Yama and the eastern hills, Osaka dreaded the decision he knew he must make.

"I have lost my friend and most valuable officer, and, without Major Koturu's help, it is futile to continue to defend the island," he murmured bitterly. "Many of my officers have been killed, and my men are wounded or too sick to fight. I will not see the rest of my men slaughtered. We are finished here."

Osaka spoke to his men. "I must order you to withdraw from your posts. We can fight no longer here, but I will lead you through the jungles of New Britain, and we will reach Rabaul."

"No, Colonel," a soldier pleaded, "let us stay here. We will die for our emperor if we must, but let us stay." He looked around him. "Some of us are too weak to follow you, but we are still strong enough to fight."

Osaka knew the soldier was right; some of his men could not last through the difficult journey he knew lay ahead. "I will leave only those men who cannot walk. All other men must follow me."

The Japanese commander regrouped his bedraggled troops and, in the last days of January 1944, withdrew them from the western end of New Britain.

Brigadier General Adams, flanked by the officers under his command, tugged at his lip and studied the map. The rain that dulled the faraway noises had momentarily stopped, and the tent flaps of his command post were rolled up, inviting any stray breeze to enter.

"Gentlemen, we've captured the airstrip and eliminated the possibility of a Japanese counteroffensive into our further operations in New Guinea and the Solomons. Our objective on New Britain is essentially over. However, it's apparent the Japanese have pulled their men out of here, perhaps as many as twenty-five hundred. We can't be sure where they are headed. If we allow them to escape, they'll probably join forces with other garrisons somewhere on New Britain. I've discussed this with General Post, and we've decided we must not allow that to happen. We must locate them."

Col. Edward Taggart pointed to the map of New Britain. "This is where the main force is headed, Cape Hoskins. I'm sure of it."

"Why are you so sure?"

"Because it's the shortest, most logical route to Rabaul, the strongest base on New Britain."

Adams moved from the table and walked back and forth inside the tent. "Yes, you could be right. It's possible they could make it to Rabaul."

Taggart continued, "As long as there are Japanese troops in this area, we should make sure they're put out of action for the remainder of the war. I don't want to fight these same troops again."

"I agree with Colonel Taggart," Jacobs said. "We have them on the run now, and I say we go after them. We should finish them off before they have a chance to join forces with those at Rabaul."

Adams paced the floor. "Jacobs, Jackson, what's the possibility of the main force heading south toward Camp Busching, perhaps Arawe? Could they use Government Trail and attempt to escape by sea? It's unlikely they'd try, but we can't ignore the possibility."

Jacobs interjected, "Sir, surely the Navy can keep that from happening. The Navy can patrol the entire coastline, all the way from Cape Gloucester to Cape Merkus—all the way around to New Guinea if necessary."

Adams pulled at his lower lip. "Yes and no, Colonel. The Navy could patrol the Dampier Strait, but the Navy would argue that patrolling the coast isn't on their priority list."

Adams stopped pacing the floor. "Our objective is to make sure they don't escape, and we've got to find where they are and where they're headed, whether it's Rabaul, Cape Busching, or wherever."

"I agree," Jacobs said. "We have to locate and destroy Osaka and his troops."

Jacobs pointed to the map and traced the ridges and coast line with his finger. "General, the new men from the Twenty-ninth have me back up to regimental strength. I can send out patrols to find Osaka. I can get my men to this area, and if you'll…"

"Colonel, your men got hit hard at Hill 666. They're not ready to take on another campaign. They need to dry out, if that's possible, and get some hot food in their bellies. Your regulars need more time to catch their breath before they start back, even if that time to rest is here in this godforsaken jungle."

Adams looked back at the map and frowned in deep thought, pursing his lips as if he were preparing to give a trumpet solo.

"Sir," Taggart said, "as far as we know, Osaka is alive and still in command. He's smart. He's proven that. When his men couldn't keep us from landing and taking the airfield, he pulled his men into the jungles and used the natural terrain as effectively as anyone could. He's a master in jungle warfare, moving his men from bunker to bunker so we could only fight individual pockets. His troops got the shit kicked out of them, but he still managed to give us a tough fight. When it came time to withdraw, he had an escape plan. Probably had it before we ever hit the beaches."

"What's your point?" Adams questioned.

"Osaka will take the quickest, maybe not the easiest, route through Cape Hoskins and then on to Rabaul."

"Colonel Jackson? You got anything to add?"

"I'm convinced there is but one answer. Cape Hoskins gets my vote."

"All right, Colonel Taggart, I want to use the Fifth for the assault group. Get me a plan of action. We'll review it, but I'll have the final say. Send out your reconnaissance patrols. We need Division Intelligence in on this. I want them to furnish us with all the information they can."

Adams rubbed his eyes. The sudden pain was excruciating, and he turned away from his officers. "Let's get back on this at 0800 tomorrow."

Taggart returned to his tent and sent a runner for Captain Slator. When Slator reported to Taggart's tent, the colonel was standing beside a small wooden table. A map was draped over the top.

"Come in, Captain, over here if you will."

Slator bent low and stepped through the opening.

Taggart and Slator had a close and personal relationship. They had served together on Guadalcanal, and there was mutual respect for each other. Taggart had earned a Silver Sar, and Slator had earned a Purple Heart and a Bronze Star. His actions on Nigiri Ridge would win him another medal, possibly the Congressional Medal Of Honor.

Slator had the reputation of being an honest and sincere officer. His men liked him, and he had shown them he was not a "shit tail," a term reserved for an officer whose lack of courage was substituted by bravado in command of others. If he told one of his men to do something, he expected it to be done. His men knew he wouldn't ask them to do anything he wouldn't do himself under similar circumstances. His company had fought well in combat, and his casualties had been the lowest of any company in the Second Battalion.

Taggart's finger drew an imaginary circle around the western tip of the island. "Slator, this part of New Britain is secured. The Japanese have withdrawn, but the question is where are they going? Will they try to get all the way to the other end of the island, or will they stop to fight? It's my guess Osaka won't fight unless he's forced, or in the unlikely event he gets reinforcements from Rabaul."

Slator stepped closer to the map. "From Rabaul? That's a long way to bring reinforcements."

Taggart sat down at the table. "Right now, Osaka's men are physically unable to make much of a fight, and he'll wait until the odds are more in his favor. I believe the Japs will work their way along the coast toward Cape Hoskins and Talasea. I don't believe they'll get to Rabaul, but it's a possibility. Our job is to outmaneuver them and catch them before they escape."

Slator studied the map closely as Taggart spoke. "You want me to take reconnaissance patrols and see if I can locate their route?"

"That's exactly what I want you to do. I need to know if the Japs are withdrawing as a single group or if they're doing so as stragglers. It's my guess Osaka will keep his men together as much as the terrain will allow. See if you can learn anything about their weapon supply and their physical condition. They should be short on supplies unless they've picked up food and ammunition stored along the way. Osaka may have anticipated the possibility of a troop withdrawal and stashed supplies."

Slator's eyes were still focused on the map. "That's true. Osaka could have done that."

"Captain, your objective is not to fight them but to determine their route and to get answers to as many of the questions as you can. Pick your men, no more than a squad of men for each patrol. You have five days to find those answers and report back to me."

Slator looked at his watch and then stooped down and peered under the rolled-up flaps of the tent. "I think we can get that information for you. I've got a few more hours of daylight to get my men together, and we'll be on our way. I'll have Sergeant Tucker pick volunteers, and I'll brief him on the objectives. Anything else, Colonel?"

"No, just let me know when you're ready to leave. Let me know if you need anything. Good luck."

Sgt. Sammy Tucker had proven to be an exceptional leader in the fighting at Cape Gloucester. He had shown bravery and intelligence from the moment he went ashore. His men considered him a tough son of a bitch when he wanted to be, and to them, that was most of the time.

"Sergeant Tucker," Slator said, "pick ten volunteers and rations for five days. Divide your men into two patrols of five men each. Your area of responsibility will be from Sag Sag to Gilnit, and then down to Arawe. How and where you disperse your patrols will be up to you, but I want the area covered."

"How many Japs will be in the main group, providing I find them?"

"The estimate is between two and three thousand. You may find small segments of stragglers, but Taggart is only interested in where the main group is headed. If they're in your area, they probably plan to escape by sea. If you do confirm this, report back to the colonel as soon as you can. The general will alert the Navy to step up their patrol along the coast. Taggart will get word to me if you return before I do."

"Where will your patrol be, Captain?"

"I'll search from Natamo to Iboki and points south. I'll concentrate on the low country. The jungle cover is thick and the terrain is rough, but that's what Osaka will need for an escape. I'll have one patrol from Fox Company searching the high country just in case he's decided to go that way. If I confirm the route the Japs are taking, I'll report to Taggart and then get word to you. Any questions?"

"Well, none that I can think of right now, sir," Tucker replied. "But, if I may say so, you've got the area the Japs will take. No way will the main group try for an escape by sea. Even if their ships did slip in, they'd get their little asses blown out of the water by our Navy—that's just my opinion. Well, anyway, I'll see you back here in five days, if not sooner."

Mack, Pappas, Gil, and Manny volunteered for Slator's patrol and gathered their gear and enough rations for five days.

"Pappas, if you eat all your steak and potatoes before you get back, don't ask for none of mine," quipped Manny.

"Damn, wouldn't a big ol' juicy steak be good right now. I'd eat all they could serve and as many as I could eat of some hot biscuits, smothered with butter and strawberry jelly. You know, I'd have a hard time choosing between all that and sex right now," Pappas remarked.

Mack laughed. "I hope I don't ever get that hungry."

"And while you're thinking of food, how 'bout adding some corn on the cob, right out of the field like we eat back home, and maybe a good fresh green salad from the garden and maybe a dozen country eggs to go along with the steak," added Manny. "What I wouldn't give for some of my mama's homemade biscuits."

"Don't forget a pitcher of cold sweet milk and some fresh fruit and some strawberry cobbler," Gil said.

"Why the hell did you have to start all this, Manny?" Pappas asked. "Youse guy are making me so hungry I'd try eating one of those Texas crossbreeds of a chicken with rabbit ears."

"They're mighty tasty, George," Mack added. "Right now, I'd be satisfied with the south end of a northbound goat. Did you ever eat a goat, Pappas?"

"Hell no, I've never eaten goat. Why would anybody do that?"

"I'd give my last dollar for a little *cabrito* right now," Mack said. "Wouldn't it be nice to have a little *cabrito* right now?"

"Well, that's a different story. I'd give that some thought, even though I am sorta engaged to a girl back home."

"*Cabrito* isn't what you think, George. *Cabrito* is a young goat that's tender eating." Mack laughed as he pulled his poncho over his head. "Come on, let's go. The captain said we needed to be leaving in a couple more minutes."

Gil picked up his M-1 rifle and started walking toward the waiting volunteers. "Right now I'd settle for a pair of dry socks and clean skivvies. I never knew it could rain so fucking much for so long in all my life. I'll bet sure as hell my toes are grown together."

Slator ordered the patrols to meet for a final briefing outside his tent. "Sergeant, step inside a minute."

When they were inside the tent, Slator said, "Sergeant, there's danger in what I have asked of the men. I don't anticipate any trouble, but have everyone be on the lookout for snipers, especially up in the trees. Some gung ho son of a bitch may be looking for one last Marine to take with him to his pagoda in the sky."

"Oh, I plan to make sure we don't give him the opportunity to do that," Tucker said. "I aim to be real careful. I got a pretty little gal back home I want to see."

Slator smiled. "Yeah, me too. I told the colonel where we'll search and the men assigned to each patrol. He'll know where to start looking if we're not back in five days. Let's go, I want to get started before it gets too dark."

Slator walked outside to where his patrols were waiting and, as he strapped on his .45 pistol, began talking. "Men, your NCO has briefed you on what we're doing on this mission, but I want to add a few comments. You may meet some of the island natives as you get further inland. They should be friendly, but there's no guarantee on that. They can help us if they will. If you see a Jap, take him prisoner. He probably won't talk, but if he's hungry enough and wants to eat, he will. If he can walk, bring him back to Colonel Taggart for questioning. This is a fact-finding mission, nothing more. Remember this isn't a gung ho operation. I don't want any fuck-ups, and I sure as hell don't want anyone killed. Everybody understand?"

"Captain, what do we do if he can't walk? Do you still want us to bring him back?" Pfc. Robertson asked.

"That depends on if you want to carry him. Any more questions? OK, then, let's move out."

Slator's patrol walked single file into the muggy jungle, following seldom used trails through the dense underbrush.

The continuous rain made the ground slick, and their boondockers felt like dead weights, as with each step more mud stuck to their soles. They walked through puddles of captured water and fought swarms of mosquitoes that kept pace with their every step.

For three days, the patrol picked its way through the dense jungle, walking along one narrow, winding trail until it joined another.

"Captain, there's a Jap canteen and two empty cartridge belts over here. There were some pieces of a uniform a little ways back," King said.

"Yeah, I saw that, but I've seen nothing that looks like a large group."

"Holy shit!" Pappas yelled. The native who had stepped into the path just twenty feet ahead of the patrol stood motionless, then slowly lifted his left hand in a gesture of friendliness.

Slator stopped and motioned for the men behind him to do the same. The Marines stood for a moment, watching the native ahead of them. When Slator returned the hand gesture of friendliness, the native cautiously advanced toward them, his black skin glistening from the rain, his wide feet caked with mud. In his right hand he carried a machete, and around his waist hung the remnants of a Japanese uniform. Red betel juice overflowed his mouth, staining his chin and his bare chest. He approached the Marine captain and smiled broadly, showing his darkened teeth.

"Me Dendie," he said simply.

"Slator," responded Captain Slator, and saluted.

Dendie grinned in approval. In broken English and by motions with his hands, Dendie told Slator a large group of Japanese soldiers had passed through his native village only a week before.

"We go your village?" Slator asked.

Dendie smiled broadly. "You come," he said, and in an easy trot, led the Marines along the path. From time to time,

Dendie stopped and listened, then resumed his pace. When he finally stopped, he turned to Slator. "You come." He pushed the branches apart, stepped over a fallen log, and disappeared.

"Where the hell did he go?" Mack asked. "He was right there in front of us."

"Beats the shit out of me, but he must have gone this way," Slator said, and pushed the branches apart. "Come on, we can't lose him now."

The dense foliage opened to another, narrower but heavily used path completely hidden from view. Dendie stood waiting, his black body glistening from sweat and rain. He grinned and spit betel juice through his red lips. He turned without a word and trotted down the path.

Slator trotted behind Dendie, matching his easy pace step for step. Mack followed, then Gil, and Pappas and Manny brought up the rear. For almost two hours, they alternated their pace from a jog to a trot. Their breathing got heavier as the jungle closed over them, changing daylight to dark. Dendie finally slowed his pace to a walk, and the Marines slowed theirs, grateful for a chance to catch their breath.

"Jesus Christ," Pappas breathed in short gasps, "I didn't think he'd ever stop. My ol' butt is dragging."

"You're not the only one," Manny panted. "That feller could pull a plow all day and still win a hog-calling contest."

The path gradually got wider and then opened into a small clearing where four huts were clustered around one larger hut. Slator slowed his walk and stopped near the edge of the clearing.

Dendie stopped in front of the largest hut, and Slator's eyes searched the area for signs of a trap. A tall man with gray hair pushed back from his black forehead stepped from the hut. His muscled body was erect, and it was obvious he was the chieftain of the small native village. He looked toward the Marine patrol as he listened to Dendie.

Slator stood at the edge of the clearing and held up his left hand in a gesture of friendliness as Dendie had done when they first met on the jungle path. The gesture was returned, and the Marine officer and the native chief walked toward each other.

Gil and Manny stepped just into the clearing and turned to face the rear. Mack and Pappas walked toward the center of the village, their weapons ready to fire.

Slator walked toward the chieftain and very slowly turned to his patrol and motioned for them to move into the clearing where he was standing. As if by some silent signal, native men emerged from the far end of the jungle. Each man carried a machete, the blade sharpened like a razor.

The natives whispered to each other as they looked and pointed at the Marines. The chieftain called to them, and each man held up his left hand in a gesture of friendliness.

Manny grinned and returned the gesture, and the tension disappeared.

Slator talked with the chieftain for several minutes, and when he could not understand, looked for Dendie to translate. The chief pointed to a plot of crudely tilled land that had once been a small vegetables garden. Slator could not understand the chieftain's words as he pointed to the broken stalks that littered the ground, but understood the anger in the man's voice.

The chief led Slator to the entrance of a large hut and motioned for him to enter. Dendie stood in front of the opening and, every few minutes, spewed a stream of red juice that misted the air around him.

Slator emerged from the hut and motioned for Gil and Manny to follow. They walked behind one of the smaller huts and waited as Dendie motioned with his machete for them to look at an area near the edge of the clearing.

Almost instantly, Gil turned away and gagged as he tried not to vomit. What Manny and Slator saw made them gasp, and they turned away, a grim expression on their faces.

"Good God!" Gil whispered. "There's at least five Jap bodies hanging from the trees, hanging from their feet, with their heads and arms chopped off."

Slator turned to leave. "I've seen enough. Let's get the hell out of here."

When Slator walked back to the old chieftain, he spoke with the same broken English used by the natives. The native once more lifted his left hand in a final salute. Slator saluted as he would salute a senior officer. The old chief smiled and nodded his head in appreciation and then did his best to return the salute.

Slator turned to Dendie and raised his left hand. Dendie smiled and tried to salute as his chief had done. Without a word, the Marines walked out of the village and back down the path from which they had come.

On the morning of February 28, the rain splattered against the top of the tent where Brigadier General Adams and his officers were seated. Adams got up from his chair and walked to the open door. "Damn miserable rain. It never stops." He returned to the table in the center of the tent. "All right, Colonel Taggart, get on with it. Let's hear your report and action plan."

Taggart rose from his chair and stood before the group. "I've asked Captain Slator, George Company, to give you a firsthand report of what his patrols found. Go ahead, Slator."

Slator walked to a crude easel placed before the table where the officers were seated. He secured a map of the western portion of New Britain to the board and began his report. Slator's words were explicit.

"Sgt. Sammy Tucker, George Company, Second Battalion, led two patrols over a wide area, searching the area from Natamo to Sag Sag to Gilnit. His patrols found only small groups of stragglers, nothing to indicate a large withdrawal of troops, and nothing to indicate the Japs planned an escape by sea. Two other patrols, including my own, made a wide search of the area from Natamo to Iboki and points south."

"Captain, would you show us where those places are on the map?" Colonel Jackson asked.

Slator studied the map for a second. "Here is Iboki, and this is Natamo."

Slator continued, "On the third day out, my patrol met a friendly native who took us to his village, a place they call Kiosi." Slator pointed to a spot on the map. "This is the location of the village, about twenty-five miles southeast of Iboki. Our reconnaissance maps don't show it, and we wouldn't have found it if the native had not taken us there. The village chief told us a large group of Jap soldiers came into their village. He said they were sick and wounded, starving, eating snakes, lizards, anything they could catch. The Japs stole the native's food supply and raided their gardens. They even ate their dogs."

"Jesus Christ," Adams murmured.

"Were any of the Japs still there?" Jacobs asked.

"We found several decomposed bodies of Jap soldiers. The natives hate the Japs. They've been under their harsh rule for too many years, and they took out their revenge on the sickly, retreating soldiers, and killed as many as they could with their machetes and spears. What we saw was unbeliev-able. I saw at least fifty Jap bodies the natives had killed, and with vengeance, I'd say."

"And with just cause," Jacobs added.

"The natives believe if they cut off the heads and arms of someone and then bury the body parts away from the torso, the soul will wander for all time, searching for the complete man, and will never come back to harm them again."

"Could you get an idea of how many Japs were there?" Jacobs asked.

"The chief told me there were about nine hundred soldiers in the first group that passed near their village, and two days later twelve hundred more passed along the same route. He described an officer, a 'number one boss man.' The descrip-tion fits that of Colonel Osaka. Both groups were headed toward Cape Hoskins. Many of the last group went into the village to plunder what they could, and the natives killed them. After we left the village, my patrol found evidence of still another large group, which confirms in every way what they told us. There's no doubt they were all headed toward Cape Hoskins."

Slator waited for questions.

General Adams unconsciously pulled his lower lip. Damn good Marine, Adams thought as he watched and listened to Slator's report. He was pleased with the information. The decision he would make on the next phase of the combat operations depended on its accuracy.

"Captain," the general said, "if the Japs are in such poor physical condition, will they survive to reach Cape Hoskins?"

"I don't know, sir. Osaka will get some there if anyone can," replied Slator.

"Captain, did you find any other route?" asked Colonel Jacobs. "Any evidence of an attempt to escape toward Camp Busching or Arawe?"

"There is no other route, Colonel." Slator replied.

General Adams shifted his chair. "All right, Colonel Taggart, let's hear your plan. Spell it out for us."

Taggart walked to the map of New Britain. "The code name for the plan is Appease. We will use a series of troop landings, leapfrogging from one to the next along the northern coast of New Britain, eventually landing at Talasea, sixty miles up from Cape Gloucester. If we don't stop Osaka, he'll reach Rabaul with at least a thousand or more of his troops. The most logical route will take him through the Talasea pass." Taggart pointed at the location of Talasea on the east side of the Willaumez Peninsula.

"Intelligence reports show a small airdrome at Talasea, large enough to accommodate fighter planes that could harass our other Pacific operations. We must knock out the airstrip as well as go after the Japs. If we follow the plan I propose, we can do both—block Osaka's escape and capture a strategic airfield."

"How do you propose to do that, Colonel?" Adams asked.

"We can use fresh platoons, landing from LCMs at strategic points all along the coastal shores. The men will then secure the immediate area and wait to be leapfrogged to another critical point further up the coast. Doing it this way, we will use only ten LCMs and jungle trails to move five thousand men, their supplies, and equipment to the base at Talasea."

"Talasea?" questioned General Adams. "Why there? Why not go directly to Cape Hoskins if that's where the largest concentration of Japs is located?"

"By landing at Talasea we can cut off their escape route without unnecessary losses," Taggart responded. "Talasea is at the eastern junction of the Numundo Peninsula and the mainland, and if the Japanese take this route, they'll pass this junction on their way to Cape Hoskins and on to Rabaul."

"What's the estimate from Intelligence on the number of enemy troops at Talasea?" Adams asked.

"About two thousand. Osaka's troops would add another thousand or so. Osaka's men will not add much strength to the existing garrison, not after their trip through the jungle, but if Osaka gets there, his presence will mean a lot. It's doubtful that troops will be sent down from Rabaul, and I can't see many troops leaving the main fortifications at Cape Hoskins to go to Talasea. Maybe a few, but not many. It's far more likely the Japanese command will try to withdraw troops from Talasea and send them to Cape Hoskins, rather than sending reinforcements from Cape Hoskins to Talasea."

General Adams listened intently, constantly pursing his lips as if to play a trumpet solo. He turned to his staff. "I like it. Anybody see a problem? How about you, Captain Slator?"

They shook their heads. "None I can see now," Jacobs replied.

Colonel Jackson said, "No, General, I think Ed has a good working plan."

"Sir, what about the garrison at Cape Hoskins?" Slator asked. "Will we pursue them too, or is this just a Talasea fight?"

"Good question, Captain," the general replied. "No, we won't pursue them. When we secure the airstrip at Talasea, we neutralize the Japs all the way to Rabaul, and Rabaul can be bypassed. We'll leave the fucking Japs to sit out the war right there. They can't hurt us, and I'm not going to keep after the bastards all the way to Tokyo. Our mission on New Britain will be accomplished when the strip at Talasea is secured and the Japs are no longer a threat."

Adams pushed his chair back from the table. "Colonel Jackson, First Regiment will be backup to the Fifth. Make your plans to do that, and we'll talk later. Right now I want to get this operation with the Fifth underway. March 6 will be D-day at Talasea." Adams's tone was a dismissal.

"We'll be ready. I'll need the air support for the landing we talked about earlier."

"You'll get it. Fifth Air Force will be your cover and support. Anything else? OK, let's get it done."

General Adams sent a cryptic report to Tenth Army Command, attention General Frederick D. Post, Commander of the Southwest Pacific Area: "Fifth Marine Regiment ordered to seize and occupy Talasea and patrol southward to Numundo. D-day March 6, H-hour 0800. Signed, Brigadier General Wilford T. Adams, First Marine Division, Cape Gloucester, New Britain."

24

The sunlight that warmed Talasea, New Britain on the first day of March 1944 was a welcome change from the incessant rain. Deep in the jungle forest, a clatter of familiar noises, punctuated by the ever present, shrill bird chatter, greeted the rising sun.

Captain Kiyamatasu Terunuma, 132nd Imperial Infantry Division, buckled his sword around his waist. He read again the orders from the South Pacific Regional Command at Rabaul, New Britain: "To the attention of Senior Regimental Officer, Talasea, New Britain. Hold your ground. Defend your position. The American forces must not be allowed to advance. Every Japanese soldier is to defend his position and, if necessary, give his life for the emperor to fight for the glorious cause of freedom."

At last, he thought, he could serve his emperor as he had been taught since birth and, as a final gesture, if need be, give his life. The duty at Talasea was Terunuma's first command. He had been passed over in three previous post assignments, and his promotion to captain had come only after a letter from his uncle in the central intelligence office in Japan had reached the Rabaul Command Headquarters.

The Japanese Command in Tokyo realized the American forces had gained control of Cape Gloucester and the western sector of New Britain and believed the Americans would make another landing somewhere along the coast of New Britain. Every garrison had received the same orders Captain Terunuma now read with pride and anticipation.

Terunuma decided to survey the fortifications for the defense of Talasea. He buttoned his coat, inhaling to do so, and was angry to find the button nearest his waist was missing. The next time I go to Japan, I'll find a better tailor, he thought. He walked out of his command post and strutted past the guards on his way to the beach.

He was overweight for his short frame, and as he walked jauntily along the sandy shore, the tip of his long sword dragged the ground. He was in an unusually good mood, and the sun felt warm on his shoulders. The deep sand made walking difficult, and he stopped to rest. He made a mental note that his soldiers must do more morning exercises. Perhaps that will improve their physical shape and their morale, he thought. The sun will be good for them, and I'll demand that they see the rising sun each morning, and I'll be with them. As an afterthought, he murmured, "At least on those mornings when it's not raining."

The sun was hotter than he expected, and the sand was difficult to walk through. He was out of breath and decided he would inspect the shore installations at another time.

Terunuma wiped the sweat from his face and returned to his post. I'll finish the inspection tomorrow morning, when it's not quite so hot, he thought. I'm sure the gun emplacements are as good as we can make them. Certainly not as strong as needed, and I definitely need more men, but if the Americans attack, we must do the best we can with what we have. Perhaps I should write Uncle to see if he can persuade Rabaul to increase my garrison of men.

Terunuma's requests for more troops from Cape Hoskins had been ignored. The garrison had been strengthened by remnants of the Seventy-ninth Division from New Guinea, but his uncle had written that the division had been soundly defeated by the Americans, and the military command in Tokyo, disgraced by the defeat, had assigned the soldiers to the less important post at Talasea instead of the stronger garrison at Cape Hoskins.

When Terunuma first took command at Talasea, he considered trying to train the soldiers, but there was such a lack of discipline, he decided he would do nothing until he asked his uncle what to do. Terunuma had never before been associated with a defeated Japanese Army, and he had no idea how to proceed.

Just before dusk on the evening of March 5, when the shadows were at their longest, the convoy of units from the Fifth Regiment got under way for the landing at Talasea. The northern coast of New Britain had treacherous uncharted rocks and shoals and was as dangerous as any in the Solomons, and the Navy commanders continually searched the warm Pacific waters for signs of danger. The men aboard the first transport ship had mixed feelings, some dreading the night's end, others anxious for morning's dawn.

Boog Marshall lay in his canvas bunk. He had chosen a bunk about shoulder level so he could more easily cram his massive body into the confined space. He closed his eyes, but was unable to sleep. He tried counting sheep, but when that didn't work, he started counting the women in his life.

He remembered his last night of liberty in San Diego. God, what a hunk of ass that Army nurse had been, he thought. He recalled their first night, when they went to the hotel room and she had marveled at his body, hidden beneath his green Marine uniform. As they stood by the bed, she rubbed her breasts against his chest and felt the muscles of his shoulders and arms harden and crowd the seams of his coat. "Oh honey, I can't wait," she said. She felt the muscles in his arms and breathed in his ear. "I hope another part of your body gets as hard." When he took off his trousers, she had been surprised, and the expression on her face showed she was more than a little doubtful of his sexual prowess.

"Is that all there is?" she exclaimed.

"Don't worry about the size," he assured her. "Just worry about whether you can hang on when I give you a real Texas bronc ride.

"My dick may be undersized," he admitted. "But dynamite comes in small packages."

Having a small penis had always bothered his ego, even when he was just a kid. He remembered his first time, when he was on top and really getting into the swing of things when she had pleaded, "Put it in, now!"

"I am in already," he said. He had been embarrassed so many times that once he tried to make his penis longer by tying one end of a string around it and, with the other end of the string tied to a door knob, slamming the door. The string broke, and all he had to show for his efforts was a bruised penis. He even considered tying a string to a brick, then tying the string to his penis and throwing the brick off the porch, but at the last moment, decided against it.

Even when he got older, he masturbated at least once before going out on a date, thinking he was putting his penis in training.

As he recalled that night with the Army nurse, he rubbed his hand across the fly of his dungarees. His day dreams became more real. He was jolted back to reality when he felt a sudden shove from the bunk below.

"Hey Boog, you beating your meat again?" Corporal Fulter muttered. "Christ, what a time to beat your meat! That's disgusting. Knock it off. I'm getting seasick watching your bunk jumping up and down."

In another part of the compartment, Mack lay in his bunk, cursing the heat and the stink that filled the air. Someone in the bunk across the passageway to his left let out a fart that sounded like a bassoon. Two bunks to his right, a deep reply sounded. "Sounds like two bullfrogs on either side of a pond sounding their mating call," Mack said in a low voice. "Just my luck to get caught in the middle of an affair gone sour."

In a distant corner, a high-pitched fart sounded. "That's a Yankee fart," Mack said, and rolled over on his stomach and covered his face.

It was almost dawn, and H-hour, the moment for the invasion to begin, was near. Sgt. Sammy Tucker walked along the passageway and shouted, "George Company, let's move it! Topside! Full gear! First platoon, move it out!"

The Marines crawled out of their bunks, but few eyes met. Fear was evident in their empty stares. The air was charged with tension as the men put on their combat gear. Some men tried to joke, and there was an occasional laugh. Some were quiet, and others spoke in monotones. Private Murphy, in a deep Southern drawl, sang softly.

Mack's M-1 rifle was slung over his shoulder as he stood near the ship's railing. As a veteran of Cape Gloucester, he feared what he knew the morning would bring.

Pappas pushed his way to where Mack was standing. He nudged him with his shoulder. "Damn, this rocking is getting to me. Every time I get aboard ship, I get seasick. I either throw up or have to take a crap. If we don't go in pretty soon, I'll be so sick I couldn't shoot a Jap unless he placed the end of my rifle to his head and pulled the trigger hisself."

He suddenly grabbed at his stomach. "Oh, I'm sick. I gotta find the head!"

Manny and Gil were only a few feet away, awaiting the inevitable landing.

"You can't take a crap now, Pappas," Manny said. "Sarge wouldn't let you go below. We're ready to go ashore!"

"Don't tell me when I can take a crap. I can't wait even if I wanted to." He unbuttoned his dungarees and gagged as he squatted at the edge of the boat.

"Gil, hold my arms," he pleaded. "I don't want to fall overboard."

Manny grabbed Pappas's arms. "George, if you puke on me, I swear to God I'll turn you loose."

Mack began to laugh. "I can see the headlines: 'Marine gets bullet up his ass while mooning Japs.' If the Japs see you coming ashore that way, they'll think we have a secret weapon. You haven't been eating Irish stew, have you?"

"Oh hell, why'd you mention that?" Gil groaned. "I can sympathize with you, Pappas."

"I don't need sympathy. I need toilet paper," Pappas said.

"We don't have any. Use your rifle butt," Mack laughed.

"Gill, loan me a dollar bill," Pappas begged.

"You won my last bill in blackjack last night," Gil said.

Pappas pulled himself back onto the deck of the boat and pulled up his dungarees. He forced a smile. "What the hell, I'll crap in them the first time a Jap shoots at me anyway."

25

The hum of the landing crafts' engines was so monotonous it gave a sense of false security. Mack looked at his watch, now almost 0630. He heard a change in the engine noise as the landing craft tanks (LCTs) slowed their forward motion.

Through the dim light of dawn, Mack saw the outline of Little Mt. Worri, rising over thirteen hundred feet above the jungle floor. He looked to the south where he saw Big Mt. Worri, higher by some three hundred feet. When the landing craft slowed, the backwashes from the other landing crafts mechanized (LCMs) and LCTs caught and then passed beneath, causing the bow and the stern of the landing boat to bob up and down and rock with the same alternating motion.

Mack rested his hand on the canteen that hung from his cartridge belt and looked intently into the early morning shadows that partially hid the shore. As they neared the shore, he could see the thick jungle vines that hung loosely from the trees, but the dark, lush green of the trees and hanging vines blended with the shadows and made a dark curtain over the dangers that lay behind the water's edge.

Taggart scanned the skies and listened for the sound of the promised fighter planes from the Fifth Air Force. "Dammit, where the hell are the planes? They're supposed to strafe the beaches before we go ashore. Adams promised we'd have those planes," he said disgustedly. "He knows we need them to get our supplies unloaded."

The colonel looked at his watch. "We should have gone ashore twenty-five minutes ago. Captain Slator, we're going in without the goddamn fucking air force. Goddamn it to hell! All we're doing is giving the fucking Japs time to set up their defenses. Shit!" He turned to the Navy operator of the LCM. "Take this son of a bitch into shore!"

The LCM-tank gunboats opened with a shattering burst of fire, raking the beach with machine-gun fire. Some of the land mines on the beaches exploded with great upheavals of sand, mud, and rock.

The sudden noise of machine-gun fire startled Gil and Manny, and they instinctively fell to the deck. It was a moment before they realized the machine gun fire had come from their own craft.

The landing crafts drove in under 90 mm mortar shells and sporadic Japanese machine gun fire. Gil and Mack were only a foot apart when they heard a Marine behind them scream. Mack whirled and saw Corporal Fulter crumple to the deck. The left side of his face was missing, and blood covered the deck. Fulter became the first casualty of the Talasea campaign.

Another burst of gunfire from the assault ships into the rapidly nearing coral beach had the desired results. Most of the

Japanese soldiers on the first line of defense forgot about the glory of dying for their emperor and ran toward the greater safety of the jungle. Within ten minutes, over five hundred Marines had landed.

Mack ran across the coral beach and moved further from the water's edge toward the intended cover of the jungle. He dived to the ground and lay panting, his heart racing. He looked to see if Gil had followed and saw him lying half-buried in the coral sand near a mass of fallen and tangled trees.

"Gil, Gil!" Mack shouted, and when he saw him slowly raise his head and look in Mack's direction, he knew his friend had made it to shore through the machine-gun and mortar fire.

"Gil, get over here. Get off the beach."

Gil scrambled to his feet and ran toward the jungle where Mack lay. They both ducked as a mortar shell exploded behind them.

Pappas heard the whistle of an incoming shell that fell to the ground only a few feet from where he and Manny lay. Coral sand from the mortar shell sprayed over them, and Manny spit sand from his mouth as he got to his feet and ran with Pappas across the beach toward the cover of the tangled trees.

Slator crouched behind a shelter of rotted logs and tangled vines. The ground, similar to the jungle at Cape Gloucester, was marshy and smelled of decaying matter and of rotted wood, wet from countless days and nights of rain. He looked back over his shoulder and saw Tucker running toward him.

"How many men have we lost?" Slator asked.

"Corporal Fulter and the new kid from Oklahoma, Private Stephens. Several wounded. I don't know how many yet. I'll let you know."

"The first two hundred yards came easier than I expected," Slator said. "Some of the fucking boats landed at the wrong beach, just like at Gloucester. Otherwise, things seem not too bad, not yet anyway. We'll make D plus two before dark at this rate."

A Japanese mortar shell whistled and whined overhead, exploding with a deafening blast only a short distance in front of where the men lay.

"Sons of bitches getting too close to suit me! Let's move up," Slator said as he picked up his M-1 and ran forward to the next bank of protection. Tucker was with him, step for step. The enemy mortar fired again, this time closer than before, to the left of where they crouched, and Slator and Tucker buried their bodies beneath the partial safety of the logs. Slator could hear the chatter of machine guns and knew his men were moving in.

The captain and his men pushed inland. Baker Company moved its way further inland and established its forward line another hundred yards from the shore.

The First Battalion was taking only light casualties from intermittent rifle fire and steadily pushed forward through the fringes of the jungle bordering the beachhead. Two hundred yards inland, Easy Company began to meet stiff resistance and temporarily stalled before pushing forward and driving the Japanese further inland.

Rear echelon troops, raked by Japanese mortar fire, began unloading supplies and equipment on the beaches. When the Marines answered with 60 mm mortars, the Japanese troops left their gun installations, and the Marines pushed forward.

One hundred yards away from where George Company began moving through the thick jungle, a young Japanese soldier, only eighteen years old, crouched beside another soldier. The young soldier's heart pounded as he fed the ammunition belt into a machine gun. He was serving his first military duty at Talasea as a member of a machine gun crew, and this was his first combat experience since his enlistment in the Imperial Army.

Because of his youth and inexperience, the young Japanese boy had been teased by the more seasoned soldiers and been the brunt of countless pranks. He had defiantly declared he was as brave as any of them and would give his life for his emperor as graciously as the bravest, but they continued to tease him.

He had tried to make his comrades believe their cruel jokes had not mattered to him, but the truth was they hurt him deeply. He tried to ignore the constant harassment and, on this day, had been happy to be in the jungle away from the main garrison.

The young Japanese soldier despised the man who lay beside him, a man who had been especially cruel to him and reportedly one of those who had deserted his post while in combat on New Guinea with the Seventy-ninth Army Division.

As the Marines approached, the two Japanese men flattened their bodies to the ground. A shell exploded along the edge of the jungle, and the man beside the young Japanese boy jumped to his feet and ran into the deeper jungle, away from the approaching Marines.

The young boy's heart beat rapidly and he tried to swallow. The machine gun, nestled behind a tree stump, was hidden from the view of the approaching Marines. The Americans were within a hundred yards when he opened fire, and two Marines fell to the ground. He felt no joy or pride in the fact that he had taken the lives of two men. Perhaps, he thought, they were young, like me.

Gil Everson squinted his eyes. "Mack, can you see where those shots came from?"

"I couldn't tell. It's too dark."

Gil raised his head. "Two of our men are hit. I can see them on the ground up ahead. They're both trying to crawl for cover. If that Jap sees them they'll be killed for sure. We gotta knock out that machine gun."

The Nambu started firing again, and leaves fell from the branches above where Gil and Mack lay.

"I saw where the machine gun is." Gil pointed. "By that tree stump.

"Yeah, I saw it too," Mack whispered. "Too far away to throw a hand grenade."

Gil looked back over his shoulder. "That stream we just crossed, doesn't it run toward where the Nambu is? If I crawl back to the stream, I can work my way down the ditch where I can get a shot or throw a grenade."

"You might, but there may be another machine gun pointing right where you'd be running. Don't try it," Mack cautioned. "Wait till we can take him out with mortars. Tucker will be here in a minute with mortars."

"Those Marines on the ground can't wait that long, Mack. If I can get close enough to throw a grenade, I can take the machine gun out. I'm going to try it."

"Don't try it, Gil. It's too dangerous. Keep down. Tucker will have a better plan."

Gil started moving back, crawling on his stomach. "There's a log just to my left. Give me a couple of minutes to get back to the stream, then move over here. You can get behind the log for cover. After two minutes, fire as many rounds toward him as you can. If the Jap opens up with his Nambu before then, try to keep him busy. Throw a hand grenade—anything to keep him looking this way. Keep him watching you instead of those two on the ground. I remember how you used to score a bull's-eye on the rifle range. See if you can do it here. See you later."

Mack looked at his watch. One minute had passed since Gil had left, and he pulled a grenade from his belt. The seconds ticked away, and when the two minutes had elapsed, he pulled the pin on the grenade and threw it as far as he could. He grabbed his rifle and fired as rapidly as he could toward the dark jungle cover. Immediately, the Nambu returned the fire, the bullets hitting the log in front of where Mack lay. The chatter from the Nambu gun continued, the leaves and vines fell as though cut by a scythe.

Mack put another clip in his M-1 and waited until the firing stopped. He carefully raised his head and fired again. The Nambu answered, then suddenly a loud explosion shattered the air, and all was quiet.

Mack peered over the log and looked for Gil in the dark jungle ahead. When he heard nothing, he raised up slowly, then ran forward as fast as he could. He stopped when he saw Gil standing over the Japanese soldier and the twisted metal of a machine gun. The soldier was crumpled in a bloody pile, his arms holding the useless weapon. His body was ripped by shrapnel, the uniform stained by seeping blood from a dozen places.

Gil looked at Mack, then back at the Japanese soldier on the ground. "He was just a kid, Mack, just a kid. Goddamn this war!"

Mack looked at the boy on the ground, "A kid with a machine gun. He looks about your age, Gil," Mack said, and placed his hand on Gil's shoulder. "He would have killed you if he could."

By the end of the first day, the beachhead had been extended to over two thousand yards.

The next morning and early afternoon, the Japanese troops continued to fall back, giving way to the hard-pressing Marines. Colonel Taggart directed his troops to consolidate the defenses around Waru and ordered the Second Battalion to assume responsibility for the airdrome and Talasea. K Company was ordered to set up a defense line as protection for the regimental CP.

Captain Terunuma peered through the half-open door to his command post and saw two Marines come into the open area just a hundred yards from where he stood. The gun installation just outside his quarters had been abandoned, and he realized there was no one between him and the advancing Marines. He watched them stop, then motion to the other Marines to circle the hut where he stood, and he knew it would be only minutes before they entered his post.

He knelt, his fingers playing along the sharp edge of his sword, saddened to think his troops had been unable to hold the Marines at the water's edge. He regretted his troops had not followed his orders to hold the line of defense, or if that was not to be, they should have died honorably for their emperor. How could they not do so? he wondered. Surely there was no greater honor than to give one's life for his emperor. He was ashamed that his troops had fled to the safer part of the dense jungle, leaving a gap to allow the Marines to push through and capture the airdrome. He did not know the capture of Talasea would block the route for Osaka's troops in their flight to Rabaul.

He prepared himself for what he was about to do. He thought of his family in Japan, wished them well, and then with his last thoughts and a final tribute for his sacred and beloved emperor, fell forward on the sharp point of his sword.

Manny and Boog cautiously pushed open the door of the hut. Through the semidarkness, they saw an officer lying on the floor, a sword half-embedded in his stomach. Blood seeped from the wound, and the stain on the uniform spread, and then slowly, blood covered the floor where he lay.

"Poor bastard's war just ended, didn't it?" Manny said.

"That takes guts, I guess," Boog said, "but I'd try taking the enemy with me rather than killing myself like that."

"Yeah," Manny nodded, "but I wish all the Japs would do the same thing. It'd make our job easier, wouldn't it? Let's get out of here."

On March 9, 1944, General Adams read the report from Colonel Taggart: "Talasea secured. Marine losses are 17 killed, 114 wounded. Japanese losses are 150 killed, remainder of garrison deserted."

Adams studied the results of the Talasea Campaign. The death of so many of his men weighed heavily on his conscience. He reflected on the losses as opposed to the expected gains. "I've lost seventeen good Marines," he whispered. "I pray to God it was worth it."

The next morning, Adams sent a report back to Taggart: "Your heroic actions have given us the best and strongest position to prevent the escape of the Japanese forces, and you have blocked their escape to Rabaul. Congratulations on a job well done, signed Brigadier General Wilford T. Adams, First Marine Division."

Colonel Osaka's patrols were surprised to find small groups of Japanese soldiers in the dense jungle a few miles from Cape Hoskins. Most suffered from dysentery, and only a few of them still carried weapons. He ordered an officer to bring one of the soldiers to him. He listened as the Japanese soldier related the American capture of Talasea.

"Our troops fought with uncommon valor, Colonel Osaka," the soldier stammered. "We were outnumbered, and our brave soldiers were willing to die for our emperor and our country, but our commander, Captain Terunuma, ordered us into the jungle. We had planned a counterattack, but we waited when we learned you were here."

"Yes, I understand," Colonel Osaka said, "and where is your captain now?"

The soldier hesitated. "I...I do not know, Colonel."

Colonel Osaka studied the soldier before him. He saw the ragged, dirty uniform and looked at the half-starved expression of a soldier he did not believe. His eyes betrayed the truth. Can this be the once proud defender of our great and honorable nation? he thought.

He started to angrily denounce the soldier for deserting his command, then realized he and his troops were also attempting to escape from the Americans. He thought the two situations were different, but he could not reprimand the frightened soldier before him.

"I can see you are ready to engage the enemy," Colonel Osaka said, unable to keep a tinge of sarcasm from his voice, "but this is not the time or place."

He motioned for the soldier to leave and turned to the officer beside him. "We must change our plans. If we are to reach Rabaul, we must take a more southerly route through the more mountainous and difficult terrain. That is not the best way, but it is the only way."

Osaka realized his planned escape route by way of Cape Hoskins and then to Rabaul was closed. He knew his tattered and weary men must face more hunger and disease, and he feared only a fraction of the original two thousand soldiers would ever reach the garrison at Rabaul.

He looked toward his homeland. "With Buddha as my witness, we will meet these Marines again, and when we do, things will be different."

26

On March 10, General Adams sent a message to Colonel Taggart: "The Fifth Regiment is ordered to establish a camp at Talasea and remain there until the First Marine Division returns to a rest camp area prior to the next operation. Tents, cots, and other camp equipment will be shipped from Cape Gloucester. Further supplies will be sent as requested and needed."

As soon as the supplies arrived, tents were erected, and for the first time since the beginning of the New Britain campaign, the men escaped from the infinite rain. A galley, hot food, canvas cots, and a covered mess hall began to change the soggy bivouac into a camp. Poles were cut from the jungle and used to construct raised flooring around the cots.

Mack and Gil crowded around the bulletin board outside Lieutenant Blevins's tent and looked for their names on the list of the next week's work details.

"What the hell does 'Native NCO' mean?" Mack asked.

"I don't know. I wonder if it's better than my duty. I'm on mess detail." Gil answered.

"Ain't this a hell of a note?" Pappas said. "I've been given the awesome responsibility of getting pits dug and latrines built for the officers. I'm going to order the holes in the two stoolers cut big enough so that Lieutenant Blevins will fall through some night. Trouble is, we wouldn't be able to find him in all that shit, would we?" he laughed.

"Yeah, and you'll spend a few days in the brig, too," Manny cautioned.

"They couldn't prove I did it on purpose. How the hell should I know how big to cut the holes? I don't know how big an officer's ass is. What am I supposed to do, ask Lieutenant Blevins to bend over so I can measure the size of his ass?" Pappas asked.

"You're always eyeing everybody else's ass when we're taking a shower," Manny joked. "It's just not safe to drop the soap and bend over when you're in the same shower."

"Get out of here, Manny, or I'll tell the corpsman you're not taking your atabrine tablets."

"Why don't you write your folks and tell them you've been promoted to Captain of the Head? Or maybe Colonel of the Urinal," Manny asked.

"It sure as hell beats the detail they put you on," Pappas laughed. "NCO in charge of picking up cigarette butts! I can just see it happening someday; your little boy asking you, 'Hey Daddy, what did you do in the war?' and you telling him you fought hard to keep all the butts picked up." He threw his cigarette to the ground. "Pick it up," he laughed.

"Pick it up yourself. I don't start till Monday. Picking up butts sure as hell beats digging shithouses. I can just see you telling your little boy you dug shithouses during the war," Manny said, and threw a handful of mud at Pappas.

Mack joined in the ribbing. "I wish we could get a correspondent to take a picture of you, standing by one of the latrines. The headline could read, 'Ohio Marine discovers way to keep outhouse odorless.' You'd be famous."

Pappas thought a minute. "How would I keep it from smelling?" he questioned.

"You could stand guard and keep someone from taking a crap in it."

Boog Marshall kicked mud from his boondockers. "I wonder why we haven't had any mail. The last mail we got was back in Cape Gloucester. Lolita promised me she'd write."

Two days later, when mail finally arrived, Boog's name was called more often than anyone else. When the last letter was handed out, the men returned to their tents where they could read about home and relive the dreams that had been a part of so many of the lonely hours since the last good-bye.

Cpl. Robert Munday sat on the edge of his cot, reading the first of four letters from his wife. He looked at the postmarks, and arranged them in the order they had been written. The first letter was dated December 1943, two more letters were dated January 1944, and the last letter had been written in April.

"I think I'm missing some letters from my wife," he said, and looked at the postmarks again. "I should have more letters than this. There's not a single letter dated February and March."

As he read the first letter, he laughed out loud. "Listen to this. My wife says that Bobby—that's my son—tried to tie his shoes, but got so frustrated he pulled the laces out of his shoes and threw them in the commode."

Munday laughed again. "Listen to what my wife says about my little boy. She says, 'He handles problems just like you, Bob. If he can't do what he wants to do, he tries to find another way, regardless of the consequences.' I guess that's the way I am." Munday handed a picture to Manny. "Want to see my boy?"

"He was eight months old last October when I left the States. I've watched him grow through the pictures my wife sends me."

Manny handed the picture back to Munday. "He's a good-looking kid, Bob. So's your wife."

Munday looked at the picture again. "It's hard to realize he's almost a year and a half old. He's got my eyes and hair the same color as his mother. He's a handsome boy, just like his mother was beautiful."

"I know you're proud of both," Manny said.

"Yeah, I am. I sure do miss them, that's a fact."

Munday stared a long time at the picture of his wife standing beside their son. "I wish I could hold her, feel her hair against my cheek, smell the scent of her perfume."

Munday lay back on his cot and closed his eyes, lost in the memory of his wife's arms around his body as they had made love on his last night before leaving for the Pacific.

Mack lay on the cot next to Munday and removed his soggy boondockers. He read one letter after another, hardly stopping between letters before he tore open the envelope of the next letter. He opened one letter from Anna, and a picture slipped from the envelope and fell to the green blanket that covered the cot. He found the picture and looked at it again.

"Wow! My gosh almighty," Mack said. "If you want to see something, take a look at this."

Gil looked up from the letter he was reading and saw Mack smiling broadly at the picture. Gil got up from his cot and held out his hand. "Let me see."

Gil's eyes widened at the picture of Anna standing near the edge of a swimming pool. She wore a black swimsuit, and her long black hair fell around her shoulders. Her shapely legs were silhouetted against the blue water. Her smile was more of a tease, and the tilt of her chin was a provocative gesture.

"Man, that'll get your heart pumping," Gil said.

Mack grinned and took the picture from Gil. "There's something written on the back you don't need to see. You're too young."

"What'd she say on the back? Don't tell me. Let me guess. She probably said something like, 'Getting ready to cool it off,' didn't she?"

Mack grinned. "Something like that," he said, and turned and looked at the other men. The smile left his face when he looked at Bob Munday, reading the last of the four letters from his wife. Munday's face was pale, and his hands were visibly shaking.

"Bob, what's the matter?" Mack asked.

Munday groaned, and the letter fell from his fingers. He buried his face in his hands, and his voice trembled. "Oh my God, my wife wants a divorce. She says she's found someone she loves and wants to marry him." Tears rolled down his cheeks. He looked up. "A fucking sailor! She's filing for a divorce, and her attorney will send me the papers to sign."

The tent was quiet except for the sound of Munday crying. Manny walked to Munday's cot and stood helplessly beside his friend. He patted Munday's shoulder. "I'm sorry, Bob."

Mack motioned for Pappas and Gil to leave with him. In a few moments, Manny came out of the tent. "Poor guy, he's really hurt, and he doesn't know what to do. He said he wanted to be by himself to think things through. I told him to talk to the chaplain. Any of you got any ideas?"

"You did the right thing, Manny. It'll take time for him to get his thinking back in order," Pappas said. "The chaplain can help if anyone can."

"He looked like he was ready to pass out," Gil said. "Did you see how pale he was? That's a tough letter to get from your wife, saying she wants a divorce. What can you do?"

Munday walked out of the tent, the letter from his wife clutched in his right hand, the picture of his son and his wife held tightly in his left. His lips quivered. "Where's the chaplain's tent? Anybody know?"

"I think it's a little past Colonel Taggart's, on the same side. Want me to go with you?" Gil asked.

"I'll find it. Thanks anyway. I'll see you guys later." Munday walked away, his head lowered and his shoulders slumped.

"Damn, it's tough enough for a guy to have that happen to him at all, but to have it happen when he's over here and can't do much about it! He can't talk with his wife to see if maybe they could make it up, all he can do is what she asks him to do and let it go," Manny said.

"What'll they do about their son, I wonder? Bob talks about him all the time, and he thought his wife was the greatest woman in the world," Pappas said. "I never proposed to Fay before I left the States. I'm glad now I didn't. If she finds someone else while I'm gone, I wouldn't want her to be tied to a promise."

"It'll be a long war for Munday, you can bet your sweet ass on that," Mack added. "I'm going back to the tent. There's nothing more we can do, is there?"

27

Before the war, Talasea had been a coconut plantation, owned and operated by the Australian Coconut Enterprise, headquartered in Melbourne, Australia.

When the Japanese invaded New Britain in early 1942, the Australian civilians at Talasea escaped to Australia, and the natives fled to the hills. Most of them eluded the invaders, but those unfortunate enough to be captured lived a harsh life as slave laborers. Many of them died from starvation or were killed by the Japanese soldiers.

The island natives had a deep hatred and fierce contempt for the Japanese and were grateful to the Marines for the return of their homeland.

Shortly after the area was secured, the plantation manager

for the Coconut Enterprise returned to Talasea and regrouped the natives who had remained during the Japanese occupation. Sensing both the need and the use of labor to build the camp, the Australian contracted with the Marines to use the natives.

Few of the natives could speak English, and those who did spoke in broken dialect with a pronounced Australian accent.

Mack was put in charge of a detail of natives whose job was to cut large bamboo poles and branches from the abundant jungle trees and to bring them back into camp for use in the construction of officer's quarters and a mess hall.

A light rain fell on the first morning the natives reported to the Marine camp. The natives, led by their chieftain, walked down the jungle trail in single file with smooth rhythmic steps, insensitive to the mud that caked their wide feet. Each man was dressed in a brief, loosely hanging loincloth, and each carried two possessions: a machete sharpened to a smooth razor's edge and a small pouch containing a supply of betel nut. The chief was dressed the same, except he wore a short, carved wooden ornament around his neck.

They walked down the rain-drenched path toward the camp, and from time to time, the chief slowed his pace, and listened carefully for any unfamiliar sound from the jungle. His eyes searched for signs of danger, and when he was satisfied there was none, he motioned for his men to follow. When the natives reached the outskirts of the Marine camp, the chief motioned for his men to stop. He stepped to the last shadow at the jungle's edge and listened.

The Australian plantation owner, who had received permission from the Marine officer of the day to escort the natives into camp, waited for them at the first guard post. He watched the chieftain standing in the shadow behind a bush and was not surprised at the caution the natives showed in approaching the Marine camp. He called softly to the leader in his native language, and the chief motioned for his men to follow.

The natives emerged from the early morning shadows of the dark jungle as quietly as the vapor from the morning mist.

Their lean black bodies glistened from the noiseless water that dripped from the drooping tree branches. They were all similar in stature, with muscular chests and forearms, and kinky short hair framed their black faces like dark curtains around a stage. Their dark eyes were separated by wide nostrils, and the only contrast of color on their ebony faces were their teeth, tainted red by chewing the ever present betel nut.

The Australian led the natives into camp, and when they reached the edge of the first row of tents, he ordered them to wait.

Mack walked from his tent to greet them. He remembered that Dendie, the native who had led Slator's patrol to visit his village, had held up his left hand as a show of friendship. Mack lifted his left hand, and the chieftain returned the gesture. Mack walked to the chief and saluted him, and the chief smiled.

"My name is Corporal Mack. I will call you General Boss Boy." A mutual feeling of trust developed between the two men.

Each morning following that first day, twenty natives came to the camp before daylight and waited patiently for Mack to give them their orders for the day's work.

With the construction of the wooden buildings, the camp became quite livable. The danger of an occasional Japanese sniper still existed, and the unrelenting rain was inevitable, but for all practical purposes, the Marines were enjoying their assignment at Talasea.

As the early morning light first crossed the sky, Mack walked from the mess hall toward his tent. He strapped his poncho to his pack, adjusted it on his shoulders, and buckled on his cartridge belt and canteen. He slung his rifle and walked toward the native chieftain waiting at the edge of the camp. Mack saluted the chieftain as he had done each morning.

"General Boss Boy, before we start, there's something I must tell you. We don't need to build any more buildings for the camp. This will be the last day we will cut poles, and this will probably be the last day that you and your men will report to our camp."

The chief frowned, then shook his head slowly. "General Boss Boy not happy. Marines leave?"

"Yes, I think so. I don't think we'll stay here much longer. I won't be happy to go. You are my friend. I will miss you."

The chief turned toward the path that led into the jungle. "Come, we go now."

They walked along the shadowed trail, and Mack followed close behind the old chief, his feet stepping into the same prints. Behind them came the natives, single file, each man stepping into the footprints of the one before him. The morning was quiet except for the familiar sounds of the jungle and the soft, muffled sound of the falling rain.

The ebony chief led the men farther into the jungle than they had ever gone before, and Mack wondered why they had not stopped to begin cutting the poles so abundant along the trail. The deeper they went into the jungle, the further the natives would be required to carry the poles back into camp.

When General Boss Boy stopped, he said, "This place I show only you. No other white man see. I show you, but you no say to others. You come follow me."

He left the trail and made his way through dripping branches. He pushed them aside with his machete and walked into a large clearing. In the center of the area was a native hut, constructed almost ten feet above the ground. It was surrounded by a prolific growth of orchids and beautiful assorted flowers. The ground was bathed in vivid colors of blue, green, yellow, and red.

"Good God! Would you look at that!" Mack stared at the magnificent display of color. "I've never in my life seen a more beautiful place. What is this?"

"This where our souls come when we die."

"It's…it's so peaceful. I'm honored you'd bring me here."

The chief motioned for Mack to follow him to the front of the hut.

"Do you go inside?"

"Only our spirits go there. I not been inside, but my soul go one day."

Mack was touched. "Thank you for bringing me here."

"You are friend. Come, we go now. We cut poles." The black man turned and walked back toward the path where the others waited.

At the end of the day, after the poles had been cut and the natives had carried them back to the camp, Mack asked the chief, "Could you and three of your men show me and my friends where we can hunt wild pigs? We want to go to another island, over there, on the horizon. We need a boat and guides to take us there. We've heard that when the Aussies left the island, they left pigs and other livestock, and some may still be there. If you'll go with us, I'll ask the Australian owner for permission for you to take us there."

"We go with you," the chief replied.

Mack got permission from the plantation owner for four of the natives to accompany the Marines to the island to hunt wild pigs, and on the following Sunday morning, Mack, Pappas, Gil, Manny, and Boog gathered their gear for the hunt.

"Munday," Mack asked, "are you sure you don't want to come along? We can make room for one more in the canoe. Why don't you come with us?"

"Yeah, you could have my place if you wanted to," Boog added. "I'm not too fucking sure I want to go. There may be Japs on the island, and I sure as shit don't need to be looking for any more than I've found already. Besides, I don't feel as safe as Mack does with those gooks. He says they're his friends, but that don't make them mine."

"Bob, we'll be leaving within the hour. I saved you a place in the canoe, but I told Doc Wharton he could go in your place if you didn't go. You're sure you don't want to come along?"

"No, Mack, I don't want to go. I don't feel like hunting. Thanks for asking me anyway. It's not a bad idea taking a corpsman in my place anyway. I'll see you when you get back."

Mack picked up his rifle. "If you change your mind, come on down to the beach." He waved at Munday and walked toward the beach where the chieftain and four of his natives waited in their canoe.

The outrigger, approximately forty feet long, had been hollowed from a large tree trunk. Long poles tied with another larger pole extended from one side and served as a stabilizer.

Mack waded into the shallow water and sat behind General Boss Boy sitting in the front of the canoe. Manny, Boog, Doc, Gil, and Pappas took alternate seats behind the natives. Mack looked one last time to see if Munday had decided to join them and then motioned for the canoe to move from shore.

The weather was remarkably favorable for their wild pig hunt, and the sky had none of the usual rain clouds. The breeze across the water was cool, and the wind was to their back. The paddles dipped quickly into the blue-green Pacific, and the outrigger glided across the smooth water toward the distant island.

The outrigger slowed as they neared the shore. Boog ducked his head when a spray of water splashed across the canoe, and when he looked up, he saw one of the natives rise to his feet and take a hand grenade from the cloth bag on his shoulder.

The native pulled the pin from the grenade, and Boog screamed, "My aching ass! He's gonna kill us!"

When Boog screamed, Manny and Gil fell forward in the dugout. Pappas and Doc fell to the bottom of the canoe and covered their heads with their arms. Boog jumped to his feet and put one foot on the side of the canoe and started to leap into the water.

The chieftain yelled, "No danger! No danger! Sit down! No jump in water!" He motioned for Boog to sit down, and he shouted something to the native sitting beside Boog.

The native grabbed Boog by the legs and tried to pull him back into the boat. Boog kicked his feet and screamed, "He's trying to kill me," and both men fell to the bottom of the canoe.

Mack jumped beneath the Chieftain's legs and covered his head.

The native holding the grenade was so startled that he dropped the grenade in the canoe. The chief shouted and jumped over Mack and frantically searched for the grenade. He found it and threw it as far as he could, and the grenade exploded just below the surface of the water.

The sound of the exploding grenade was deafening, and a fountain of water covered the men and the boat.

The natives started laughing and pointed at Boog in the bottom of the boat. Boog raised up and peeked over the side of the canoe.

"We eat fish," General Boss Boy proudly proclaimed to the Marines, and the natives gathered the fish that had floated to the surface.

Pappas was still shaking when he crawled back to his seat on the canoe. "You're the headhunter, Mack, you organized this safari. What do we do now?"

"As soon as Boog cleans the crap out of his dungarees," Mack laughed, "we'll divide up into three groups, two hunters to a group. Each group will hunt in a different part of the island, and we'll meet back at the abandoned plantation house at four this afternoon."

"Who's hunting with who?" Pappas asked.

"I'll hunt with Manny, and we'll go to the west, Pappas and Gil to the east, and Doc and Boog will go directly north from the old plantation quarters. If you see any Japs, or if there's any trouble or danger, the signal will be two fast shots, followed by one shot, then two more quick shots. Everybody understand?"

"Mack, where the fuck will those gooks be? Somebody ought to stay here and make sure they don't leave us," Boog said.

"General Boss Boy won't leave us here. I promise you don't need to worry about that."

"Yeah, like I didn't think I'd have to worry about getting my ass blown off by a hand grenade," Boog replied.

Gil and Pappas were more impressed by the hundreds of banana trees with their hanging stalks of fruit than they were with the prospect of killing a wild pig.

"What the hell will we do if we kill a pig?" asked Pappas. "I'm wondering how we'd get the thing back to the plantation house. You're nuts if you think we could carry a five-hundred-pound pig very far. I'm not too sure I'll shoot one even if I get the chance."

"Do you know how to gut one?" Gil asked. "You said your father was a butcher, so you should know how to butcher a pig."

"I never worked in the butcher shop. My father wouldn't let me. I've never gutted an animal in my life, let alone some wild pig."

"I wouldn't know what to cut out and what to keep," Gil admitted. "I think I read where you dress a deer by starting at the asshole and working toward the ear, or was it the other way around?"

"I know which end you eat first," Pappas said.

"I got an idea," Gil said. "Let's cut some stalks of bananas, take a long nap, and maybe explore the island. If we see a wild pig, we can decide if we want to shoot him or not."

"Yeah," Pappas grinned, "Let's gather bananas. I know how to peel a banana."

Four hundred yards from where Gil and Pappas sat eating their bananas, Doc and Boog walked cautiously through the thick growth of vines that had inundated and almost reclaimed the plantation.

Boog moaned, "I wish to shit I'd never come on this trip. Some friggin' Jap may have decided to wait out the war right here on this island. I wouldn't blame the son of a bitch. I'd do the same thing, except I wouldn't know when the war was over and when to go home. I damned sure wouldn't try to make it home in one of those outrigger canoes. That fuckin' gook shouldn't have scared me with that hand grenade. How the hell was I to know he caught fish that way, and besides, I didn't bring an extra pair of skivvies and now I've got to go all day with crap in my drawers."

"Boog, why do you think I've kept you downwind all day? You smell like shit," Doc said.

Boog said, "Yeah, that's OK for you, but how 'bout me? I can't get away from the smell."

Boog felt a raindrop. "It's starting to rain, and I forgot to bring my poncho. What the hell happened to this beautiful day we started out with? Now I gotta worry about a sniper shooting me in my wet ass."

Boog ducked under the cover of one of the banana trees as the rain fell heavier. "Look at the size of the vine on this tree. Funny-looking color, isn't it?" He leaned against the tree and felt something move.

"Shit!" he yelled. "That's no vine, that's a snake!"

Boog stumbled over the thick brush and tried to run. He fell to his knees and dropped his rifle when he fell. He was too excited to stop and pick it up and tried to put as much distance between himself and the boa constrictor as he could. In less than a minute, he had run two hundred yards, and only then did he stop to catch his breath. He realized he was alone, and he yelled as loud as he could. "Can you hear me Doc? Hey Doc, can you hear me?"

There was no reply, and Boog tried again. "Hey Doc, listen, can you hear me? I'm lost, damn it, answer me," he pleaded.

The only sound he could hear was the falling rain, which had turned into the heavy deluge of a tropical storm. "I should go back to find my rifle, but I'm not getting near that damn snake again. To hell with it," he said disgustedly. "I'm going back to the plantation house."

He walked in the direction he thought he had run, but the

heavy rain made it difficult for him to see where he had been. He continued to call out for his friend, but he heard no response to his calls.

Mack and Manny walked so they could always be in sight of each other. Both men had hunted wild game before, and they searched for signs of the game they were hunting.

Manny saw pig droppings and motioned for Mack to be on the alert. Mack saw a pig wallow and knew the game they sought would not be too far away. The heavy rain slowed them down, but they pushed forward. They knew the rain would muffle any sounds they made as they moved closer to where the pigs were feeding. Manny spotted them first and motioned to Mack that they were just ahead. Mack signaled he would approach from the side where he could shoot before the pigs scattered. As Mack crept forward, he remembered the days when he hunted on the ranch with his friend Felipe Ramirez.

Mack stopped and looked for Manny. He heard a pig squeal and searched the underbrush. A huge wild pig, grunting and moving the black soil with his impressive snout, was less than twenty yards ahead of him. He waved his hand for Manny to see and pointed toward the pig. Manny motioned that he also saw the pigs, and both men raised their rifles to their shoulders.

Two quick shots sounded simultaneously, and two wild pigs fell to the ground. Mack saw a young pig run for the protection of thicker foliage and, with one shot, killed it.

The huge boar with tusks four inches long ducked his head and charged. Manny fired, but the .30-caliber bullet missed the vital spot between the eyes where he had aimed, and the bullet hit the boar in the shoulder. The wild pig spun around and lunged toward Manny. Manny fired again, and the massive boar fell dead at his feet.

"Are you OK?" Mack shouted.

"I am now, but this big ol' daddy wouldn't give up. In another step, he would have ripped my legs with those big tusks. How about you? Did you get one? I heard you shoot when I did and again before I shot ol' papa here. Took two shots to bring him down."

Mack looked at the battle-scarred hide of the boar that had charged Manny. "That pig must be the granddaddy and as tough as a wild pig can get. We'll give that one to the officers' cook. I got two before the rest scattered. Three pigs ought to feed the entire camp for a meal."

"Have you heard anything from the other guys?" Manny asked. "I don't know how far a sound would travel in this dense undergrowth, but they can't be too far away."

Mack took out his knife and began to gut one of the pigs. "I haven't heard anything, but after we finish here we better find them. There's no telling where Boog might be. He came so close to jumping overboard when the native pulled the pin on the hand grenade."

Mack laughed. "I wouldn't admit it to Boog, but for a second, I almost did the same thing."

"Look," Manny said. "Here comes Doc, but I don't see Boog. They were supposed to stay together. They must have gotten separated. Damn, that means we gotta go find Boog before we go back to camp."

"Maybe he'll come in with Gil and Pappas," Mack said.

When Boog failed to find his hunting partner, he became more frightened and thought he would be lost forever. "What the hell happens if I can't find the others?" he asked himself. "And what happens if night comes and I haven't found them?" he moaned. He stopped. "I wonder if any Japs are still here," he whispered.

The rain stopped almost as soon as it had started, and Boog could once again hear the sounds of the jungle. He listened for a voice, but he could only hear the jungle sounds. Then suddenly, he heard the distant sound of rifle fire.

He counted the shots. "What was the signal if anyone spotted a Jap?" he whispered. "It was two, then one, then two shots. Oh no," he moaned. "That's the danger signal. There's

Japs here, and they're going to kill me, and all because I was stupid enough to come on this fuckin' pig chase."

Boog fell to his knees and crawled toward the thickest part of the underbrush. He stopped crawling and listened. "Oh my God, I hear footsteps. It's a Japanese patrol party. I know it is." He lay as still as he could, and his heart pounded so loud he was afraid it would give away his hiding place. Several minutes passed, and when he could not hear any noise except that of the jungle, he cautiously lifted his head, and squinted his eyes.

"If I can crawl up one of these banana trees, I can see more and hide better, but how the hell do I fight without a rifle? The only thing I can do is throw coconuts and bananas." He was almost crying. He gathered as many bananas as he could and stuffed them inside his dungaree jacket. He examined the tree nearest where he was hiding and made sure that the vines hanging from the upper branches were truly vines and not snakes. His agility in climbing the tree was assisted by his fear of the moment, and he climbed into the thick branches near the top of the tree. He balanced his feet on two limbs of the tree and tried to squat, but his feet kept slipping, and he feared he would fall to the ground. He unbuckled his cartridge belt and wrapped it around one leg and a limb of the tree and worked his boondockers into the tangled vines. He tested the belt on his leg and smiled at his ingenuity in securing himself to the tree.

When Gil and Pappas heard the shots fired by Mack and Manny, they didn't relate the number of shots to the signal for danger.

"Sounds like someone has some luck, if you can call it luck," Gil said.

"It was probably Mack and Manny. Boog would run if he saw a wild boar," Pappas said. "We better find them. If they've shot a wild pig, they'll need help when they start back."

They walked through the jungle for several minutes, then stopped to get their bearing. "I believe we're going in the right direction," Pappas said, "but I wish I could see something familiar."

"I don't see anything that looks familiar," Gil admitted. "Look. What's that up there?" Pappas whispered.

"Where? Where you looking?"

"Up there, in the top of that tree, something white. It's moving, but I can't tell what it is. Do you think I ought to take a shot?"

"Not without knowing what it is," Gil said. "Let's get closer."

Gil and Pappas carefully moved closer, and Pappas shook his head. "I've never seen anything like that in a tree before. Do you think it's some kind of animal? Maybe it's an orangutan. I'm sure I saw a banana fall."

"I can't tell yet. Keep your rifle ready. If it tries to get away, blast hell out of it. We can figure out what it is when it drops to the ground."

It was at that moment that Boog pitched another banana peeling to the ground and then yawned and stretched his arms above his head.

Below, on the ground, Gil shook his head in disbelief. "Well, I'll be damned. That's Boog up there!"

Pappas grabbed his sides in laughter. "I'll never make my grandchildren believe this. I'm not too sure I do. I can't wait to hear what kind of story Boog will tell."

"Yeah, and aren't you glad you didn't shoot without knowing what it was?"

Pappas sat on the ground and wiped the tears from his eyes. "Jesus Christ, am I ever, but what a trophy it would have made."

28

Lieutenant Blevins hurried toward the officers' mess hall. He passed the tent assigned to Williams, Everson, King, and Pappas and looked with envy at the stalks of fresh bananas, brought back from the pig hunt, that hung outside the tent. "Those enlisted men shouldn't be allowed to keep all that fresh fruit," he muttered.

Blevins wanted to get to the mess hall before the other officers came for evening chow. It had been over four months since fresh meat had been served, and Blevins didn't know how many of the wild pigs had been cooked for the officers.

Blevins stood on his toes and looked over the serving trays. He could smell the aroma of meat cooking, and his mouth watered.

"Evening, Sarge," Blevins called to the mess sergeant. "That fresh pork sure smells good, doesn't it? Is there enough for all the officers? I'm glad those enlisted men remembered to bring us some of the meat. Of course, it was government ammunition they used, so it was only right that they saved us some. Are you roasting or frying it?"

The cook didn't like the lieutenant, but he was smart enough not to show it. "I'm roasting it, Lieutenant."

"Good, that's the way I like it. You sure there's enough?" Lieutenant Blevins looked around the mess hall to see if they were alone. Blevins leaned as far over the trays as he could. "Sarge," he said in a hushed voice, "if you can set aside an extra piece of the loin, I'd see to it that you get a bottle of whiskey from the officers' next liquor ration."

"OK, Lieutenant, I'll do that. Colonel Taggart asked for a piece of the loin too, but I think there's enough for both."

The lieutenant forced a laugh. "Of course if you get a bottle of whiskey, that's not something we need to let others know about, is it? You wouldn't tell anyone where you got it if they found out, would you Sarge?"

"No, Lieutenant Blevins."

"How much longer before you start serving?"

"We're about ready, maybe another five minutes."

When chow call sounded, Blevins was the first to fill his tray with potatoes and Navy beans and grinned as he waited for the mess sergeant to serve the meat. When the sergeant put a chunk of meat on his tray, Blevins winked and found a table in the back of the mess hall. No sense in letting the other officers know I've got the best part of the pig, he thought.

He tried hard to push his fork into the piece of meat, but the fork bent. He tried cutting it with his knife and then gave up and picked the meat up with his hands. He tried to bite off a piece, then clamped his teeth on the meat and pulled. He started chewing, but it seemed that the longer he chewed, the bigger it became. He looked at the table where Colonel Taggart and Captain Slator were sitting and tried to see if they were able to chew their meat. Blevins pulled the wad of meat from his mouth. "Damn that mess sergeant," he cursed. "He gave me a piece of somebody's boondocker."

In the enlisted men's mess hall, Manny licked his fingers. "Man oh man, that was the best meat I've eaten in a long time."

"My piece was so tender I could cut it with my fork," Boog said. "That pig hunt turned out to be better than I thought."

"I wonder how the officers are doing eating the old boar?" Pappas grinned.

Mack laughed. "I hope the mess sergeant gave Lieutenant Blevins a part of the round steak."

Boog looked up from his tray. "What round steak? I didn't know you could get a round steak from a pig."

"I'm talking about the round piece of meat with a hole in it," Mack said.

With Talasea secured and the danger of snipers no longer a threat, Mack, Gil, Manny, and Pappas worked to improve the comfort and appearance of their tent. Coconuts were painted with whitewash and aligned in winding rows along the pathway to their tent, and Manny and Mack constructed crude but efficient writing tables.

It was a time when lonely men recalled treasured memories and wrote letters to their girlfriends, and some, when they looked at the Southern Cross in the star-filled Pacific sky, proposed marriage.

With so much time to relax, the men became restless and hungered for any type of sports activity. On the promise that bats and balls would be sent from the Red Cross at Cape Gloucester, the enlisted men cleared an area large enough for playing baseball.

Manny looked at one of the black, hot sinkholes on the edge of the clearing. "That mud is so hot it's bubbling. What caused all these hot pits anyway?"

"Most of these islands were caused by volcanoes," Mack said. "The steam coming out of the ground means there's hot lava not too far below."

"You mean we're sitting on top of a volcano?" Pappas asked. "What would we do if it erupted? Jesus Christ, first we gotta fight the frigging Japs and now you tell me we may get our butts roasted."

"I don't think that will happen," Mack replied, "but if it did, we'd be up shit creek without a paddle—no place to go and no way to get there."

Manny threw a coconut in the pit. "Look at that, it's already burning. It'd be tough to fall in one of those, wouldn't it? I heard that some Marine in Able Company fell in one. They say he really got burned before they got him out, and they had to take him back to the Division hospital at Gloucester. We have hot weather back home, but at least we don't have any hot mud holes like these."

"Texas has hotter and bigger holes than these," Mack boasted.

"Baloney," Manny said. "You're full of crap."

"Are you calling me a liar?"

Manny grinned, "Yeah, and someday I'm going to finish the fight we had aboard ship."

"If you think you're ready, why not try it now? I could use some physical exercise." Mack smiled. "I've been wanting to finish that fight myself."

Manny pulled his dungaree jacket from his shoulders. "I just believe I'm ready," he said, and lunged for Mack's waist.

They fell to the ground, and Mack twisted and turned, attempting to pull free from Manny's arms around his neck. Manny pulled his arms tighter, and Mack was powerless to get out from under Manny's body. Mack worked his right leg between Manny's and, with his left foot, rolled Manny on his side. With an extra surge of strength, he flipped Manny to his back and then wrapped his arms around his neck. Manny tried to roll back, but Mack pushed with his feet and held Manny in a scissors lock. They rolled over again, only inches away from the hot, bubbling mud pit. Manny strained to break Mack's hold, and Mack used every muscle to keep him from doing so.

Pappas and Gil heard the noise and ran to where the two men fought. Pappas yelled, "They're at it again! Grab Mack's feet and pull. I'll get Manny's."

"Pull them away from the pit," Gil screamed. "They'll get scalded if they fall in."

Boog heard Gil and Pappas yelling and helped pull Mack and Manny from the edge of the boiling pit.

"You two guys are going to kill yourselves if you don't cut out this damn fighting," Gil said.

"We can't be around all the time to pull youse guys apart," panted Pappas. "Whatever it was you were fighting about couldn't be worth scalding yourselves."

Mack breathed heavily and grinned at Manny. "You want to fight some more, or will we call this a draw like the last one?" he asked.

Manny got to his feet. "We better call it a draw. Seems like a man can't have a good fight anymore without Gil and Pappas ruining it." He walked to where Mack sat and helped him to his feet.

"You must have wrestled bears back in Carolina," Mack said. "You're as big as a bear, and you just might be as strong. I'm sure glad I don't have to fight you every day."

"I'll say the same to that. What do you say we just agree neither one of us can whip the other and let it go at that?" Manny suggested.

Mack laughed and put his arm around Manny's shoulder. "That's fine with me. Let's leave it that way."

Two weeks later, Taggart received the order from General Adams for the Fifth Marines to break camp, board the waiting ships, and join the rest of the First Division for their departure from New Britain.

Mack stood by the railing of the ship as it moved away from land. He was sure he saw a lone native standing just at the edge of the jungle, waving his hand in a last salute. Mack could see a carved wooden ornament, worn only around the neck of a chief, and knew it was his friend. The native waved one last time and then turned and disappeared into the shadows of the dense jungle.

"So long, General Boss Boy," Mack said softly.

On April 14, 1944, General Adams made an entry in his diary.

> *On this day, I ordered all units of the First Marine Division to prepare to leave New Britain. By the first week in May, the move should be complete.*
>
> *With the capture of New Britain, the gateway through the South Pacific for the Japanese forces to invade Australia has been finally and completely closed. The American forces can now plan for the further advancement toward Japan."* He put his pen down for a moment to rub his eyes, and then wrote again.
>
> *The price paid for the capture of Cape Gloucester and Talasea was steep. Over 300 Marines were killed and nearly 1,100 more were wounded.*
>
> *The First Marine Division has achieved a degree of perfection in jungle warfare never before equaled. The actual fighting at Cape Gloucester lasted a little over two weeks, and only four days at Talasea, but for those who were here, they will be forever unforgettable days and nights, of misery, of death, and of unbelievable courage and sacrifice.*
>
> *The island is secured. Our objective has been accomplished. I am proud to have been their commander.*

The general closed his diary and put it in his footlocker.

On another part of New Britain, Mack finished writing a letter to Anna.

> *Well, I'll finish this so I can get it ready for mail call. I have no idea how long it takes for one of my letters to get to you, or how much is censored, but I*

hope you're getting all my letters. Last week was the first mail call we've had in over a week, and I got five letters from you at the same time. Well, I'll say again how much I love you and how much I miss you. I wish it were possible for me to hold you in my arms, and someday, God willing, I will.

The scuttlebutt is we'll be leaving for a rest camp in a few days, but some of my buddies that came on this invasion won't be going home. For some, this was our first combat experience. We shared tormented moments and death was our companion. We saw friends stumble and fall, and for those who gave their lives, the war is over. They can rest now. I am one of the survivors, the lucky ones, and I will forever remember the sight of death, and I will always remember the crying of the wounded.

Good night. I love you,
Mack

PART III

29

The troopship from New Britain edged closer to the shore of Pavuvu, part of the Russell Islands. The four friends leaned over the ship's railing to see the lush green island with a halo of white sandy beach surrounded by the deep blue of the Pacific. Ocean waves broke over the reef that sheltered the shore, and beyond the beach, water from the morning rain still dripped from the trees and tropical plants.

Gil stared at the empty canoe houses with long, sloping thatched roofs huddled beneath the tall palms that swayed with the gentle winds. "Would you look at that? If I didn't know better I'd think we got us a pretty place for a rest camp, but there's no telling what it's like once we get ashore."

"Yeah, it is pretty. You know why?" Williams asked. "It's

because every other island we've seen has had the hell bombed out of it."

"All the islands looked like this before the war," Manny added. "It looks so peaceful."

"Yeah, and in some ways, it's kinda sad," Pappas said. "After we land, the island and its people will be changed forever."

Mack watched the waves breaking over the white sand. "The Japanese have already done that. They did that when they started using the Solomons for military bases."

The savage Pacific war had bypassed Pavuvu, only sixty miles from Guadalcanal, and the beauty of the ancient people who had first settled the island had been spared. The natives of small villages still subsisted on yams, sweet potatoes, fish, and copra. The land crabs, which would become such a nuisance to the Marines, were caught and eaten by the natives. Breadfruit, coconut, and bananas grew in great abundance, and a drink made from kava was the favorite drink of the simple people.

Brigadier General Wilford T. Adams, aboard the flag ship USS *Quantos*, sat across the table from his regimental and division officers. He pulled at his lower lip in deep thought and studied the official report, a description of the resources and advantages of using Pavuvu as a rest camp for the men under his command. He rubbed his temples, closed his eyes for a moment, and placed the report on the conference table.

"Gentlemen, I want you to know the reason the division is here in the Russell Islands and why Pavuvu has been chosen as the site for our rest camp. The Sixth Army decided a return to Australia was out, and after scouting several of these islands, Pavuvu was chosen. General Post and his staff agreed with that choice, and I support that decision."

"Sir, the island may have its advantages, but isn't it too small for training maneuvers?" Colonel Jacobs asked. "Did we do any reconnaissance work ourselves? We'll have to build our base camp from the ground up, and right now our men need to rest more than they need to work as seabees."

"No, Colonel, we didn't do any reconnaissance. I haven't seen the other islands the Army scouted, but I probably would have made the same decision."

Jacobs shook his head. "It may turn out to be better than I expect, but I'm skeptical when the Army chooses anything for a Marine Division. I wouldn't be surprised if they just flew over the island and based their conclusions on what they saw from a thousand feet above the tallest tree."

"Jacobs is probably right," Colonel Jackson added. "Although I don't see anything to say it's not a good choice."

"Whether or not you believe it was a good decision doesn't matter. The decision has been made," Adams retorted. He leaned across the table. "Jacobs, you're in charge of unloading operations. Major Evans will stay aboard ship, and the two of you will coordinate unloading operations until all units, equipment, and supplies are ashore. See that we get unloaded as soon as possible."

He pushed his chair back from the table. "Colonel Jacobs, it's also your responsibility to set up camp. Our new replacements are on the way, and we've got to get them trained for our next operation."

When the officers left, General Adams took two pills from a box in his pocket and swallowed them. He closed his eyes and rubbed his temples until the pain behind his eyes diminished.

George Pappas and Manny waded through the last few yards of the shallow water at the shore's edge. Their heavy packs pulled at their shoulders as they found firm footing on the sandy beach.

"A little better than the last time we went ashore on an island, isn't it?" Pappas said.

"Yeah, at least we don't have to dodge shrapnel."

"If the Army was coming ashore here," Pappas said, "they'd get a commendation for bravery. 'Coming in under enemy fire,' the citation would read."

When the men reached the shore, Sergeant Tucker ordered George Company to follow him. As they walked, mud stuck to the bottom of their boondockers.

A narrow roadway had been cut through the coconut trees for the incoming motorized units, and each truck that came ashore deepened the ruts in the soft surface.

A weapons carrier, loaded with heavy equipment, dragged bottom and came to a stop.

"All right, let's all push," Tucker yelled. "Let's get this truck out of here. Pappas, get over there."

Pappas cursed under his breath. "Ain't this just dandy? This fucking place is no better than Cape Gloucester. I thought we came here to rest."

"Quit your bitching, Pappas, and push," King said.

"Yeah, yeah, I am, I am," Pappas replied. His feet slipped in the mud, and he almost fell. "I don't remember seeing a poster of a Marine doing this when I joined."

Tucker checked his map and looked around at all the mud and water. Everson asked Williams, "What are we stopping here for? This can't be where our camp will be. There's at least four inches of water standing everywhere you look. This is nothing but a frigging swamp. We can't build a rest camp here."

"Maybe we're just going to bivouac here," Williams suggested.

The sergeant checked his map again. "All right, this is George Company's area. String your hammock. There won't be hot rations until we get our mess hall set up. I want a guard posted at each side of our bivouac. Pappas and Marshall will take the first watch, and Williams and Everson the second watch."

Boog looked at Pappas. "I know you're on Tucker's shit list, but why do I have to share that distinction with you? Why in hell do we need to post guards at a place like this? It's bad enough to think this is where our camp will be, but to post guards to protect it is stupid."

Pappas shook his head. "Boog, you just don't realize the value of things or the importance of being a good Marine. If we didn't post guards, some gook might steal all our coconuts."

Pappas looked slowly from side to side, staring at the shadows. "Boog, another reason is that some Jap from Guadalcanal might be hiding here, maybe planning to steal your dirty skivvies."

"If a Jap wants my dirty skivvies, he won't have to fight me for them," Boog replied. "I'll give him the ones I wore on the pig hunt."

The rain fell, slowly at first, then with greater intensity, until it came down in torrents. Pappas and Everson struggled to string their hammocks in the deluge and then crawled inside in their muddy and wet clothes, too weary to take them off.

The relentless rain fell for hours, and Pappas unzipped the mosquito netting and crawled out of his hammock. He stood in the downpour, and water dripped from his soggy dungarees.

"What are you doing out there?" Gil called.

"Trying to get dry. There's more water in the bottom of my hammock than there is out here. Aren't these great to sleep in?"

"What are you going to do? Stand out there all night?"

"No, I just thought how I'll get the water out of my hammock." Pappas took his K-bar knife and poked the blade through the bottom of the hammock. "There, now the water can just go on through." He crawled back inside. "Good night."

The next morning, Sergeant Tucker sloshed his way through the pouring rain. He cursed under his breath at the miserable conditions. "Okay, let's go, let's go," he yelled. "You ain't staying in the Pavuvu Hilton, we got work to do. We're on the first detail on the shore party. All of you just volunteered to unload amphibians from the supply convoy. Come on, Marines, you ain't got all day."

Boog stuck his head out the flap of his hammock. "Aw come on, Sarge, give us a break."

Pappas crawled out of his hammock. "Don't we have time for chow?"

"Get moving, Pappas, get the lead out of your ass. You'll get C rations at the beach." Tucker stared. "What the hell is the matter with your face? You look like a shriveled prune."

"You'd look like a prune, too, if you'd slept in water all night. Somebody better show me again how to hang that damned hammock."

Pappas whispered to Everson, "I just love Sergeant Tucker, don't you?"

Everson wiped his muddy hands on his wet dungarees. "Love him or not, you'd better get your butt in high gear. Tucker's hemorrhoids must be bothering him today."

Bulldozers from the Seventeenth Engineering Group had cleared a long but narrow area for stacking crates and boxes from the supply convoy, and the men unloaded boxes of ammunition, tents, poles, galley supplies, and an assortment of equipment to be used in establishing the rest camp. "Jesus," Pappas said. "What the hell is all this stuff? You'd think we're building a town here."

"We may do that before we get through. Look here at this box of raincoats. Must be for the officers. Did you ever see an enlisted man wear one? All we get are ponchos, and they sweat as much on the inside as they do on the outside," Mack said.

Boog Marshall pulled at the sides of the box. "You're going to see an enlisted man wear one just as soon as I can break open the crate. Anyone else want one?"

"Boog," King said, "you'll stick out like a sore thumb wearing a raincoat. Only officers have them, or at least all but the officer that was going to wear the one you just stole. How are you going to wear it without getting caught? You could get a court-martial for stealing, you know."

"I didn't steal a raincoat. The case just broke open, and I put it on to keep this one out of the mud," Boog said. "I'll wear it under my poncho."

Pappas found a small raincoat. "If you're going to have one, I'll have one, too."

Manny searched through the pile of raincoats. "Yeah, in boot camp, our DI said anything we could steal was ours and if we couldn't carry it off we could lay down beside it and claim it."

Everson held up one of the raincoats, "Just my size," and hid it under his poncho.

"I think our detail is being relieved, thank God," Williams said. "I'm tired. I want to get back and fix my hammock. I'll sure be glad when we can put up tents."

On the following day, Mack, Pappas, Gil, and Manny received their first mail since leaving Talasea. Some of the mail was postmarked March and April. Mack stacked his letters in chronological order, reading the letter with the earliest postmark first. Some of the men shared their letters with each other and, in doing so, shared parts of their lives.

Mack read three letters from Anna, and then opened an envelope from his mother. Inside was a letter with a military postmark. He studied it for a moment, trying to recognize the handwriting.

"Pfc. Juan Hernandez, Company A, 142nd Infantry, 36th Texas Infantry Division," Mack said. "I don't remember anyone by the name of Juan Hernandez."

Mack shook the envelope. "That's strange, no letter from Mom, but a letter inside from someone I don't know." He studied the envelope again.

"Why don't you open the letter?" suggested Gil. "Most of the time they're easier to read if you do."

Mack grinned. "Yeah, good idea, Gil."

Mack started reading the letter and said, "Oh no," and his shoulders slumped forward.

"What is it, Mack? What's the matter?" Gil asked.

"My friend, Felipe, is missing in action."

"Who's Felipe?" Pappas asked.

"Felipe Ramirez is my best friend from back home," Mack replied.

"You told me about him," Gil said. "Isn't he the one you went home to see before he joined the Army?"

"Yeah, we've been friends almost all our lives."

Gil walked to Mack's cot, saying, "Mack, I'm sorry," and sat on the cot beside him. "I'm sorry," he said again.

"Felipe was one of the best. Maybe I never told the two of you," Mack said to Manny and Pappas. "Felipe is my age, and he and his dad worked on our ranch. Carlos—that's Felipe's father—crossed the Rio Grande from Mexico into Texas when Felipe was just a young boy, and they came to our ranch. Dad put Carlos to work, and the ranch was their home as it was mine."

"Missing in action doesn't mean he was killed," Pappas said. "Maybe he just got separated from his unit. Maybe he's been captured by the Italians or Germans. That's not good, but it would mean he's still alive."

"Juan Hernandez doesn't think so," Mack replied. "He thinks he was killed."

"Do you know the man who wrote the letter?" Manny asked.

"No, I never heard of him," Mack replied. "He says he was in the same company with Felipe, and Felipe was his friend, too. He knew Felipe and I were friends, and he wanted me to know."

Gil reached for the letter. "Can I read it?"

"Go ahead," Mack said. "Read it out loud."

Gil began reading the letter. "'Dear Mack, I wish I did not have to tell you what I believe you should know. The Army has said your friend Felipe Ramirez is missing in action.'"

Gil frowned and pulled the letter closer to his face and said, "I can't make out some of the words. The handwriting is hard to read." Then he continued reading, "'The Army don't know what I know. Our platoon leader told me the Army is saying Felipe is missing in action, but I think he got killed. The German guns hit us bad, and the German soldiers kept coming at our lines. We was all doing what we could. The last time I saw Felipe he was with some of us men fighting the Germans and then a shell hit where they was and I know he was killed at that time. He was a good soldier. We all liked him and he was always a very brave man. I think he was a friend to all of us in his company. He treated me good like I was a man. He talked about you and told me how you were friends. He told me when he go home after the war, he go back and work on the ranch. I am sent this letter to your mother and ask her to sent it to you. Your friend, Pfc. Juan Hernandez, 142nd Regiment, Company A, 36th Division.'"

Gil folded the letter and handed it to Mack. "I can see why he meant so much to you."

"There isn't anything any of us can say," Manny said, "except we're sorry. I know his father will take it hard—any father would—but I hope that when he thinks of his son and cries, he can remember the times he laughed with him, too."

For the next week, the Marines were divided into work details, putting up pyramid tents, digging latrines, getting a galley operational, putting up mess tents, gathering rotted coconuts, and pushing jeeps and trucks out of the mud.

The pyramid tents and canvas cots, stored in an Army depot in Australia, were so rotted they were hardly fit to use. The first night Boog slept on one of the cots, the canvas bottom ripped and he fell to the deck.

The tents leaked from the constant rain, and nothing stayed dry. Tent pegs, driven into the wet ground, pulled out as easily as they were driven in, and tents collapsed over the sleeping men. Boog and Manny slept in their hammocks rather than in the dripping tents, and the men kept their personal belongings dry by rolling them in their ponchos.

Everson and Pappas stole wooden crates from the supply depot and built wooden platforms for their cots.

Pavuvu, like so many of the islands in the Pacific, was an atoll formed from coral. At an area inland from the camp, bulldozers pushed the thick mud away, and the coral was scooped and loaded into ten-wheel trucks. For the next two months, a continuous line of trucks hauled coral rock for tent decks for the officer quarters, then for roads, and eventually for campgrounds.

At the end of the first week, Colonel Jacobs went to General Adams's quarters.

"Sir, I'd like to make a request. Let's make Sunday a 'no work' day. It would be the first day the men have had off since we landed, and I believe it would be good for morale."

"You are the one who put the men on work details," Adams protested. "If their morale is not good, it's your fault, not mine. The selection of Pavuvu as a rest camp has proven to be a poor one, just as I suspected, and as I recall, one you believed to be a good one."

Jacobs was surprised. "Sir, I had no part in the selection of Pavuvu as a rest site, and the work details have been necessary to get this camp operational in the allotted time you've given us."

"I'll give your request some thought, Colonel Jacobs. Is that all?"

"No, sir, I have another suggestion," Jacobs replied. "I've heard there are wild cattle in the hills. I suspect they've been left from before the war by the plantation owners. I've got a few cowboys from Texas in Able Company, and Taggart has some in George Company. With your permission, I'll have them get us some fresh beef. I could add the extra incentive that each cowboy that brings in a beef will get two days off from work details, and I assure you we'll get fresh meat, something our men haven't had in a long time."

Adams thought for a moment. "Well, it might be something I could do for the men. Yes, fresh meat would make the enlisted men realize I'm as concerned about their comfort as I am about their training. You do understand the men must know it's my decision for them to have Sunday off? I want them to be proud to be under my command."

"Yes sir, I'll make sure the men know. The men will appreciate your thoughtfulness."

"All right, your request is approved."

"I'll let the other officers know. Thank you, General." Jacobs moved toward the door.

"Colonel Jacobs, you will deliver on your promise that we have fresh meat?"

"Yes, sir, we'll have fresh meat."

Jacobs started to leave, and Adams called, "Colonel Jacobs, can you order up better weather while you're at it?"

"Yes, sir, I will," Jacobs answered.

Jacobs stepped out of Adams's tent, and scratched his head. "What the hell is the matter with Adams?" Jacobs said under his breath. "He knows the Army chose Pavuvu as a rest camp, and that General Post and his staff approved it. Adams knows I had nothing to do with that."

Mack found a pair of dry skivvies and a relatively clean pair of dungarees. It was good to see the sun shining for a change, and morale was high over the news fresh meat would be served. "Gil, are you about ready to go see Billy and Donald? I'm anxious to know how they are."

"I am too," Gil replied. "From what I hear, the Seventh had it pretty rough on Cape Gloucester. I hope Billy and Donald didn't get hurt."

"I made a promise to Harris I'd write his mother if something ever happened to him, and until now, I haven't had the chance to find out how he is," Mack said.

"I'm ready when you are," Gil said. "We can still make it back for chow if we leave pretty soon."

When Mack and Gil got out of the jeep, Mack waved to the driver, "Thanks for the lift, corporal. You saved us a lot of walking."

Gil looked around him at the mud and puddles of water. "This area is no better than where we are. I can see we weren't the only ones that got a swamp for a campsite."

"Yeah," Mack said, "and I can see they have rats and land crabs, too. I don't know which I hate the most. Last night I woke up to see a land crab riding bareback on a big rat."

Gil grinned. "You sure he was just riding?"

"Do you think they can crossbreed?"

"I hope not," Gill laughed. "Either one is bad enough, but a crossbreed is something I'd hate to see."

They found where I Company was camped, and Gil said, "Now all we have to do is find Billy's tent. I'll ask in here."

A skinny Marine playing a harmonica looked up when Gil walked into the tent.

"We're friends of Pfc. Billy Harris and Donald Woodson. Do you know where we can find them?"

The Marine frowned. "Harris is bunked in the third tent. You might find him there. What outfit you from?"

"Fifth Regiment, George Company," Gil answered. "We joined the Marines with Harris and Woodson. We went through boot camp together."

"Good luck, fellows," the Marine said, and started playing his harmonica again.

When Gil and Mack found the tent, Gil stuck his head inside. Harris was sitting on his bunk, writing a letter.

"Hey, Marine, what the hell you doing?"

"Gil! Mack!" Billy shouted, and jumped from his cot.

"How are you, Billy?" Gil said. "Gosh, it's good to see you."

Mack was grinning, too, as he grabbed Billy around the neck. "We hadn't heard anything from you or about you since before we boarded ship at New Guinea. How are you doing?"

"I'm doing great. Gil, the last time I saw you, you were in the sick bay in San Diego. Are you and Mack in the same outfit?"

"Yeah, we're in the Fifth, George Company."

"Mack, I intended to get over to your outfit as soon as I could, but I haven't had the chance," Billy said. "This is the first day I haven't been on a work detail since we landed."

Gil laughed, "Everybody has been on a work detail since we came to Pavuvu."

"I'm glad to see y'all made it. I heard the Fifth Regiment was in some of the toughest fighting at Gloucester, and we heard y'all got the added duty at Talasea. At least my company didn't catch that part of the fighting."

"Where's Woodson?" Gil asked. "Is he here?"

Billy stopped smiling. "You had no way of knowing. Donald didn't make it."

"When? How?" Gil asked.

"January 13, Hill 666. Donald didn't get killed, not physically, anyway. I don't know how to say this. He…he couldn't go on. He just couldn't fight anymore. I knew he was having a hard time, but I didn't realize how bad off he was until it happened."

"How what happened?" Mack asked.

"Sergeant Smith had just given us the orders to go back up on the line. We'd been through some pretty tough fighting with lots of casualties—maybe forty or fifty percent, I'm not sure—but none of us were in very good condition, and we sure didn't want to go back. We'd been on K rations and most of us had lost weight, but Donald lost a lot of weight. You could see it, and I tried to get him to eat, but he wouldn't do it."

Billy sat down on his cot. "I blame myself for not doing something."

"You shouldn't blame yourself. What could you have done?" Gil asked.

"I don't know, but I should have thought of something."

Mack sat on the cot beside Billy. "What happened?"

"Well, you both remember how quiet Donald was. Even in boot camp, he never talked to anyone, stayed by himself most of the time. While we were in New Guinea, and then after we landed at Cape Gloucester, we talked some. He told me a little about his mother and stepfather. He said he joined the Marines to get away from his folks, mostly his step father. He really hated him."

"We never knew, did we?" Gil said.

"One night, he told me that when he was a kid, he found out how lonely life could be, and he started crying, and then he wiped his face and said, 'What am I doing this for? I'm too old to cry.' Donald was really hurting, and I should have helped him."

Everson shook his head. "Why didn't he tell us the way it was? If we had known, we might have been more understanding."

Billy continued, "The night before we went back up on the line, he came over to where I was sleeping, and he wanted to talk. I know now he was really bad off. He told me he was afraid of getting killed, but we all have that fear.

"The next day, when the orders came to go back to the front, Donald just cracked up. He said he couldn't go. I tried to help him, but he couldn't even stand up. His legs wouldn't hold him up. He started crying and saying something, but I couldn't understand what he was trying to say. Sergeant Smith knew what had happened and ordered Donald sent back to the States."

"I'm sorry," Mack said. "I really am. I don't feel good about saying it, but Donald and I were never good friends. I couldn't get close to him, and I never gave him a chance. It's too late now to tell him I'm sorry. Did you write his folks?"

"No, Donald told me a long time ago that if anything ever happened to him he didn't want anyone to write his folks. Mack, I had told him of our agreement to write if something happened, and I asked him if he wanted me to tell anyone if something happened to him. He said no, he didn't want me to."

"There was no one he wanted you to write to—a friend or girlfriend—nobody?" Gil asked.

"No, he didn't, but he talked a lot about a girl he met back at the beach on New Guinea, a Red Cross worker. He met her just before we boarded ship for Cape Gloucester. He went to see her one night and planned to see her again, but we shipped out the next day. We didn't know we were leaving so fast, and he never got her address. He didn't know her very long, but Donald said he liked her more than any person he had ever known. From what Donald said, she liked him, too."

"Do you remember her name?" Mack asked.

"Yes, her name was Sarah, Sarah Randolph."

"Where is Donald now?" Gil asked.

"Sergeant Smith said they would send him back to the States, to some Navy hospital, but he didn't know where. Sarge did say that...he said that Donald might be mentally hurt for the rest of his life. Mack, he was so bad off he didn't know me and didn't even know where he was. It really hurt seeing him that way."

"Oh goddamn," Gil said. "That would almost be as bad as getting killed, maybe worse. Even if he gets well, he'll always know that he didn't…or couldn't…you know what I mean."

"Donald isn't the only one relieved from the front lines," Mack said. "We had a man that shot himself when he was told he had to go back to the front, and other companies probably had men that did the same thing. Damn, I just don't see how someone could do that."

"In Donald's case, it had nothing to do with lack of courage," Billy said. "I think his mind just couldn't take it anymore. He was under more pressure than any of us realized, and he cracked up."

"Well, the three of us made it. That's something to be thankful for," Gil said. "I don't know how many more of these invasions we'll have before the war ends, but we made it through one," Gil said.

"Yeah, I was writing Laura when you came, telling her about how some things were, but I didn't tell her how bad it was in combat. I didn't tell her about Donald, either. Someday maybe I'll tell her about him, but not now."

Mack shook Billy's hand. "Well, we better be getting back to our camp. I'm glad you're okay. I see you're still wearing your scarf. You sure it hasn't grown to your skin?"

Billy grinned and replied, "Nope, not yet." He shrugged, "I've worn it so much now I wouldn't feel right without it. It's my good luck charm."

30

After three months of continuous and difficult work details, living conditions at Pavuvu improved, but the monotonous diet of dried potatoes, powdered eggs, spam, corned beef hash, and hard tack, was still as predictable as the constant rain.

The fighting in the rotting jungles of Cape Gloucester and Talasea and the never-ending exposure to the rain and mud had taken its toll. Many of the veterans still suffered from "jungle rot," where re-opened wounds failed to close and sores refused to heal. Those who had not swallowed the bitter atabrine tablets had contracted malaria and suffered from the chills and fever of that dreaded disease.

Some of the veterans had been with the division since before Guadalcanal and had been in the jungles for over a year, and mental fatigue was almost as common as physical fatigue.

Boog Marshall aimed his M-1 at a rat beneath Gil's cot. "Hold still, Gil, I've got the little fucker's eyes in my sights."

"Hey, Boog, put that damn rifle down. You're not that good of a shot. You can't get rid of them that way," Gil shouted.

Boog lowered his rifle. "We've tried every other way, and it hasn't worked. Maybe if we all shot ten rats a day we'd get rid of the ugly bastards. Every time one is killed, two more come back. They're driving me bananas."

"There's almost as many land crabs as there are rats. You want to shoot them, too?" Mack asked.

Manny sat on his cot, his chin resting in his hands, and nonchalantly watched the land crabs crawl sideways across the tent. "Did anyone ever notice that some of these land crabs are faster than some of the others?"

"They may be fast," Pappas muttered, "but I know one that won't move fast anymore. That son of a bitch that crawled inside my boondocker last night scared hell out of me when I put on my boondocker this morning."

"They probably heard your scream over in Fox Company," Mack said.

Gil rubbed his chin as he watched the land crabs scurrying across the deck. "That one with a missing claw is pretty fast— maybe the fastest of all. I like his style."

Gil pretended to draw a sword from a scabbard and waved the imaginary sword toward the crab, "I dub thee 'Captain Hook.'"

"Why don't we train them, make racers out of them?" Mack suggested. "We can't get rid of them, so we might as well have some fun with them. We can each choose a crab and have races, maybe do a little betting."

"I don't have anything to bet," Gil replied. "Pappas keeps winning all my money at blackjack."

"You could bet your beer ration," Mack proposed.

There was no denying that even without one claw, 'Captain Hook' was the fastest land crab in the tent. Gil's crab consistently won the races held in the evenings after chow.

"OK, Mack," Gil offered, "what do you want to bet tonight? Do you still want to swap your next Coke ration for my next beer ration?"

"I don't know. You've won my Coke ration until 1952, and I've washed your dirty skivvies twice already. If Captain Hook keeps winning, he may have an untimely and mysterious ending. If I bet, I gotta have something to boot. Besides, my crab isn't feeling too good. He didn't finish all his hard tack, and he looks kinda pink around the belly button," Mack replied.

Pappas scratched his head. "Crabs don't have belly buttons, do they?"

"Pappas, stay out of this. This is between Gil and me. Just because your crab got squashed by a jeep yesterday doesn't give you any right to interfere with serious negotiations."

"Yeah, too bad it wasn't 'Captain Hook' that got run over," Manny complained. "I'll never have another beer ration."

"Well, I aim to get me another crab," Pappas admitted, "just as soon as I have a chance to watch them run tonight. There's no sense picking one unless he can run. Poor Ralph was fast, but he had no business being out of the tent. I should have tied the string tighter so he couldn't get away, so it's part my fault he got squashed. By the way, the funeral is scheduled for Sunday morning just after chow. Munday has agreed to say a few words. Manny, are you still going to sing that hymn you used to sing at your church?"

"I didn't know they had funerals on Sunday," Mack said.

"He's beginning to stink. I can't wait any longer," Pappas said.

"Manny, what song is it, the song you're going to sing?" Mack asked. "I used to play a trumpet, and I learned the words to 'Onward Christian Soldiers,' so I can help you sing."

"I'm going to sing 'On This Rock I'll Build My Church'," Manny said.

"I don't know that one," Mack confessed, "but the words to 'Onwards Christian Soldiers' will probably fit in with what you sing."

"Come on, Mack, get back to the bet." Gil thought for a moment. "Suppose you give me your Coke ration for 1953 and agree to bring me morning chow on Sunday if you lose. That sound fair?"

Mack said. "I've got to have some boot. I'll tell you what, I'll bet my next Coke ration against your next two beer rations, providing there will be two more, and if there aren't, then I'll take your next beer ration plus you stand guard duty for me the next time, providing it isn't raining. How about that? Is it a deal?"

Pappas said, "What did he just bet?"

"Beats the hell out of me. I don't know what he said, but yeah, it's a deal. I don't like beer anyway," Gil replied. "By the way, Pappas, who's coming to the funeral?"

"All the guys from this tent and two from the next tent are coming. You want to be a pallbearer, Gil?"

"Naw, funerals break me up. I might have to leave if it gets too sad."

"Well, I need to get to sleep," Manny said. "I'm tired. Sergeant Tucker put us through the ropes today, and I'm hitting the sack. Somebody wake me up for chow in the morning. Since it's Sunday, we get the day off and I may want to sleep all day, but just in case they got something besides powdered eggs I don't want to miss it."

"Yeah, me too," Mack said. "I'm too tired to write Anna tonight, and that's pretty tired."

"KAPOW!" The sound fractured the night's calm.

Mack opened one eye and squinted in the darkness. He looked across the tent at his sleeping buddy.

"Gil," he said. "Gil," he said again.

"What?"

"Did you hear it?"

"Yeah"

"You getting up?"

"Yeah, guess so."

Mack raised up on one elbow. Manny and George were already sitting up on their cots.

"Is Boog up yet?" Manny asked. He yawned.

"Shake him. Kick his cot," Gil said.

George walked to Boog's cot and kicked it. Boog groaned. "Leave me alone. I'm dreaming."

"Which one is it this time?" George asked. "The blonde from Dallas or the redhead from Waco?"

"Neither. Leave me alone."

"You got another one this time, huh Boog?" quizzed George.

"It's a Mexican gal from San Antonio. Now leave me alone," Boog said.

George mumbled, "Jesus Christ, he's got all the luck. I can't ever dream like he does."

Gil stood by his cot, scratching his rear. It was hot, and as was Gil's custom, he slept bare-assed. He put on his boondockers, still unlaced, and stepped toward the corner of the tent.

"Is it ready?" he asked.

Mack looked up at the hole in the tent. "Think so," he said. "Made a pretty good-sized hole in the tent when the lid blew off."

Manny had his canteen cup in his hand. "I'm first this time. You damn Texans drink too much when you say you're just sampling. Last time there was hardly enough for thirds when Mack got through sampling."

Boog sat on his cot, yawned, stretched, and said, "This better be good. Lolita was just starting to dance when you kicked my cot," he said as he looked at Pappas. "You ever see a naked Mexican gal dance?" he asked.

"What kind of dance?" George asked.

Manny interrupted, "Forget about the Mexican gal, let's see if it's ready yet."

Mack lit a match and held it just close enough to look into the water can, now filled with jungle juice. "Can't see too much. I'm afraid to get the match too close. Remember what happened the last time?"

"Yeah," Gil said. "You held the match too close and you blew the whole fucking tent apart."

"Yeah," Pappas said, "that would have been some jungle juice. I'll bet we'll never make another batch that good."

"Manny, hand me your canteen cup and your cigarette lighter," Mack said.

"Yeah, here," Manny said, handing the cup and lighter to Mack.

"Help me tilt it," Mack said as Gil walked over. "We sure as hell don't want to spill any," Mack said. Together, they emptied a small amount of jungle juice into the cup, and Mack carefully poured a small amount from the cup into the fuel tank of the lighter. He screwed the cap back and with his thumb, flicked the lighter. A blue flame three inches long erupted from the lighter.

"Looks like a pretty good batch this time, doesn't it?" Mack said. He grinned. "Somebody go wake up the guys in the next tent."

Gil walked out of the tent, naked except for his untied boondockers, and went to the next tent to awaken their friends.

Manny filled his canteen cup with the jungle juice and raised it to his lips. Everyone in the tent waited for the verdict. Manny took a small sip, then a larger one, then emptied the cup in fast gulps.

"How is it, Manny?" asked George. He looked at the second hand on his watch.

Manny stood very still. His mouth opened, but no words came out. Everyone looked at the expression on Manny's face.

"Someone light a lantern so we can see his face better. We can't judge good jungle juice in the dark," Boog said.

"Ask him again how good it is, George," Mack said.

"How is it, Manny?"

Again, no sound escaped his opened mouth.

"Great!" Mack said. "We got us a winner this time."

The Marines moved eagerly toward the water can and held out their canteen cups to be filled.

One Marine from the other tent asked Mack, "What'd you use?"

"The best dried apricots and dried peaches the cook could get. About three quarts."

"How much sick bay alcohol?" asked another Marine.

"Doc could only get two pints."

"Is Manny still standing?" some one asked.

"Yeah, he's still standing. He's still trying to talk," Boog said. "He's still moving his lips."

"And still can't talk? That's great. How long has it been? George, you're the official timekeeper," Mack said.

"It's been four minutes and forty seconds. Mark one!" he said.

"Man oh man, this must be a really good batch," Boog said. "Lolita, you've gotta wait!"

"How long did you let it age, Mack?" a Marine from the other tent asked.

"Before the lid blew or after?" inquired Mack.

"After."

Mack looked at George. "How long, George?"

"Ten minutes, more or less," George said.

"That's plenty long enough," Boog said, and took a very small sip. "WOW!" he said in a hoarse whisper. "That is some good…"

Manny was still standing, and George looked at him. "He's got that stupid intelligent look on his face. I think he's about to come out of it."

For the next hour, there was a continuous line of Marines in front of the can of jungle juice, waiting for a refill of the potent stuff. Manny had recovered enough to stand in line for seconds before the can needed to be tilted and the last drop was drained. There were twelve Marines in the tent now, all in a happy stupor. Some sat, while others remained standing as if frozen to the spot where they had taken their last gulp.

Gil said, "Mack, let's go get the chicken. I think it's time. Right now. You agree?" His speech was slurred.

"Yeah, let's go do it," Mack replied.

"You're going to catch hell from Lieutenant Blevins if you do," Munday said. "He's had that Rhode Island Red hen ever since he got transferred over from Fox Company, ever since it was just a baby chick. You better not do it," he warned.

Gil picked up his helmet and removed the inside liner. "Much lighter now," he declared, and put the outside shell on his head. It wobbled from side to side, and Gil had to steady it with his hands.

"I'm telling you, Lieutenant Blevins is proud of that hen. You've seen him every morning, when the lieutenant takes his chicken for a walk," Munday said.

Pappas started laughing. "Yeah, the first time, when he tied a string around one of the chicken's legs and the two of them walked down the muddy street in front of the officers' quarters, I thought I was going to flip."

Manny said, "You got to give the lieutenant credit. At first it was just a jumble of flapping wings, loud squawks, and flying feathers, but Blevins taught that hen to walk beside him. It sure is a pretty sight, the lieutenant and that hen strolling down the muddy street in front of the officers' quarters. Makes me homesick for my chickens back home. I sure do miss my chickens."

Each morning, Blevins fed the chicken the crumbs his orderly gathered from the mess hall. The mess cook was not pleased when Blevins ordered him to bake a special bread, insisting that only the best available corn and flour be used. Blevins gave the cook a standing order that if a supply of fresh grain arrived, it was to be used first to make a special bread for his Rhode Island Red.

Munday tried again to stop Mack and Gil from leaving the tent. "Mack, you know no one is allowed to feed the chicken except Lieutenant Blevins, and it's strictly off limits for anyone to make too much noise during the early morning laying hours."

Mack said, "I heard the hen is as yet childless."

"There may not have been any eggs, but the lieutenant is still proud of that hen," Munday said.

Gil and Mack staggered out the tent toward their destination. Gil saw an ammunition cart outside one of the weapons supply tent. He started pulling it, and Mack asked, "What the hell you doing? What you going to do with that cart?"

"Don't know, but you never can tell when you might need something like this, so I'm going to take it," replied Gil. The two Marines laughed and stumbled together.

Gil started singing. "Old Soul of Mira, la la la la, Old soul of Mira, la la la la." He sang it again, totally off-key.

"Goddamn it, Gil, don't you know any other words to that fucking song?" Mack asked.

"Don't need any more," Gil said, and stumbled and fell to the ground. He struggled to his feet and started singing the song again.

When they neared the lieutenant's tent, Gil stopped singing and placed his index finger to his lips. "Shhh," he whispered.

"Shhh," Mack said very softly, repeating the same gesture.

"Now what?" Gil asked.

"I got a plan," Mack replied.

"What is it?" Gil asked, trying to keep his helmet from falling off his head.

"You go steal the chicken," Mack said.

"That's a good plan," Gil agreed.

Gil located the cage and carried the hen several yards before he stopped and asked, "Mack, why don't I put the cage on the ammunition cart and you pull it?"

"Shhh," whispered Mack. "The cart would be too heavy. Come on."

Gil placed his index finger to his lips and then followed the cart Mack was pulling.

When they returned to their tent, Gil said, "What we going to do with the chicken? We can't let Boog have it. I know what he'd do."

"I've got another plan," Mack said.

"What is it?"

"Get a GI can and fill it with water. We're going to make chicken soup."

"That's a good plan," Gil said, as he almost fell.

Manny, Boog, and George heard the noise outside the tent, and joined Mack and Gil. When the plan was explained to them, they gladly searched the galley and found a ten gallon GI container. They poured five gallons of water into the container, and then as an afterthought, Manny added a small amount of jungle juice that had been left in a canteen cup.

"That's for flavor," he said.

"Do we need to heat the water?" Pappas asked.

"Certainly we need to heat the water. You ever try to eat a raw chicken? Somebody build a fire," commanded Mack.

Gil asked, "We gonna pluck 'im first?"

"You must think I'm stupid or something. Hell yes, we're going to pluck 'im," Mack said.

At the first yank of feathers, the bird squawked so loud the Marines were afraid it could be heard throughout the entire camp. Manny tried to hold his hand over the chicken's mouth.

"Whoops, we forgot something," Mack said, and then tried to wring the chicken's neck. The frantic bird flapped its wings, and feathers flew in all directions.

The chicken ran into the tent, and Mack and Gil were only a step behind. "This is like trying to catch a kite in a dust storm," Mack said. "We can't let it get away now."

The chicken was cornered beneath Gil's cot, and Gil grabbed the squawking bird by the neck and carried it outside. The violent movement of the flapping wings contributed to its early demise, and when the hen hung limp, the five Marines started pulling the feathers from the carcass.

Gil pulled a feather. "She loves me, she loves me not, she loves me, she loves me not," he said, plucking the feathers one at a time.

"What'll we do with the feathers?" asked George.

"Make a feather pillow out of them," replied Gil.

The water heated to a boil, and Gil said, "What do we do now?"

Mack said, "We throw the chicken into the water, stupid."

"You sure you've done this before?" he asked Mack.

"Yeah. Nothing to it. I used to watch Mom make soup all the time," answered Mack.

"We do take the guts out, don't we?" George asked. "And the head and feet, do we cut them off?"

"Naw, wouldn't be enough left of the chicken to make good soup if we did all that," Mack said. "We're just going to throw the whole thing in." He dropped the chicken, with more than a few feathers still attached, into the boiling water.

The Marines who had been drinking the jungle juice were now gathered around the roaring fire and watched the lonely chicken bob up and down in the steaming water.

Mack said, "How long we been cooking, Pappas?"

"Well, not more than twenty or thirty minutes. Don't really know. I'm still so dizzy the hands on my watch don't look right. Probably not running anymore," he said and put the watch to his ear. "Yep, it's going ticktock, ticktock."

"I'd say the goose is cooked. Time's up. Soup's on," Mack said. "Everybody get your canteen cup."

"We cooking a goose instead of a chicken?" Boog asked.

"Chow down for the troops," echoed Gil.

They dipped their cups in the water, now a somewhat brownish color, and Manny was the first to taste it.

He swallowed a big gulp.

"Well, how is it?" Mack asked.

Manny spit a chicken feather from his mouth. "Needs more salt," he replied.

When reveille sounded the next morning, twelve very sick Marines lay in their sacks.

Munday opened one eye. "George," he said, "I'm going to miss the funeral."

Pappas groaned. "My aching ass. My head hurts. Forget

about the funeral. I'll cremate Ralph. Manny can't sing too good anyway," he said, and rolled over in his cot.

The shrill voice of Lieutenant Blevins could be heard throughout the camp. "Where's my chicken? Who stole my chicken? Somebody is going to get a court-martial if a single feather has been touched. I want someone to tell me where my chicken is, and they better speak up loud and clear. Sergeant Tucker," he shouted, "get the platoon out here for roll call. I want to know who is and who isn't present. Get them out here on the double."

"Gil," Mack said, "did you hear Lieutenant Blevins?"

"Yeah, I heard," Gill said. "How could you keep from hearing? Goddamn, his voice hurts my head. I don't think I can get out of the sack. If I do, I'm going to throw up sure as shit. My head hurts, my stomach hurts, and I ache all over. That was one helluva batch of jungle juice. Wow! I wish I was dead. I may be dead, for all I know."

"You gonna tell the lieutenant we did it?" asked Mack.

"What did we do?" asked Gil.

"Stole Lieutenant Blevins's chicken. You telling?" Mack asked.

"Not if you don't. I'm not sure we did it, anyway. I don't remember much about last night except drinking all that jungle juice, and I vaguely remember being attacked by a chicken. You don't suppose we could plead self-defense, do you?" Gil said.

When the platoon was assembled in front of their tents, Lieutenant Blevins walked along the ranks, looking each Marine in the eye. Each time he looked into bloodshot eyes, he stopped and smelled the same foul odor of soured fruit. When he stood in front of Gil, he said, "Whew," and almost fell backwards. He nodded, understanding the significance of the horrible smell.

"Sergeant Tucker, I want to see these twelve men outside my quarters," Blevins said, pointing to each man with the foul odor. "You can dismiss the rest of the platoon."

When the twelve men gathered outside Lieutenant Blevins's tent, he called them to attention. "Men," he said, "it's a criminal offense to steal government property, and my chicken was the property of the United States Marine Corps. I can only guess that one of you, maybe all of you, have something to admit about the disappearance of a certain piece of government property. I may not be able to retrieve what's been lost, but I do intend to find the party responsible for the theft. I can be as tough as you force me to be. If the guilty party will step forward, the rest can return to your tent, and I'll discipline the guilty party according to the circumstances."

All twelve men stepped forward.

"I see," Blevins said. "In that case, you will all stand extra guard duty until we board ship for the next invasion. I will discuss this with Sergeant Tucker, and he will post the guard duty roster. You're dismissed."

When the Marines turned to leave, Blevins said, "Corporal Williams, I'd like a word with you. I don't suppose there is any sense in asking if my hen is still around?"

"I wouldn't know, sir," Williams replied.

"No chance at all?" asked the lieutenant.

Williams hesitated, then said, "Lieutenant Blevins, it was a rooster."

31

In early August, Brigadier General Wilford Adams paced the floor and waved the paper in front of his regimental officers.

"The reason you're here this morning is for me to tell you about this report from the Joint Chiefs. The Army has moved up their plans to attack Mindanao." Adams placed the paper on the table. "Before the invasion of the Philippines begins, Peleliu must be secured as a fighter base."

Adams unfolded the map of Peleliu, and placed it in front of his officers. "The Army is anxious to return to the Philippines, and the commander in chief of the Pacific—CinCPac—has agreed to their accelerated plan. Operation Stalemate, the attack on Peleliu, will begin September 15. I assured General Post that the First Marine Division will secure the island in a matter of days, and the Army will have their fighter base."

Colonel Jackson looked incredulously at his commanding officer. "Sir, may I ask what information you have to promise General Post that Peleliu will be secured in just days? The last report from Division Intelligence was that over twelve thousand Japanese could be there, and I'm sure that's a low estimate."

Colonel Jacobs interrupted, "Sir, how can we possibly expect to take the island in two days?"

Adams slowly turned to look at Jacobs. "Colonel, General Post believes, as I do, that a chunk of coral only six miles by two miles can withstand just so much from the preinvasion shelling."

"But General, sir," Jackson protested, "intelligence confirms there's probably several thousand Japs on other islands in the Palau group. They could join with the ones on Peleliu. If they're willing to fight and die for their emperor as they did at Saipan, we'll have a hell of a fight on our hands. We can't expect them to surrender. I'd like to share your optimism, but I can't believe we can secure the island in a just days."

"Once we're on the island, we can keep the Japanese from landing any additional support troops," Adams insisted.

Taggart started to ask a question, but the general waved his hand to cut him off. "The island will be fortified, and you're correct about the number of troops there, but our shelling will render the Japanese forces incapable of defending the island."

"We have less than a month to complete our amphibious training and get all men and equipment on board, and that concerns me," Colonel Taggart said. "Every morning, we have men reporting to sick bay with jungle rot and malaria."

"Then get your men ready to fight," Adams demanded. "That's what they're here for. Besides..." Adams looked directly at Colonel Jacobs..."your Pavuvu island paradise, as you thought it would be, is getting to some of the troops. They want to get back into combat."

Jackson tried not to show the anger he felt toward his commanding officer. "Sir, if the Army has moved up their invasion plans of the Philippines, what change will there be in the air and naval support promised for Peleliu?"

"None. The Navy is positive their massive preinvasion shelling will destroy the beach installations, and CinCPac will bring in heavy bombers to destroy those installations and troops in the inland terrain."

The general shrugged his shoulders. "The enemy will dig in, there's no question about that, and they'll certainly take advantage of the coral terrain to construct caves and bunkers, but when we pound them with artillery and bombs they'll be so demoralized they won't fight."

Adams paused. "Of course, if some do survive the bombardment, then the fighting may take longer. I don't believe that will be the case."

Jacobs was frustrated. "General..."

Adams waved his hand. "Just a minute, Colonel. Let me continue. We know our March bombing destroyed their airfield, and they can't use it, so they know what's in store for them when we really hit them. The Army is not going to change their timetable to invade the Philippines, and there will not be any delay in taking Peleliu. General MacArthur told me personally at our meeting on Oahu that he will keep his promise to the people of the Philippines."

Adams slapped the table with his hand. "The Army needs Peleliu's airfield, and the First Marine Division is going to give it to them."

"And the Japanese Navy? Any new information on that?" asked Colonel Jacobs. "What can we expect from them? What happens to our troops once we get ashore if their Navy breaks through?"

"You tell me," Adams replied sarcastically. "You know the answer to that question without me telling you, Colonel."

Jacobs tightened his fists in anger and looked at Jackson and Taggart.

"Do we know which Japanese fleets are there?" Jackson asked.

"Yes, the Japanese Second Fleet. We believe Tokyo will keep Vice Admiral Naha Koturu's central carrier fleet out of the Peleliu operations. They want Koturu's carriers to protect the Philippines. General MacArthur is not going to bypass those islands, and the Japanese know it."

Adams motioned for his officers to join him around the mock-up of Peleliu constructed from aerial photographs. "OK, let's get on with it. Let's review your landing orders."

The officers gathered around Adams at the table. "Now I know you're familiar with your assignments for D-day, but as we cover them, if you see a problem, speak up."

Adams turned to Colonel Jackson. "The First Regiment will cross the reef and go ashore on White Beach One and White Beach Two at the north end of the landing zone, then drive straight inland for five hundred yards and swing left to attack the low-lying ridges dominating the shoreline. Any problems?"

"No sir. I understand. My officers are prepared, and the men know what's expected of them."

"Colonel Taggart, your Fifth Regiment will hit Orange One and Orange Two, then push straight ahead toward the airstrip. Understood?"

"Yes sir, I understand."

Adams faced Jacobs, "And you, Colonel Jacobs, you will land with the Seventh Regiment on Orange Beach Three, move across the island to protect Taggart's flank, and then move to the right to take on any Japs on the southern tip. Do you understand your orders?"

Jacobs frowned. "Yes, General, I understand. I'm aware of what we're to do once we get ashore, but…"

"But what?" Adams interrupted.

"Well, General, our first obstacle is getting across the reef. We haven't had an actual reef to use in our training maneuvers. Our men have practiced transferring from the LSTs into Higgins boats and then into amtracks, but I'm wondering if we've done enough. We should discuss again how we're to cross the reef."

General Adams sighed. "Are there conflicts that I'm not aware of? Are there problems in the reef crossing that need discussing?"

"Yes sir, there are," Taggart answered. "Aerial photographs show that the reef is almost six hundred yards long in some places. That's a lot of coral to cross. The Navy will have to make the trip several times under enemy fire. The reef could give us more problems than the Japs, and I'm not sure our plans include enough amphibious tractors. Without those amphibs, there's no way we can get across the reef. If the Japanese gun installations haven't been destroyed before we go in, and if we lose too many amtracks, there will be no way for the remaining troops to get ashore."

"I made the decision not to ask for any more amtracks from the Army," Adams said defensively. "There's room for only thirty Sherman tanks and fifty amphibious tractors, and since space on the landing ship docks—the LSDs—is limited, I prefer to have more tanks and fewer amphibs."

Adams looked at his officers. "Don't worry, we'll get across the reef. My main concern is to get enough men and equipment ashore on the first two waves so that even if we do lose a few, we'll still have a landing force that can stay."

"Two waves of men and equipment can't stay on the shore indefinitely," Jacobs argued. "They must have support, and that means more troops coming ashore. If we're not successful in getting across the reef with all our men and equipment, we're going to have one hell of a lot of casualties."

Adams, obviously annoyed, leaned over and placed his hands on the table. He looked directly at Jacobs. "The reef will not be a problem."

Adams moved away from the table and started pacing the floor again. "There are several factors in our favor. First, our big guns and bombs will demolish the Japanese stronghold. Second, the reconnaissance photos show the island will be of low elevation. Japanese mortars and artillery won't be coming at us from some fortified hilltop, and third, the aerial reconnaissance photos show there aren't any swamps and jungle like we experienced at Cape Gloucester, fourth…"

"General," Jacobs interrupted, his voice louder than he intended. "I don't agree. I've studied those photographs, and they don't prove there aren't any swamps. All they show is greenery. We don't have a true idea of what the terrain is like beneath all that foliage, and that scares the hell out of me. Those reconnaissance photos are useless to our ground troops."

"Jacobs is right," Taggart said. "If the terrain beyond the beach is not flat, we'll have problems from the high grounds. We need much more information on the terrain before we go in."

"Our offensive strategy is based on the fact we don't expect anything other than low-lying terrain," Adams said, his face turning crimson. "We have absolutely no reason to change that strategy at this point."

Taggart tried to appear calm. "General, with your permission, let Jacobs, Jackson and me study the reconnaissance photos again. We'll let you know if we have anything more to add."

Adams ignored the suggestion from Taggart and moved his face only inches from Jacobs's face. "One thing we do know is we can concentrate all our fire power at Peleliu. We know where and when we will attack, but the Japanese don't. That, Colonel Jacobs, is always the advantage of the aggressor. The Japanese must scatter their forces across the Pacific in case we attack at some place where they are not expecting us."

Taggart jumped to Jacobs's defense. "General, in this case, there is a very definite advantage to the defender. The Japanese are fanatics. They are willing to die. They can and they will tie down our forces. Their promise of eternal life if they die for their emperor makes every battle more difficult. The closer we get to Japan itself, the more fanatical the enemy will become."

"Even if that's true," Adams argued, "the advantage we have is that we know where we'll be landing, and they don't.

Once we're ready to attack, they won't have the time or the reason to fortify the entire island."

Jacobs did his best to control his frustrations. It was apparent that Adams would not listen to their opinions, and it seemed useless to argue further, but he tried one last time to change Adams's thinking. "I still think we need to be more concerned about their air power. The Japs know why we're taking Peleliu, and they'll do everything they can to keep us from gaining the airstrip. Their medium bombers have the maneuverability, speed, and range to fly from their bases on Okinawa. Their fighter planes are the fastest and most maneuverable planes in the air. The Zero can fly over a thousand miles without refueling, which means it could fly from a carrier or a land base—a real tough opponent for our Hellcats and a definite threat to our operations."

Adams's jaw tightened. "We have the advantage of more planes and better-trained pilots. The Zero's armor is light, and the plane can become a torch if a bullet hits the fuel tank. I assure you that what our Grumman Hellcats lack in speed and maneuverability is offset by the training and capabilities of our pilots."

"In other words, all our Navy pilots have to do is aim at the fuel tank and we're safe. That's real consoling," Jacobs said, sarcasm in his voice.

"Any resistance from the Japanese air power won't be from Peleliu," Adams shouted, and threw his pencil to the table. "General MacArthur hasn't forgotten that his forces in the Philippines were hit by fighters and medium-range bombers from Peleliu, and he won't let the Japanese forget it, either. Since last March, our planes have virtually destroyed the runways and hangars there. Our photos show nothing but rubbles of steel and rock. No, by God, Peleliu is not the fighter base it was when the war started."

"Then why in the name of God are we going to Peleliu? If the fighter base is destroyed, what's the purpose in landing Marines?" Jacobs asked, his voice trembling with anger.

"Because," Adams shouted, "the Army wants the First Marine Division to take Peleliu for a fighter base for their invasion of the Philippines."

Jacobs was too angry to stop his words. "You know what I think? We're assuming everything will be in our favor, but if it's not, we could get the shit kicked out of us. That, sir, makes my asshole pucker."

There was an awkward silence as General Adams studied the remark. "Colonel Jacobs, I am told that the ship's store has a supply of assholes in the event you need another one."

The knuckles on Colonel Jacobs's clenched fists were white. "I don't suppose we need to requisition any more assholes. We already have a few too many. Present company excluded, of course."

General Adams sat very still for a moment, glaring at Jacobs. The intense pain behind his eyes blurred his vision. His face was ashen. He turned slowly in his chair and rubbed his eyes. "I only hope the enlisted men are more anxious to fight this war than, apparently, the officers are. That's all for today. I'll not further discuss your concerns about our landing. Have your men ready to board the LSTs on September 3. We weigh anchor on September 4. D-day will be September 15, and H-hour will be 0830."

When the officers left, Adams felt his way to his bunk and lay down on his back. He was nauseated, and vomited on the floor. He tried to get up, but he was too dizzy to get out of his bunk.

Outside the general's tent, Taggart motioned for Jacobs and Jackson to follow. Taggart stalked inside his tent, then wheeled around and stared into Jacobs's face. "You dumbass, what the hell got into you? You can't talk to a superior officer that way. You know that. He was too mad to think, or he would have court-martialed you on the spot. I'm surprised he didn't. You made him look like a fool in front of all of us. Don't you see what you've done?"

Jacobs's face was livid. "But you heard what he just said to us. He practically called us cowards."

Jacobs stared at Taggart and Jackson. "And he promised General Post and the entire Army that we can take Peleliu in a matter of days. Goddammit, he had no right to do that. Hell, you both know we can't take Peleliu in two or three days! The Japs will fight until they die, and that means they'll take a hell of a lot of Marines with them."

Jacobs threw his helmet to the deck and then shook his head and said, "Aw, crap, I guess I really blew it, didn't I? But dammit, he's not rational, not just about Peleliu, but about other things. I've seen him this way before. Hell, he even blames me for picking Pavuvu for our rest camp."

Jacobs continued to pace the deck of the tent and then said, "I'm scared, Ed. I'm scared and I'm concerned for the whole division. Something is *wrong* with Adams, terribly wrong, and I don't know what to do about it. He's not thinking things through. We could have major problems. I know Peleliu won't be as easy to take as he says it will. We all know it. I'll bet my ass on it."

Jackson put his hand on Jacobs's shoulder. "Al, you may have already done that. I'm afraid you've just shit in your mess gear. Adams is not one to forget."

"Well, what the hell," Jacobs said in exasperation. "Maybe I'm wrong, maybe it'll be like he said. I don't know what to do about it now. I guess we'll just wait and see how it all works out."

On the morning of September 4, 1944, an armada of ships over thirty miles long lifted anchor and sailed toward Peleliu. Sixteen thousand Marines of the First Marine Division, reinforced to over twenty-eight thousand men, crowded onto LSTs, transports, and LSDs and watched Pavuvu disappear behind the horizon. They turned their faces toward their next amphibious assault, two thousand miles away and two thousand miles closer to the Japanese Empire.

32

The Americans' relentless advance across the Pacific moved them ever closer to the Japanese homeland, and it was certain the Americans planned to invade the Philippines. The fighter base on Peleliu, a tiny coral rock in the Pacific, was strategically located for their defense, and American bombers had targeted the coral runways and bombed the military installations.

The Imperial War Command in Tokyo agreed that Peleliu must be defended at all costs, and the selection of an officer to command the forces stationed there was extremely critical. The war council searched their military roster and chose Colonel Kushi Tameichi Koturu.

Colonel Koturu's exuberance and fanatical dedication to his emperor and his country were unquestioned. He had advanced in military rank at a rapid pace, and his reputation as a brilliant officer was beyond question. The council was impressed with his uncanny astuteness in solving problems, but would have been surprised to know that before his plans were put into action, he always tried to consult with his father, Vice Admiral Naha Koturu.

In the spring of 1944, Colonel Koturu placed his most prized possession, a small photograph of his father, in the breast pocket of his uniform and left Japan with seventy-five hundred troops to reinforce the garrison of six thousand men already at Peleliu.

Major Kazuma, the senior officer on the island, was envious of Koturu's reputation and was reluctant to relinquish the status of his position to the new commanding officer. He dreaded Koturu's arrival but knew he had no choice but to accept it.

As soon as Colonel Koturu arrived at Peleliu, he requested Major Kuzuma to accompany him as he surveyed the protected northern edge of the airfield.

"As you can see, Colonel Koturu, the American bombers have destroyed our hangers and barracks. Our headquarters building is nothing but rubble."

"What about the radio and cable communication center?" Koturu asked.

"They were underground and not severely damaged."

"And the electric power plant and machine shops? Were they also underground?"

"Yes. They were damaged, but they have been repaired."

The two officers walked through the concrete boulders that had once been the two-story headquarters building. Major Kazuma stepped over a twisted mass of steel and pointed toward a massive concrete structure. "That is where our cisterns for storing rainwater are located. Our water supply is intact."

Koturu and Kazuma returned to the airfield and stood on the edge of one of the two runways. "When the Americans come, Major Kazuma, this is what they will fight to obtain, two strips of hot, white coral rock."

"And this is where they will die," Kazuma boasted.

Koturu shook his head sadly. "Yes, and so will our men. We must rebuild the airfield for our own planes, Major. It must be operational in a matter of weeks. The Americans will come. I know that. We must be prepared to defend this base at all costs."

When Koturu and Kazuma returned to the main defense bunker that Koturu had chosen as his command quarters, he asked to see a map of the island. He studied the location of the airfield, only five hundred yards from shore, and the two runways, one six thousand feet long and the other thirty-five hundred feet long.

He looked at the island and the reefs that bordered the coral atoll. "This is where the American troops will come ashore, here on the southwestern side of the island. The reef and the beaches are where we will aim our mortars and artillery." Tameichi studied the island and looked particularly at the hundreds and hundreds of caves, carved by centuries of typhoon winds. "Major Kazuma, there are changes that must be made."

Kazuma stiffened. "What changes do you propose, Colonel Koturu?"

Koturu pointed to the map. "We will use these caves in the defense of the island. Have your men install thick metal doors in them. And these, along the beach where the Americans will come ashore, must be reinforced with thick logs and coconut trees. See that the passageways are just tall enough for a man to stand."

Koturu took his pen and marked the caves farther back from the shore. "In these, change the entrances so that they have sharp turns to protect our men against flamethrowers and artillery."

Koturu looked carefully at the map. "These larger caves must be stocked with ammunition, rice, canned fish, and containers of water. Here, along the beach, tank traps are to be constructed, and land mines are to be placed along the steep slopes. Do you understand what must be done?"

Major Kazuma bowed. "Yes, Colonel Koturu. We will do as you have ordered."

Koturu surprised Kazuma with his next order. "I will commit only twenty-five hundred men to repel the landing. The rest must remain in the caves and bunkers. It is there they must fight to the end."

Major Kazuma frowned. "Colonel, our garrison now has over thirteen thousand men. Is it wise to have so few to defend the landing? Should we not have more soldiers to keep the Americans from our shore?"

"The Americans will come ashore. We cannot keep them from doing that, but we can fight the enemy from the caves and bunkers. The enemy will pay dearly for every step he takes."

Major Kazuma bowed again and turned to leave. "Major," Koturu called, "I must have your help. You must trust me. It is the only way."

During the next three months, under the watchful eye of Tameichi Koturu, Peleliu turned into an island fortress.

In early September, Koturu ordered Major Kazuma to assemble the garrison on the two runways of the airfield. "Have them there tomorrow, just before sunrise, facing toward Japan and toward the rising sun."

Koturu waited until just before dawn to climb a tall platform, and when he reached the top, he looked down on a sea of faces. Over thirteen thousand soldiers stood at attention. He waited until he saw the first glow of the sun on the horizon before he spoke.

"Soon the enemy will come to these shores. We have prepared our defenses as best we can, and we can do no more. When the enemy is on the horizon, you must be brave. When the enemy comes ashore, we must fight to defend the beaches, and then we must fight from the caves and ridges. We must defend every inch, every foot, and we must fight with all the courage we can bring forth from our hearts, and then…we must fight until there are none of us left."

The sun's rays streaked through the sky, and Koturu had timed his words for just this moment. "Now," he shouted.

"Now, my soldiers, we must dedicate our lives to the emperor and to Japan. And now," he shouted as loud as he could, "now is the moment to offer your soul to Buddha. Banzai! Banzai! Banzai!"

The crescendo of voices shouting banzai increased until it was a roar. Koturu saluted the thirteen thousand Japanese soldiers who were willing to die for their emperor, climbed down from the tower, and joined his men to wait for the Marines of the First Division.

"Commence firing!" Admiral Higgins flashed the order, and at 0530, September 13, the Navy guns blasted the white coral beaches with thousands of shells, stripping the inland hills and valleys of their jungle cover.

For the next two days, Dauntless bombers dropped napalm canisters that opened in red bursts and scorched the earth, and Hellcats fired their .50-caliber machine guns while screeching rockets splattered the white rock below.

Adams tried to focus his binoculars on the distant island, but the smoke from the bombs hid the land from his view. "No return fire from shore. That's good." Adams smiled triumphantly. "After two days of shelling like that, the Japs won't fight very long. I knew they couldn't withstand our naval barrage."

At 0830, September 15, D-day, Adams signaled the landing assault to begin. In a flurry of activity, LCMs, LSTs, assault personnel armoreds (APAs), LCTs, and auxiliary dock personnels (ADPs) unloaded men and equipment. Marines crawled down cargo nets into bobbing Higgins boats. Two thousand yards from the island, the men transferred from the Higgins boats into waiting amtracks, and then the first wave of infantrymen crossed the barrier reef and headed for land. DUKWs, vehicles aptly named for their ability to travel on land and sea, and specially equipped with rockets, began leaving the ships and joined with the assault waves. Operation Stalemate was underway.

Pfc. Billy Harris sat huddled in the amtrack with other infantrymen from I Company, Thirrd Battalion, Seventh

Marines. He watched the faces of his friends crouched beside him. This was the first combat experience for some of them, and they tried not to show the fear inside.

The smell of diesel and the rocking motion of the amtrack had already made one of the men sick, and Billy knew how the chain reaction would begin. Soon they would all be vomiting on each other.

He remembered how it had been when he and Donald Woodson went into combat for the first time at Cape Gloucester. Then, as now, he had been in the first wave, and for a moment, he thought about Donald, how fearful he had been, how sick they had all been, how the first sight of death had changed so many, and on that first day, how the war had robbed them of their youth.

Here, as on Cape Gloucester, the first wave would be riflemen, and behind them in the second wave, more riflemen and machine gunners, followed by men carrying heavy flamethrowers, gunners with bulky bazookas, and finally, men carrying the 60 mm mortars. As it was then, some would not live through the day.

Billy closed his eyes and tried to shut out the noise of the churning tracks. His body swayed with the motion of the amtrack as it dipped into the waves. He felt no fear, only apprehension. In his mind's eye, he pictured the beach ahead, and he could almost hear the explosion of the dreaded mortar shells on the coral beach that awaited them. His thoughts returned to the last invasion, when his platoon had been dumped into the churning water, yards from shore. They had fought the sea to gain the land, swallowing salty sea water while gulping for air.

At Cape Gloucester, he had killed to keep from being killed. He would always feel that was not right, but it was his only means of survival. He wondered if the memories would haunt him for the rest of his life. He knew the war had forever changed him, and he had aged beyond his years, transformed from a boy into a man. He felt the assault craft slow its thrust and knew shore was only a few yards away. He took a deep breath and waited for the killing to begin again.

The range of the Japanese mortars and field weapons had been predetermined, and the accuracy of their aim made direct hits on many of the amtracks, and moments later, bodies of Marines floated in the foaming sea. A mortar shell exploded just as one amtrack touched land, and the survivors staggered through the shallow water and ran across the coral sand. Panicked and confused, the men lost contact with their officers and gathered in shell holes and waited for orders.

On White Beach One and Orange Beach Three, the Japanese troops remained hidden in the fortified caves and camouflaged bunkers covered with fallen coconut trees. They waited until the first wave of Marines stepped on the beach, and then opened with a deadly burst of fire. The Japanese shelling intensified, and many of the Marines fell in the sand as they stepped from the landing craft.

As soon as the amtracks were unloaded, the drivers frantically turned from the beaches and raced back across the coral reef. Higgins boats waited just beyond the reef to unload the next group of infantrymen. Casualties mounted, and fewer amtracks joined the circle of boats. Higgins boats rammed the sides of other boats, and mortar shells dropped among the helpless Marines.

Sgt. Wally Smith, I Company, Seventh, in the first amtrack to land on Orange Beach Three, stepped into the churning water and sand. He was the first to see the Japanese troops leave their caves and bunkers to man their guns.

Smith yelled, "Git off'n tha beach. Move up! Move up!" He grabbed the dungaree collar of one of the frightened men, and pulled him from the crater. They ran toward the first cliff that would offer more protection from the shells and mortars falling along the water's edge.

Billy Harris clutched his M-1 rifle and followed Smith across the hostile shore. "Come on," he yelled, "do what Sarge says. Move up! Let's go!"

He stumbled and fell into a bomb crater, still hot and smoking from the impact of the exploding shell. Other Marines crouched in the shell crater, too frightened to move.

"Come on, get up! Get off the beach," Harris yelled.

When he crawled from the crater, the other men followed. They ran toward a steep cliff a hundred yards away. and when they reached the cliff, they flattened their bodies against the smoldering coral.

Twenty yards ahead, Captain Brit, I Company, crouched against the same coral ridge. A piece of shrapnel grazed his arm and tore away part of his jacket. He squinted in the growing haze, motioning for the sergeant to move his men further inland, and Smith nodded that he understood.

On Orange Beach One, a mortar shell exploded near Sergeant Tucker, King, and Pappas as they ran ashore. They jumped into a shell hole as .50-caliber bullets kicked the coral rocks around them. Devastating fire from hidden caves raked the shore, and in a matter of minutes, as far as the eye could see, the beaches were littered with bodies and wounded men.

When Mack Williams, Gil Everson, and Boog Marshall came ashore, they jumped over fallen comrades and raced across the beach. All along the glistening sand, frightened men filled shell holes and waited for a chance to run toward the inland ridge.

A mortar shell exploded two hundred feet to the left of where they lay, and then another, and another, and with each succeeding shell, the sound of exploding shells come closer.

Everson lay with his head in the sand and heard the whistling sound of a mortar shell. "Son of a bitch, they're getting closer."

Sand and rock showered them, and Gil raised his head to see the smoking coral. "Mack, we can't stay here. The Japs have the range. They're getting closer!"

Mack shouted, "Let's get out of here."

"Which way?" Gil yelled.

"Hell who cares, just run," Mack screamed.

The two men, oblivious to the danger about them, ran as fast as they could across the soft wet sand. They were too scared to know they were running directly toward a Japanese machine gun.

Sergeant Tucker heard the staccato fire of the Nambu machine gun and stared at Mack and Gil running toward the enemy caves.

"Look at that!" Tucker yelled. "That's what I call courage! They're not afraid of anything. They're running right at the Japs! Come on, men, let's show them we're with them!"

Mack and Gil ran for over a hundred yards, unaware they were several yards ahead of the nearest Marine. When they came to a cliff they couldn't climb, they fell to the ground and gasped for their breath.

Tucker ran to where Gil and Mack lay on the ground by the cliff. "Damn." He grinned and slapped Everson on the back. "I'm proud of you and Mack. You led the way, we'd still be on the beach if it weren't for you." Tucker pointed to the men coming toward them. "Here come the rest, now we'll show those Japs how a Marine fights." He scrambled to his feet and ran toward the next coral cliff.

Mack looked at Gil. "What the hell was he talking about?"

"Beats me. He said something about us leading the way. If I was leading the way, I didn't know it. Did you?"

"Just keep it to yourself, Gil, just keep it to yourself," Mack laughed. He grabbed his rifle and got to his feet. "I don't know about you, but I'm through leading."

Aboard the command ship, General Adams looked through his binoculars at the barrier reef protecting the shore. "Oh my God, that shouldn't be," he whispered.

He was horrified to see the Japanese artillery shells crashing into the Higgins boats filled with Marines. Amtracks exploded as mortar shells found their mark.

Adams kept adjusting his binoculars, trying to see the landing beaches through the early morning light and the haze and smoke from the phosphorous shells. He could just see the steep hills, coral ridges, and sheer cliffs.

Adams's hands were shaking. "The aerial photographs didn't show any of that! Oh God."

On shore, Sergeant Smith witnessed the massacre of his men. He inched forward, staying as close to the ground as he could. Billy Harris crawled over the cutting sand, not feeling the pain in his bleeding hands.

The second wave of Marines with 60 mm mortars now reached the shore and raced to a spot where they could set up their weapons, and soon, their shells rumbled over the heads of the advancing front line of Marine infantrymen.

Progress was slow across the deep crevices, and each time a man tried to move, a Nambu machine gun fired. Eventually, riflemen crawled near enough to throw grenades, and finally, searing tongues of fire from the flamethrowers licked the openings of the caves and bunkers. The coughing sound of mortars and streaks of tracer bullets from machine guns joined in the battle against the entrenched Japanese soldiers, and foot by foot, the Marines advanced. All through the morning, they fought their way across the rugged terrain. By noon, the temperature reached 120 degrees, and the stifling heat began to take its toll. Coral dust from artillery fire floated in the air and filtered the scorching sun.

Boog Marshall wiped his forehead with the sleeve of his dungaree and pulled the back of his helmet cover down over his neck. His eyes burned, and his lips were parched, and he licked them with his tongue. He gulped the last swallow of water from his canteen and held it above his mouth, waiting for the last drop to fall. He crawled over the sun-heated coral rock to where Mack lay.

"Mack, you got any water left in your canteen?"

"Not much. I saved some. I remembered the time in boot camp when the Corporal Allen made us do without water. You got any left?"

"I drank all mine. I'm dehydrated, and I'm having stomach cramps. I'm about to throw up. I gotta find some water."

Boog crawled to where a dead Marine lay and unfastened

the man's canteen from its pouch. He shook the canteen. It was almost full. "You don't need this, but I do." He put the canteen to his lips, and the water, hot from the blazing heat, burned his throat as he swallowed. Boog wiped his lips with the back of his hands and looked at the dead Marine. "Thanks, fellow."

When the shadows faded, the longest day eventually turned to night, and the exhausted Marines blessed the cover of darkness and the absence of the blistering heat.

"Get foxholes dug," Tucker instructed George Company. "We're staying here till morning. It ain't as hot at night, but that's when the Japs will come out of their caves and try to infiltrate our lines. Don't be surprised to see one of them in your foxhole with you before the night is over. If one does come into our position, don't do any more shooting than you have to 'cause you're just as apt to shoot one of your own men as you are to shoot the enemy. Fight with your knife and your hands."

Mack and Gil dug foxholes in the hard rock and waited. They listened to the staccato sound of a .30-caliber machine gun just beyond the next ridge and heard the sharp bark of an M-1 rifle punctuate the night. The enemy returned the fire with their guns and mortars, and after a moment, the flash from the 105 mm howitzers of the Eleventh Marines pierced the darkness, and the night air was shattered by the sound of the shells exploding against the coral rocks where the Japanese waited.

Mack watched the yellow cast of light from an illuminating flare float down toward their foxholes. "Don't move," he cautioned. "Snipers will shoot at anything that moves."

The parachute flare swung back and forth, and each stump and boulder caught in the eerie glare cast a shadow that transformed every object into a crawling Japanese soldier, attempting to infiltrate the American lines.

From a distant cave, the Japanese began firing their 90 mm mortars into the Marine positions. The shells landed just beyond where Mack and Gil lay side by side in the shallow foxholes dug in the white coral rock.

"My hole isn't as deep as yours. Wanna trade for a while?" Gil whispered. After he waited for an answer, he joked, "I guess that snickering sound means you won't trade."

A shell exploded a few feet from their foxhole. Mack felt a stinging sensation on his left ear, and when he touched his ear, the tip was missing.

Another shell exploded, and a piece of shrapnel hit Mack in the upper thigh,

"Oh, I'm hit!" he cried.

"Are you hit bad? Where?"

"The top of my ear and my leg. I can't tell how bad," Mack moaned. He felt his trousers. "I can't feel any blood on my leg. I can't feel any pain."

"Maybe it went clear through your leg and it's numb," Gil said.

"Yeah, and maybe part of my leg is blown off," Mack sobbed.

"Can you feel it? Is it there?"

"I'm afraid to see," Mack groaned and slowly moved his hand down his leg. "My leg is still here, but there's no pain."

"How do you know you've been hit if you can't feel any pain?" Gil asked.

"Hell, I felt something hit my leg, that's how I know."

He felt something hot on his thigh and held up a piece of jagged shrapnel. "Here's what hit me, a piece of shrapnel. It didn't even tear my dungarees. How about that for luck?"

"You're lucky, all right. We're both lucky to have missed those mortars," Gil answered. "I'm glad it's almost daylight. I don't like the dark. The thought of a Jap crawling in my foxhole scared the hell out of me."

Mack cocked his head to one side and listened. "Gil, do you hear what I hear?"

"Oh my God," Gil answered. "Jap fighter planes. They're coming in to strafe."

"No, look! They're Navy Corsairs," Mack shouted, and waved at the gull-winged, blue F4U's that streaked overhead.

Gil scrambled to his feet and waved with both arms. "That's the best sight I've ever seen."

The planes dived toward the Japanese bunkers and dropped half-ton bombs, then the pilots returned for a strafing run, their six machine guns shooting a constant stream of .50-caliber bullets into the Japanese lines.

Gil shouted, "Give 'em hell," and started laughing. Suddenly, he stopped laughing and looked around him.

He frowned and, with a puzzled look on his face, whispered, "Hey, where is everybody?"

Mack slowly rose to his feet. "No one's here!" He grabbed for his rifle. "I don't know about you, but I've led all the attacks I intend to. I'm getting the hell out of here."

The two men jumped out of their foxholes and raced back toward the rear lines.

"Halt!" a voice shouted ahead of them, and Mack and Gil fell to the ground.

Manny King lowered his rifle from his shoulder. "Mack! Gil! Is that you? I nearly shot you. Where the hell have y'all been? Tucker ordered us to pull back last night. Didn't you get the word?"

"You mean we were on the front lines? All alone?" Mack asked.

"It's a wonder you didn't have a Jap in your foxhole," Manny snickered.

Gil took off his helmet and scratched his head. "What are we going to tell Sarge? He'll chew us out if he hears we didn't get the word."

Mack thought a minute. "We'll tell him we've been out scouting the enemy lines."

33

Darkness covered the island of Peleliu on D-day, and General Adams, still aboard his command ship three miles offshore, waited for the casualty report from each of his regimental commanders. He paced the deck and rubbed his forehead.

"Sir," a voice said, "the reports are..."

"Give them to me," Adams interrupted and grabbed the papers from the lieutenant's hand.

Adams stared at the reports from Colonel Jacobs, Colonel Taggart, and Lieutenant Colonel Jackson. He shook his head in disbelief. "My God," he whispered, "92 killed, 58 missing, 1,148 wounded. The casualties in just this first day are almost as many as we took the entire Cape Gloucester campaign."

Adams looked at the lieutenant. "There's...only a handful

of men…left…in some companies." He swallowed hard and walked across his stateroom, fiercely pulling at his lower lip. "This isn't the way it was supposed to be. Oh my God, my God," he cried softly. Adams closed his eyes and rubbed his temples. His head throbbed, and the pain intensified.

The lieutenant said nothing and backed out of the room.

Lieutenant Brown, H Company, and Captain Burleson, Easy Company, sat on a rocky ledge, talking in hushed voices. Captain Slator, George Company, and Captain Flint, Fox Company, stood beside them. Flint's dungaree trousers were ripped from the near miss of a piece of shrapnel in the landing the day before, and Slator's helmet was dented by a spent rifle bullet. He rubbed his fingers along the barrel of his .30-caliber carbine and waited for Colonel Taggart to speak.

"We've been ordered to enlarge the perimeter of control around the airfield and to secure the northern sector," Taggart began. "The lead group in the assault will be Captain Slator's George Company. Captain Flint, your company will be on his right flank. Lieutenant Brown, your company will move to the left flank, advance across the lower end of the strip, and then swing north along the base of the first ridge. Captain Burleson, Easy Company took some pretty heavy casualties in the landing, and I'm keeping you in reserve."

He studied his men carefully. "When all three companies move out, you'll have tank support to back you up as you cross the open runways. Continue toward the northern end of the airstrip. If our preinvasion shelling was effective, you might not get enemy fire from the higher ground beyond the airstrip, but don't count on that too much. Keep me advised at all time. I'll order more tanks and artillery if they're needed. Easy Company can be called up when needed. That's all for now. Meet with your NCOs and prepare your men. You've got a couple of hours before daylight."

The officers turned to leave, and Taggart spoke again, "The landing yesterday was tough. The taking of Peleliu won't be easy."

Dawn's light was just beginning to appear when Mack Williams and Gil Everson followed Sergeant Tucker across the airstrip. Shermans from the First Tank Battalion with armor-piercing 75 mm cannon and .50-caliber machine guns clanked out on the runway. Armor-plated landing vehicle tank-armored (LVT-A) amtracks, mounted with flamethrowers that could squirt a stream of fire over two hundred feet, lumbered behind.

When Pappas and King neared the open area surrounding the airfield, small arms fire, rifle and machine gun bullets came from hundreds of caves. Corporal Everson trotted behind a Sherman tank, and enemy bullets flicked the coral dust on the ground around him. A Japanese machine gun opened fire from the far side of the airstrip, and three Marines running behind Gil fell to their knees, then pitched forward on their faces in the gravel rocks. Everson, Williams, and Pappas, blinded by the smoke and dust, crowded as close as they could to the side of the tank.

"Keep moving," shouted Tucker. "Stay close."

The tank commanders turned their cannons toward the first ridge and fired shells into the rocky terrain. The Eleventh Marine Artillery Division joined in the barrage, and the Japanese moved their men and weapons back into the protection of the caves.

The temperature was over a hundred degrees already and continued to climb, reaching 115. The searing heat from the sun's rays burned their faces, and the reflection off the white coral rocks burned their feet. When the machine gunners and mortar men carried their weapons on their shoulders, the metal was so hot it burned their hands. They ripped off pieces of their dungarees and folded the material under their weapons to keep the hot metal from blistering their skin.

The push toward the more fortified north end of the airfield began, and Marine F4U Corsair fighters and Dauntless dive-bombers began their air strikes, dropping bombs and strafing the enemy positions in the concrete rubble of the control tower. The bombardment was deafening, and bombs and shells exploded just ahead of the advancing Marines. The Corsairs strafed one end of the airstrip while other planes landed on the secured end of the strip and loaded more bombs for the next run. Tanks and riflemen, aided by the smoke screen of phosphorous shells from the mortar group, moved forward.

By nightfall of D plus two, the Fifth Regiment secured the airfield and reached their first objective in the invasion of Peleliu.

By the morning of D plus three, George Company reached the far end of the airstrip, and Williams and Pappas took cover in the wooded area to the northeast. Grotesque stumps were all that remained of the trees and brush. Rocks broken into smaller fragments from hot coral and sand from the pounding of thousands of shells covered the bodies of Japanese soldiers scattered in the rubble of concrete and steel.

Pappas held his nose. "Whew, they stink."

Williams made a face and looked at the bloated body of a dead soldier. "You'd stink, too, if you'd been dead in this hot sun for two days."

Tucker knelt beside Captain Slator and squinted at the rocky ridge beyond the airstrip. "It's too dark to climb the hill now, Captain. We should wait till daylight."

Slator rubbed the stubble of beard. "Yeah, we have some protection where we are. Set up trip flares around the perimeter; the Japs might decide to make a counterattack during the night. At daylight I'll get our 60 mm mortars to shell the ridge. We'll move up on my command."

Dawn lifted the darkness around them, and Williams, Pappas, Everson, and King waited at the bottom of the rocky hill.

"Anybody seen Boog?" Manny asked.

Gil motioned with his head. "Over there. He's still asleep. How he can sleep at a time like this beats me."

"Probably dreaming of that Mexican gal he's always talking about," Pappas said.

King pointed at the ridge ahead of them. "Even in this light, I can see caves up there. Tucker said that's what we gotta take."

Tucker walked through his platoon, looking at his men. "Just hold here until I give you the word. Everson, don't you and Williams get gung ho and charge the hill until I give the order."

Mack ducked his head and looked under his helmet at Gil. "I sure hate to hear that, don't you, Gil?"

"Yeah don't I," Gil replied.

The 60 mm mortars began shelling the upper terrain, and Slator motioned to Tucker. "Sergeant, if your men are ready, start them up the ridge."

Tucker nodded. "All right, Captain, we're as ready as we'll ever be."

Tucker motioned for his riflemen to start their climb, and the attack on the caves and enemy positions began.

Pappas and Williams were the first to start climbing, and when they reached the first cave, Pappas pulled a hand grenade from his belt and pulled the pin. He counted to three and tossed the grenade into the opening. When the smoke and dust settled, Mack fanned the dust from his face. He spit the coral dust from his mouth and looked toward Pappas.

"You going to see what's in there?"

"You want to go first?" Pappas answered.

"No." Mack shook his head. "You."

Pappas shrugged his shoulders and crawled slowly on his hands and knees through the entrance. The room was still filled with smoke, but Pappas counted four enemy soldiers crumpled on the floor of the cave. He crawled out of the cave and saw Everson kneeling beside the entrance of another cave.

"Nothing alive in this one," Gil said. "They smell like they've been dead a couple of days."

Williams looked toward the cliff up above. "Yeah, but there's more caves. There'll be some live ones up there."

Colonel Tameichi Koturu lay on the ground just inside the entrance to one of the caves on the highest part of the ridge. He breathed deeply and watched the Marines climb the foothills of the ridge where over three hundred of his men waited. His cave, like many of the others on the ridge, was constructed with a long tunnel and a concealed exit that opened into the next valley.

The sweat began to roll down his forehead and into his eyes. He pulled a rag from his pocket and wiped away the salty moisture. He took his binoculars from their case, and with the same dirty rag he used for his face, he wiped the white dust from the lens.

From where he lay, he had full view of the approaching men. He searched their uniforms, moving from one to the next, hoping to find an officer's insignia. He decided he would wait for just the right moment, and when he saw ten Marines grouped in one area, he signaled for his men to open fire.

Bullets whined and ricocheted off the rocky slope, and mortar shells exploded among the advancing Marines. Everson and Williams leaped behind a large boulder for protection.

"Can you see where the shots came from, Mack?"

Mack squinted into the blazing sun and then looked down and rubbed his eyes. "Damn, that sun will cook your eyes if you look at it."

Gil's hands were shaking. "I can't see to shoot."

Down below, 60 mm mortars started firing, and the shells shattered the scraggly rocks above their heads.

Mack ducked his head as pieces of coral fell around them. "Son of a bitch, those shells are close."

Pappas and Manny, thirty feet to the right, huddled behind a boulder.

A Japanese soldier stepped from a cave only a few feet away and raised his rifle to his shoulder.

"Look out," Pappas yelled.

Manny lunged at the soldier's feet, and they fell to the ground and rolled down the slope. Manny tried to pull his K-bar knife from its scabbard, but it slipped from his hands and rolled down the coral ridge.

Mack watched Manny and the Japanese soldier wrestling near the edge of the steep cliff, and when he saw Manny's knife fall from his hands, he started sliding down the rocky ledge toward them.

Manny wrestled on top and pushed the soldier's face into the coral rock as hard as he could. He struggled to his feet and grabbed the barrel of the soldier's rifle and jerked it from his grip.

Manny swung the rifle like a club, and when the butt of the rifle crashed down on the soldier's neck, he screamed in pain and tried to get to his feet. Manny swung his club again, and the impact cracked the soldier's skull, and he pitched to the ground and lay still.

Manny raised the rifle above his head once more, then stopped and slowly lowered it. He gasped for breath, then looked at the bloody weapon in his hands. Part of the stock had split from the impact. Manny threw it to the ground in disgust and stared at his hands. He wiped them on his dungarees and looked at Williams standing beside him.

Williams saw the look on Manny's face. "I know, Manny. He would have killed all of us. You had to do it."

Manny fell to his knees, and began to vomit.

All through the day, the four friends fought side by side on the rocky slope. As each cave was located, grenades and dynamite charges were thrown into the openings, and by day's end, the caves and the Japanese soldiers who had defended them were destroyed.

Some of Slator's men were barely able to stand. Their eyes were wide, and their faces showed the strain of the deadly fight. The sooty gray coral ash had turned the green Marine dungarees into a bleached, lifeless color, and the sharp coral rocks had torn and ripped their boondockers.

Slator turned when he heard Tucker's voice behind him. "We won, Captain."

"Yes, we did. Take the men to the edge of the airstrip. Colonel Taggart is sending Third Battalion up for relief."

Corporals Williams and Everson, Pappas, and King, walked toward the rear lines, too exhausted to know if the blood on their jackets was their own or that from the enemy soldiers who lay nearby. Salty sweat hardened the shoulders of their torn and bloody jackets. Uncontrolled stains of urine and bowel movements showed on their pants legs.

They passed a row of Marines, covered with ponchos, lying on the ground, and Pappas looked down at a young Marine, still untanned from the tropical sun.

"Manny, he's about the age of my younger brother back home." Pappas looked away to keep Manny from seeing the tears in his eyes.

General Adams ordered Lieutenant Colonel Jackson to report to him.

"Colonel, I'm not happy with the way things are going. We've got to secure this island right away. I promised General MacArthur he'd have the airfield for his invasion of the Philippines. I want the First Regiment to continue their assault on the ridges along the western shore and then sweep eastward. You've got to join up with the Seventh on the northern end of the island, and I want you to go from one ridge to the next, clearing out all pockets of Japanese defenders. Do you understand?"

"General, we're moving ahead as fast as we can."

"It's not fast enough."

For the next three days, the First Regiment continued to encounter strong resistance from the Japanese defenders, and casualties mounted. In just three days, the First Regiment had more than twelve hundred killed or wounded, almost equal to the division's total casualties after fighting for 123 days to capture Guadalcanal.

By the end of D plus six, the First Regiment had suffered so many casualties that Lieutenant Colonel Jackson met with General Adams and handed him a report.

"General," Jackson said, "two of my three infantry battalions lack the manpower to continue fighting, and my third battalion is both physically and mentally incapable of further combat. My men have fought every hour of every day since they've landed, and they're sick with malaria and dysentery. Some of them have sores and jungle rot on their legs and feet. I can't ask anything more of them. They've given all they can. I'm making a formal request that the First Regiment be pulled from the lines. It's all in the report." He added, "For the record."

General Adams stiffened. "It was not necessary for you to send a copy to CinCPac. I will determine when one of my regiments will be relieved, and until the island is secured, your regiment will stay. Your request to be relieved from the front line is denied."

On the afternoon of September 20, Adams was informed that CinCPac had ordered the Army's RCT 321st of the Eighty-first Division on Angaur to begin loading LSTs to replace the First Regiment on Peleliu.

Adams, believing CinCPac's order had been instigated by the casualty report from Jackson, was furious that his authority had been undermined. When the Army came ashore the next morning, Adams reluctantly ordered the First Regiment be relieved from combat.

Jackson's regiment, with its ranks decimated by disease and thinned by Japanese fire, returned to Purple Beach One for transportation back to Pavuvu.

The general was determined not to let the Army's Eighty-first Division win the battle of Peleliu and sent orders to Colonel Jacobs: "The Seventh Regiment is hereby assigned the responsibility of securing the northern part of the island. You are to encircle the remaining Japanese defenders and advance to the west and to the south."

The Seventh Regiment was entrenched along the southern edge of the highest coral cliffs. The ridges were strangely quiet, and the officers took advantage of the calm to evaluate their position.

Captain Brit, I Company, looked toward the scorched hills where vegetation once covered the uneven and tortuous terrain.

Sgt. Wally Smith watched Captain Brit. "Shore do look quiet, don't it, Cap'n? Ya'd think there's nothin' up there a'tall. Them friggin' Japs are purty good 'bout stayin' in tha caves till they wanna come out. Ah'll give 'em credit fer that. When things git quiet, they git dangerous, and them ridges are gonna be dangerous."

Brit nodded his head. "Yeah, they're dangerous. The Japs in those caves will fight until they die, and some of us will die with them."

"Now Cap'n," Smith said, "some of us will, but ah guess if'n ah'm gonna be one, ah sure 'ntend ta take as many with me as ah kin, and ah figure ta git at least a dozen or so, jist ta make it more even for the rest of muh platoon."

"We'll find out tomorrow, I guess. Keep plenty of guards posted, Sergeant." Brit walked away.

Smith returned to his men and sat down beside Pfc. Harris. Smith watched Harris clean his M-1, watched the quick and knowledgeable way he put the parts back together. "Harris," he said, "ya still write that li'l gal back home? Tha one ya show'd me tha picture of back on Cape Gloucester? What was her name?"

Billy grinned, "Laura. Laura Bently," he said.

"That's uh pretty name," Smith said.

"Yeah. She's a pretty girl," Billy said. "I look at her picture a lot, but it got wet a long time ago, so it's not very good, but I can still see her the way she looked when I told her good-bye. I write her every chance I get. Of course, I haven't had a chance since we left ship, but I will as soon as we get some place where it's kinda quiet, and I have a moment to think about her. I just can't start writing what I want to write. I got to think a while, then I don't always say what I really want to say. You know what I mean? Do you have that problem, Sarge?"

Smith rubbed his chin. "Ah guess ah do. Ah'm not much good at writin' either."

"Sarge," Billy said, "you've never said anything about your girl, or maybe your wife. You mind me asking about that?"

"Nah, ah don't mind. Ah had a gal once, a long time ago, back when ah played football in college."

"What happened to her? Do you still write to her?" Billy asked.

"Nah, she married uh cheerleader 'stead of me." He laughed. "Ah guess ah wasn't her type."

"Harris," he said after a moment. "Yore a good gyrene. Stay lucky, ya hear, so's ya kin git back ta that purty li'l gal back home."

Adams was acutely aware he had promised a swift victory in the capture of Peleliu. On D plus twelve, September 27, Adams advised Lt. General Frederick Post that the American flag had been raised over the cinder block headquarters building of the First Marine Division. The Marine line officers knew the fighting for control of the island was far from over, as did Colonel Kushi Tameichi Koturu, commanding officer of the Japanese forces on Peleliu.

34

Colonel Tameichi Koturu used the cover of the night to move his men from cave to cave and bunker to bunker, instructing his unit leaders of the next day's plans.

Koturu reduced the daily food ration for his men to one bowl of rice and a few pieces of dried fish. Water, generally stale and dirty, was available, but in small portions.

The Japanese colonel slept little and used his uncanny awareness of the strengths and weaknesses of the Marine battalions to determine how to slow the Americans in their ceaseless battle for control of Peleliu.

A reinforcement of five hundred troops from the Japanese garrison on Babelthuap slipped ashore to join the main forces on Peleliu, and Tameichi Koturu advised Tokyo that the

Marines had not captured his island of rugged coral ridges and tortuous valleys.

In the second week, monsoon rains added to the misery of the Marines on the front lines. Steam arose as the rain fell on the hot coral rocks, and smoke from exploding phosphorous shells, made putrid from the stench of decaying bodies, made breathing difficult.

Each morning, General Adams sent the same orders to Colonel Taggart and Colonel Jacobs: "Move up with maximum fire power and continue to advance."

On the evening of October 4, Colonel Jacobs made a decision. He knew the men in his battalions who remained from the initial landing were mentally and physically unfit to fight any longer. Many of his men had diarrhea, and greenish blue flies were their constant companions. There had been almost fifty percent casualties, and Jacobs knew the survivors had dodged death too often and were so fatigued they could no longer fight or defend themselves.

On the morning of October 5, Adams received a report marked "Urgent and Confidential" from Jacobs: "Absolutely urgent that I meet with you. The outcome of Peleliu Campaign is dependent on confidential matter, signed Colonel Alfred Jacobs, Regimental Commander, Seventh Regiment. cc: CinCPac"

Jacobs did not wait for a reply before he jumped in his jeep and sped across the rocky road toward the general's command post. The jeep stopped, and the white dust from the bumpy road settled like falling snow, covering Jacobs with fine powder. Jacobs brushed the dust from his arms, climbed from the jeep, and walked toward the general's private quarters.

He waited at the entrance of the tent, unsure if he should enter without being ordered to do so. He looked inside the tent and saw that the general was alone. Jacobs walked through the entrance and stood before his commanding officer. There was silence for a moment, then Adams, pretending to ignore the purpose of the visit, said, "Come in, Colonel Jacobs. Your request to see me, I assume, is as urgent as you said it would be?"

"Yes, sir, I'm making a formal request that the Seventh Regiment be relieved from further combat. A casualty report and a status of my regiment's strength is included. It should be clear that my regiment is far too undermanned to be effective in further combat. Some of my companies are down to half strength, and the survivors are in no condition to fight any longer."

"War is hell, isn't it, Colonel?" Adams said arrogantly.

Jacobs ignored the comment. "We're in about the same condition as the First when they were relieved, maybe much worse. We haven't had as many killed, and probably not as many physically wounded, but my men are mentally beat. My officers tell me some of their men are about to go 'Asiatic' on them. They've been on the lines too long without relief. The Army is here. Why not have them give my men relief?"

Adams rose from his chair, his face crimson with anger. "Colonel, it's not your responsibility to tell me when or where the Army will relieve your regiment, and for you to compare your losses to those of the First Regiment has no bearing on when or if I order you from the front. The taking of this island is our responsibility, and by God, I will not allow the Army to come in at this late date and take credit for doing something we were assigned to do. Your request is denied."

Jacobs stood for a moment, the muscles in his jaw tightening. He moved closer to Adams. "General, I respectfully request that you reconsider. I know you earlier denied Colonel Jackson's request, but CinCPac rescinded your order. You reconsidered, shall I say, when the Eighty-first Army was ordered to occupy First Regiment's front line position. Just so we understand each other, a copy of my request has been forwarded to CinCPac. They will see the casualty list and the status of my battalions—what's left of them. I believe they'll understand the Seventh has given all that should be expected of them, and if they are not relieved from the front, many will be killed needlessly, not because they won't fight, but because they can't."

Jacobs took another step toward Adams. "General, if you order my men to stay on the front lines, CinCPac will overrule you. We both know that. I wouldn't think a brigadier general would want his combat orders overruled."

Adams glared at Jacobs. "Colonel, you will not talk to me that way. You can be court-martialed for insubordination for this. You know that, don't you?"

"No sir, I don't, but if it comes to that, I'll go before a court-martial and tell them what I've said to you. If you don't relieve my regiment from combat, I'll ask General Post for a hearing, and you and I will go before him and his staff. If that happens, our careers could be finished, but I'll take that chance if I can save the lives of my troops. The choice is yours. Either relieve my men from the lines or press charges against me. And General," Jacobs said, "if you're thinking of relieving me of duty and keeping my men on the lines, I suggest you reconsider that also. I hope you don't command me to do that."

Adams was livid with rage. He stalked across his tent, fiercely pulling at his lower lip. "And if I should give that command, what would you do?"

"Don't take that chance, sir," Jacobs said in a soft, almost inaudible voice.

Adams looked into Jacobs's eyes for a long moment. "Colonel Jacobs, you are…as of this moment, commanded to…" He paused and walked to the other side of the tent. He turned to face Col. Jacobs. "You are commanded…to return the Seventh Regiment to…Purple Beach One, and as soon as transportation is arranged, board ship to return to Pavuvu." His face sagged. "I will advise the Army to begin replacing your men on the lines. The Seventh Regiment is hereby relieved of further action, only…and I mean only…after the Army has taken over your position. You may go now."

Jacobs stormed from the tent, and Adams slumped on the end of his cot. His breathing was heavy, and he gasped for air.

He fell back on his cot. The pain behind his eyes was excruciating and made him sick. He gagged and the vomit covered his clean dungaree jacket.

The Japanese forces had withstood the bombardment from the Eleventh Artillery, and the Marine Second Battalion, Fifth, was ordered to assault one of the steeper ridges.

Mack and Gil walked side by side toward the front, searching for a familiar face in the line of Marines from the Third Battalion, Seventh, returning to Purple Beach.

"Hey, there's Billy Harris," Mack shouted and ran toward his friend.

"It is Billy!" Gil exclaimed.

Billy grabbed his friends around their necks. "Boy, am I glad to see y'all," he cried. "I didn't know if you were still alive. Gosh, it's good to see both of you."

"We didn't know about you either, and I couldn't tell for sure if that was you, but when I saw those size eleven boondockers, I knew it had to be," Gil kidded.

Billy grinned. "Me and my size eleven boondockers have had all of Peleliu we want. Guess you heard the Army has taken over our lines and we're returning to Pavuvu?"

"Yeah, and I wish we were going with you," Mack replied. "Sergeant Tucker said we weren't shot up enough to be relieved. Where we're going won't be a picnic, and when we finish, maybe we'll qualify for relief. Some joke, isn't it?"

"Sergeant Smith said the Fifth will be relieved any day now. Heck, you have to be relieved soon, the Fifth is the only Marine regiment left on Peleliu. Sarge said the Army is moving in more troops and when they do, you'll be leaving for Pavuvu."

"We better be," Gil stated.

"Look, you two guys take care," Billy said. "I gotta run catch my outfit. I don't want to be left behind. I'll see you when we get back to Pavuvu."

Mack touched the scarf around Billy's neck and grinned. "Still got it, I see."

Billy smiled, "Still got it. Needs washing though. Well, so long y'all. See you at Pavuvu. I hope it's not too rough up there. Good luck," he said, and ran to catch his company.

When the Seventh Marines reached Purple Beach One, Billy Harris fell on his cot, too exhausted and mentally fatigued to remove his torn and dirty dungarees. Eyes that hadn't closed for days refused to stay open any longer, and for the first time since the landing began, he slept without fear.

Colonel Tameichi Koturu's troops were as weary as the Marines. His men were in desperate need of food and rest, but the colonel knew they would endure, because they believed, as he did, that their hardship was either the atonement for sins committed in the last existence or the education necessary to prepare for a higher place in the life to come.

Their food was almost gone, and Koturu had to make a choice between starvation or survival. He put his men on a daily ration of four hundred grams of polished rice, thirty grams of canned meat, twenty grams of bean mash, and an equal amount of soy sauce. Ten grams of sugar and salt would be added once every fourth day. A candy ball made of puffed rice and black sugar would be given to each man once a week.

Two days after the Seventh Marines were relieved, the Army First Battalion was ordered to move along the west road toward a pocket of Japanese on one of the higher ridges.

Tameichi Koturu, aware that his soldiers now faced the Army instead of the Marines, planned a counterattack.

When the Army's Second and Third Battalions came under enemy fire for the first time, they pulled away from the high ground for the safer flat areas below, leaving the eastern flank of the First Battalion vulnerable.

The colonel was quick to seize an opportunity for one last victory against the American forces, and three hundred of his men charged from the caves and bunkers on the ridges into the opening left by the retreat of the Army's two battalions. In just three hours, Koturu's men regained what the Marines had fought so gallantly to win with days of bloody fighting.

General Adams read the report marked urgent and signed by the commanding general of the Eighty-first Army Division: "Japanese troops, estimated to be over a thousand men, have penetrated our lines. I have ordered the Eighty-first Army Division to move into the more strategic and more defensible areas in the lower elevations. If the Japanese Army is not contained, the enemy will recapture the entire northern end of the island. It is urgently requested all available combat personnel from the First Marine Division come to our support."

Adams was outraged at the Army for allowing the Japanese troops to recapture what his Marines had won. "Go to hell," the general said under his breath. Then he stopped and thought. If he sent his Marines back to the front, CinCPac could never give credit to the Army for the capture of Peleliu, and the victory would belong solely to the First Marine Division. He summoned Colonel Jacobs to his quarters.

An hour later, Jacobs stalked out of General Adams's tent, his eyes glaring, his jaw set, face red from anger. He threw his helmet onto the floorboard of the jeep, slammed it into gear, and drove toward Purple Beach One, where his men were packing their equipment to return to Pavuvu. He sent a runner to find Major Haarken, Third Battalion commander, with orders for him to report on the double to his tent.

When Haarken arrived, Jacobs motioned for him to enter. "What I'm about to tell you will not be what you want to hear," he said. "The Japs have broken through the Army's front lines, and are about to overrun the northern end of the island. It isn't clear how strong the Japanese forces are. The Army commander says 'over a thousand' but we can't confirm that. The Army believes the entire operation on Peleliu is in jeopardy. Consequently, I'm ordering the Third Battalion to return to the front lines. I'm taking every man that isn't wounded or too sick to fight from the First and Second Battalions and assigning them to your command. You won't be at full battalion strength, but it's the best I can do." He looked at his watch. "I want you and your men to start moving out within the next two hours."

Major Haarken looked at Jacobs in disbelief. "Colonel, did I understand what you just said? You're asking me to get my men off the beach and send them back to the front lines? My God, Colonel, I'm not sure the men can handle that, or the officers either for that matter. Goddamn, Colonel, it's unbelievable that you can ask me to send them back. The men have been relieved from combat, and we've had over fifty percent casualties, and now you're telling me to send them back to the lines?"

"Goddammit, Major," Jacobs said, "if you can't do it, I'll get an officer that can. Do you think for a minute this is my idea? I've been given an order, and by God, I'm giving you an order. Either you obey that command, or I'll strip those major insignias off your collar and you can report to the brig. Which is it going to be?"

Haarken swallowed, and his eyes met those of his commanding officer. "I fought with you on Guadalcanal and Cape Gloucester, Colonel," he said, his voice shaking. "You know where my men go, I go. I'm sorry I said what I did." He turned to leave. "I'll have my men ready to move back to the front."

After Haarken left the tent, Jacobs sat on his cot and put his face in his hands. He had not intended to speak to Major Haarken the way he had or to say the things he did. They had been friends since officer's training school before the war, and neither man had ever doubted the honor or courage of the other. The pressure of combat makes a man say and do odd things, he thought.

Sergeant Smith went from tent to tent, telling his men they were returning to the front lines. Some of the men began to curse, while others, too tired to care, quietly started gathering their gear. Many thought it must be some kind of cruel joke and refused to believe the order to return to combat until they saw others getting ready to leave, and then they too put on their shoulder packs, picked up their weapons, and wearily trudged from their tents to join the other men.

Smith ran to the entrance of Billy Harris's tent and yelled, "C'mon, Harris, what's holdin' ya up? We ain't got all day, git yer gear on. Let's go."

"Sarge," Harris said, "I can't find my scarf. I've looked all over for it. I washed it and put it out on the tent post to dry. I know that's where I put it, and now I can't find it. I've gotta find it."

"Harris, ah don't got tha time ta hep ya look, and ya ain't got tha time ta look any longer yoreself. We're loading up right now, and ya can't hold up tha whole company. Git outside and git on tha truck, 'cause we can't wait."

Moments later, Billy heard the trucks beginning to leave and ran to join the other men returning to the front lines.

By the end of the second day, the Third Battalion recaptured the part of the island lost by the Eighty-first Army.

Colonel Jacobs held the speaker phone of the field radio to his ear and waited to talk until he heard General Adams's voice through the static. "General Adams, Colonel Jacobs here. You read me? Over."

"Go on, Colonel, I read you. Over," Adams replied.

"General, we're not able to move up the slope as you've ordered. We have the Japs bunched in one pocket, but they're dug in, and to finish them off will take hand-to-hand combat. My men are too beat to do that. A direct hit with a 105 or a flamethrower might get them out, but we can't get either one in a position to do what we need. Their caves are too well built and protected. I'm requesting artillery be brought up, and if they can blast the Japs out of some of the caves, we can get to the remaining caves and drop explosives."

Jacobs paused. "General, I've lost good men today trying to get up the hill. The Japs are fanatics and don't give a damn if they're killed or not. We must have some help. It's going to take hand-to-hand combat. There's no other way to get them off the hill, and without support from the artillery, with the men I have, I can't do what you've asked me to do, over."

"Colonel, let's have an understanding. I'm not asking you, by God, I'm telling you what you're to do. You know I don't have any relief for you. You've got to do with what you have. You already have 75s and mortars at your command, and in my opinion you don't need the fucking artillery doing your job for you. Where are your men now? Over."

"At the base of Hill 111. We had to pull back when it got too dark to see what we were doing. Over."

"Colonel, by now I expected you to be at the top of the hill, not at the bottom. Get your men up and move out first thing in the morning. I want that goddamned pocket of Japs out of there, do I make myself clear? I want that entire hillside cleaned out of every Jap that's there, and I want them out of there no later than tomorrow night. You've allowed the fucking Japs to hold up the entire offensive for two days, and that's two days too long. Don't tell me they are better fighters than our Marines, and I'm not going to let them think so either. Now, you get moving by 0800 in the morning and get those damned Japs one way or the other. I don't give a shit how you do it, but by God, you'd better do it. Do you understand what I'm telling you to do? Have I made myself clear? Over."

"All right, General, but I want you to understand we'll take a hell of a loss. By this time tomorrow, there may not be enough of the Third Battalion to go on. Have I made myself clear on that, General?"

Colonel Jacobs slammed down the speaker phone, cursing under his breath. He sat with his head down, his hands over his face. He knew his men would do as he ordered. He knew they would understand the sacrifice he had to ask them to make. He got up slowly, put his helmet on his head, and looked about him. "Goddamn this stinking heat," he said out loud. "Goddamn this whole fucking island."

Jacobs ordered Major Haarken and his company officers to meet with him, and for the next half-hour, he questioned them about their casualties and the condition of their men. He did not tell them of his latest conversation with General Adams.

"Men," Jacobs finally said, "the enemy has enough artillery and mortar fire in that pocket to prolong this fighting for God knows how long. We must get up that hill and clean out the caves, fight it out hand to hand. We must clean out every cave and kill every Jap that's in them."

Captain Brit, I Company, was the first to speak. "Colonel," he said, "that's what we've been trying to do for the last two days. How can we expect to do that now, with half the men we started with? There's no doubt the Japs are not as strong as they were—we've had some success—but they're still back in the caves where we can't hit them. The terrain is the worst we've had to fight in. It's their ally, and it's our enemy. The only thing I can think of in our favor, I guess, is we know where most of their caves are. After two days we should know, shouldn't we? As long as they stay in their caves, we can't do anything. If any of my men get close to a cave, the Japs in some other cave catch us where we have no protection."

"Then we'll try something different," Jacobs said. "We're not going to wait till daylight. The Japs expect us to come at them at daylight, just like we've done the last two days. We've got to be up the cliff and in their caves before sunup. If we wait, we don't have a chance. Do any of you see why we can't start out at midnight tonight?"

"Tonight?" Brit asked. "My God, Colonel, that cliff is dangerous in broad daylight. It would be impossible in the dark. Even the Japs would agree to that."

"That's the best thing I've heard," Jacobs stated. "If the Japs think it's impossible, then that's what we'll do. I don't expect it to be easy, and if it should not succeed, I'll take full responsibility."

Jacobs waited a moment and watched the expressions on the face of his officers, then continued, "Major, considering the number of casualties we've had in the battalion, I've decided there are just two companies, I and K, that are capable of getting the job done. This is what I propose. I want Captain Brit to have I Company at the base of the slope at midnight.

The men will carry their weapons and knives and as many phosphorus and shrapnel hand grenades as they can."

Captain Brit looked at Captain Story, then he looked at the colonel.

Jacobs continued, "I want some of the men to carry satchels of high explosives of fused TNT and all the men to carry only what they'll need for hand-to-hand fighting. Whatever they carry, I want it secured to their body. I don't want anything hanging loose."

Jacobs turned to Story. "Captain, K Company will follow I Company if I so order. Nobody is to begin shooting or dropping hand grenades in the caves until Haarken and his men get up the slope, and only when Major Haarken gives the signal. On the way up, if anyone is discovered, if the enemy can be killed quietly, that's the way I want it done. If your men are discovered and they open fire, I'm afraid it will all be over. Tell your men if they rattle rocks or equipment on their climb, and the enemy hears it, there won't be a chance for any of them to survive. I can't afford to send any other men up to help you. The more men on the slope, the greater the danger that someone will slip and they will know we're coming."

"If that happens, God help us," Brit stated.

"Major, the success of this mission obviously rests on you, on Captain Brit, and the men under your command. You know what needs to be done, and I'm confident you can get it done. Tell the men I'm the one to ask them to lead the way, and I have full confidence in their success. Do any of you have any questions? Speak freely."

"I don't have any questions, Colonel," Haarken replied. "We'll get our men ready to move at midnight. I'd like to talk with my men, and then I'll get back with you."

"Go ahead, Major, you do that. I'll be waiting to hear from you. You don't have much time, you know," Jacobs warned.

Story and Brit stood in the darkness outside Taggart's tent. Brit looked at Story. "I guess…" He swallowed and looked up at the sky. "Not many stars out tonight."

"Brit, I wish I was going with you," Story said. "We've been together a long time."

"Yeah, we have, since Quantico."

Story held out his hand. "I'll see you when you get back."

"Yeah, sure. Take care of yourself," Brit said hoarsely.

Haarken waited until Story and Brit were beyond hearing his voice. "Colonel, I'll tell you right now we're about to lose a lot of men. This hill is the most fortified hill we've faced. Our objective was to secure the airfield, and we've done that." Haarken shook his head. "Colonel, is it necessary to risk so many lives over one hill that may not mean that much to the objective?"

"Major, you and I both know our orders are to take the hill. Let's let it stand at that."

When Sergeant Smith was told of Colonel Jacobs's orders, he stared at Captain Brit. He licked his lips and shook his head. "Son of a bitch, ah jist reckon we done got us uh Medal of Honor battle comin' up. Ah kinda wish we had some of them split-toed shoes tha Japs wear. They don't last long in tha coral rocks, made of jist heavy cloth, but they shore don't make no noise."

When Smith saw Billy Harris slumped over his rifle, he touched him on the shoulder. "Awright, Harris, ya been sleepin' and restin' long enough. We got us uh job ta do in a li'l while, and we better start gittin' ready ta do it now. Ah want I Company NCOs ta gather up. Since yore tha senior rankin' PFC, ya git ta sit in too. Git word ta tha others ah want 'em here in ten minutes, ya got that?"

Harris rose to his feet. "Yeah, I'll get them," he sighed. He picked his way through the coral rubble, and his foot slipped on a rock.

"Harris," Smith called after him, "learn ta walk without kickin' rocks with those big feet of yore's. Ya'll live longer if'n ya do."

At midnight, the major spoke to Captain Brit and to Captain Story. "Brit, get your men ready to move. I'm going up first. When I give the signal, have the men begin with their grenades. If for some reason I'm not able to give that signal, then you take my place. Remember that if we're discovered before I get to the top, we fight where we are. Good luck to you and to your men. Captain Story, if the colonel sends you up to help, good luck to you, too."

Sergeant Smith looked at the tortuous ascent of the ridge. "No way ta go but up," he muttered, and ordered the men of I Company to follow him. "Spread out, don't bunch up, an' keep quiet."

He slung his rifle over his shoulder and carefully began pulling himself up the slope by grabbing any rock or tree stump that would hold his weight. The men watched Smith begin crawling up the slope, straining to gain a foothold in the jagged rocks, and one by one, they followed.

Billy Harris inched his way upward, groping with bleeding hands, frantically clinging to the side of the steep cliff.

At the top of the ridge, in a concrete blockhouse with walls four feet thick, two Japanese soldiers, exhausted from the never-ending battle, slept soundly beside their Nambu machine gun aimed at the men below.

Haarken's Marines crawled up the face of the ridge. Only once did a small rock fall from the cliff, and all the men froze where they were, afraid that the enemy had heard. When no sound came from the sleeping Japanese, the leathernecks resumed their climb.

The major crawled on his hands and knees. He was almost to the top, and he took long deep breaths, gasping for air. His hands felt moist, and he saw they were bleeding. The sharp rocks had torn away the flesh, and he wiped his hands on his dungarees before he resumed the climb. He reached the top of the cliff, and he knew his men had reached their positions outside the many caves and bunkers and were waiting for him to give the signal for the battle to begin.

Haarken took slow and careful steps toward the concrete blockhouse and peered inside. He could see the two sleeping

Japanese soldiers, and his heart pounded as he took a deep breath, and he exhaled slowly as he took a hand grenade from his belt. He took another deep breath, knowing when he pulled the pin and dropped it beside the two Japanese soldiers, his men would soon be fighting for the right to live or to die.

He pulled the pin, held the primed grenade in his hand for what seemed an eternity, then dropped the grenade inside. A fraction of a second later, there was a deafening sound, and the entire hillside exploded as the Marines threw phosphorous and shrapnel grenades into the caves and bunkers.

The Japanese, those not killed by the flying shrapnel, ran screaming from their cover. All along the steep side of the ridge, the survivors fought in a hand-to-hand struggle, and they were either killed or they killed the ones they fought.

The short but decisive battle ended as it had begun, with the Marines standing alone, victors on the rugged coral rock.

Sergeant Smith, his dungaree jacket bloody and torn, surveyed the hillside. The sound of exploding grenades and the sharp crack of BARs and M-1 rifles had subsided, and he tried to see how many of his men had survived the battle. Some of his men lay still on the dirty gray coral, and Smith knew the cost in lives would be high.

He felt pain in his left arm and saw it was bleeding. The most important thing, he thought, was that he was among the living, and the objective had been won. He crawled down the side of the hill and grasped the jagged rocks to keep from sliding down the steep cliff.

The survivors of his company knew the battle was over, and limped down the hill beside him.

Halfway down the steep side, a Japanese soldier, his uniform still smoking from the burns of a phosphorous grenade, stepped from a concealed cave. His automatic weapon was aimed at the nearest group of Marines, and he opened fire, and three Marines fell and rolled to a ledge just below the entrance to the cave.

On the other side of the cave, Sergeant Smith fired his M-1, and the head and shoulders of the Japanese soldier flung violently backward, hands extended. He made no cry. Smith watched him sink to the ground and then roll down the cliff. Smith crawled to where his three comrades lay and knew at once two of his men were dead, but one moaned and moved an arm. Smith knelt down beside him.

"Harris, it's me, Sergeant Smith. Kin ya hear me?"

"Sarge?" Billy asked. "I'm hit."

"Jist take it easy, Harris, we're goin' ta git some hep. Jist take it easy, now," Smith said gently.

Smith looked at Billy's dungaree jacket and saw four bloody, jagged holes in Billy's chest. He looked at Billy's legs and saw one leg crumpled beneath him in an awkward position. He started to move Billy's leg, but moved closer to where Billy lay and eased his head up on his lap.

Billy cried out, "Sarge, it hurts. I can't breath, Sarge."

"Corpsman, over here! Corpsman," Smith shouted.

Smith looked down at Billy. "Now, ya look here, Harris, ya jist hang on till tha corpsman gits here. Don't go givin' up on me."

Billy coughed, and tried to swallow. "Sarge?"

"Yeah, Billy. Ah'm here."

"Sarge," he said again, very slowly, "Do you remember on Gloucester, when Woodson , when Woodson…?"

"Yeah, ah remember," Smith said.

Billy's breath came in short gasps. "Woodson said…he was too old to cry. I'm not too old…am I?" he whispered.

Smith felt Billy's body relax. "Uh man's never ta old ta cry, Harris, ain't never ta old."

The corpsman knelt by Sergeant Smith and looked at the Marine in his arms. He knew there was nothing he could do for either of them.

Smith looked up, with tears rolling down his face. "Never mind," he said. "Never mind." He moved Billy's head from his lap and gently placed it on the coral rock. He rose to his feet, picked up his M-1 rifle, and joined his men in their final descent down the coral ridge.

Jacobs sent a short report to General Adams: "Twenty-seven killed and wounded. Hill 111 secured as ordered."

The list of those killed included the names of Major Haarken, Third Battalion commander, Captain Brit, I Company, and Pfc. Billy Harris of Pampa, Texas.

After the last cave was sealed and the hill was finally secured, the exhausted Marines were ordered to evacuate from the front lines. The Army's Eighty-first Division was called back to the front, and when they met the returning Marines, they stopped and watched the silent Marines walk by.

Some of the Army soldiers stood at attention and saluted the men with their dirty dungarees, covered with coral dust, torn and tattered, the soles of their boondockers cut from the coral rocks, and their camouflaged helmet covers hanging limp over their necks to keep the hot, blistering sun from turning their skin into parchment. Their bloodshot eyes stared but seemed not to see, and their lips were parched and bleeding, but they were alive.

The assault on Hill 111 was their last combat mission of the Peleliu campaign, and for them, the battle was over.

On October 14, the Eighty-first Army began taking over the positions held by the Fifth Regiment, and the last of the Marines returned to Purple Beach.

The General read the final report from Col. Taggart: "In just twenty-nine days, the Fifth Regiment had thirteen hundred killed and wounded, forty-two percent of the original landing force. The survivors will forever remember the battle they fought and the comrades they left behind."

General Post, at his CinCPac office in Hawaii, studied the report from General Adams. "The First Marine Division has bravely and courageously won the battle for Peleliu. This conquest will take its rightful place among such victories as

Guadalcanal, Tarawa, and Saipan. The Marine casualties of over 6,350, with 1,120 killed, 5,142 wounded, and 73 missing in action testify to the brave courage and the resolve of the First Marine Division to win this conflict of aggression against the Japanese empire. Operation Stalemate has been completed. Signed, Brigadier General Wilford T. Adams."

Adams neglected to mention that although the original purpose for Operation Stalemate was to gain a base for fighter planes in the invasion of the Philippines, that invasion had started and ended before a single fighter plane flew from the coral runways of Peleliu.

General Post dropped the report to his desk and shook his head. My God, he thought, what a terrible loss of lives. He immediately dispatched a communiqué to General Adams: "The people of the United States of America will forever owe you and the brave men of the First Marine Division their gratitude and a debt of honor for a job well-done for the capture of Peleliu. Upon the return to Pavuvu, the First Marine Division will receive a presidential citation to commemorate their bravery. Signed, Lt. General Frederick D. Post, Commanding General, U.S. Marine Corps."

There was a separate note stamped "Personal and Confidential" and signed by Post: "Brigadier General Wilford T. Adams is hereby ordered to fly at earliest convenience to CinCPac Headquarters, Oahu, Honolulu, where he will be awarded the Navy Cross for his personal gallantry and bravery in leading the First Marine Division in the victory at Peleliu."

On October 30, the final remnants of the First Marine Division boarded the USS *Sea Runner* and left the shores of Peleliu and set a course for Pavuvu.

On November 25, almost two and a half months after General Adams ordered the American flag to be raised over the island of Peleliu, Colonel Kushi Tameichi Koturu sent a message to Tokyo: "Of the thirteen thousand Japanese soldiers who defended the island of Peleliu, there are only 301 survivors. The struggle is over."

Koturu pulled his kogai from his belt, looked at the slender, blunt knife his father had given him, and placed it with his other personal belongings on the table along the wall of the cave. He took the photograph of his father from his pocket and placed it beside the knife. He untied the waist band of crimson thread and, for a moment, held it in his hands. His mother had made the traditional charm to be used against enemy bullets when he was in the military academy.

He knelt on the ground, and his fingers gently touched the gold cloth as he folded the band and placed it beside him. In his final sacrifice for his country and his emperor, he disemboweled himself, and as his body fell forward, his fingers reached for the charm of one thousand stitches.

35

The leathernecks of the First Marine Division watched the shore of Pavuvu come closer, and even from a distance, they could see changes had been made since they had left for the invasion of Peleliu.

When they went ashore, they were surprised to see Red Cross nurses, dressed in clean and starched uniforms, waiting to hand them chilled lemonade. The men stumbled over each other in an effort to get closer to the women and grinned and stared when they reached for the cups of juice. The more adventuresome Marines tried to find something to say to the nurses to encourage further association.

Mack smiled and took the container of juice from one of the girls. "That's the prettiest smile I've seen since I left the

States. I hope to see it again sometime. My name is Corporal Mack Williams, from Texas."

"Hi, I'm Sarah Randolph, from Iowa."

"The name sounds familiar," Mack replied. "I've heard it somewhere. If you'll give me the chance to see you again, I'm sure I'll remember."

Sarah smiled. "Sure, I'll bet you have."

Boog Marshall elbowed his way to the front of the stand, and pushed Mack to the side. "Say, good-looking, what's a pretty girl like you dishing out this stuff for?" He flexed his muscles and inhaled to make his huge chest seem even larger. "I've got a bottle of jungle juice that will knock your panties off. What time should I come by tonight?"

"Thanks, but lemonade is all I ever drink. Would you like some more before you move on?" Sarah asked.

Mack took a few steps, then swung around and ran back to the Red Cross stand. "Sarah. Sarah Randolph. Now I know where I've heard your name! I knew that name was familiar. Does the name Donald Woodson mean anything to you?"

Sarah looked startled. "Yes. Do you know him?"

"We joined the Marines and went through boot camp together. I need to talk with you. There's something you need to know."

"Can you come to my quarters? Tonight?"

Boog Marshall said, "Sure, we can come. What time?"

"I'll come tonight if I can. Alone," Mack added, looking at Boog. "If not tonight, I'll come just as soon as I can. I'll find your Red Cross quarters, and I'll find you."

"Is he…? Is he all right?" she questioned.

"I've got to go for now. I'll talk with you just as soon as I can," Mack replied.

"Wait," Sarah begged. "Tell me. Is he all right? Is he here?"

"I'll talk to you tonight," Mack said and ran to catch the men of his platoon.

The Marines were amazed to see the changes in the camp.

There were wide roads, packed hard with coral rock, neat rows of tents, walkways leading into each tent, and wooden elevated decks for the cots. Each battalion had a galley and mess hall and closed latrines and fresh water showers. A large movie screen with coconut logs placed in rows had been constructed in a cleared and coral-packed area, previously a muddy quagmire. A basketball and volleyball court had been constructed for each regiment. The rumor was there would be periodic beer and Coke rations, and the best rumor of all was that mail would be flown in from the States each day.

The Marines were assigned their quarters, and Mack, Pappas, King, Everson, and Boog Marshall were assigned to share the same tent. Boog dumped his pack on the deck by his cot and watched Mack out of the corner of his eye. "How'd you know to ask that Red Cross babe what you did, Mack? How'd you get her to ask you to her tent the first night you're here? Christ a'mighty, I almost creamed in my jeans just looking at her. Do you realize how long it's been since we've been close to a white gal?"

"Well, some of us use the subtle approach, and then there are others that use the more direct approach, like saying you'd knock off her panties," Mack laughed. "Damn, Boog, you can't talk to a decent girl that way and expect her to fall for you, and before you ask, the answer is no, you can't go with me tonight. I really do know someone she knows, someone she likes, and the tough part about all this is she's going to be very hurt by what I'm going to tell her."

Gil said, "Mack, she really is going to be hurt. I don't know what you're going to say, or how you're going to say it, but from what Billy Harris said, she was in love with Donald. Do you know what you're going to say? Are you going to tell her the truth about Donald?"

Mack answered, "I don't know what I'll tell her. I'm going to find out how much she thinks of Donald before I tell her anything. If she really thinks a lot of him, maybe I'll tell her the truth or maybe I won't. I don't know."

After chow, Mack left his friends and caught a ride to the area where the Red Cross nurses were located and found the tent that Sarah shared with three other Red Cross women.

Sarah smiled when she extended her hand. "Hello again. I'm glad you came. I don't remember your name and really had no way of knowing how to find you in the event you didn't come back. I'm glad to see you. We can go to the mess hall and have a cup of coffee, if you'd like."

"Sure, that's fine. If you don't remember my name, I didn't make much of an impression on you," he laughed. "My name is Mack Williams."

They poured their coffee and sat across the table from each other. "You didn't tell me if Donald Woodson was here," Sarah said. "Is he here?"

"Sarah," Mack said, "could we go outside? I'd like to walk, if you don't mind. This is one of those special nights when it's easy to see the Southern Cross. On a night like this, even the coconut trees have their own special beauty. Would you like to walk down to the beach?"

"You've not answered my questions about Donald. There's something wrong, something you don't want to tell me, isn't there?"

"Sarah, Donald isn't here on Pavuvu, but he's alive."

"Thank God for that. Where is he? Please tell me."

"You think a lot of him, don't you? I know he thought you were something special."

"Thought?" she asked, stepping back.

Mack saw the hurt look on her face. "Sorry, I didn't mean to put it in the past tense. I'm sure he thinks as much of you now as he ever did."

Mack took Sarah's hands. "Sarah, Donald was hurt on Cape Gloucester, before Peleliu. I think it was in January. I wasn't with him at the time. He was in another regiment, but I have a close friend that was there when it happened. Donald was sent back to the States."

"Was he wounded? Was it bad? It must have been if he was sent back to the States."

Sarah looked at Mack, with tears in her eyes. "Was it...very bad?" she asked again. "I have to know."

Mack felt her fingers tighten. "Yes," Mack replied. "I don't know how to say this, or even if I should, but I believe Donald has a place in your heart. From what I was told, you and Donald met on New Guinea, just before the invasion of Gloucester. I don't know if you and Donald had the time to fall in love, but who am I to say? What I'm going to tell you may change the way you think of him. If it does, then I'll never know if I did the right thing by telling you."

Sarah pulled her hands away. "You must tell me. Let me be the judge of how I feel."

"I'm sorry. You're right. Well, I first met Donald when we joined the Marines. There were four of us that went through boot camp together. When we shipped overseas, Donald and one of the men, Billy Harris, were assigned to the Seventh Marines. I was assigned to the Fifth Marines with the other man, Gil Everson. That's why I wasn't with Donald on Cape Gloucester."

"You may be surprised," Sarah said, "but Donald told me about all of you and that he wanted to prove he was just as good a Marine as any of you were."

"Well, I know he tried, but I was never in combat with him, and I never knew how he would act under fire. He tried to make us believe he could handle any situation. I was never sure he could."

"What are you trying to tell me?" she demanded.

"I don't like having to tell you, but Donald couldn't handle the pressure of being under constant fire, and he reached a point when he wasn't capable, mentally or physically, to continue fighting. He had a mental breakdown. He was evacuated from the lines, and sent back to the States for treatment."

"Oh no," Sarah cried softly. "Oh no."

Mack reached for her hand. His voice was soft. "Sarah, every day we're in combat, the law of averages is bound to catch us all. We know that. We just don't know when or where it might be. We either accept it, or we let it get to us as it did to Donald. Battle fatigue is as deadly as a sniper's bullet, and it can happen to any of us. He wasn't a coward, and no one has said that he was."

"I'm so sorry," she whispered, and brushed the tear from her cheek.

"Billy Harris, the friend who was with Donald, told me when they were on Cape Gloucester, their company had been under constant fire for several days, and a lot of men had been killed or wounded, and every day more men were lost. It was tough."

Sarah wiped her eyes. "But you said he wasn't a coward. Everyone can't be a war hero. We all have a breaking point. Some of you can go on fighting until you're killed, and some can't do that. Donald's breaking point was different than yours or your friend's, but it doesn't make him less of a man to me. Must a man go on killing, or go on fighting until he's killed to prove he's a man?"

"No, but I know this war can be won only by those who can take the pressure, by those who can go on killing until there's no one else to kill. They may not be braver than the others, but they're the ones who'll still be standing when the fighting is over. Sometimes luck and the law of averages play a part in whether a man survives, but most of us who live through this war will do so because our determination to live will be greater than the Japanese soldier's determination to die."

They walked along the water's edge, not saying anything, each lost in their own thoughts. The night was still except for the sound of the waves reaching for the shore.

Sarah stopped and faced Mack. "I wanted to write Donald so very much, but I never knew where to send the letter. I don't know if he ever tried to write to me. Do you know where I can write him? I must find him."

"No. He's probably in some Navy hospital back in the States, but I don't know for sure."

"I'm due to return to the States myself," Sarah replied. "I'm going back home to Iowa. I'll be leaving soon, but I wanted to wait until the First Marine Division returned before I left, hoping I might get to see him again."

"You think that much of him, to delay going home just to see him again?"

"I want to find him, Mack. Perhaps some officer or doctor in his regiment knows where he is. There must be someone who can help me locate him. Will you help me?"

"I'll tell you what," Mack said, "let me see if I can find out anything. I'm going to talk with Billy Harris, my friend that was with Donald on Cape Gloucester, and I'll talk to the doctors. If I learn anything, I'll let you know."

"Please try," she said, her voice breaking.

"What will you do when you go back to the States?" Mack asked.

Sarah tried to smile. "Oh, I'll do something in the war effort, but I need to do something different. I've seen death and loneliness and fear and heartache. I've listened to stories about wives and girlfriends and dreams of going home. I need to get back home, too. We all feel that way after being overseas a long time, don't we?"

"Yes. We all want to go home someday. Most of us have someone we hope to go home to."

Mack stood beside Sarah and listened to the waves splash the sandy beach. The night was clear, and he searched for the Southern Cross in the sky. Moonlight filtered through the palms of the coconut trees, and pieces of coral rock glistened in the light from the brilliant stars. For a moment, he was captured by the raw beauty of the tropical island, and his thoughts were of a girl he had long ago kissed good-bye.

"Do you have someone back home?" Sarah asked. "Mack, is there a girl waiting for you?" she asked again.

"Yes. Someday I hope to marry her." They stood for a long moment. "We'd better go back now," Mack said.

When they returned to Sarah's quarters, Mack said, "If

you leave before I have a chance to find out anything about Donald, how can I write you?"

She wrote her home address on a piece of paper and handed it to him. She stood on her toes and kissed his cheek. "Good night, Mack. I'll pray that you make it through the war, and I hope your girl will be waiting for you when you return."

"And I hope you find Donald. I'll help if I can."

Mack turned to leave, then looked back. "Sarah, if you really and truly think a lot of Donald, and I believe you do, perhaps someday you'll be able to help him. Perhaps you can help him where others can't. I would like to think you can. Good-bye, Sarah."

For the first three days on Pavuvu, the enlisted men unloaded and transported gear to be used in setting up camp. The weather, unlike the first tour on Pavuvu, was dry and generally pleasant, and the temperature, in the eighty to ninety degree range, was a pleasant relief from the blistering heat on Peleliu. Most of the rats and crabs that had been such a nuisance had somehow been exterminated, and the coral streets were free from the mud that had clogged the wheels of trucks and weighted the men's boondockers. Living conditions and morale were the best since the division had been in Australia.

The first day Mack and Gil were not on a work detail, they left their tent and walked along the coral-packed road.

"You remember where the Seventh Marines camp is?" Gil asked.

"Yeah, I think so. It's hard to believe this is the same island, isn't it?" Mack replied. "When we were here before, there was nothing but mud, rats, and crabs."

"And falling coconuts," laughed Gil. "Lieutenant Blevins did a good job of making the camp livable while we were on Peleliu. Do you think he got another chicken?"

"Oh hell," Mack laughed. "What a night that was when we stole his chicken. My head still hurts every time I think of all the jungle juice we drank that night. I have to admit we'll never make a stronger batch."

"If we do, count me out," Gil said. "The soup wasn't any good, either. You and your soup-making. I'll bet you never saw your mother make chicken soup in your life, and if you did, you sure didn't see her put in the head, guts, and feet."

"We ate it," Mack laughed.

"Only because we were so drunk we didn't know better," Gil confessed.

Mack pointed, "Isn't this where the Seventh Regiment was before, and Billy's company was just ahead? What you want to bet he's wearing his scarf when we see him?"

Mack and Gil stopped at the first tent and peered inside. "Is this I Company, Seventh Marines?" Mack asked.

"Yeah. Who you looking for?" a Marine asked.

"Pfc. Billy Harris," Gil answered.

The Marine rose from his cot and walked to the entrance to his tent where Mack and Gil stood.

"You're friends of Billy's?" he asked.

"Yeah, we joined together. We're in the Fifth. Where is he?" Gil asked.

The Marine stood silent for a moment. "Billy was killed on Peleliu. He was my friend, too. I'm sorry."

Mack stared at the Marine. "Billy Harris is dead? You must be wrong. We saw him heading for the beach to return to Pavuvu. The Army had already taken over the lines. You must be talking about someone else. Billy Harris can't be dead."

"I'm sorry, it's true," another man said. "We were together when he was killed."

"But how? He was going back to the beach. How could he have been killed? Was he killed on the way back to the beach?"

"No. We returned to the beach and were waiting to board ship, then the Japs broke through the Army lines and we had to go back to the front. He was killed the last day we were on the lines," the Marine said. "The very last day."

"Oh God," Mack cried. "Oh God, no."

Gil bowed his head. "Billy, Billy," he said, his voice breaking. "Why Billy?"

"Y'all want to come in a while?" the Marine asked. "You're welcome to come in and sit, if you'd like."

Mack tried to say something, but the words were not there.

Gil shook his head. "No thanks. I think we want to go on back. Maybe later we'll come back and talk to some of you who knew him."

Gil put his hand on Mack's shoulder. "You ready to go?"

Mack nodded, and they walked toward the Fifth Marine camp, their heads bowed, trying to recapture the memory of their friend.

"Mack, do you still have Billy's home address? You promised Billy you'd write to his mother, if…if he…got killed."

"Yeah, I've got it. I'll write her tonight. I wish I could say something that would help ease the pain of losing a son, but there isn't anything I could say that would do that. It's like a wound that will never heal. I know how I felt when my friend Felipe Ramirez was killed. The words his Army buddy wrote to me didn't mean as much as the fact he cared enough to write. I'm sure the war department has notified Billy's mother so she already knows by now."

That night, Mack walked alone to the cleared area where the weekly movies were shown. It was quiet, the area abandoned. He sat on a coconut log, and for several moments, as he stared at the Southern Cross in the sky, his thoughts were of Billy.

He remembered the first time he had met him, the first time he saw the tall, freckle-faced kid with the big feet. He thought of Billy's quick smile and friendly voice. He thought of boot camp, the long marches, the difficult training, the liberties in San Diego, and he smiled when he thought of the time when he, Billy, and Gil had decided to go to the Hollywood Canteen to see the movie stars. He laughed out loud, recalling how they had hitched a ride to Los Angeles in the back of a pickup truck that belonged to a pig farmer.

He remembered Billy talking about Laura Bently, his high school sweetheart, saying how much he loved her and how he wanted to return to her, and Mack hurt inside, thinking of how the news of Billy's death would also change her life forever.

He thought of the night, on the boat going overseas, when they had talked about home, and Billy expressed his love and respect for his mother and talked about the sacrifices she made for him after his father died. It was that night that he promised Billy he would write his mother if he were killed.

He could never forget the scarf, the good luck scarf, that Billy always wore because it was a gift from his mother and because it made him think of the girl he loved, and Mack wondered if Billy was wearing it when he was killed. He thought of all the good things to say about Billy, how much of a friend he was and would always be.

Mack sat on the log for a long time and, finally, in the stillness of the night, said good-bye to Billy.

The camp was dark and the men asleep when Mack walked back toward his tent. He knew now all that he had remembered would be the things he would write about in his letter to Billy's mother. He quietly entered his tent and sat on his cot. He turned the light from the lantern just bright enough to see the page and wrote a letter to a mother about her son— a friend he had known and a friend he had lost.

36

In late October and early November of 1944, new recruits filled the vacancies from casualties in the Peleliu campaign. Marines who had been overseas since the first of the war and fought on Guadalcanal, Cape Gloucester, Talasea, and Peleliu became eligible for rotation back to the States, and the veterans gathered on the hard coral parade ground to pass in their final review before the division officers.

There was a feeling of sadness in leaving friends who would be staying to fight yet another battle in the conquest of the Pacific.

The new replacements, anxious to become a part of the famed First Marine Division, took their position in the ranks and proudly marched behind the color guards carrying the Stars and Stripes and the division banner.

A feeling of pride touched the men when the division was awarded the presidential citation, and the recruits watched solemnly as the enlisted veterans and officers paid homage to eight of their friends awarded the Medal of Honor for courage on Peleliu. Major Haarken was one of four awarded the Medal of Honor posthumously.

Brigadier General Wilford T. Adams, wearing the Navy Cross with his many other battle ribbons and medals, pinned the Silver and Bronze Stars on the chests of recognized heroes. The Purple Heart was given to those wounded in battle, including one Marine who had cut his finger on a C ration can.

When General Adams pinned the Bronze Star on Col. Alfred Jacobs, the colonel deliberately turned his head and stared at the Navy Cross on General Adams's chest. The muscles on Jacobs's jaw tightened, and he gritted his teeth. The scowl on his face was barely perceptible, but when he looked again at Adams and saw the grimace on the general's face, he knew Adams had seen, and understood his feelings toward the commanding officer.

Immediately after the presentation, Brigadier General Adams was reassigned to the Marine Corps. Depot in San Diego and was replaced as commanding officer of the First Marine Division by Major General Warren Valley.

At General Valley's first staff meeting as commanding officer, his officers expected him to discuss military planning and discipline, but instead he said, "I want to keep the First Marine Division not only as good as it's been, but make it as good as it can be. I have the highest respect for the enlisted men and the job they do, and every officer and enlisted man will have my support in any job done for the best interest of the division."

Jacobs straightened in his chair and glanced at Taggart.

"I understand the camp conditions are greatly improved over what they were when the division was here before," Valley continued, "and now I'm ready to start improving the physical and mental health of the men we will be leading into the next battle. I believe when a man's body is healthy, his mental attitude will also improve. Do you agree, Colonel Jackson?"

Jackson looked surprised. "There's no denying that, sir."

"Now there are certain things upon which I will insist, and one of them is that every able-bodied man will participate in morning exercises. Sick bay will be for treating the sick, so if anybody believes they can report for sick call to get out of physical exercises, they should now plan to do otherwise. Baseball, football, and basketball equipment will be flown in from the States, and I'm encouraging the battalion and regimental officers to form teams to compete with each other. Colonel Taggart, you played football in college, you'll be head coach."

"Well, that's something I'd like to do." Taggart grinned. "I haven't had my hands on a football in a few years, but that sounds fine to me."

"The men will train and work during the week while we're here on Pavuvu, but until further notice, every Sunday will be considered a day of rest and recreation," Valley stated.

"Colonel Jacobs, I'm open for suggestions on how to improve the health, morale, and mental attitude of our men."

"General, it's been months since our men last tasted fresh beef. When we were here on Pavuvu, before Peleliu, we rounded up some wild cattle, and although it tasted like tough shoe leather, the men appreciated it. Any chance of getting the Navy or Army to share some of what they get? We could swap them some of our corned beef and hard tack for a side of beef. That will be as new to them as fresh beef will be to our men."

"I'm sure the Army wouldn't make that trade," Valley laughed, "but getting a shipment of beef is one of my first priorities. The men will have fresh beef. It's already on the docks, and lamb and mutton, certainly not the men's first choice of meat, will be flown in from Australia and New Zealand once a week."

Colonel Taggart laughed. "Colonel Jacobs, while we were

at Talasea, one of my battalions had wild pig. I know for a fact the enlisted men got the tender pieces, because the piece I tried to eat was so tough I would have traded it for the sole of my boondocker."

"General Valley," Jackson said, "we haven't had any new movies since the day we came back to Pavuvu. We've even tried running some in reverse to break the monotony. I don't know how difficult it would be for us to get a change in the movies we have, but it's something we might think about."

"I kinda like watching some of those western movies when we show them backwards," Taggart grinned, "but I'd agree with Jackson, we've seen enough of the Three Stooges."

"And we don't need any more movies on venereal disease," Jacobs added.

The general laughed. "Colonel, a general has certain privileges, and one of them is to pull rank on a subordinate. If it's done by crossing military branches, it makes it all the better. I have a long-time friend who's in the Army, a college roommate who owes me a favor. He's the recreation officer at Fort Bragg, and nothing would please me more than to see that we get the same movies shown to his men. I think that problem can be solved. What else do we need?"

"Mail is getting here about once a week," Jackson said. "Can we improve on that? Letters from home mean a lot to these men. I know it does to me."

"I can't promise that mail from the States will get here every day, but I hope it will," Valley replied.

"What about beer and soft drinks for the men?" Jacobs asked.

"The enlisted men will get beer and soft drinks at least once a month, more often if possible. If it doesn't come that often, the officers will donate their supply of whiskey to the enlisted men. Anything else, Jacobs?"

"The morale of our men could be greatly improved if some USO group from the States would visit Pavuvu. Is there a possibility that we could get one here for Christmas?"

"It will happen. Bob Hope and his group are scheduled to come here before Christmas."

"It all sounds too good to be true. The men won't know what to think about all this," Jackson commented.

"If it all happens as you say it will," Jacobs added.

"It will happen. That's a promise. Now, let's talk about the replacements that are coming. Our division is filled with young men who need to be trained for fighting here in the Pacific, and we must do that before the next invasion. The experience you veterans have gained in earlier combat will be invaluable in our training exercises. This division has fought in places where even angels fear to tread, so I'll rely heavily on you to share with the others what you've learned."

Valley rose to his feet. "I believe that's all I wanted to discuss with you today. Thank you gentlemen for your input. The next time we meet, I'll present ideas for the training phase of our men. I look forward to working with each of you."

When the mail call was over, Mack shook the package he held in his hands. "It's marked 'Do not open before Christmas,' but just in case it's food, I'd better open it now."

Manny moved closer, "If it's cookies, they're probably stale, but I'll help you eat them if you want me to."

Pappas got up from his cot. "Yeah, me too. I've never seen a homemade cookie I couldn't eat. Why don't you open it up so we can see what kind they are?"

Mack tore away the wrapping paper and saw the note inside from his mother. "Dear Mack," he read, "I know the Marines give you the things you need while you're overseas, but I wanted to send you something special for Christmas. I was afraid food might spoil by the time you got this package, so I'm sending you something different. I want you to share it with your friend, Gil. Love, Mom."

"It's not food?" Boog Marshall scowled. "Damn, I was looking forward to some homemade cookies, but what I'd really like right now you couldn't put in a box anyway. Food would be my second choice. Come to think of it, I'm going to write Lolita and see if there's some way she could box up what I need and send it to me."

Mack laughed. "Boog, don't you ever think about anything but sex? You know Lolita can't send that in a box."

Pappas frowned. "Boog, isn't Lolita that Mexican gal from San Antonio you used to dream about? I didn't know she was real. I thought she was just someone you dreamed about. Is she real, Boog? Is she?"

Manny looked at Pappas disgustedly. "Hell, who cares, Pappas, what difference does it make? Go ahead, Mack, open the box."

Mack felt inside the box and pulled out a handful of dirt.

Boog looked surprised. "What the hell is that?"

Mack started laughing. "Well I'll be, this is the best Christmas present I could hope for."

"Dirt is the best thing you could hope for?" Boog asked incredulously. "You've been overseas as long as I have, and dirt is the best thing you want right now? Well, you've never met a girl like Lolita, that's for sure. Boy, I gotta wonder about you, Mack."

Pappas shook his head, "Mack, I'll admit your priorities are a little different from the rest of us. Dirt isn't very high on my list either."

"Hell, y'all don't understand," Mack said. "This isn't just plain old dirt, this is Texas land! The best land in the world. You can see how valuable it is just by looking at it."

Boog leaned closer. "I don't see anything different about it, and I'm from Texas." He turned away. "I'd still rather have what I'm thinking of than a box of dirt."

Pappas looked at Boog. "Boog, if Lolita can send you a box of what you want, will you ask her to include just a little bit for me too?"

Gil felt of the dirt and started laughing. "Yeah, Mack, we can stand on Texas land. We can be on hometown dirt at Christmas time. That's the best gift we could have, but only a Texan could be smart enough to understand that."

Boog looked back at Gil, "Do you believe the other Texans feel the same way?"

"Sure, every true Texan would give his last dollar to be able to stand on Texas soil, you can believe that."

Boog thought a moment. "How about me spreading the word that we'll let every Texan stand on Texas dirt if they'll give us their next beer ration?"

"Nope, this is sacred land, and only Gil and I are going to stand on it," Mack declared.

On Sunday morning, Manny sat on his cot and rubbed his head. "I wonder if there's fleas around here. My head itches so bad I may have to shave my head. Too bad we don't have a barber around here. Everyone in the tent is beginning to look like a shaggy dog."

"If I had a pair of clippers I could cut your hair." Mack grinned. "Shouldn't be much different than shearing a sheep."

Manny looked doubtful. "I'm not too sure about that, but my hair is getting so long, I'm tempted to let you try. Think maybe someone has a pair of scissors we could borrow?"

"I'll bet we could get a pair from the Red Cross people," Pappas suggested. "Mack, you know someone there. Why don't you see if you can get us a pair of scissors and a barber's comb? I'm like Manny, my head is itching, too."

Mack shook his head. "Nah, Sarah has returned to the States, but it wouldn't hurt to ask her friends. Are all of you sure you trust me?"

Manny thought for a minute. "I've got an idea. If you can get some scissors, I'll tell Lieutenant Blevins you're an experienced barber and see if he'll let you cut his hair. I saw him this morning, and his hair is longer than mine. After you cut his hair, if it looks right, I'll let you cut my hair. What do you think?"

Pappas rubbed his head. "Yeah, I could use a haircut. Count me in, too. What about you, Gil?"

"I'll be fourth in line. After Mack cuts your hair, he'll have enough experience to cut mine."

When Mack returned that afternoon with a pair of scissors in his hand, he grinned. "Manny, go talk to Lt. Blevins." He clicked the scissors in the air. "This may be as good as stealing and cooking his chicken."

The next evening, Lieutenant Blevins came to Mack's tent. He peered inside and said, "Is Corporal Williams here?"

Mack walked to the entrance. "Yes sir, I'm here, Lieutenant Blevins."

"Corporal, is it true you were an experienced barber before you enlisted in the Marines?"

"Well, sir, I've held many a pair of clippers in my time. Why do you ask?"

"Well, my hair is getting too long. I can't get down to see the officer's barber as often as I'd like. I always have to wait in line behind all the captains, majors, and colonels. Think I could get you to cut my hair?"

"As a favor to you, I would. You're the only officer whose hair I'd cut, and that's the truth," Mack replied. "I'm ready now, if you want me to cut it."

Mack studied the blades of the scissors. "Lieutenant Blevins, these have always been my favorite pair of scissors. They've hardly been out of my sight for as long as I've owned them. They kinda have sentimental value to me."

Blevins leaned over and looked at the scissors in Mack's hands. "You must have taken good care of them. They look new. How long did you say you've had them?"

"I really can't say for sure. You know how time flies. Seems like only yesterday I got them for my very own."

Pappas clapped his hand over his mouth, pretending to cough, and ran from the tent.

"I think I'd better get going," Manny almost choked with laughter. "I've got things to do," he said, and he too slapped his hands over his mouth and ran from the tent.

"Have those men been to sick bay?" Blevins asked. "Their coughing sounds pretty bad. I hope it's not contagious, I'd hate to get what they have."

"They just won't go to sick bay, Lieutenant. They don't want to miss the morning exercise." Mack clicked the scissors in the air and smiled. "I love to hear the sound of scissors clicking. Well, I'll start cutting your hair if you want me to." He stepped through the opening of the tent. "I'll carry this water can outside for you to sit on."

Mack started trimming and cutting, and the higher he cut on the left side, the more he needed to cut on the right side. He stared at the top of Blevins's head and realized that where he had cut the left side had met the place where he had cut the right side. He looked at the pile of hair by his feet and picked up as much as he could and stuffed it into the pocket of his dungaree jacket.

Blevins rubbed the top of his head. "You're not cutting off too much, are you? I told you I just wanted a trim."

"No, Lieutenant, just snipping off the ends like you wanted." Mack looked again at Blevin's head and started to laugh. He tried to hide his laughter by coughing with his hand over his face.

"Sounds like you're getting the same thing your friends have. I sure hope I don't get what all of you have. You be sure all of you go to sick bay tomorrow. I'll excuse your absence from morning calisthenics."

"Thank you, Lieutenant, we sure will," Mack said.

Mack stood behind Lieutenant Blevins, trying to keep from laughing so he could face the officer. Mack saw Boog walking toward the tent and began waving for him to go back. Boog stopped and stared at Mack and then looked at Blevins's head. "What the hell is going on?"

Mack frantically motioned for Boog not to say anything more and for him to leave.

Boog looked again at Blevins sitting on the water can and couldn't keep from yelling, "Oh my God, the chicken man rides again." Then he started singing, "Have you seen the chicken man, the chicken man? Have you seen the chicken man that lives on Drury Lane?" He stopped, turned back to look, then started crowing like a rooster.

"What brought that on? Is Marshall all right? He isn't getting 'Asiatic' is he?"

"He may be, sir. He sometimes thinks he's a chicken. We sometimes feed him bread crumbs to keep him happy."

Blevins rubbed the top of his head again. "Seems like you cut quite a bit off the top. Is there a mirror around here?"

"No, Lieutenant, the enlisted men don't have mirrors. You can see here on the ground there's not as much hair as you might think."

Blevins looked at the black hair on the ground, "Well there's not as much as I thought there would be from the way my head feels. Well, thanks for cutting my hair. You're a good Marine, Corporal." Blevins walked toward his tent, whistling, "Have you seen the chicken man, the chicken man…"

Moments later, a scream could be heard from one end of the camp to the other. "Corporal Williams, where are you?" shouted Blevins, running from his tent with a mirror in his hand. "Corporal Williams! Where are you?" he shouted again and ran to where Mack had cut his hair. He dug around in the coral rocks, grabbing up pieces of his hair. "Corporal Williams! You'd better come out of that tent!"

Pappas stuck his head out the entrance to the tent. "Corporal Williams said you told him to report to sick bay," he said, and began coughing as he walked back inside his tent. He kicked Mack's cot. "You can come out from under your cot now. He's gone."

The Second Battalion Fifth Regiment "Gyrenes" and the Third Battalion Seventh Regiment "Leathernecks" were undefeated in the division tag football games which had begun in early December. Interest had mounted as each team advanced through the play-offs toward the final game.

The First Marine Division championship trophy, a large coconut mounted on a white coral rock, had been on display at each of the regimental mess halls and was an ever increasing topic of conversation as rivalry mounted between the regiments.

Officers and enlisted men stood side by side on the sidelines when the final game was played. The score was tied 21-21, and the players, even without pads, became more intense in their blocking and tackling.

Mack Williams knelt in the center of the huddle and explained the next play. "The game's almost over. If we're going to win the trophy, this next play has to be it. Let's try 43 fake pass left, and somebody has to block that big defensive guard that keeps knocking me on my ass before I ever get the ball."

Mack stood up and looked at their opponents line, then squatted down in the huddle. "Boog, on this next play, try a cross block. Manny, you pull out, and you and Boog double-team him. Pappas, as soon as you center the ball, fill the gap after Manny pulls out. Block anybody that gets through the line. Gil, stint-block their left end, then lead interference for me when I cut toward the sideline. Their linebacker is almost as big as their left guard, but you're going to have to block him for this play to work. Everyone know what to do? This next play will decide if we win the game."

Boog breathed hard. "Hell, I've been trying to block that guy, but he's tough."

"Well, then pretend he's some jerk trying to sleep with Lolita, and if you don't block him on this next play, Lolita will let him."

Boog gritted his teeth. "That big dude ain't going to sleep with my Lolita, you can bet your sweet ass on that. I'll kill 'im." He started running toward the defensive guard on the line of scrimmage.

"Boog," Mack shouted and grabbed his arm before he could make contact. "Wait till the play starts."

Mack pulled him back toward the huddle. Bob Munday, the umpire, had his red flag in his hand, ready to call a penalty if Boog had taken another step.

"Just wait!" Boog shouted. "You ain't sleeping with my Lolita. Just wait till I can push your head through your neck."

The big guard raised up and looked at one of his teammates. "Who the hell is Lolita? What the fuck is he talking about?"

Boog shook his fist at the big guard. "Lolita doesn't give a shit about you, and you ain't sleeping with her, you hear?"

Mack yelled, "Hurry up everybody, line up. Hurry, we're going to be penalized for delay of game."

The men were in their position and Pappas centered the ball a fraction of a second before time expired for the play to begin.

Before Manny had a chance to pull out and do his part of the cross block, Boog threw a vicious block into the big guard, and the two men fell to the hard playing field. Manny ran past the two Marines on the ground and blocked the defensive end that charged into the Gyrenes backfield. Pappas stepped back to block the first man that broke through the line, and Gil ran toward the Leatherneck linebacker, the only man between Mack and the goal line. Gil blocked the linebacker just as he reached out his arms to tackle Mack.

When Mack crossed the goal line, he looked back at his team members. Everyone except Gil was jumping up and down shouting, "We win the game! We win the game."

The Leatherneck linebacker Gil had blocked was cursing, his face only inches from Gil's face. Mack ran to where they stood and stepped between them.

"Calm down a minute, I want to whisper something in your ear." Mack leaned over, his mouth almost in the linebacker's ear. He whispered something and stepped back, and the two men stared at each other for a minute, then the linebacker shrugged his shoulders and turned and walked away.

"How come you whispered to him, Mack?" Gil asked as they walked off the playing field.

"I didn't want to start a riot. Tensions were already pretty high."

"What did you say to him?"

"Nothing much. I just told him you were my buddy, and I'd beat the shit out of him if he didn't back off," Mack panted. "Good block, Gil, you won the game for us."

By the middle of January 1945, the First Marine Division was back to full combat strength, and preparations were underway for the next assault against the Japanese empire.

The Marines realized they were being trained for a different type of warfare when the jungle strategy of earlier invasions was replaced by methods in street fighting and emphasis was placed on tank-infantry maneuvers. The veterans were the first to realize the significance; the battle front had moved closer to the inevitable assault on the Japanese mainland.

The final battle loomed on the horizon.

37

General S. Barlow, commander of the Tenth Army, looked at himself in the mirror. His uniform, starched and perfectly pressed, was tailored to fit his ample girth. His orderly had polished the four stars on his uniform, and his battle ribbons were properly placed on the tunic of his uniform. His shoes reflected the light almost as much as his polished brass belt buckle.

"General Barlow, sir, the other officers are waiting in the meeting room," his orderly said.

"Good, I'll let them wait for another half-hour. Is General Post wearing his battle ribbons?"

"Yes, sir, all the officers are."

Thirty minutes later, Barlow walked into the meeting room and returned the salutes from Lt. General F. Post, commanding officer of the Third Amphibious Corps, Lt. General Wayne Stratton, commanding officer of the Twenty-fourth Army, General H. Arbour of the Third Air Wing, and Vice Admiral Lesley Higgins, commander of the Fifth Fleet. He called each of them by their first names. "Sorry to keep you waiting, gentlemen, but it couldn't be helped."

"Congratulations on your promotion to vice admiral, Lesley," Barlow said when he returned Higgins's salute.

Higgins beamed. "Thank you, sir."

Barlow strode to the large table, and acknowledged the Marine generals from the First, Second, and Sixth Marine Divisions, the division officers from the Seventh, Twenty-seventh, Seventy-seventh, and Ninety-sixth Army Divisions, the flight commanders of the Third Air Wing, and the Navy commanders of the Fifth Fleet. He sat down at the end of the table and placed his hands palm down. He cleared his throat, a sound much like the combination of a grunt and a growl.

"Now then, I asked you here for our final strategy meeting for Operation Iceberg. The largest amphibious operation so far in the Pacific is only a month and a half away. General MacArthur had planned to be here but was called to Washington. I will act in his capacity."

Barlow cleared his throat again. "Those of you who know General MacArthur know that he demands complete obedience and cooperation from his subordinates, and..." Barlow smiled..."and since he's a five-star general, that means we're all his subordinates."

Some of the Army officers laughed obediently, but General Post was not accustomed to being referred to as a subordinate and failed to find any amusement with the remark. His back stiffened as his shoulders lifted.

"Some of you junior officers who don't know me should know that I believe, as General MacArthur does, in the creed of 'Duty, Honor, Country,' something we lived by at 'the Point.' I've always said obedience should be added to that. Wouldn't you agree General Stratton? But then you weren't at the Point, were you?"

"Yes, General Barlow, obedience is necessary in the military, and no sir, I did not attend West Point. I chose to attend Texas A & M to get my military training."

General Post couldn't suppress a soft laugh.

"Yes, well…" Barlow sniffed, obviously piqued at Stratton's comment. He pulled his chin back against his neck and brushed a speck of dirt from the sleeve of his uniform.

"Now, let's get on with why we're here," Barlow announced. "There will be over half a million men taking part in the invasion of Okinawa, and I must stress the importance of coordination. General Post, I expect you to coordinate Marine activities with the officers of the Third Amphibious Group and General Stratton, the same applies to you and the Twenty-fourth Army Corps, and to you, General Arbour, with the Third Wing. Admiral Higgins, the coordination of over thirteen hundred ships of the Fifth Fleet will be a monumental job."

Barlow leaned back in his chair and looked at each of the officers. "When I was placed in charge of this operation, I asked for each of your files. I was impressed and pleased with what I saw, and I have no doubt that you will all do your job well. I expect Operation Iceberg to be a success, and I cannot overemphasize the importance of coordination and precision timing between the four branches of service. If any of you have any negative feelings about the Army being in command of all land operations, you can dismiss it. There absolutely cannot be any challenge to my command. I trust I make myself clear."

"You'll have the Navy's support, General," Higgins said.

General Post sat stiffly in his chair, his body erect, his eyes never leaving Barlow's face. "It's not the first time the Marines have been under the Army's command, General. The Marines will do what's expected of them. You'll have our cooperation."

Barlow cleared his throat again. "Good. I'll keep each of you informed as much as I can. I always say an informed group is a prepared group. I learned that at the Point." Barlow glanced at Stratton and emphasized the words "the Point."

For the next hour, the officers talked about the logistics of such a major undertaking, and finally, Barlow rose from his chair. "As I said before, an informed group is a prepared group, so you can decide what part of our strategy should be passed down to the junior officers of your command."

Three days later, General Valley called Taggart, Jackson, Jacobs, and Armstrong to his quarters.

"Gentlemen, when we met with General Barlow last week, we discussed the logistics of Operation Iceberg." Valley gave a short laugh. "It was quite a meeting. The next morning, General Post asked us to review every detail for our landing on Okinawa. In any operation as monumental as this, there could be some overlooked circumstance, but I'll be damned if I can see one now. Nevertheless, we'll run through our plans again. I want to be certain that for every potential problem, we've an alternate strategy. I don't want a repeat of any of the surprises the First Marine Division had on Peleliu.

"I have not discussed Peleliu with General Post, but you should know my feelings about it. I've studied the records and I'm privy to things perhaps even you don't know. Crossing reefs in an invasion, when the enemy is pounding the hell out of you, is never easy, but at Peleliu there were major casualties that shouldn't have occurred. I'm not blaming anyone for what happened there, but CinCPac could have made some changes, and they chose not to.

"When I served in China before the war, I learned a few things from the Chinese. The Japanese believe they're superior to the Chinese, and in many ways, they are, but the Japanese understand and use the wisdom of the ancient Chinese. A saying from Sun Tzu's writings that makes good sense to me is 'It's bad to repeat the same mistake and worse to repeat it the third time.' The mistakes at Peleliu will not be repeated under my command."

Valley went on, "Another strategy of Sun Tzu's was 'When the opponent thinks high, hit low, and when he thinks low, hit high.' The top secret plan devised by military intelligence for the invasion of Okinawa uses that philosophy.

"The Second Marine Division will make a mock landing on the southeast beaches, and if the Japanese move their troops to that sector, as we believe they will, they'll be grouped on the southern third of the island, and we'll not have a prolonged fight on two fronts.

"Most of the population is already in the southern part of the island, with the majority living in Naha. We'll land in the central area, where the island is narrow, and move inland to the Yontan and Kadena airfields. Once we capture these, our planes can have a land base. After the northern part of the island is secured, First and Sixth will move south.

"Colonel Armstrong, your artillery will be able to reach either end, but I hope your guns will be facing south throughout most of the fighting. The Army will turn south after landing and move toward the southern pocket. Any questions?"

"I'm sure we'll get some resistance from the Japanese Air Force," Jackson said, "and certainly from their Navy. We're too close to their homeland to expect otherwise. The high command understands that, doesn't it?"

"Oh, there's no doubt about that," General Valley replied, "but the size of our sea and air power is great enough to destroy most, if not all, the enemy can throw at us."

"Seems like I've heard this before," Jacobs muttered.

"If the ruse by the Second Division works," Valley continued, "most of the Japanese will be in the southern part of the island when we land our invasion forces. I think it's fitting we've chosen April Fool's Day as the day we go ashore."

"It's also Easter Sunday," Taggart reminded him. "We hit Cape Gloucester on Christmas of '43, and now on Easter of '45, we hit Okinawa. Ironic, isn't it?"

"Yes, it is," General Valley replied. "Perhaps the time is near when we'll spend New Year's back home with our families."

The general moved to the other side of the table. "Communications between you, me, and General Post will be all-important. General Barlow, as central commander of the Tenth Army, will coordinate all military land operations. Vice Admiral Higgins will command the Fifth Fleet, the largest naval force ever put to sea. There are no changes in what you already know about the assault team. The First and Sixth Marine Divisions and Seventh and Ninety-sixth Army Divisions will be the assault force, and one Marine division and one Army division will be held in floating reserve. We'll be landing over one hundred and seventy-five thousand combat personnel and over a hundred thousand service troops along a five-mile stretch of beaches on the west coast."

"Any change on the estimate of Japanese on Okinawa?" Jacobs inquired.

"Our best guess is about eighty-five thousand, but there will be another fifty thousand on other nearby islands. We will have full supremacy of the skies and the sea. That is an undisputed fact, but it doesn't guarantee the Japs won't try to contest it. Our combined sea and air power will not allow the enemy troops on the nearby islands to reinforce the garrison on Okinawa."

"There once was a time when I would have been skeptical of that remark." Jacobs shrugged. "I'll never feel good about being under the Army's command, but in this instance, I can't complain about the size of our forces."

General Valley returned to the large table covered with maps. "The island of Okinawa is the largest of the islands on which we've fought. If there is a ratio of size to the number of casualties, this could be the worst yet, but I'm sincere in telling you none of us believe there will be that correlation. If our strategy of a fake landing works, we'll get most of the Japanese in the south part of the island, and we can concentrate all our fire power there."

When the meeting was over, General Valley opened his footlocker and held a bottle in his hand. "I have a bottle of good

Tennessee bourbon whiskey I've been saving. I'd like to share it with you."

He pulled the wrapper off the bottle, and got a single glass from his footlocker. "The Japanese have a custom, called 'Kampai' which means 'dry cup.' It's a practice where one man fills the glass with sake and gives it to a friend. When the cup of sake, or in this instance, whiskey, is emptied, the cup is refilled and passed to another. It's a meaningful ceremony to the Japanese, symbolic for extending trust and good wishes. I offer it to you with the same feeling."

The officers drank the bourbon and passed the glass from one to the next. General Valley said, "Before you leave, I have one more question, personal in nature, but one I'd like to have answered before this invasion begins. The First Marine Division has fought in the Solomons, New Britain, and Peleliu. All of you have served your country with distinction, and you three infantry commanders were eligible for rotation back to the States, yet each of you rejected the opportunity. I think I know why, but do any of you want to say why you didn't return to the States when the opportunity was there?"

Colonel Jackson said, "Sir, I'm a professional Marine. There will come a time when I'll go home, but not until the war is over. My family knows that. I want to be in the fight until it's finished. I wouldn't have it any other way."

"That's pretty much the way I feel," Taggart said. "I don't believe the war will last too many more months, perhaps it'll take years, but I don't think so. We'll go from this invasion to the next until we invade the main islands of Japan. We'll win the war, and when we do, I want to be part of the victory parade down the main street of Tokyo."

General Valley turned to Jacobs. "And you, Colonel Jacobs, why didn't you return to the States when the rotation plan was adopted?"

Colonel Jacobs looked down at his hands. They were shaking. He placed them behind his back. "On Peleliu, I asked a man to do the impossible, but he did it anyway. Major

Haarken was a brave officer and a friend, and I'm ashamed to say I questioned his courage. He gave his life in doing what few other men could have done. The least I can do is try to be as good an officer as he was, and the only place where I can do it is here in the Pacific, and here I'll stay until the war is over and the fight is won."

General Valley nodded and smiled at his three regimental infantry commanders. "I thought as much."

In early March, all personnel were issued warm, wool-lined jackets, suggesting that the next invasion would be in a much colder climate than where they had fought before. The scuttlebutt was that their next invasion would be one of the Japanese home islands, but the men could only guess which one it would be.

The First Marine Division was ordered to break camp and stand by to board ship on March 15, 1945 and to leave Pavuvu for their next assault on the Japanese military might.

On the evening of March 14, Boog Marshall finished packing his gear. "My fucking arm still hurts from all those fucking shots we took for this fucking trip."

Manny laughed. "Boog, if you weren't dumb enough to stand in both lines getting the shots instead of just one line as you were supposed to, your arms wouldn't be hurting so bad."

"Nobody told me to just get in one line. I can't stand to watch the corpsmen just waiting with those needles, and when I closed my eyes, they hit me from both sides. The next thing I remember was being in sick bay. One good thing about it was the food wasn't bad, better than we usually get, and the two days I spent in sick bay would've been all right if I hadn't felt so bad. It's a good thing I got to feeling better, 'cause that little corpsman was beginning to look pretty good to me. He had a cute ass on him, kinda reminded me of Lolita."

"Yeah, yeah, there you go again, thinking of sex," Mack said.

"Boog, which one is he? The one with a cute ass?" Pappas asked. "I may get to feeling bad myself."

"I'm thinking of something else besides sex right now. I think that good food at the hospital gave me the running shits.

I'm thinking I need to go take a Pappas," he said, looking at George.

"Fuck you," Pappas said. "Don't forget to wipe your Boog," he added.

"We're going aboard ship tomorrow," Boog said. "And there's something I've been wanting to do ever since Lieutenant Blevins gave us all that extra guard duty when Mack and Gil stole his chicken. I heard he'll be in the rear echelon again, and I might never get another chance."

"What chance you talking about?" Manny asked.

Boog laughed. "I'll let you know if I can do what I think I can do. I'll see y'all later."

"Where do you think Boog's going?" Pappas asked. "He's got something planned for Blevins, but I don't know what."

"I don't either," Mack replied. "The lieutenant doesn't need another haircut, and he never did find another chicken, so I don't know what Boog has on his mind. Whatever it is, we'll end up paying for it."

On the morning of March 15, the Marines mustered outside their quarters, waiting for Sergeant Tucker to give them the order to board the trucks to take them to the troopships.

Lieutenant Blevins, red-faced and obviously angry, hurried to where George Company waited.

"Okay, who's the wise guy?" Blevins screamed. "Last night, someone shit a streak four inches wide and three feet long on my tent. One of you men from George Company did it, I know you did. Which one of you did it?"

Mack looked at Pappas. "I told you so."

Manny tried to suppress his laughter by coughing and almost choked.

The lieutenant walked back and forth in front of the Marines. "You all know I'm not going with you, and there isn't time for me to punish all of you for doing such a mean thing, but I want the guilty person to be man enough to admit he did it." No one spoke. "The streak of shit on my tent smells, and it's not very pretty to look at, either." There was only silence.

Sergeant Tucker grinned. "Which one of you assholes did this? Somebody 'fess up before we get on the trucks."

Still silence. The Marines put on their packs and slowly started towards the trucks. Lieutenant Blevins walked beside the column of Marines. "If you won't tell me who did it, will someone at least tell me how he got his ass in position to shit such a long string?"

When they got on the truck, Mack looked at Boog and started laughing. "How did you do it, Boog?"

"It was easy. I just shit on a board and slung it at his tent."

On the island of Okinawa, the fields were filled with peasants with crude wooden hoes, working in the man-made ponds for growing the rice that was the lifeblood of the Japanese people. Each year, the fertile land waited like an expectant woman to give its blessing to the increasing demands of war. Water buffalo grunted and groaned and dragged wooden plows along the furrows of the rice patch, and just beyond, the rice mill beside the stream creaked as the narrow blades turned.

On the morning of March 23, 1945, barefoot women, bending their bodies to work in the foot-deep water, heard the drone of approaching planes. One by one, they straightened and shielded their eyes to look toward the sky. It was not the first time they had seen the planes overhead and felt the indignities of war, nor would it be the last. The horizon was shadowed by American B-29 bombers. Their bomb bay doors opened, and bombs and devastation emptied from their bellies onto the military defenses and airfields below.

The imperial war cabinet knew the inevitable was near. The American forces, only a ripple on the Pacific waters in 1941, were now a tidal wave that moved ever closer to the Japanese mainland, just four hundred miles away, and over six thousand miles from the golden gate of San Francisco.

The war lords were forced to acknowledge that Okinawa was the last staging point before the actual invasion of the

Land of the emperor God, and terror and fear reigned in the hearts of the Japanese people.

Task Force Fifty-eight from the Third Air Wing struck the airfields and harbors as far north as Kyushu, and hundreds of Japanese aircraft and ships, poised to fight in the battle for Okinawa, were destroyed. Preinvasion bombing on the western shore of Okinawa targeted military defenses. Gun installations were demolished, and antiaircraft guns and artillery cannons became masses of twisted steel and useless chunks of iron. The preassault bombardment lasted over a week, and fire support from the battleships, cruisers and destroyers continued uninterrupted, as the cities of Naha and Shuri felt the might of the American naval force. American underwater demolition teams cleared the landing beaches, and the stage was set for Operation Iceberg to begin.

The mighty American armada moved across the Pacific Ocean, and bright moonlight silvered the sea. Japanese reconnaissance planes sighted the American invasion force entering the East China Sea and alerted the Navy and Army Japanese command in Tokyo. Japanese Zeros, torpedo planes, and bombers that flew to intercept the American ships were no match for the military might of the American Navy. Vice Admiral Higgins reported to General Barlow that three of his cruisers were damaged and two destroyers sunk. He also reported that the entire Japanese air wing had been destroyed. Barlow frowned when he read Higgins's last comment: "The damage to our fleet was not from bombs or torpedoes, but from Japanese suicide planes that crashed into our ships."

Vice Admiral Higgins sat on the bridge and poured over charts. The ship was quiet, and the ocean was calm, but all eyes turned to the sky in search of the new threat from Kamikaze planes. "Tomorrow, the big battle begins," Higgins thought. "I pray to God all goes well."

The next morning, April 1, the landing force turned to starboard in the East China Sea, and the island of Okinawa was sighted on the radar screens. The battleships closed to within two thousand yards, and at 0640, the bombardment began. Artillery shells of all sizes fell on the landing shores. The roar and scream of thousands of shells was deafening, but one hour later, the shelling stopped with an equally deafening calm.

Mack Williams and Gil Everson, in full combat gear, stood on the deck of the troop transport, awaiting the order to climb down the cargo nets into the bobbing Higgins boats.

Gil nervously adjusted his shoulder pack. "These straps never seem tight enough to hold the weight where it ought to be. My back already hurts."

"Yeah," Mack grunted, "I'm tempted to leave part of my pack aboard ship, but sure as hell, I'll need what I leave. I can't see carrying our gas masks, but I learned my lesson on Peleliu when we thought the Japs were using gas and I had thrown my mask away. This jacket feels good. It's almost cold."

Pappas looked over the railing at the water below. "I hate going down those fucking nets. I keep thinking I'm going to lose my grip and fall in the water. That's my greatest fear. I don't like water, especially cold water."

"You always get sick when we get aboard ship," Manny muttered.

"Yeah, I'm just not cut out to be a sea-going Marine, that's all there is to it. Where I really get sick is in those fucking Higgins boats. Jesus Christ, I even hate to think about it."

"You're not the only one that gets sick in those little boats," Manny said. "Boog has puked on every landing. I don't even like to be in the same boat with him."

Sergeant Tucker gave the order, "First and second platoons, over the sides and into the boats. Move it out. Let's go, over the sides."

Mack said, "Gil, Manny, George, be careful and good luck. I'll see you ashore."

The Marines climbed down the swaying nets and struggled to keep their rifles and gear from becoming entangled in the ropes. The men crowded into the bobbing boats and, when the boats were filled, moved away from the transport, making room for the next boat to fill with waiting platoons.

Landing craft filled with silent, scared, brave men, formed a line four thousand yards from the western side of the mountainous and wooded island, and on one command, the Army and the Marines joined in a dash for the western beaches north of Hagushi Bay in a major invasion of the Japanese Empire.

The landing craft crossed the reef, and a school of dolphins raced alongside the ships. Men bowed their heads, and some prayed, too afraid to think of the fate that awaited them. The veterans of earlier Pacific landings braced for the onslaught of the deadly Japanese artillery and mortar shells to begin.

To the surprise of the assault troops, the landing was unopposed. At 0830, the motors of the landing craft surged, the ramps lowered on the sandy shore, and Marines and soldiers stepped onto land the Japanese believed was protected by their sacred emperor. The Easter sun rose in the morning sky.

General Valley landed with the fourth wave of Marines of the First Division and conferred by radio transmission with General Post, Third Amphibious Corps commanding officer.

"General Post, this is General Valley, can you read me? Over."

"I read you loud and clear. Over," General Post replied.

"The resistance to the First Marine Division continues to be minimal. We're already moving across the island without any opposition, and we'll be across the island before nightfall. The Yontan airfield is already secured. How are the other invasion forces doing? Over."

"General Barlow advises Kadena airfield is secured, and our planes will be flying from both airfields within the next forty-eight hours. None of the landing forces have met anything that resembles an organized resistance on any front. Our false landing was successful, and the Japanese commanding officers are either kicking themselves in the ass or considering hara-kiri for being fooled into placing all their troops in the south region. Over."

Valley smiled. "That's great to hear, General. Over."

"The Japanese land forces are holding back, as was considered a possibility, and by nightfall, we'll have fifty thousand men ashore. I've notified General Barlow that both Marine divisions will turn north. General Stratton reports the Twenty-fourth Army is turning south. The resistance will no doubt increase, but the landing went better than we could have expected. Over and out."

General Ohijima, commander of the Thirty-second Army Force, dispersed one regiment from the Sixty-second Division into the caves built in the soft limestone hills of the area north of Naha and waited for the American forces. He was furious for being fooled by the fake landing. He knew his decision to move the majority of his troops into the southern sector had allowed the American forces to establish a beachhead.

By the end of D-day, the Americans held an area nine miles wide and three miles deep.

By D plus two, the Japanese forces still offered no formidable defense to the swiftly moving Americans. When the imperial war office realized General Ohijima's mistake and learned of the lack of forceful defense, the minister of war, the commander of the Imperial Guards Division, and the admiral of the combined fleet were summoned to Tokyo.

"General Ohijima, commander of our Imperial Army on Okinawa, has made an unforgivable error. His stupidity allowed the Americans to gain a foothold on Japanese sacred soil. We must delay no longer in removing him. He must be returned to Tokyo, where he will be tried and judged by the privy council," the minister of war said.

The commander of the Imperial Guards Division was angry. "General Ohijima is a stupid bastard, a bakayaro, for making the decision to move his troops to the southern sector. I agree he must be replaced at once."

"We must choose wisely in his replacement, Okinawa must not be lost," the minister cautioned. "There is one man we can depend on, a man with bravery and tenacity, the 'Soldier of New Britain.'"

"Ah, yes, Colonel Torao Osaka," the admiral of the combined fleet said. "His reputation for survival on New Britain is well-known. His escape to Rabaul with over five hundred men was truly a remarkable feat."

"He is General Osaka now," the minister corrected. "Can we chance sending him to Okinawa by submarine?"

"It will be risky," the admiral agreed, "but it is the only way. The longer we wait, the more risk there will be. The main American naval force is still in the East China Sea. We will send an R.O. class submarine to the east coast, and we can put General Osaka ashore at Minatoga. I will also order General Ohijima to return to Japan. It is the only way."

"Then it is decided," the minister declared.

General Ohijima bowed to General Osaka when they met in the unrelenting rain on the eastern shore of Okinawa. The submarine, five hundred yards from the coast, waited for the return passenger. Osaka searched Ohijima's face, trying to find any emotion of fear or hatred. Instead, Ohijima appeared calm and almost relieved.

"General Osaka, I bow to you with respect. Your survival on New Britain is famous. It was an amazing show of courage and personal strength to lead your soldiers safely through the jungles, and to reach Rabaul was remarkable."

General Osaka politely bowed to Ohijima. "I was determined to fight the American Marines once more. There was never any doubt that I would do so."

"I regret I do not have the opportunity to show you our defenses, but as you can see, the boat waits to take me to the submarine. I must return to Japan," Ohijima said.

Osaka stepped toward Ohijima. "Yes, but first, tell me what you can about the number of troops under your command. Tell me about your supplies of food and ammunition."

"There are seventy-five thousand soldiers in the southern sector. Another five thousand men are here, but they are not combat-trained. The most experienced soldiers in the Sixty-second Division were transferred from China and are anxious to fight the Americans. In the northern area, in the Motobu and Oroku Peninsulas, there are over ten thousand seamen and armed civilians and another twenty thousand men from the territorial militia. There were many casualties from the shelling by the American fleet. The supplies and ammunition will last as long as the men can fight. Perhaps you can defeat the Americans." General Ohijima shrugged. "I could not do so."

The rain fell in a slow drizzle, and Ohijima stepped into the boat. "I wish it could have been different. Banzai," he called, and turned toward the waiting Japanese submarine.

General Osaka immediately surveyed the terrain just north of Naha and Shuri. He frowned, as if his entire mental force was concentrated on a defensive plan. He inspected the intertwining tunnels and bunkers and instructed his men to stock the caves with ammunition and supplies. He ordered units of the Sixty-second Division to pull back from their scattered defenses in the caves and commanded four regiments to occupy the ridges and natural points of defense surrounding Shuri Castle. He moved a company of mortars behind the infantrymen, and behind them, he moved his artillery and assigned a platoon of machine gunners to each point of advantage. He ordered one full division to move up behind his first line of troops and be held in instant reserve and two regiments to occupy the coastal low lands.

"When the Americans landed in the center of Okinawa, they divided our Army into two groups, but we will use the same strategy," General Osaka told his chief of staff. "We must keep the Marine divisions in the north from joining force with the American Army divisions in the south. The number of our men in the northern sector is insufficient to make a sustained frontal assault against the Marines, but units of battalion strength can occupy pockets of defense, where the terrain is favorable for a diversionary tactic. We will tie down the Marines and keep them in the northern sector and out of the more strategic area to the south where our main forces are positioned."

Osaka sent a coded radio message to the Japanese War Ministry's Office of Military Affairs in Tokyo: "I await your orders for Operation Ten-Go to commence. Signed, General Torao Osaka, Commanding Officer of Imperial Forces, Okinawa."

38

The train would be at the Sendai station for only a short time, and Vice Admiral Koturu peered through the window as the train slowed. In the faded light from the setting sun, he saw the stationmaster, his violet uniform and gold-laced cap making him look as though he were an admiral of a great ship, waiting for the train to stop and the passengers to step into his domain.

The stationmaster ceremoniously pulled his watch from his uniform pocket and nodded his approval that the train had arrived at precisely the correct time. The war had been unable to destroy such a ritual, Koturu thought.

Vice Admiral Koturu stepped to the platform and pulled his coat around his shoulders to keep out the bitter cold. The winter of 1944–1945 had been severe, especially in the mountain villages in northern Honshu, and the shrines, lamp posts, and statues were covered with straw as a protection against the cold winter winds.

Great snowflakes from the late winter storm fell softly and hid the tragedies war had brought to this once beautiful land. Koturu held out his palm and watched a snowflake float toward his gloved hand. He left the semidarkness for the darker edges of the station area and walked with his head down across the almost deserted courtyard.

He stepped carefully into the street where coolies had shoveled away the snow, and picked his way through the half-light from the lanterns. He passed a Shinto shrine, a jinja, built in a place where his people believed the spirits of lakes, mountains, and flowers bestowed their special power.

Overhead, the sky and clouds were filled with patches of almost frozen mist that hung just above the taller hills. Koturu trudged wearily along the street until it narrowed and instinctively turned into the michi, the familiar pathway that would eventually lead him to his home.

He was deep in thought. The war was going badly, and he was convinced that Japan could not win this war it had begun. He knew that the American industrial might could not be defeated, and it was senseless to continue the conflict which threatened to destroy his beloved country.

The war had completely entangled his life and all those he loved. It should not have begun the way it did, he thought, and the war lords had far underestimated the American fighting strength.

He passed the jumble of huts and crossed the meadow where flowers grew in the spring and where his three sons once played. He stopped and tried to remember his sons as they were then. He lifted his head now, for he was familiar with every foot of the way. Even in the half-darkness, he could make out the dwarfed and twisted pine trees dotting the gradual slope toward his home.

The village, before the war, had seemed almost delicate, like a porcelain vase. Here, the people still valued the simple things of beauty, like polished wood, colored paper, and old stone made shiny from rubbing.

Koturu felt relieved to be away from the mass of jinrikishas and the city noises of Tokyo, noises of civilization that lately seemed to wrap him in a thick cloak of despair.

When Koturu reached the wall surrounding his home, he opened the gate and stood for a moment looking at the small garden, draped in a blanket of snow, then walked to the entrance of his home. He wondered what he would say to his wife. She would, of course, know this was his last time to be home. She understood those things instinctively.

The wooden door opened as he reached his hand toward the latch, and his wife stood just inside, head slightly bowed, waiting for him to enter. Her silver hair was tied with a silk cord in two shining loops.

When he entered, she bowed and stepped away from the door. He wanted to touch her, to greet her in some way that would show his affection for her, but he could only bow his head. Ever since the news had come of the loss of their three sons, a smile had not crossed her face.

Takashi had never quarreled with the regimented life of a Japanese wife. She had long ago accepted the selection of her husband in the traditional manner of a Japanese woman whose husband is found through family connections. It had been many years ago, at the o-miai, when her parents first met in a formal way with the parents of her future husband. Her father had been a farmer, and his social class was just below that of the Samurai. It was difficult to change from one class to the other.

Her father eventually persuaded the Koturu family to accept her, promising she would be a good and fruitful wife who would bear many sons, but she had borne only three sons in all the years she had been married, and now all had died in this war that brought misery to her family, her people, and her country.

When she was young, she had prayed for many sons and secretly knelt before the bronze Buddha on the polished cherry wood table. She placed lotus leaves, dried and turned up at the edges, beside the ancestral tablet. She filled the green jade dishes with flowers and cried when Buddha did not hear her prayers.

Koturu removed his shoes and heavy coat and walked across the polished straw mats and down a narrow, crooked hallway into a tiny room with sliding doors made of thin paper and crossed with slender bars of wood. A plain wooden Shinto, sealed with white paper to guard it from pollution, was placed in the center of a small teakwood table. A curling mist rose slowly from the koro, the incense pot, filling the room with the perfumed sweet smell of burning sticks of incense.

It was here, before the shrine honoring the sun goddess and the emperor, where the Koturu family had knelt so many times. As she always did when her husband returned home, Takashi had placed an ikebana, a beautiful flower arrangement, in a delicate clay vase beside the table.

Takashi lit a silver-plated Bon lantern filled with rapeseed oil and watched the rising heat twist and whirl the ends of twisted braids of colored paper that hung above the lantern. She knelt silently on the tatami before her husband, waiting for him to speak. The straw mat, worn thin from years of use, should have been replaced, she thought. Takashi was puzzled when her husband poured two glasses of Toso-sake, the rice wine reserved only for very special occasions and New Year's.

"Takashi," Koturu said softly, "it is good to see you. You look well. I hope the snows have not been too high nor the winter winds chilled your body."

"The winter has been bad this year," she said simply.

Koturu lowered his eyes. "I can only stay the night. I must return to Tokyo tomorrow. I have been allowed to command an aircraft carrier. I am to take the ship on a great mission." He reached out his hand and his fingers touched her face. He hesitated. "I will not return," he said softly.

Takashi held his hand against her face. "I understand," she said, and kissed his hand.

Koturu held her hands in his. "But I had to see you this last time. We have seen many winters together, and there was always the spring that followed, but now, we must only see the winter."

Takashi felt a tear roll down her cheek, and Koturu touched the tear with his finger. "Takashi," he said gently, "a Samurai's eyes know no moisture."

"When our sons died," she whispered, "I lit candles that burned for forty-nine days, and the incense softened the air in their honor, and the heartache was deep within my breast. I prayed to Buddha to let me join my sons." She shook her head. "There is no body to rest in the family burial ground, and there is no tablet, no ihai, in the gilded shrine beneath the lotus tree. Where can I show my love and reverence?"

"The shrine must be in your heart, as it is in mine. Someday, when this war is ended, Japan will be a nation again. There will be winter, but spring will come again for the children of Japan. When that day comes, you and I and our three sons will have a garden where we can see the flowers bloom again."

Takashi nodded her head and said, "I hope that day will come soon."

Koturu lifted his glass of sake to his lips and waited for his wife to do the same. Their eyes met, and Takashi smiled.

The next morning, after her husband left to return to Tokyo, Takashi knelt on the straw mat she placed before the bronze Buddha and prayed that the journey of her husband would end in peace.

Two days later, Koturu stood by the window of the naval office in Tokyo and listened to a sweet-potato vendor, a uri nushi, singing a plaintive "Yakiimo," and watched him pull his cart of satsuma.

Koturu's eyes scanned the ko-seki, the ruins that had once been Tokyo. A few automobiles made their way through the masses of bicycles, carts, and rickshaws. In the far distance, the skeleton of buildings teetered on shattered foundations, and branchless trees, seemingly magnified in height, towered above the flattened waste that was once part of the Japanese beauty he loved. Scattered pieces of melted bottles and twisted metal were all that was left of houses and little shops and stores. Here and there, strong boxes, kuras, made of concrete or bricks and shaped like little houses, were all that remained.

Concrete troughs, once filled with water to put out the fires from the fire bombs, were empty. He shook his head in sorrow and grief over the devastation. The official news reported the damage from the fires had been contained, but as far as he could see, the earth was black from the fires that had so readily consumed the paper and wooden houses.

Our war was lost when we lost Saipan, Koturu thought. When the Americans cut off our shipping and attacked our homeland, we were left with nothing but our foolish dreams.

A secret report stated the fire bombs in late 1944 through March of 1945 killed thousands and thousands of Japanese civilians. He recalled too vividly the first night he saw the American B-29 bombers overhead and the destruction that followed. Not since the great earthquake of 1923 had so many of his people died. Then, as now, the fires raged from one flimsy house to the next, doing the actual killing. He shook his head again. The Americans know how deadly their fire bombs are, and we are helpless, he thought. What were the words to the poem he had once read? Something about the hidden flower of the heart fading so slowly?

Koturu longed for the time when the war would be over, and there would once again be time for poems and dreams. He gathered his papers and placed them in his briefcase and left the office for his assignment as commander aboard the aircraft carrier *Shuwon*.

On the evening of April 5, 1945, Koturu sat alone in the stateroom of the aircraft carrier. Koturu was a Samurai, and like his father and his father before him, he accepted death, as all warriors must, but now that his sons had died in the war, there would be no ancestor to follow. His life as a Samurai had taught him that courage and valor must be blended with serenity and composure, and life and death were inseparable, each a part of the other. He had taught those beliefs to his sons. He hoped they had remembered.

Koturu knew he must show the faith and courage of a Samurai to his men when the time came. From an early age, he had been taught true courage was to live when it is right to live, and to die only when it was right to die. Koturu knew this was that time.

The vice admiral removed his glasses and rubbed his eyes. As usual, his thick white hair was disheveled. He picked up the microphone and held it to his mouth. His voice was soft, and the crew crowded around the intercoms in every area of the ship.

"My brave and loyal men of this great ship, the final sacrifice has been asked of each of you, a sacrifice for your country and for your emperor. We are on a glorious mission to destroy the American fleet. If we are successful, Japan will still win this war. If we are not successful, and if our ship is sinking, save your life so you may fight another day."

He continued haltingly, "If there is anyone on the ship who wishes to remain ashore, he may go before the morning light." Koturu paused, then added, "The rising sun promises that we will have a tomorrow, for our tomorrow is the future of our country. May the emperor's blessings be with you, and Buddha be your companion. Banzai! Banzai!"

No crew member went ashore during the night, and at 0300 on April 6, the Japanese fleet consisting of ten ships moved from its sheltered mooring place toward the waters of the Inland Sea between Honshu and Shikoku. Two submarines of the R.O. class had moved out earlier to serve as the eyes of the fleet. As the carrier, two cruisers, four destroyers, and the largest of all battleships reached the Inland Sea on the way toward Okinawa, Koturu felt the adrenaline flowing and the excitement gathering.

The armada was under radio silence, but each ship knew its assigned course of action and its specific objective. Zero fighters lined the *Shuwon*'s flight decks, and the battleship *Fujiyama*'s guns were readied. The two mighty warships were the best and last great ships of the Japanese Imperial Navy.

The gun crews on each ship readied their weapons and pointed their guns toward the sky. Torpedoes were loaded and primed. Orders were given that when the American fleet was found, and the battle began, all ammunition and torpedoes were to be expended.

Koturu's objective was to launch his Zeros and direct them toward sinking the American carriers. If Koturu's *Shuwon* came under attack before he launched his planes, the cruisers would first protect the carrier and then the battleship as best they could. If the battle could not be won, they were to ram and sink any major American ship.

The destroyers would attack the American carriers and then join the cruisers in their fatal mission.

The carrier planes were to fly a protective cover for the Japanese fleet, then the pilots would fly low to the water and crash their plane into the flight decks and control towers of the American warships. The prime targets were the carriers and battleships. No plane was to return.

The weather bulletin promised clear weather, and Koturu frowned. He needed foul weather, not weather such as promised. One hour later, Koturu was handed another weather projection that stated a storm was directly ahead and a better than fifty percent chance of foul weather for the next several hours. Incredibly, the barometer had already begun to fall. The wind increased, and soon the sea was churning up angry, whitecapped waves. In the predawn darkness, Admiral Koturu stood clutching a rail on the bridge of his flagship.

Koturu's eyes searched the sea before him. His mind flashed back to a cold morning, only three and a half years ago when the news was broadcast to all the world. How could so much have gone wrong in such a short time? he wondered. So many sorrows, so much destruction, so many bitter memories. He recalled hearing the announcement, "Today, December 7, before dawn, the Imperial Army and Navy entered into a state of war with American and British forces in the western Pacific…" Soon the early morning news vendor was shouting "Senso! Senso!" and throughout the day, people of all nations shouted "War! War!" It was odd, he thought, that he remembered hearing the sound of tiny bells announcing extra editions of the day's newspapers from the *Domei* and the *Nippon Times*.

Koturu was now concerned that the storm was so severe his planes would be unable to locate the American ships. His planes could not search for the American fleet and have enough fuel to accomplish their mission. The Japanese destroyers pitched and rolled in the angry sea.

Koturu was convinced the Americans were aware of his every move. He was one of the few who believed the Americans had long ago been able to decipher Japanese messages. It could not be a coincidence, he thought, that the Americans were always ready and waiting when the Japanese fleet sailed. After all, he reasoned, the Japanese had been able to break the American lower grade ciphers on weather reports and routine transmissions, but lost this advantage when the Americans used their high frequency radio waves.

Koturu knew the impending sea battle would be his last and felt a sense of pride in being a part of the suicide mission. He prayed his planes would find the American carriers and would inflict heavy damage to the enemy before they could launch their planes.

If his Japanese warships were successful in locating the American ships and could sink the carriers, there would be some lingering hope that Japan could still obtain a negotiated settlement with the Allies. The peace he prayed for would come, and his people would suffer no more. If the mission failed, Japan would be defeated. Either way, the war would finally be over.

An incredible piece of good luck brought encouragement

to Koturu's mission. A radio operator on one of the American ships was sending a weather advisory, and the Japanese, skilled in the use of radio direction-finding equipment, used the transmission as a beacon to locate the American carriers.

Koturu stood in the driving rain and watched the last of his planes speed down the carrier deck and into the stormy air. Crew members shouted "Banzai! Banzai," and minutes later, the commander of the squadron informed the bridge that all planes were in formation, and the flight was turning toward the American Fleet.

Koturu looked at the storm winds from the bridge of the *Shuwon*. How fitting, he thought, that his Kamikaze planes were named in honor of two thirteenth-century storms that had driven the invading fleet of Kublai Khan away from the Japanese shores.

"Perhaps this storm is a good omen," he said.

The Japanese Navy had been unable to devise a dependable system to help its pilots distinguish friends from enemies at sea, and identification was almost impossible when visibility was poor, especially on a rainy morning like this, but Tokyo had assured Vice Admiral Koturu that no other Japanese ships lay ahead of his fleet.

If Buddha were kind, Koturu thought, the Japanese Zero pilots should be able to accomplish their mission. Japanese planes would have to penetrate the fighter defense protecting the American carriers, but the dark skies would provide cover for the Kamikaze pilots.

Meanwhile, the American fleet saw the approach of the enemy on their radar, and the order to man battle stations screamed over the intercoms. Hellcats raced into the air and headed toward the Japanese ships.

The Kamikaze planes flew just above the waves and headed for the American ships. Antiaircraft fire darkened the gray sky with dark explosive blotches, and tracer bullets streaked across the skies. Four Japanese planes fell in red bursts of flame into the sea.

An American Avenger torpedo plane headed directly toward Koturu's fleet, and the pilot released his torpedo when his plane was a hundred yards from a Japanese cruiser. The ship shuddered and smoke and flame billowed from the port side.

A Dauntless dive-bomber dropped a bomb down the stack of another Japanese cruiser, and the forward magazine exploded in a blazing inferno. Depth charges ignited in a series of shattering sympathetic explosions. The Japanese seamen staggered to the deck and watched grimly as the ship began to list. The seamen, realizing their ship was going under, lowered her colors to half-mast, and the crew, hats off, stood at attention as the ship's bow slipped below the waves.

Two Japanese submarines sighted the American ships in their cross hairs and fired their entire supply of twenty-four-inch torpedoes at the approaching enemy. Two of the torpedoes hit a light cruiser, and the bow of the ship was blown away. Three torpedoes crashed into a heavy cruiser, and the remainder of the torpedoes missed their targets.

The American cruisers and battleships fired salvo after salvo toward the *Fujiyama*, and shells swept the bridge with a murderous hail of shrapnel and splinters. The *Shuwon* turned to starboard, helpless to come to the aid of the battleship.

One of the Japanese screening destroyers reported torpedo tracks racing toward the *Fujiyama*'s blackened starboard side. One torpedo exploded harmlessly on the heavy armor belt amidships of the battleship, but the second struck her unprotected stern, jamming the rudders and wrecking the steering gear.

The battleship rocked as six more torpedoes crashed into her port side. Fires broke out below, and the Japanese sailors rushed to extinguish the flames. One torpedo exploded at the same time the third salvo from an American cruiser plunged through the armored deck amidships to the four-inch magazine. In seconds, the flash spread down to the fifteen-inch magazine, and a terrific explosion amidships seemed to lift the battleship into the air, tearing the ship apart.

The battle for the *Fujiyama* was ended, and the greatest of all Japanese battleships slowly rolled over, and twenty-five hundred sailors followed her to her watery grave. The pride of the Imperial Navy, the "unsinkable battleship," was no more.

With the loss of the *Fujiyama*, the American planes flew directly toward the now listing *Shuwon*, and like swarming hornets, dropped their payloads on the sinking carrier. The *Shuwon* was attacked from the starboard bow by three dive-bombers and by a second wave of four dive-bombers off the starboard quarter. The first hit was scored amidships, and the second hit came to the after-section of the flight deck. A large gasoline storage area in the stern of the ship exploded.

Koturu tried to turn his ship in one last effort to escape the torpedoes that raced toward him. A torpedo skimmed the water just behind the stern, and another crashed below the waterline. A mighty explosion rocked the ship, sending sheets of metal flying into the air. Fires burned uncontrollably, and water poured through a huge gaping hole in the belly of the ship.

Koturu sat in his command chair on the bridge. He found the photograph of his sons and wife in the pocket of his uniform. He kissed the photograph and leaned back and closed his eyes. He was unaware that blood dripped from the chair and formed a puddle on the deck. The pain in his side that had been so severe was gone now; his head seemed clear for the first time since the battle had begun.

His life, like all Japanese Samurai, was dedicated to his emperor, and now too, was his death. He whispered, "Tenno heika, Banzai"—long live the emperor. The flag with its red rising sun disappeared below the waves, and the once proud *Shuwon* settled to the floor of the sea. The Imperial Japanese Navy died, and the battle was finished.

39

When General Osaka received the coded message from the Office of Military Affairs in Tokyo that Ten-Go would commence on the morning of April 6, his first line of troops in the southern sector prepared to attack along all fronts. His reserve divisions near Naha moved into the defensive positions vacated by the assault regiments.

At dawn on April 6, Osaka's artillery in the southern sector opened fire, and shells from 50 mm knee mortars, 90 mm, and 150 mm howitzers fell on the Seventh and Ninety-sixth Army divisions. The surprised Army commanders moved their defenses back from the charging Japanese Army, and General Stratton, Twenty-fourth Army commander, advised the Tenth Army command that the Japanese were penetrating his line in several locations. General Barlow ordered the Twenty-seventh Army Division into combat.

The First and Sixth Marine Divisions pushed northward to secure the northern two thirds of the island.

In the fading hours on D plus six, the Fifth Regiment met scattered resistance from Japanese artillery positioned in the wooded, mountainous terrain. Sporadic machine-gun fire punctuated the relative calm, and opposition from the Japanese infantrymen became more intense as the Marines advanced northward.

A high sea wall, built to guard the beach against storms, extended along the coast above Yontan airfield. A cliff riddled with caves, almost invulnerable to bombardment from the direction of the sea, lay just behind the wall.

Sergeant Tucker pulled his pack on his shoulders and tightened the straps. "George Company, get ready to move out." He looked at his watch. "We've got an hour before it gets too dark to check any more of the caves."

A battalion of Japanese soldiers waited in the ravines just over the first ridge.

George Pappas heard the rumble of artillery and looked toward the south. "Sounds like things are beginning to pick up for the Doggies fighting around Naha. I was hoping the bombing and shelling would have killed all the Japs, but I don't guess it did."

"Have you ever seen it that way?" Manny asked. "No matter how many bombs we drop, the Japs always come out to fight."

"I hope the Army has more of the Japs to fight than we do. On Cape Gloucester, I couldn't wait to get ashore," Pappas admitted.

"Yeah, I remember. What happened to all that gung ho crap you used to have, George?"

"I don't want the law of averages to catch me. The more times we get in combat, the closer my number gets, and I'm not taking any more chances than I need to take."

"The law of averages could catch us all before the war is over," Manny admitted.

A mortar shell exploded fifty feet from where Pappas and King walked, and shrapnel dug into the coral limestone. Another shell landed among the Marines just to their left, and pieces of flesh, blood, and strips of clothing exploded into the air. A sickening layer of red and blackened body parts covered Manny and Pappas. Pappas pulled a burning piece of clothing from the top of his helmet and, with his foot, stomped the smoldering remnant of a Marine's dungaree jacket. A Nambu machine gun spewed bullets along the limestone ridge, and three Marines fell.

"Get back down the hill!" Sergeant Tucker shouted, as bullets swept the rugged terrain. Williams and Boog slid down the steep ridge they had just climbed and tumbled into the narrow canyon below. Tucker slid on his stomach down the cliff beside them and crawled behind a large boulder.

Boog's left hand was bleeding and felt numb, but he could still move his fingers. He groaned and tried to get to his feet, as bullets from a Japanese sniper splattered the boulder beside him. He fell to the ground and covered his head from the spray of rock.

Tucker shouted, "Stay where you are. Stay under cover."

A Nambu fired from the other side of the canyon, and Boog pushed his large shoulders closer to the boulder.

"Son of a bitch," Tucker cursed. "We're trapped in a fuckin' cross fire."

"Corporal King," Tucker shouted, "can you hear me?"

There was a moment of silence, then Manny called out, "I hear you, Sergeant." Tucker looked behind him and saw Manny only a few feet away.

"I need a volunteer to get word to Captain Slator that we need help. Slator shouldn't be far back, just over the last hill. You'll have to crawl out of here without being seen. It's getting dark, that'll help. Think you can do that?"

"Yeah, do you want me to tell him anything else?"

"Tell him what the situation is. We have casualties, wounded men that will have to be carried out. Tell him we need artillery, 105s at least, and tell him we can't take a miss. We're too close and there's no place to take cover."

Manny slipped his pack from his shoulders. "I'll tell him."

"King," Tucker said, "if you don't make it, we don't."

"I'll make it." Manny placed his rifle on the ground beside his pack. He kept only his knife and stepped around the boulders and disappeared.

"Mack, are you and Gil OK?" Pappas asked.

"Scared, but no broken bones," Gil answered. "Stanley got hit in the chest, and I saw Gordon fall. He slid right past me. I couldn't help him. Are you hurt, Mack?"

"I'm afraid to look," Mack cursed.

Pappas rubbed his bruised knees. "We're still in a hell of a position. All we can do is just sit here." He peeked over the boulder. "The Japs can't see us down here, but they don't need to see us. They can kill us with their fuckin' mortars and grenades. If they do, George Company will be minus at least one damned good Marine."

"It all depends on Manny getting through," Gil said.

"I'll bet my next beer ration he does," Mack replied.

When Manny started crawling toward the far side of the canyon, he stopped behind one of the battered tree stumps. He tried to see the top of the ridge, but it was too dark. He listened for any movement ahead, then crouched as low as he could and moved as quickly as he could. He knew the sooner he reached the far side of the canyon the less likely it would be for the enemy to find him.

He ran as quietly as he could in the rubble, and when he stopped again to get his breath, he looked behind him to see flashes of light that he knew were the Japanese guns shelling his friends. "Damn you, Josie," he muttered. "If I hadn't stepped in your mule shit I might still be back on the farm picking cotton."

Manny started to climb the steep back side of the canyon. He knew he must climb as fast as he could, but he also knew caution and silence were equally as important if he was to slip through the enemy net. He planted each foot in the loose rubble and, before he took the next step, made sure no rock would roll to the valley below.

For the next hour, the Marines of George Company huddled beneath the overhang of the rocky ledge. Then suddenly, 105 shells exploded into the ridge just above them. Tucker smiled when the first shell slammed into the Japanese fortifications, and seconds later, the ridge shook from the bombardment as shell after shell pounded the scraggly rocks above.

Boog grinned. "Manny got through."

Tucker shouted, "OK, platoon, let's get ready to move out. Off your ass, Pappas, let's go!"

On April 7, the Navy's battleships and cruisers trained their guns on the stronghold at Naha, and the Japanese Army was caught in a murderous barrage. General Stratton ordered his artillery guns to concentrate their fire on the enemy fortifications, and shells streaked overhead.

General Osaka realized the Americans had regained the advantage, and unless he ordered his troops to fall back into a more defensible position, over thirty thousand of his men could be killed. Osaka advised Tokyo that his effort to support Ten-Go had failed and reluctantly gave the command, "Tenshin." The Japanese soldiers turned and advanced toward the Shuri Line north of Naha.

"Here," he told his soldiers, "the battle for Okinawa will be won or lost. You must defend your position with your life."

In the center of Tokyo, a subterranean bomb shelter with bare, concrete walls, now served as the headquarters for the Japanese war ministry's office of military affairs. It was in stark contrast to the president of the privy council's office in Tokyo destroyed by the American B-29 bombers, but it was the safest place the war council could meet.

The president of the privy council had visibly aged in the last year. His hair was gray, his face sallow and deeply wrinkled.

He had called the meeting as soon as he learned the devastating news about Koturu's fleet. He looked at the paper in his hand and thought of how it had been impossible to follow Sun Tzu's advice given more than twenty-five hundred years ago that one should avoid engaging the enemy while his morale is keen and one should strike when his morale ebbs.

He sat at the large table, surrounded by members of the highest rank of the Japanese Imperial Army and Navy. On the left side of the chief of the Navy general staff sat the commander of the First Imperial Guards Division, and to his right sat the admiral of the combined fleet. The director of the bureau of naval affairs and the minister of war sat together on the opposite side of the table. The prime minister sat at the far end of the table.

"The news of the first sea battle of our Ten-Go operation off the shores of Okinawa is not good," the president said solemnly. "We lost every plane and every ship."

There was a groan among the Japanese war lords seated at the table.

"There may have been survivors picked up by the American destroyers," the president continued. "But we had nothing with which to search for our brave countrymen. Our men could not accomplish their objectives, and I am saddened to say we did not destroy the American fleet, but we have no alternative but to pursue our plans of the 'Ten-Go' operation. If we abandon 'Ten-Go' now, there will be little hope of ever stemming the tide of the advancing American troops."

"And our troops on Okinawa? How did they do in their attack on the American forces? Were they successful in overrunning the American lines?" asked the chief of the Navy.

"General Osaka could not push the Americans into the sea as we had hoped. Our troops are bravely resisting the Americans, and we occupy strong positions north of Naha, but it will be a long battle."

The president took a deep breath. "Our Kamikaze planes sank only one destroyer, two LSTs, and several supply ships and damaged two cruisers, three of their carriers, and one of their battleships. Our antiaircraft guns managed to shoot down an unverified six of their planes. Several of our Kamikaze pilots penetrated the intense naval fire, but unfortunately, many of them crashed into the sea."

The president's voice broke. "They sank our ships and shot down our planes—all of them."

He swallowed and waited until he could speak again. "The news I have told you is not good, and we must now prepare for an American landing force to attack our homeland."

"Let them try to invade our shores," the minister shouted. "We will meet them on the beaches, and they will pay dearly for the injustice wrought on our people. We can still win the war. Our people will give their lives, if necessary, to defend their country. We have the duty to protect the emperor and our nation, and we must honor our pledge to do all in our power to do so."

The admiral rose slowly from his seat and bowed to the president. "We no longer have a Navy with which to defend our country. We have lost our last and greatest warships. Our planes are lost. There are no more to replace them. Our seamen are gone. Our ships are gone. General Osaka could not defeat the Americans on Okinawa. What more do we have with which to fight them?"

"I agree with the admiral," the naval chieftan said. "We have little left to fight with, and there is no chance we can rebuild our defenses in time to resist an invasion of our homeland. Intelligence believes the invasion will begin on Kyushu, but there are some who believe the landing will be on the island of Shikoku. In either event, we cannot keep them from landing."

"We are not defeated," the commander said. "The Navy may not have ships, but you forget we have millions of soldiers and armed civilians here in Japan. The Americans may land, but they will not advance. Our women and children will fight beside our soldiers, and we can keep the Americans from moving inland. This is our homeland, and we will die, if need be, to defend it. The Americans are not willing to die as are the Japanese."

"Every member of this council has the opportunity to speak," the prime minister said. "Every member is encouraged to speak what is in his heart, but I must speak what is on my mind as well as in my heart."

The minister rose from the table. "I am concerned about the emperor's safety, but I am also concerned about public safety. Certainly our people are loyal, but before the Americans invade our shores, we should consider an alternative to continuing the war."

A look of surprise was on the faces of the council at the prime minister's words. They were aware of the importance of his position in the Japanese governmental system, and his opinions were considered in the highest esteem, not only with the privy council, but with the emperor himself.

The director leaned forward. "Do you suggest, Mr. Prime Minister, we now sue for peace with the Americans and the British?"

The council members waited for the answer.

"No, not just yet," the prime minister answered. "But it is something we must not be afraid to suggest at a later time."

"I suggest each of you consider the words of the prime minister," the president said. "When you do, give your mind as well as your heart a chance to speak. For now, return to your respective commands. I will ask you to meet with me as the war events so dictate. The fate of our nation may soon rest in your hands."

40

The Japanese seamen and soldiers in the northern two-thirds of the island were not trained in the type of warfare they were forced to fight, and one by one, the Japanese pockets of resistance were destroyed. The armed civilians and territorial militia could not hold back the combat veterans of the First and Sixth Marine Divisions, and in the last week of April, General Post advised General Barlow that the northern two-thirds of Okinawa was secured.

Barlow ordered the Third Amphibious Corps to assist the Army's Twenty-seventh and Seventh Divisions in the southern area, and the Marine divisions turned south and moved into the front line positions facing the Shuri Line.

The Japanese high command believed the caves and

intertwining tunnels north of Naha and Shuri to be impregnable, but the Japanese forces began to crumble from the unrelenting bombardment by the American forces. The war council in Tokyo realized evacuation was impossible. Still, the council ordered an increase in the Kamikaze raids on American warships and land forces.

General Osaka moved his experienced troops of the Sixty-second Imperial Division into the center of the battle line, while General Valley ordered the First and Seventh Regiments to hold their position until the Japanese forces could be targeted by heavy artillery barrage.

Valley ordered Colonel Taggart's Fifth Marines to occupy the area directly north of Shuri Castle, which was also a flank position on the east side of the entrenched First and Seventh Marines.

The rain fell gently, like spring rain in Kansas, as Bob Munday sat on the ground, his legs folded. In the last light of day, he stared at the photograph of his wife and son. How many months since she wrote she wanted a divorce? he thought. He thought of the happy times they had shared before he enlisted in the Marines and how proud he was when his wife gave birth to his first son. They named him Robert; that was his wife's idea, he remembered. He recalled the day he enlisted, when she told him how much she loved him and that she would wait forever for his return.

When the letter came telling him she wanted to marry another man, he had been terribly hurt, and the words the chaplain said to comfort him were meaningless. All he could think about then, and now, were the wonderful times they had spent together, and the love they once shared.

He wrapped his handkerchief around the photograph, a note he had written to his son, his wrist watch, and his wedding ring. He thought for a moment, unfolded the handkerchief, and placed the picture of his wife back inside his billfold. He re-wrapped the handkerchief around the note, watch, and ring and put them in his pocket.

He listened to the exploding shells from the 105 mm and 155 mm howitzers and the crash of the 81 mm mortars adding to the destruction of the caves and installations near the Shuri Castle. He heard the answering salvos of Japanese artillery and watched the .50-caliber tracer bullets arch across the sky. Like pieces of a rainbow, he thought.

He got up and walked to where Manny lay. "Manny," Munday whispered, "you awake?"

"Yeah, I'm awake. You can't sleep either?"

"No. Guess I'm thinking about tomorrow. Sergeant Tucker said we'll be moving up about daybreak. You'd think there wouldn't be any Japs left after all that shelling, but I doubt that'll be the case."

"Well, it never has been that way. There always seems to be more Japs than we ever expect, doesn't it?"

"Can I talk with you a minute?" Munday asked.

Manny raised up on one elbow. "Sure, what's on your mind?"

Munday sat beside Manny and crossed his legs. "That was a brave thing you did the other day, going to tell Captain Slator we needed artillery when the Japs had us pinned down. I just wanted to tell you it took guts to do what you did. You saved some of our lives. The Japs would have hit us with their mortars sooner or later if you hadn't gotten through their lines."

"Somebody had to do it, and besides, Sergeant Tucker volunteered me to do it. When Tucker volunteers you, there isn't much choice," he laughed.

"But you did it. That's what counted."

"Everyone else in the platoon would have done the same, but thanks for saying it."

Munday stared at the ground, and for a moment, neither man spoke.

"That's not what you wanted to talk about is it?" Manny asked.

"Not exactly, but I did want you to know I thought you ought to get a medal."

Munday cleared his throat. "Manny, we've known each other almost two years, but I don't think I've ever heard you talk about your family. I know you lived on a farm, but that's about all I know."

Manny shrugged. "I've never been much of a talker. I'm better at listening. Do you want to talk about your wife, about your divorce? Is that what you're trying to say?"

"It's all I ever think about. I haven't wanted to talk about it, but I've got to talk to someone. When the letter came from my wife, asking me for a divorce, I considered suicide, but I didn't have the guts to do it. I used to dream about how great it will be when the war ends and we all go home. It doesn't mean that much to me now, not anymore. Ever since I got the letter from my wife asking me for a divorce, I haven't really cared about going back home. Without her and my son, there's nothing worth going home for now."

"Bob, there's lots of reasons to go back. You're the father of a fine son, and nothing can ever change that. You may not think so now, but it can't be the end of the world. You owe it to your son to go back."

"Sometimes I want to see both of them so much it almost kills me," Bob said in a low voice. "I try to tell myself that if I do go back, maybe it can be the way it was, but I know it won't ever be the same. I still love my wife, but I hate her, too. You know what I mean?"

"Maybe it can't be the way it was, but it won't be the same for any of us," Manny said. "I don't want it to be. We've all changed. Why should we expect it to be any different for the ones back home?"

Both men watched the flashes of light from the artillery brighten the sky and listened to the battle's prelude, noting the increase in the crescendo of exploding shells.

"I'm not afraid of dying, are you? I mean, when the time comes, will you be afraid?" Munday asked.

"I don't know. I don't let myself think about it," Manny answered. "Worrying about it won't help."

"If I do get killed," Munday murmured softly, "it might make it easier on my wife to marry again. She's always been a strong Catholic. In the eyes of God, she'd be free to marry again."

"Did you give her the divorce?"

"I signed the papers she sent, and I haven't heard any more from her. I suppose she went ahead with the divorce and probably got married. I don't know. I never wrote her back. I didn't even write a letter to her when I sent the divorce papers back to her. I didn't know what to say that would make much sense to her. I wanted to tell her how much I loved her and how much it meant to me to have a son, but I couldn't bring myself to say that."

"The war will end someday, and we'll go home, and when we do, some of us will be disappointed in what we find, but that doesn't mean it's not worth going back for."

"I guess you're right, maybe it'll be better than I think."

"We can hope it will be, Bob."

"Well, good night, Manny, guess I'll try to get some sleep. It may be awhile before we get to do that again. Thanks for talking with me. You're a good friend."

"Bob, when you want to talk again, about this or anything else for that matter, I'll be here. Just talking to someone helps."

"Yeah, it does. Well, thanks again. Good night."

Manny lay back on his poncho, and when Munday saw Manny's eyes were closed, he slipped his handkerchief with his watch, ring, and the note to his son inside Manny's pack on the ground beside him. He got up and walked back to where he had been sitting. He leaned back and closed his eyes and waited for the night to end.

At daybreak, the artillery stopped, and there was a deafening stillness. There was no return fire from the Japanese gun emplacements, and for a moment, to the Marines of George Company, the war seemed far away.

"All right, up and at 'em, let's move 'em out. George Company, let's go," Tucker shouted.

As the push began, Navy Corsairs and dive-bombers began their air strikes, dropping bombs and strafing the Japanese fortifications. Marine tanks and riflemen moved forward under a smoke screen from phosphorous mortar shells.

Corporal Williams adjusted his pack to his shoulders. "Gil, let's go." He picked up his M-1 rifle, and the two friends ran toward the Japanese lines.

Further to the west, the First and Third Battalions started their push on the Shuri Line. The sound of 60 mm and 81 mm mortars began again, and the sharp chatter of .30-caliber machine guns signaled the beginning of the offensive push on the Japanese stronghold. Osaka's troops answered with their own fire, and the sound of knee mortars and quick bursts from Nambu machine guns increased in fury, as the intensity of the battle mounted.

Mack ran behind a Sherman tank that churned through the battle-scarred, hilly terrain. Overhead, a squadron of Navy planes screamed low to the ground and strafed the Japanese lines with .50-caliber bullets.

Boog Marshall pulled the pin from the grenade he held in his hand, reached back as far as he could, and threw the grenade far ahead of him. The exploding grenade sent chunks of dirt into the air, and a Japanese soldier ran from his hiding place and fired his rifle at the approaching Marines. From another bunker, another Japanese soldier tried to get his jammed Nambu to fire, but before he could do so, Gil Everson opened fire, and the Japanese soldier fell to the ground.

The minute Gil saw the soldier fall, the image flashed through his mind of another Japanese boy who had so briefly touched his life, the young boy he had killed on Talasea. In his mind's eye, Gil saw again the soldier who could not have been older than eighteen. The vision of his body, mangled and lifeless, would forever be imprinted on his mind.

A Marine with a flamethrower shot a stream of fire into another cave, and the scream of the burning Japanese could be heard above the sound of the exploding shells. Mack ran to the adjacent cave and threw a hand grenade into the opening and fell to the ground as the grenade exploded. He waited for any survivors to emerge from the cave, but when there were none, he ran forward to the next ridge.

His breath came in quick gasps, and he licked his lips and tried to swallow. He wiped his mouth and tried to spit dirt from his mouth. A grenade landed near him, and he hugged the side of the mound where he lay. The explosion covered him with chunks of earth scorched black and smelling of decay. He lifted his head just enough to look over the top and saw Manny and Munday running across a shallow ditch. Mack took a deep breath, climbed over the mound, and ran to join them.

For the next hour, George Company fought their way toward the outskirts of Shuri Castle. Flamethrower tanks spewed burning tongues of death, and streams of fire searched inside the hiding places. One Japanese soldier, his uniform aflame, staggered from the opening and fell to the ground in a barrage of .30-caliber bullets from the charging Marines.

The Fifth Marines fought from one mound to the next and, by midday, reached the base of the ridge before the castle.

Sergeant Tucker was the first from George Company to reach the steep sides of a shell-pocked gorge at the base of Shuri Castle. He motioned for his men to take cover and surveyed his remaining assault force. He rested on one knee. "Jesus," he murmured, realizing at least twenty percent of his company had not made it to the castle.

Tucker crawled along the foot of the cliff. "How you making it, Pappas?"

"Scared shitless, Sarge,"

Tucker smiled. "Yeah, stay that way. We got tanks coming, and we'll get some help from the artillery before we move up."

"King," Tucker said, "looks like you're okay."

"I'm all right, Sarge. Just a little winded."

Two feet away, Munday lay on his stomach in the rubble at the base of the ridge. "How you doing, Munday?" Tucker asked.

Munday looked up at Tucker. "I'm...I'm fine."

The rumble of tanks could be heard over the loud burst of artillery and mortar shells. The quick, sharp sounds of machine guns and the deeper sounds of a Browning automatic rifle added to the overture.

General Osaka's troops checked and reloaded their weapons and braced for the final battle for Shuri Castle, once the island's strongest defensive stronghold.

Tucker received Captain Slator's order to renew the battle, and the remnants of George Company began the final assault against the fortress. Manny King and Bob Munday climbed over the top of the last ridge in front of the castle and stayed as close as they could to the protection of a Sherman tank.

Bob Munday was exhausted. His brain was no longer capable of command, and his feet moved his body forward by instinct alone. He ran behind the big tank, his mouth open, gasping for air; his eyes burned and his legs were numb. A Japanese shell made a direct hit on the tank, and the Sherman stopped. The bullets from a Japanese Nambu machine gun hit the thick metal walls, and Manny King huddled closer to the tank.

Munday stopped, then stepped from behind the tank.

"No, Bob, wait!" Manny shouted.

Munday stood motionless for a moment, half of his body exposed to the Japanese fire. He starred at Manny and tried to swallow.

"Bob, come back!" Manny pleaded.

Munday stared at the castle, then looked back at Manny once more. Their eyes met for just a brief moment, and then Munday slowly turned and ran toward the castle.

The bullets thudded into Munday's body, and he crumpled to the ground and lay still.

Another tank moved ahead, momentarily shielding Munday's body from the deadly Nambu machine gun. Manny ran to Munday and pulled him back to the protection of the crippled tank. He knelt down to see Munday's torn dungaree jacket turning red where a bullet had shattered his shoulder and bullets had hit him in his chest.

Manny stared into the lifeless face of his friend and tried to say something, but the words were not there. With his fingers, he wiped a bit of dirt from Munday's cheek. He loosened Munday's helmet, then lowered Munday's head to the ground. He reached inside Munday's jacket and found his dog tags. He placed them on Munday's chest, where the graves registration personnel would be sure to find them.

Manny swallowed and managed to say in a soft voice, "Munday, you didn't have to do that. Oh God, why'd you go and do that?"

Manny knelt over Munday's body, and his lips whispered a prayer. He patted Munday on his shoulder and picked up his M-1 rifle. "So long, Munday, I gotta go now." He ran toward Shuri Castle.

When darkness settled over the battle scene, the Marines had captured the strategic Japanese stronghold, and General Osaka's Japanese forces had forever lost their chance to win the battle of Okinawa.

The following morning, Manny reached inside his pack for a box of K rations, and his fingers felt the folded handkerchief Munday had slipped inside the pack the night before. Manny looked at the handkerchief with a puzzled frown on his face. He unfolded the cloth and found the note, the ring, and the watch. At first, he couldn't understand how they had gotten in his pack, then he saw the initials RM engraved inside the watch. He looked inside the ring, saw the inscription, "All my love, Jean," and realized the ring belonged to Munday.

Manny got to his feet and looked back in the direction where he had left his friend. He read the note Munday had written to his son. He felt a tear roll down his cheek as he folded the note and put it in his pocket. He looked again in the direction where he had left his friend. "You put these in my pack last night when we talked, didn't you? You gave your life for your son, and for her," he whispered, "She'll never know how deeply she hurt you and how much you cared."

After the loss of Shuri Castle, General Osaka knew the strength of his remaining Army was not sufficient to hold back the Americans, and his troops could not long endure the relentless assault by the American forces. For almost two weeks, his soldiers had been pounded by artillery and the Navy's battlewagons. Planes had strafed and bombed his installations.

The food supply for his men was exhausted, and they had lived on the insects they could catch and bark and roots they could find.

Prior to the invasion of Okinawa, Osaka had ordered his soldiers to stock the many caves on the Oruku Peninsula with food and ammunition. Knee mortars and small artillery pieces had been placed in the connecting tunnels. Now Osaka ordered his commanding officers to withdraw all troops from the Shuri Line and move them to the last underground defensive position in the southern region his troops could occupy.

In early June, when Vice Admiral Higgins received the morning weather report, he cursed under his breath. "Damn, just what we need, a full-blown typhoon." He issued storm warnings to all ship commanders, and preparations were made to disperse the fleet.

The typhoon hit Okinawa at midmorning; the rain fell in a wall of water, and the wind flattened the trees. The Marines struggled to find protection from rising water in the gullies and ravines, and field supplies and equipment were tossed in the air by the howling winds. All day and into the night and next day, the savage storm battered the island, and the American advance came to a halt. The Japanese in the caves heard the sound of the fury and, for the moment, were spared from the constant barrage of artillery shells.

After the winds passed over the island, the American Army and Marines salvaged as many supplies as they could. The recovery of the field equipment and usable supplies was hampered when the trucks bogged down in the slick mud, and the mud caked on the tracks of the tanks.

General Barlow, when advised of the deplorable field conditions, ordered the postponement of the assault of the Japanese forces until field maneuverability was restored.

For almost a week, the battle for Okinawa waited, and finally, the tanks and trucks could move to support the ground troops, and the war began again.

General Torao Osaka had never known any other way of life except that of a soldier in the Imperial Japanese Army. He had served his country with pride and distinction in China, Sumatra, and once before, here at Okinawa. His only loss of honor had been at New Britain, by these same American Marines he now faced.

When the First Marine Division came ashore at Cape Gloucester in December 1943 and defeated his elite troops of the Imperial Army, he vowed he would someday face them again. His prayer was to humiliate them as they had humiliated him. It had been this obsession that had driven him to lead the remnants of his once proud garrison through the jungles of New Britain and to eventually reach Rabaul.

When Osaka was chosen to take command on Okinawa, he thanked Buddha for the opportunity to fight the Marines again, but now, just two months later, Osaka knew he could never defeat the Americans. The American forces that had come ashore on Easter Sunday had been too many and too strong. Once more, he felt bitter and ashamed.

On June 21, General Osaka radioed a message to the war ministers in Tokyo. The message was brief, but its meaning was clear: "I can no longer defend my command."

Osaka stood at the entrance of his cave and looked toward Japan. "I can never return to my homeland." He gritted his teeth in anger. He considered his options. "I will never surrender to the Americans," he vowed. "I could commit hara-kiri. To die by the sword is the honorable thing to do. That is expected of an officer of my rank."

He listened to the shells exploding behind him, but they seemed not to matter now. His hatred for the Marines was even greater than his honor for dying as was expected of him. His eyes glared. "I will die as a soldier defending my command," he murmured defiantly.

General Osaka dressed in his most distinguished uniform as one of the highest officers in the Japanese Imperial Army. He fastened his sword to his belt, took two hand grenades and placed them inside his tunic, and gave one last tug to his coat. He bowed toward the east, toward his country and, with a white flag waving above him, walked from his command post and waited for the Marines to come, as he knew they would.

Colonel Alfred Jacobs watched the Japanese officer emerge from the cave and walk toward him. He recognized him immediately as the commanding officer of all the Japanese forces on Okinawa. Jacobs saw the white flag and ordered his troops to hold their fire.

Osaka faced his enemy and walked slowly across the battle-scarred ground. Jacobs, his dungaree jacket and trousers dirty and torn, his boots caked with mud, walked toward the immaculately dressed Japanese general. Osaka saw no officer insignia on Jacobs's jacket, but as he watched the man come toward him, he knew he faced a man of rank in the Marine Corps.

Jacobs stopped twenty-five yards from the general and motioned for Osaka to stop.

Twenty-five yards to the left of Colonel Jacobs, Sgt. Wally Smith stood with his M-1 rifle in his hand. He watched Osaka carefully and frowned at the appearance of such an impressive Japanese officer.

There's somethin' jist not right, Smith thought, but ah' jist can't figure what. He nervously rubbed the stock of his rifle and lifted it closer to his shoulder. "Colonel," he said under his breath, "Ah shure as hell hope y'all know what y'all are doin'."

The frown on his face deepened as he tried to understand what it was that bothered him. He saw Osaka take another step toward Colonel Jacobs, and then another step. They were now less than twenty yards apart.

Suddenly Sergeant Smith knew. Everything about the general's uniform was perfect, except one thing. His tunic did not fit his body as did the rest of his uniform. There was a slight bulge on one side, and when he saw Osaka move his right hand to a gap between two buttons near his waist and slip his hand inside his tunic, he knew.

"Git down, Colonel!" Smith shouted, and lifted his M-1 rifle to his shoulder and fired. The impact from the bullet spun Osaka around, and he fell to the ground and rolled onto his stomach.

Jacobs wheeled around to see who had defied his order not to fire.

The blast from the two hand grenades lifted Osaka's body in the air, and Jacobs threw up his hands to shield his face as he was knocked to the ground by the concussion.

Jacobs lay on the ground for a moment, then raised his face and stared at the mangled body before him. He slowly got to his feet and looked back to see Sergeant Smith with his rifle in his hand.

"I'm glad you saw it was a trap, Sergeant. I'm also glad you're a pretty good shot."

By the end of June, and with the death of their commanding officer, organized resistance by the Japanese forces on Okinawa had ended. Some of the soldiers chose to take their own lives, but many realized the futility of continuing the fight and surrendered.

Out of the original Japanese garrison, seventy thousand troops and eighty thousand civilians were lost. There were seventy-seven hundred Americans killed and almost thirty-two thousand wounded.

The battle for Okinawa was over, and the American forces were less than a sunrise away from the Japanese mainland.

41

On the morning of August 5, 1945, Takashi Koturu stepped from the train at the depot in the center of town. She was unaccustomed to travel, especially in cities as large as Hiroshima, and she would have preferred to stay in her village in northern Honshu.

The letter from her uncle was unmistakably clear, and if Takashi wished to see her aunt before she died, she must do so without delay. Of all the members of the Koturu family, her aunt was Takashi's favorite relative.

After the death of Vice Admiral Naha Koturu, Takashi begged her aunt and uncle to come live with her, but they refused and insisted that Takashi visit them before the snows in northern Honshu made travel more difficult. The urgency in the letter from her uncle forced her to make the trip in early August.

Takashi carried her small bag across the station platform, becoming more frightened by the push of the crowd. She was confused by the hurry of so many people, seemingly moving in all directions.

She tried to remember where she had been told to go for her uncle to meet her, but the frenzy of people pushed her toward the arched entrance leading to the front of the station.

Takashi held her small case to her body and struggled to free herself from the mass of people that jammed the exit ramp. A man brushed her face, and her glasses fell to the floor. She attempted to stop and find them, but the crowd pushed her along. She managed to work her way toward the less crowded side of the terminal.

"Excuse me, I am a stranger. Can you help me please?" she begged the young girl by her side.

"How can I help?" the girl asked.

"I am to meet my uncle, but I…" She lowered her head. "My eyes cannot see the hands on my watch. Can you please tell me the time?"

The young girl smiled at Takashi. "The time is 8:13."

Laura Bently folded diapers while she listened to the music on her radio. She was singing the words to "I'll Be Seeing You" when the music stopped. She heard a man's voice. "We interrupt this broadcast to bring you an important message from the White House in Washington, D. C. Please stand by."

Laura walked to the radio and waited.

The voice said again, "Ladies and gentlemen, the President of the United States, Harry S. Truman."

Radio stations throughout the world interrupted their programs, and interpreters stood by to broadcast Truman's message.

Laura sat beside the radio and turned up the volume. "My fellow Americans, this is your president. On August 6, 1945, at 8:15 Tokyo local time, the United States of America dropped an atomic bomb on Hiroshima, Japan's eighth largest city. The bomb was dropped from an altitude of over thirty-one thousand feet, and was timed to occur nineteen hundred feet above ground. The bomb was equivalent to twelve and a half thousand tons of TNT. The center of Hiroshima was vaporized, killing over seventy-eight thousand people. The United States urgently asks that the Japanese government surrenders unconditionally, and this terrible conflict be ended."

Throughout the world, President Truman's message had captured the minds of all people, and military and political leaders hurried to determine what history would be.

When the bomb exploded, some of the Japanese people, consumed in a wilderness of abandoned faith, believed the world was coming to an end, and the devastation could not be a part of the Pacific War. The Japanese government and war ministers refused to make a decision.

"What the hell is an atomic bomb?" George Pappas asked when he heard the news about Hiroshima. "How can one bomb do as much damage as they said it did? The scuttlebutt is there were thousands of people killed and thousands injured. I'll believe it when I hear it from Tokyo Rose."

"I heard a news broadcast on the jeep communication radio myself," Manny argued. "The announcer said the report had been confirmed, and I don't believe they'd broadcast a story like that if it wasn't true."

"If it's true, the war will end," Mack admitted. "If one bomb can do what they said it did, Japan will have no choice except to surrender."

"If the war doesn't end, and we have to invade Japan itself, the people will fight us from every street and from every house," Manny said. "We've seen them die on the islands in the Pacific rather than surrender, and they'll be more fanatic on their home soil."

"It could still be a trick of some kind," Boog argued. "Like when we made them think the Second Division was landing on the south end of the island."

"Captain Slator told Sergeant Tucker the bombing was confirmed. Do y'all realize what this means?" Gil asked.

"Who's gonna tell the Japs up on the lines the war is over?" Pappas asked.

"It's not over yet, Pappas," Manny cautioned, "not until the Japs say the war is over. I don't want the last bullet of the war to have my name on it, and you don't either, do you?"

Mack, Gil, Pappas, Manny, and Boog crowded around the radio on the communication jeep, listening to the announcement that on August 9, a second atomic bomb had been dropped on Nagasaki and thousands of people had been killed instantly, and before the day was over, thousands more had died from the aftereffects of radiation, heat, and fire. The report of "lingering death" at Nagasaki was the same as from Hiroshima.

"The war can't go on, not after this," Gil said. "I was afraid to hope at first, but not now."

"Whatever an atomic bomb is, I'm glad we have it instead of Japan," Manny added. "Can you believe that 24,000 people could be killed by just one bomb?"

"I pray that the war is over soon," Pappas whispered.

"The war is going to end," Mack said. "It just has to end. Japan can't go on fighting now."

The Soviet Union declared war on Japan on August 8, 1945, one day before the second atomic bomb was dropped.

The next day, the Japanese Supreme War Guidance Council met in Tokyo to decide the future of the war and of Japan. Some of the council wanted to accept the Potsdam Agreement, others wanted to continue fighting, but the final decision to end the war could only be made by the emperor. On August 10, Hirohito met with the council, and in a voice unfamiliar to millions of people in the Japanese empire, he told them that Japan must now surrender.

General Valley called his officers together. "Gentlemen," he said simply, "today, August 14, 1945, President Truman has advised CinCPac that Japan has accepted the terms of the Potsdam Agreement calling for unconditional surrender. This bloody Pacific war has ended."

.When the announcement was made that the war was over, Pappas and Boog started jumping in the air. "Japan has surrendered!" Pappas shouted, and the two friends danced and laughed and shouted the words again and again.

"The war is over, the war is over! We're going home!" Gil screamed and grabbed Mack's hand and pumped it up and down.

Mack hugged Manny, and tears of joy filled their eyes. Mack swallowed, and his voice broke. "It's over, Manny. We made it through the war."

Sgt. Wally Smith removed his helmet and knelt and bowed his head. "Ah thank ya, God."

Boog threw his helmet high in the air, and yelled at Mack. "I've got some whiskey, let's go have a party. The friggin' war is over!"

Gil laughed. "Mack, let's go steal another chicken from Lieutenant Blevins!"

The celebration lasted on into the night, and every bottle of jungle juice, bottle of whiskey, and beer ration was opened and shared. The thought of going home was foremost in the mind of every Marine.

Aboard the battleship USS *Missouri*, the Japanese delegation stood before the seated Allied commanders and awaited their fate as unwilling representatives of a defeated nation.

Major General Warren Valley, Lt. General Frederick Post, and Vice Admiral Lesley Higgins stood behind the seated Allied commanders. Immediately behind them, Colonel Jacobs stood beside Lieutenant Colonel Jackson and Colonel Taggart. The other Marine officers stood nearby.

The Japanese officers, their uniforms as weary as the bodies that sagged inside, faced their captors. The Japanese foreign minister, his top hat mockingly out of character for the occasion, stood wavering on his cane and grimaced, a prisoner of silence, as the surrender documents were signed.

At the same moment, the minister was thinking that what he must do this day was more of a humiliation to his emperor than to his nation. He had been the one who had tried to save His Majesty the torture of defeat by insisting that Japan would not accept the Potsdam declaration unless emperor Hirohito remained as the sovereign ruler of the Japanese people, but the Allies had refused.

He did not expect the conquerors of his world to treat his people with dignity, but he dared to hope that from this day forward, September 2, 1945, Japan could become a nation of progress rather than a nation of despair.

He looked up at the American flag, seeming to float in the gentle breeze, and his shoulders sagged ever so slightly. He wondered how it would have been if the flag was of the rising sun. He heard the Allied commander say, "A world dedicated to the dignity of man and the fulfillment of his most cherished wish for freedom, tolerance, and justice."

The minister thought about those words, and remembered that only two weeks before, at noon on August 14, he and the entire Japanese people were astounded to listen to a completely unfamiliar high-pitched voice speaking a dialect of Japanese so rarefied as to be incomprehensible to all but the most educated. He had listened to the words, "We declared war on America and Britain out of our sincere desire to ensure Japan's self-preservation and the stabilization of East Asia. Despite the best that we have done, the war situation has developed not necessarily to Japan's advantage. The hardships and sufferings to which our nation is to be subjected hereafter will certainly be great. We must unite our total strength and devote our energy to construction for the future. We must cultivate the ways of rectitude, foster nobility of spirit, and work with resolution so that we may enhance the innate glory of the Imperial State and keep pace with the progress of the world. The time has come to endure the unendurable."

Moments later, when the proceedings were over, the Allied commander, in a different tone, said, "Let us pray that peace will now be restored to the world, and that God will preserve it always."

42

Pappas and Manny looked out the window of the ancient train and were fascinated by the beautiful countryside of mainland China. Coolies working in the fields behind water buffalo and oxen straightened up from their back-breaking labor, and laughed and shouted at the passing train.

When Pappas waved, the peasants in the fields waved with pieces of clothing or their straw hats, and children dropped their primitive tools and ran toward the train clapping their hands.

"I didn't want to come to China to disarm the Japanese troops when the war ended," Gil said. "But now that we're here, I'm glad we came."

Manny watched the flooded fields of rice paddies as the

train rocked along the track. "This is a place I've read about but never thought I'd get to see."

"I'm going on liberty as soon as they'll let me. Forgive me, Lolita," Boog said.

The train slowed when it neared the depot in the center of Peking, and the curious Chinese people stared at the Marines leaving the train with their packs on their shoulder.

A Chinese woman, her padded coat torn and dirty, her feet bound with black cloth, hobbled close to a Japanese soldier standing at the gate entrance and spat on the soldier's feet. She cried in anguish, screaming at him and gesturing with her fist. The Japanese soldier cursed and lifted his hand to strike her, but several Chinese men and women hurried to her side and added their voices to the old women's anger. A Chinese man, bent from the waist in a deformed body, shook his fist in the soldier's face and also spat at the Japanese man's feet.

Boog saw the Japanese soldier and stepped out of formation and started toward the crowd.

Mack shouted, "Boog, get the hell back here. The war is over. Leave the son of a bitch alone. You'll start the war all over again."

Boog stopped and held up his middle finger at the Japanese soldier. The old Chinese man looked questionably at Boog, then grinned and lifted a bony finger and pointed it toward the Japanese soldier. Boog laughed and motioned for other Chinese men and women to make the same gesture, and one by one, they held up their fingers. One woman helped her young child lift his middle finger and shake it at the soldier. The crowd applauded and clapped their hands, and the soldier turned and walked away, lost in the crowd and excitement of the arriving conquerors.

The regiments and battalions were quartered in various parts of Peking, where suitable accommodations could be found to house the many thousands of Marines of the First Division.

Parts of the Fifth Regiment were lodged in the wooden buildings formerly used by the Dutch Legation, and Mack and

Gil were assigned a room with two wooden beds, a black coal stove, and a small table. Pappas, King, and Boog moved their gear into adjoining rooms.

Pappas said, "Hey, these rooms aren't bad. Do you guys realize this is the first time in about two years we've had a bed to sleep on, and inside a house too? I won't know what to do, sleeping inside. Boog, I hope you don't try to pee from your bed like you do from your hammock. You're back in civilization, you know."

"Sergeant Tucker said the whole town is giving us a banquet celebration tonight," Mack said. "Boog, I've heard the fish eyeballs are really good, and they say they do the same as oysters for your sex drive, and you'll like the way they season up some of their other food, too."

"Yeah?" Boog said. "Like season their food with what?"

"I think I'm not going to ask," Gil said. "All I'm going to eat for a month are fresh eggs."

"Tell them how to cook Irish stew," Mack suggested laughingly.

The banquet food was a variety of vegetables, rice, pork, duck, and fish parts, all served with an unlimited supply of hot sake and wine, and beer was consumed faster than the waiters could bring it to the tables. A Chinese man sat at each of the tables and spoke in English to the Marines, showing them how to hold the chopsticks and how to eat the various foods that filled the table.

Boog gave up trying to eat with chopsticks and raked the food from his plate into his mouth. He drank the hot sake and bottles of beer until his elbow slipped off the table and he fell out of his chair.

"Mack," Boog said, "I think I'm just drunk enough to eat some of your chicken soup. This sake and beer make as good a drink as the best of the jungle juice. Wow!" he said, looking at Pappas. "Unless there are two of you, I think I'm seeing double. I hope I'm seeing double 'cause when I sober up, there'll only be one Pappas, and one's enough."

"Yeah, I only see one of you, Boog, but I hope when I sober up I won't see any of you," Pappas said, and slipped under the table.

It was late when the last food on the table was eaten and the Marines drank the last of the sake and beer.

Boog squinted his eyes, then opened them as wide as he could. "Damn, I must be real sober 'cause I can't see Pappas," he giggled. "Where'd he go? The last time I looked, there were two of him, and now I can't even see one Pappas."

"I think he's under the table," Manny said, and bent down and looked under the table. "He's sound asleep."

Boog tried to focus his eyes on the Chinese man and asked, "How does a man go about getting with a woman?"

The man frowned a moment, then laughed, "Oh, you mean a geisha?"

"Geisha, goosha, whatever," Boog answered.

"There are many geisha. If you like, I will take you to place. You go tomorrow? I think too late for tonight."

Before Boog answered, Mack said, "You think right, tonight we're taking my friend back to our barracks. He'll have to settle for dreaming about Lolita tonight. Manny, you get Pappas up, and Gil and I'll try to steer Boog in the right direction."

A skeleton roster was listed for guard duty, and Marines swarmed the streets of Peking. Liberty was allowed every other night, and the Marines walked out the front gate. Every other night, they slipped through a hole they cut in the wall surrounding the legation. Rickshaws waited at both places and raced through the streets, carrying the men to the geisha houses, bars, and restaurants, not always in the same order. The shop owners stood outside their doors, motioning the Marines to "come see," and beggar children, who learned quickly of the generosity of the Marines, walked beside the Marines, pleading with outstretched hands. "No money, no chola."

Gil and Mack stepped out of their rickshaws and handed money to their drivers.

"Wow, that sake is stronger than a goat's breath," Mack giggled. He squinted at Gil. "Either your hat's on backwards or you're facing the wrong way."

Gil stumbled, then regained his balance. "Mack, was this an authorized liberty tonight or did we slip through the hole in the wall? If we did, we have to slip back the same way. I hear they're going to keep a list of who goes on liberty and check off names when we come back to the barracks. Did we leave by the gate tonight?"

"Tiger picked us up at the gate. He knows where to take his rickshaw to meet us and where to bring us back. Quit worrying."

The following night, before Mack and Gil climbed into the waiting rickshaws, a small man walked toward them. "Honorable Marines," he said, "my name is Tong, and I am a servant with many years experience. I speak good English, and I am a hard worker. I will work for you if you will let me. I will keep your clothes and your house clean, and I will not be expensive. I ask that you allow me to be your servant."

"If we hired you, we couldn't get you inside the barracks," Mack said.

"If you will let me work for you, I will get inside, and I will not cause you any trouble. My cousin and I worked for the Dutch people when they lived in this legation, and he and I know how to enter the building. He now works for other Marines in the legation, and they are happy. I will do the same for you."

Gil looked at Mack. "Let's give it a try. We'll get Manny, Boog, and Pappas to go along with us, and Tong can work for all of us."

"Will you be willing to work for five of us? We all live in the same building, and there is no one else living with us," Mack asked. "How much will we pay you?"

Tong bowed his head, and said, "I will gladly work for all of you. You will not be sorry. If you can bring me a little food from your table, I will work for that, and if you will bring me perhaps a little more than I can eat for my wife and small son, I will be forever grateful."

"We'll do better than that. We'll pay you in our occupation money, it doesn't change in value like Chinese money, and we will bring you all the food you can eat and food for your family. If you will agree to that, we will use you, starting in the morning," Mack said.

Tong bowed again and said, "I am very grateful. I will work hard to please you. You will not be sorry you allowed me to be your servant."

The first evening Tong worked for the Marines, he polished their shoes and washed their skivvies. He brushed their uniforms and placed them on their beds. He bowed and asked Mack, "Liberty tonight?"

"Yeah, Tong, liberty tonight. In fact, liberty every night. Just plan on us going on liberty every night unless we tell you," Mack replied. "We brought you some food from the mess hall, and there's a container filled with more of the same for your family. This is Marine chow, so your family may find it strange, but it's good food. If you don't like it, we'll try to get you the kind of food you do like."

Tong bowed again and said, "It is very good of you to bring me food. I will work extra hard for you."

A few minutes later, Gil returned to his room and called to Mack, "Hey, Mack, come look what Tong has done. You won't believe this," he said.

"I'll be damned," Mack laughed. "That's what I call a servant who knows his masters' wishes."

Boog stepped into Mack's and Gil's room. "What'd he do?"

"He's shined our shoes and made our bunks in a way our boot camp DI would have approved," Gil said. "And he's placed all our gear on our beds for inspection before we leave for liberty, and that includes rubbers."

Boog hurried to his room. "I better go see if he did the same for me."

"Did he?" Gil yelled.

Boog returned to Gil's room. "He did, but he only put out six rubbers. I'll have to tell him I need more than that for a night."

Mack laughed. "Boog, Tong thought he was putting out a week's supply, not just for one night."

When Mack and Gil left the legation that night, Tiger was waiting with his rickshaw at the gate. "Same place? Same geisha house?" he asked in his limited English.

"No, we're going to a movie tonight. We gotta slow down. Gil is losing too much weight. Take us to a theater for a change," Mack replied.

Tiger frowned. "I no understand," he said.

"Wait, I'll get Tong to tell him," Gil said and ran back inside the legation.

When Tong returned with Gil, he spoke to Tiger, and Tiger nodded his head. "Yes, I now understand. I take you."

Mack and Gil stood at the ticket booth, trying to understand how much money they were supposed to pay for their tickets. Gil said, "I don't have any idea what she's trying to tell us, and she doesn't speak English."

A soft voice behind him said, "May I help you?"

Gil turned and faced a young Chinese woman, dressed in a silk dress that almost reached the floor. Gil stared at the young girl with ebony hair and light yellow skin. Her lips were painted a pale pink, and her eyes were darkened with a faint touch of olive color. "May I help you?" she asked again.

Gil stammered, "I...I don't know what I'm supposed to pay for the ticket, and when I try to give her money, she keeps shaking her head. I keep putting more money on the counter, but she keeps shaking her head."

The Chinese girl smiled and spoke in Chinese to the girl in the ticket window, then said to Gil, "Money is not necessary for you and your friend. You are a guest in our country, and you are welcome to go inside."

"I'd like to pay for your ticket, if you will let me. My name is Gil Everson."

"A guest is not allowed to pay. The Chinese people are grateful to the Americans for returning our land to our people," she replied.

Gil saw the small boy by the girl's side. "Is he...is he your son?"

Soo Ling laughed. "He is my brother."

"I'm glad," Gil said, and they laughed together.

"You didn't tell me your name," Gil repeated.

"It is not proper for me to introduce myself to a stranger," the young girl replied.

"Do you speak English?" Gil asked the young boy by the girl's side.

The small boy nodded his head.

"Do you know your sister's name?" Gil asked.

"Soo Ling."

Gil looked at the girl. "You are no stranger to me now. Can you tell me your name, now that I know who you are?"

"My name is Soo Ling." She bowed her head and stepped to the window to purchase her ticket and a ticket for the small boy by her side.

"Is it okay to sit by you?" Gil asked.

Soo Ling frowned. "I speak English, but I do not know the meaning of 'okay.' What do you ask?"

Gil laughed again. "Okay means is it all right? I'm sorry, but I don't know any Chinese words."

"May I sit with you?" he asked again.

Soo Ling said, "I...I do not think it best. My brother and I will sit alone."

"But Soo Ling, I mean no harm to you," Gil pleaded. "Why won't you let me sit by you?"

"My father would be angry if I allowed you to do so. I do not wish to give my father displeasure."

"Why would he be angry? Doesn't he like Americans?"

"My parents are grateful to the Americans, but they are concerned for my safety and for my little brother."

"I'm not going to harm you or your little brother. I just

want to talk with you and to understand your people. Won't you please let me sit with you? Besides, your parents wouldn't know if you didn't tell them," Gil said.

Soo Ling smiled at Gil and looked down at her little brother. "He would know," she answered and looked back at Gil.

"Yeah, I think I understand," Gil said.

"You are the first American Marine I have spoken to," Soo Ling said. "My father and my mother would not allow me to be on the streets for the celebration. They have forbidden me to leave the house alone."

They walked into the theater, and Soo Ling said, "If you do not speak Chinese, perhaps you will not understand what they say in the theater. The words are spoken in Chinese, but sometimes the English words are written below."

Gil looked at Mack, then looked at Soo Ling. "We didn't know that. We saw it's an American-made movie with American actors, and we thought it would be in English. If I sit by you, you could tell me what they are saying. That would be a polite thing for you to do for your guest."

Soo Ling's brother tugged at her dress and motioned for them to enter the theater. "Yes, my brother is right. It is time to go inside. I will explain to you what the people are saying."

Inside the theater, Gil sat beside Soo Ling and could smell the fragrance of sweet perfume. His eyes never left her face. He moved his head closer and listened to her soft voice.

When the movie ended, and the lights came on, Gil extended his hand to help Soo Ling from her seat. He walked by her side toward the door of the theater.

"Your parents are probably doing the right thing, not allowing you to be out on the streets alone. The Chinese women are the first civilized people we've seen in two and a half years. If you will let me, I'd like to take you to your home. I think three of us can get in a rickshaw."

Mack said, "Three but not four, you mean, so I'd better find my way back to the barracks. Good night, Soo Ling, maybe I'll see you again."

"No, wait, please," Soo Ling said. "I do not live far, and my brother and I will walk. My father would be angry if I rode in a rickshaw with an American Marine."

She held out her hand. "Good night. We will go now."

"Wait, Soo Ling," Gil said. "If you don't want to ride in a rickshaw with me, can I walk with you to your house? I really would like to know you better, and if your parents won't object, I'd like to visit you. Maybe we can go out to eat, and of course your little brother can come too, and you both will be my guest."

"No, that is not possible. My father would not allow you to come see me. Please, I must go now," she said. "Come, little brother."

"Soo Ling," Gil called, "I must know how to find you again."

"I am sorry, but my father will not allow that," she replied and hurried down the darkened street and was lost in the shadows of the high walls and ancient buildings.

"Damn," Gil cursed. "I don't have any idea how to find her again. I don't know where she lives and don't even know her family name." Gil looked in the direction she had gone. "She was beautiful, wasn't she?"

"She was, no doubt about it," Mack agreed. "I don't know how you'd ever find her again in a place like this. Peking is a big place with no telling how many people. Come on, Tiger is waiting with his rickshaw, let's get back to the barracks."

Early the next morning, Sergeant Tucker went into the barracks where Gil, Pappas, King, Boog, and Mack were quartered, "I'm putting all of you on alert. We had problems at the China Gate last night, and if there are problems tonight, I'll need you. Don't go on liberty or leave your quarters until I say so."

"What's the problem, Sarge?" Mack asked. "The Japs don't want to give up their weapons?"

"It's not the Japs, it's the Chinese communists. They're trying to hold up our coal trucks passing through the gates.

Last night, they wouldn't let the trucks come through for almost two hours. If they try it again tonight, we'll go there, so be ready. If I call you, come with your combat gear and weapons. There could be trouble."

"You taking the whole company, or just some of us?" Gil asked.

"Just enough for a show of strength, for now," Tucker answered. "But I'm putting George Company on standby alert."

Boog frowned. "Let's go shoot the shit out of them if they give us any more trouble."

"And start another war?" Pappas asked.

Boog scowled. "Hell, so what if it starts the war all over again. We'll end up fighting the Russians sooner or later, anyway. We're over here now, and we're still geared for combat."

"I'm pissed that Russia didn't declare war on Japan until we dropped the atomic bomb and the war was won," Mack admitted, "but I don't want to get into a shooting war with Russia."

At 1800 hours, Tucker ran to the barracks. "Let's go. The communists have stopped our supply trucks. Get your weapons and load up on the double. Trucks are waiting outside the compound."

When the three trucks with segments of George Company arrived at the China Gate, they heard a driver of one of the stalled supply trucks shouting at the communist guards. "Open the gates and move the fuck out of the way, you bunch of communist pricks."

The communist guards watched the armed Marines approach the gate and heard Sergeant Tucker order his Marines to disembark from the trucks and face the communists.

Sergeant Tucker walked in front of his Marines and ordered, "Platoon, attention. Port arms." He walked to the Chinese officer. "Do you speak English?"

The officer shook his head.

Tucker said, "I think you're lying and you do understand English, so I'm going to give you thirty seconds to instruct your men to move from the gate and allow our trucks to come through. At the end of thirty seconds, I'm going to instruct my men to start firing. You'll get the message."

He returned to his men. "Platoon, ready, aim." He turned to face the Chinese officer and held up his arm to see his wrist watch.

The Marine drivers ran toward their trucks and climbed into their seat. The Chinese officer nervously looked at his guards, then back at Sergeant Tucker. The guards began backing away from the gate, and Tucker began counting, "Thirty, twenty-nine, twenty-eight,..." The Chinese officer shouted to his men, and they turned and ran from the entrance.

The Marine drivers revved their motors and shifted gears, and the trucks rolled past the guards and through the gate.

Tucker waited until the last supply truck had cleared the gate, then shouted, "Port arms," and ordered his men back on the trucks.

"Jesus Christ," Pappas said. "I don't know if Sarge had the authority to give the order to fire if that Chinese officer hadn't pulled his men away from the gate, but he made me think he would have."

"I don't just think, I know he would have given the order to fire," Mack said. "Sarge wouldn't back himself into a corner without having the authority to fire. If he hadn't called their bluff, we'd be coming here every day. I don't believe the communists will want to take a chance by stopping our trucks again, but I don't mind telling you I was sweating. Boog, do I smell what I think I smell?"

December of 1945 in Peking was cold, and a blanket of white snow fell softly, covering the dirt and waste that littered many of the streets. The basic beauty of the ancient city was seemingly restored, and the sculptured walls and buildings built in times of earlier dynasties by coolies and slaves of the reigning emperors sparkled in the sunshine of the day and glittered in the light of night.

Mack, Gil, Pappas, and King spent more time seeing the Forbidden City and the Winter Palace than they did patronizing the bars and geisha houses. They visited one of the wonders of the world, walking the centuries-old path on top of the Great Wall, worn smooth by ancient war lords and millions of feet.

"I keep thinking I might see Soo Ling at some of these places," Gil sighed, "but her father must still be keeping her locked in her home."

"She wasn't locked in her home, Gil," Mack said, "just restricted from going out alone."

"What's the difference?" Gil replied. "She's not going to be visiting places or walking the streets without her little brother tagging along, and that's about the same as having her locked up. I've seen about all of these wonders of the world and visited all the bars and geisha houses I care to. I'm about ready to go back to the States."

"The scuttlebutt going around is a rotation plan will be used and the ones with the most points will be the first to return to the States," Mack said. "I heard we'd get a point for each month overseas, five points for each combat we were in, and points for other things, but I don't know what. We've been overseas and in combat as much as anyone and more than most, and you and I, and Pappas, King, and Boog would all be in the first rotation."

"I sure would like to see Soo Ling before I go home," Gil said, "but I doubt I'll ever get to do so."

They stood before a wall with dragons carved in the stone and covered with leaves of gold.

"It's beautiful, isn't it?" Manny murmured.

"Yeah, it is if you just look at things and not at the people," Pappas replied. "Since winter came, I've seen hungry people dying on the streets, probably freezing as well as starving. I saw an old man lying along the road the other day, and the Chinese people just stepped around him. I don't know if the communists are causing the hunger or if it's the nationalists' fault, but it sure is terrible to see such misery and poverty. Beggars are everywhere, and if you give something to one of them, you're swamped by others that want you to give them something too."

"Christmas is coming, and the season of giving is almost here. Christmas is only two weeks away. Do y'all realize this will be our third Christmas overseas? I'll bet the Chinese people would be happier with food than they would presents. I feel sorry for them, and I think we should give Tong something in addition to food," Manny said. "He's really been good to all of us."

"Me too," Pappas agreed. "But I don't know what we should get him. Probably something for the family rather than for him. I doubt if he'd keep something just for himself, but he might if it was for his family. Mack, you got any ideas?"

"I'd say it's gotta be something like clothes, or blankets, or something useful," Boog suggested.

"I don't agree with that," Mack said. "It should be something extra nice that Tong wouldn't ordinarily buy, like a fine piece of porcelain for his wife, and maybe a piece of jewelry, maybe a watch for Tong. The only trouble is, how will any of us know we're buying the best for a fair price?"

"That sounds like a good idea to me," Pappas admitted. "We have a few more days until Christmas. Let's do some looking and maybe ask around."

"I'll ask my favorite gal at the geisha house," Boog volunteered.

"Hell, I wouldn't trust your geisha gal as far as I could throw a bull," Pappas grunted. "She'd screw you twice, once in bed and once at the store."

For the next two weeks, Gil asked Tiger to take him in his rickshaw to the theater where he first met Soo Ling. He sat in the rickshaw outside the theater until the last person entered the movie, hoping to see Soo Ling, and when she failed to come, he asked Tiger to take him back to the barracks.

In the last week of December, Gil waited in the rickshaw with his parka pulled over his head. The snow fell in lazy flakes that covered the street.

Tiger stood before his rickshaw, his padded coat pulled tight against the cold, his head covered with a worn cap that covered his head and neck.

Gil watched the Chinese people purchase their tickets to the theater and looked at Tiger. "I don't think she'll be here tonight. We'd better go back to the barracks."

Tiger picked up the wooden rails of the rickshaw and started pulling it through the snow.

"Wait!" Gil shouted. "Go back. I see her."

Before Tiger could stop, Gil jumped from the rickshaw and ran toward the theater entrance.

"Soo Ling," he exclaimed and ran toward the Chinese girl and her brother.

Soo Ling stopped and turned to see Gil running toward her. "Gil Everson! I am happy to see you again." She looked down, embarrassed that she had shown such emotion, and then smiled, "Oh I am happy to see you."

"Not as happy as I am to see you," Gil answered. "You have no idea how many times I've wanted to see you, and I had about given up any hope of seeing you again."

He smiled at Soo Ling's little brother. "I'm even glad to see you again, little brother. I have something for you." He pulled a candy bar from his coat pocket. "I saved this from the evening meal at the mess hall. Here, it's for you."

"Soo Ling, please let me sit by you tonight," Gil pleaded. "I still can't understand Chinese. Is it okay?"

Soo Ling laughed. "It is okay, and I will tell you what the people are saying."

The movie started, and Soo Ling, embarrassed in knowing that Gil's eyes were on her face, lowered her head. Gil touched her hand and, when she did not pull it away, held her hand as she spoke in a soft voice.

When the movie ended, Gil walked with Soo Ling and her brother to the exit. "Soo Ling, I must talk with you," he said. "You have to let me say something to you. We will be returning to the United States before too much longer, I'm sure of that. You must let me walk you to your house tonight. If your father is angry, I'll talk with him, but I won't take no for an answer, not tonight. Besides, I have a favor to ask of you."

Soo Ling answered softly, "My father knows of you. I told him how we met. He was not angry."

"You mean I can come see you?" Gil was surprised.

"No. No, my father would be very angry if you did that. You must promise you will not try to come to my house."

They walked along the edge of the street, and Tiger pulled his rickshaw through the snow behind them.

"Soo Ling, the favor I want to ask of you is very important to me and my friends. In our country, Christmas is a time of giving, and a time of believing. I don't know if you are a Christian or not. It doesn't matter, but my friends and I want to give a gift to a Chinese man and his wife, and I would like for you to go with me to a fine shop and help me buy a man's watch and a porcelain vase for his wife. Will you go with me tomorrow?" Gil asked. "We…we will be leaving soon, I'm sure," he continued, "and I would like to get the presents as soon as I can. Will your father allow you to go with me if you tell him what I have told you?"

"I will ask him," Soo Ling replied. "If I can go with you, I will meet you tomorrow, here at the entrance to the theater. The shop is not far. You must not follow me home tonight. If my father will permit me, I will be here in the evening, at the time we met tonight. There will be time to buy the gifts you spoke of before the shops close. If I am not here, you will know my father would not give his permission."

Soo Ling pulled her hand from Gil's hand and turned and walked into the shadows of the night.

Gil told Mack, Pappas, King, and Boog that he had met Soo Ling. "I asked her to help me buy the presents for Tong and his wife. I don't know if her father will let her, and if she doesn't come, I'll never see her again."

"Gil," Manny said, "will you do me a big favor? If she comes to meet you, will you ask her to help buy something for me?"

"What is it you want me to buy?" Gil asked.

"I want to buy some material for a dress, for my mother, the finest silk in China, enough to make her the best dress in Carolina. I made a promise to myself I'd do that someday. Will you do that for me?"

"Of course I'll ask her," Gil replied. "If she comes."

"I have a feeling she will," Mack said. "Go wait for her."

Gil and Tiger arrived early at the theater, and the snows were heavier than the night before. Gil stood outside the rickshaw and walked along the street, looking into the dusk and falling snow.

He looked at his watch and groaned. It was ten minutes later than when he had met Soo Ling the night before. He put his watch to his ear to see if it was still running, then looked back in the direction he had seen Soo Ling come to the theater the night before. The snow covered his heavy parka, and he pulled the cape over his head.

His heart beat with anticipation, and when the time to meet her passed, he looked at Tiger. "She's not coming," he said. Tiger shook his head excitedly and pointed toward the shadows.

Gil ran to Soo Ling and grabbed her in his arms. "No, you must not do that," she said, and pulled away.

"I'm sorry I am late," she said. "My father would not give his permission, but my mother asked him to grant me this favor."

"Bless your mother, tell her I appreciate her getting your father to give his permission. Well, do we ride in the rickshaw, or do we walk?" Gil asked happily.

"It is not too cold. I would like to walk," Soo Ling said. "The store is near."

Gil reached for Soo Ling's hand, and they walked along the street, past shop windows filled with carved wooden pieces and polished jade, and all the priceless things that only the wealthy could buy.

They stepped through the drifts of snow and entered the tiny store at the end of the block.

"We will buy your presents here," Soo Ling said. "The owner is a good man. He will give you a fair price."

Gil chose a gold watch for Tong, a small porcelain vase for Tong's wife, and the material for Manny's mother.

"Soo Ling, will you let me buy you a gift, something to remember me by?" Gil asked.

Soo Ling blushed and lowered her head. "I need no gift to remember you," she replied softly. "I will not forget you."

"Nor will I forget you," Gil said.

They walked back to where they had met, and Gil said, "Soo Ling, I don't want to get you in trouble with your father, but I want to walk you to your house. Just this last time."

Soo Ling nodded her head and whispered, "Just this last time. My father forbids me to see you again after this night."

They stopped in front of a wooden gate in front of a darkened compound. "I must go now. I cannot stay," Soo Ling said.

"Please, Soo Ling, can't you do what you want to do? Do you have to always do as your father says?" Gil asked.

"I must always obey my father. He will choose my husband, and then I must obey my husband. It is the way of the Chinese people," she said quietly.

Gil took both of her hands in his hands and stood looking into her eyes for a long time. "So, this is the way it all ends. The war, the duty here in China, my life as a Marine, here with you, a girl I met, a girl I love," he said simply.

"You must not say that," Soo Ling begged. "You are an American, and I am Chinese."

"Does it have to matter that much?" Gil started to kiss her, but she held her hand between their lips. "Please," she said, "Please do not kiss me. Our worlds are far apart."

Gil touched her hair. "I love you, Soo Ling,"

Soo Ling whispered, "You must not say the words in your heart, as I must not say what is in my heart. Love is not important to a Chinese woman. I will marry a man my father chooses for me. It is the custom, and I am bound by the custom of my ancestors."

When she looked up, Gil saw tears in her eyes.

Soo Ling backed away from Gil and touched her finger to her lips, then touched Gil's lips. She turned and entered the gate, and Gil heard her footsteps as she walked through the snow on the cobblestone pathway. He stood at the gate until the sound of her steps was gone and then walked to the waiting rickshaw.

When Tong opened the present from the Marines and saw the gold watch, tears came to his eyes. "This is the most wonderful gift I could ever imagine," he exclaimed. "I can never repay you for your generosity and kindness, and my wife will treasure this vase always. It is so beautiful."

"Well, since we're leaving the first week in January, we've got you some food, enough for you and your wife," Manny said. "There's canned goods that will last, and the sugar, flour, and spices will last a long time, too. It's our going-away gift for you."

Tong bowed his head and touched the moisture on his cheek with his finger. "There is much food, and I will share it with my family and my brother and his family. All of you are good men. I wish I could give you something, but I have nothing to give."

On January 6, 1946, Pappas, King, Mack, Gil, and Boog boarded ship for their return to the United States.

Gil was the last on board, and he looked toward the shore for a long time after the ship pulled away from the dock. He stood on the deck and watched the lights of China fade into the darkness.

The voyage across the Pacific was smooth, but it seemed to the Marines the trip took twice as long as it should have taken. Finally, the Marines stood on the deck of the ship and watched the shore of California come closer.

Boog unfastened the life preserver he had worn every day while at sea. "I don't need this anymore. I could swim the rest of the way to shore if I had to." He threw his life jacket as far out into the ocean as he could.

The jacket floated on the water, then gradually sank below the waves. Boog stared, then started laughing as the jacket disappeared. "A hell of a lot of good that jacket would have done if I had ever needed it, and to think I wore that stinking, dirty piece of crap, believing it would hold me up if the ship sunk."

"When it was new, I'm sure it worked, but not now. I'll try mine." Gil threw his jacket in the ocean and watched it disappear. "I'm glad I didn't know they wouldn't float. Thank God we never had to use them."

Pappas said, "Tomorrow we'll land, and I imagine we'll get our discharge and be on our way before the week is over. I'm anxious to get back home."

"What will you do when you get back to Ohio, Pappas?" Mack asked.

"I want to see Fay and my folks. I'll see if I can get my job back in the steel mill. If there's any money left from what I sent home for my younger brother to go to college, I may go to college myself."

"I'm going to college when I get back to Texas," Gil said. "And then, well, who knows."

Mack looked at Manny. "How about you, Manny?"

"I'll probably go back and work on the farm. I'm sure my dad can use my help. I'll go see my girl, and I'll give my mother the material for her dress. Hell, I'm even anxious to see my mule Josie." Manny thought for a moment. "It's been two and a half years, almost three years that we've been together, and I'll never forget any of you."

"Three years ago," Mack said, "we were nothing more than boys, some of us were just seventeen when we joined. We're all a little older now, maybe a little wiser. We've all changed since that first day we met, at least I know I have. When you see what we've seen, done the things we've done, you have to change."

"Yeah," Gil laughed. "We've come a long way since that first day in Lubbock when I ate the Irish stew." He paused,

"Mack, what happened to Donald, and to Billy, to Munday, to a lot of our friends, could have happened to us. We were lucky, you and I."

Mack looked down for a moment, then said, "I wish I had been a little more understanding of Donald. I could have been a little more of a friend. And Billy, well, I'll never forget him, or any of you for that matter."

Gil was quiet for a moment. "It all has to end, doesn't it? Whether we like the way it ends or not doesn't matter. We can't change some things, even if we wish we could."

Boog said, "I don't have any regrets. I'm just happy to get back in one piece, and talking about a piece, that's what I intend to get plenty of. I intend to get me a hotel room and me and Lolita are going in and we're not coming out for a week. Hell, maybe a month. If Lolita gives out before I give up, I'll know she's been screwing while I've been gone."

"What are you going to do, Mack, when you get back to Texas? You going to see Anna first thing?" Pappas asked.

"No," Mack said. "I'm going home first. I want to see my folks, go out to the ranch, be by myself for a couple of days. Do some thinking. I want to write down some of our experiences for the past three years, maybe someday I'll write a novel. There's lots to remember, and there's lots to forget."

The shore came closer, and Mack turned and looked back toward the Pacific Ocean. "We lived through some pretty tough times, but we made it. Some didn't. I'm glad the war is over."

Epilogue

The early morning bus from El Paso turned into the driveway at the Greyhound station in the town of Crockett, Texas. A lone Marine carrying a small bag stepped from the bus and walked into the cafe.

He placed his bag on the floor and took a seat at the counter. He looked around at the empty tables and chairs, the pictures on the wall, and the nickelodeon at the far end of the room. He could see no difference from the last time he had been in the cafe almost three years ago. Some things never seem to change, he thought.

The man behind the counter placed a glass of water in front of the Marine. "What'll you have, soldier? Cook ain't here yet, so if you want breakfast you'll have to wait."

"Just coffee will do."

"Just got discharged? You live around here? You kinda look familiar," the man asked.

"I used to live here. My family does," Mack replied.

"What's your name?" he asked.

"Williams. Mack Williams."

"You one of those Williams boys? Your daddy has the Williams ranch don't he?" the man asked.

"Yes."

The man placed a cup of coffee on the counter. "That'll be a nickel. What are those medals and ribbons for?"

"One medal is the Purple Heart. The other is a Silver Star."

"Where'd you get them? You earn them?"

"They say I did," Mack replied.

"Guess you were in combat. Where about? Were you in the Pacific or over in Europe?" the man asked.

"Pacific. Cape Gloucester, Talasea, Peleliu, Okinawa, then China."

"I only heard of China," the man said as he studied the Marine. "Wasn't that hired hand that worked on your ranch—the Mexican boy—wasn't he killed in the war?"

"Yes, Felipe Ramirez was killed in Italy," Mack replied.

"Sure was a bunch of boys got killed in the war. Course I was too old to go to the service myself. I wanted to though," the man behind the counter said.

"Yes, there were many men who died in the war. I left several of my friends on the islands in the Pacific," Mack said.

The man looked at Mack a long time. "I guess the Good Lord sometimes has funny ways of choosing who gets killed and who don't," he said as he picked up the nickel that Mack had placed on the counter. "Look like some of the trash we got should'a got killed rather than them good boys."

"Yes, I suppose the Good Lord knows," Mack said, and he looked toward the table where he and Felipe had sat the night Felipe had left for the Army. He reached for his bag and walked out into the morning sun, already turning hot.

"It's a beautiful morning. I should be at the ranch before nightfall. It will be a fine day," Mack said to himself, and he started walking along the dusty road that led back home.